ASCEND

SWATI M.H.

Kismet Publishing

Cover: Cover Me Darling

Editing: Silvia's Reading Corner

ALSO BY SWATI M.H.

<u>Elements of Rapture Series</u>

Adrift

(Forbidden, single-dad, nanny, grumpy/sunshine, forced-proximity romance)

Ascend

<u>Feel the Beat Series</u>

My Perfect Remix

(Single-dad, friends-to lovers romance)

My Beautiful Chaos

(Fake-relationship, second chance romance)

<u>My Darling Neighbor</u>

(Enemies to lovers, surprise pregnancy romance)

<u>Fated Love Series</u>

Kismet in the Sky

(Slightly forbidden, second chance romance)

Surrender to the Stars

(Enemies to lovers, hospital romance)

I cannot fix on the hour, or the spot, or the look, or the words, which laid the foundation. It is too long ago. I was in the middle before I knew that I had begun.

— MR. DARCY, PRIDE AND PREJUDICE

Chapter One

GARRETT

"She's cute. Who is that?" Troy eyes my phone with both brows raised before taking his seat to my right in the cockpit.

I glance at the picture again, a smile playing on my lips as I turn the screen off, slipping the phone back into my pocket. "A friend's daughter."

Troy hands me the dispatch release, and I review it before we both start our preflight procedures and panel scans in relative silence while the flight crew begins the boarding process.

I look over my shoulder a few minutes later, only to catch Ally's suggestive smirk with my frowned reply. *Just my fucking luck.* Even changing jobs—flying for a private airline to now a commercial one—can't get me far enough away from my past.

Once we've finished initial climb procedures and are cruising, I make my welcome announcement to the passengers on-board. "Good morning, passengers. This is your captain speaking. I'd like to welcome you onboard *Blue Breeze* flight eighty-two from Oakland to Las Vegas. We're cruising at an altitude of thirty-three thousand feet, flying at a speed of four hundred knots. The skies are clear and sunny on this

Thursday in January, so I'm expecting an on-time arrival into Las Vegas in the next hour and ten minutes. The cabin crew will be coming around to take your drink orders shortly. Until then, sit back, relax, and make good decisions now while you're still sober."

With that, I disconnect the intercom and switch back to listening to ATC while Troy updates the flight management system.

"So, any updates on that woman you were trying to talk to the last time we spoke?" Troy leans back on his chair, wiggling the knot of his tie looser. "Your sister-in-law's sister or cousin or whatever?"

While pilots generally tend to run into the same crew after years of working for the same airline, I've only been at *Blue Breeze* for the past year. The staff is still relatively new to me, save for Troy and *Unfortunately Ally*. She's *Unfortunately Ally*, because well, I unfortunately ran into her a few years ago, and by the way she licked her lips earlier, while pointedly staring at mine, I get the feeling she wants us to *run into each other* again. And by running into each other, what I mean is with her bent over the sink in the tiny airplane lavatory with my dick inside her.

I *ran into* a few women back in the day–a reputation I'm still trying to escape–but fortunately, *Unfortunately Ally* was the start of my self-imposed sex ban and reformation.

Her, and the fact that I'd met a purple-haired pixie . . .

It's been a few weeks since Troy and I flew from San Francisco to New York on a six-hour flight, but his memory is as sharp as a tack. Though, I get the feeling he remembers more about my love life–*or lack thereof*–because of his own being so stable.

Troy is a family man–a father of three girls and married to the same woman for over twenty years. I suppose it's fun to live vicariously and experience the instability of someone else's love life when your own is rather unchanging. It's the same reason the romance book and film industry is thriving. Most of those readers and viewers aren't riding a romance roller coaster with their stomachs in their throats, not knowing where the next three-hundred-foot blind drop will be—because they've already survived the drops, loops, and uphill climb to the heavens and are in steady relationships. Now, they just enjoy watching new passengers empty the contents of their stomachs mid-ride as they find their own happily-ever-afters.

Unfortunately, it's looking like I'll be stuck on this infinite loop for the long haul. One where I'll be loveless and sexless until . . .

Until *she* decides my fate.

I shrug, thinking about the woman Troy is referring to. Little does he know, the *update* is always the same when it comes to her—*unavailable*. "My sister-in-law's cousin. Good memory." I nod before shaking my head. "Nah, no updates, really." I take a sip of my coffee before placing it back into the cup holder and looking ahead at the open blue sky through my aviators. "I saw her over Christmas, though."

I don't mention the other time, two weeks ago, when Bella frantically called me to see if I could pick Meera up from preschool. Apparently, Meera was having a bit of a coughing spell, and the preschool asked that she be picked up right away. As it so happened, Bella was stepping into a big meeting at work at the same time. In previous, similar situations, Bella relied on her mom for help, but on that particular day, she also happened to be out of town, and I happened to live near Meera's preschool.

Luckily for me, it was my day off and all I had on the docket for the day was spending time at the gym and getting laundry done. It wasn't the first time I'd received a call from

Bella to ask for help, but I'd be lying if I said my heart didn't beat like an off-key drum when I picked up.

It's been four years since I've known . . . Four years that I've tried—at every family gathering and event—to have her eyes settle on me for more than a fraction of a moment. Four years that I've hoarded every word she's uttered in my direction, like some sort of amateur coin collector waiting for the day to cash it all in for a big payout.

Because moving on when it comes to her isn't in my wheelhouse.

Meera and I spent a portion of the time at the grocery store, where she helped me buy hearty essentials like tater tots, Goldfish crackers, and cotton-candy-flavored ice cream—she claimed her mother always gave her ice cream when she had a cough, and I pretended to whole-heartedly believe her lie—before we went home and binged her favorite show, Dora the Explorer. *She even taught me how to eat potato chips 'the right way'—by crushing them into melted ice cream and spooning them into my mouth.*

"Isn't it so yummy, Uncle Garrett? I love the crunchies." Her hazel eyes blinked up at me behind her pink-framed glasses, and I tried not to fault her for the asshole who had a hand in giving her that eye color. She had more in common with her mom, anyway.

"It's pretty darn yummy, Meerkat. I can't believe I've been eating cotton candy ice cream the wrong way all this time! I'm lucky you steered me in the right direction."

"Dora says all you need is a map to go in the right direction. Do you use a map when you fly, too?"

I nodded, giving her small head a pat, which was lazily lying on my bicep while we sat on my carpeted floor against my sofa with our bowls in our hands and our legs splayed out in front of us. Dora blabbed in the background about some kleptomaniac fox named Swiper who, in my opinion, seemed to be in serious need of a good ass kicking. "I do. I use something called an aeronautical map when I fly."

She seemed to think about that for a moment before taking

another spoonful of the melted and crispy cream, spilling a few drops on her flowery shirt. She frowned at the mess before seemingly deciding it wasn't worth stressing over. "I'm going to be a pilot like you when I grow up. I'm going to use a naughty map, too."

I cringed, articulating the word again. "Aeronautical."

Jesus, this would be the last time Bella called me to take care of her kid if she started repeating words like that.

Meera blinked up at me slowly, pursing her lips. It was a condescending look I'd been the recipient of many times over the course of four years—a look she generally reserved only for me because she knew it would also have me guffawing when I received it. It always did. "That's what I said. Aero-naughty maps. You just can't hear that well anymore, Uncle Garrett, because you're old."

Oh, wow. So, she's going to go with the age card.

But just like that, she had me bursting out with another laugh.

Maybe it was the mischief that constantly surrounded her like her dark and tangly, long hair, or her all-too-sassy remarks, or the little lies she'd tell, thinking she'd outsmarted everyone else. I knew even before that day that, while her mother might never claim the entity beating inside my ribs, her daughter had already made a permanent home in it.

"Oh yeah?" Troy pulls me out of my musings. "You really seem to be pining for her, man. Why don't you do something about it?"

I chuckle. "Believe me, I've tried. Over the holidays, my brother and sister-in-law rented a large cabin in Tahoe and had us all over for a couple of nights. I tried talking to her a few times but . . ." I rake my teeth over my bottom lip. "No change. The woman's a fortress."

Troy chuckles. "One of those stand-offish types, huh? Let me guess; she's been burned by some douche and now she doesn't trust anyone with a dick."

My jaw ticks at the mention of said douche. "Something like that."

I do a quick scan of the fuel gauge before we get into conversation about yesterday's news report about a flight that had to make an emergency landing because a woman went into preterm labor.

"Looks like you're not going to be with me on the flight to Kansas City," Troy states as we start preparing for our initial descent into Las Vegas. "You staying in Vegas or headed back home?"

I make an announcement to let the cabin crew know I've turned on the seatbelt sign and that they need to clear the cabin before answering Troy, "Nah, I'm actually spending the weekend in Vegas with my twin brother and a couple of friends. I fly out on Sunday, work the whole week, and then get back home the following Friday."

"Nice! Have fun, man. I'll see you next time. Who knows, maybe you'll find someone in Vegas to take your mind off that other girl. Hell, maybe you'll win the jackpot and never have to work another day in your life! Anything's possible in Vegas."

Little did I know, as I prepared the aircraft for landing, how true Troy's words would ring.

Indeed, anything was possible in Vegas.

Chapter Two

GARRETT

I nod a curt farewell to *Unfortunately Ally* before trying to scoot past her on my way out of the aircraft. "Excuse me."

I don't get very far before her hand softly lands on my bicep. "Hello, captain."

I discreetly look around at the rest of the crew to see if they are paying attention to us. Thankfully, they're all busy cleaning up the cabin for the next round of passengers.

Pulling my arm out of Ally's touch, I create some distance between us. "Hope you're well, Ally. I didn't realize you were working for *Blue Breeze* as well."

Her blue eyes shimmer with mischief before she tucks her chocolatey brown hair behind her ear, biting her bottom lip. It's a wonder how I ever found that inviting. I mean, by all standards, she's an absolute smokeshow and definitely has the whole sex-kitten thing down to an art but . . . she's missing something.

Like purple tips in her hair and a set of dimples so fucking deep, you envision diving into them.

Or licking them.

She shrugs, coyly. "My life got a little . . . *complicated* a few years ago, so I hopped around companies for a while, and then recently found this job at *Blue Breeze*." She scans me from under her overly-long fake lashes, giving me a sultry smile. "I'm glad to see you here, though. Maybe . . ." she looks around the aircraft, speaking in a hushed tone, "we can hang out again sometime?"

My brows furrow, and I know I need to deplane before this gets even more uncomfortable. "Uh, I don't think that's a good idea."

"It was a good idea when you fucked me inside the lavatory. On more than one occasion, and on more than one flight, I might add."

I wish I could go back in time and punch my old self for the mess he created for my current self.

I squeeze my eyes shut. "Listen, Ally. That was years ago, and I know we haven't seen each other in a while, but I'm not that guy anymore. I'm also not really available right now."

"*You're not that guy any more?*" Ally's expression turns taunting, like she's trying to keep herself from snickering. "Please. It takes a lot for a tiger to change his stripes and walk into a party pretending to be a meek little cat. And what does 'I'm not really available right now' even mean? Either you are or you aren't, *captain*."

She's got me there, but since I don't have a better answer for her, I keep my mouth shut.

"Anyway, I'm glad to see you, and I don't want anything to be weird between us since we'll probably work together again, but just know," her smile turns sultry again, "the offer is still on the table."

"Uh, thanks," I reply before walking down the jet bridge. A part of me wants to argue with her—to tell her that I'm not the guy she met four years ago—but the other part realizes it's not my prerogative to change everyone's mind. There's only one woman whose opinion I give a shit about, and it's not her.

Fuck, I hope the other crew members didn't hear any of that. The last thing I need is for more of my idiotic past reputation following me around.

Sure, I moved to *Blue Breeze* because it was based out of the Oakland airport instead of the smaller one in Tahoe—even though that's where the rest of my family lives, aside from my mom, stepdad, and Grams. But I also changed jobs because I wanted a chance to reinvent myself, to put my past 'deeds' where they belong—in the past. I couldn't get away from them while I was at the previous airline, not when all they did was follow me around like a dark storm cloud.

The bustling sights and sounds of Harry Reid International airport, with its chiming slot machines and flickering lights, invites me as I exit the gate, still reeling from the strange conversation with Ally. I pull out my phone, taking it off airplane mode, to find a whole slew of missed messages from my brother Dean, and our friends, Rohan and Hudson.

> Dean: Meet me in baggage claim, assholes.
> We can take an Uber from there to the strip.

> Rohan: I'm in baggage claim. I don't see
> you.

> Rohan: Wait, I see your stupid man bun now.
> It's like a beacon.

> Dean: It's a beacon, alright. A beacon that
> 'beckons' all the ladies. See what I did
> there? I also have another *beacon* in my
> pants. It's even bigger than the one on my
> head.

Hudson: I have no idea what the fuck you just said, but you need to keep your shitty pickup lines under wraps until we get to the club tonight.

Rohan: You're truly an idiot. Where's Garrett? Why hasn't he chimed in yet?

Dean: @Hudson, you wouldn't get it, old man. How old are you turning, ninety-six?

Dean: @Rohan, he's probably still in the air.

Hudson: @Dean, clearly, all that firefighting burned off those brain cells. I'll be forty-three, asshole.

There's a message twenty minutes after the previous ones.

Dean: @Garrett, we'll see you at the casino, brother. We're going to go check-in. Call when you get in, and we'll tell you where we are.

I send them a response, letting them know I just landed and will be headed to the casino soon. I'm smiling down at the three thumbs-up signs I receive in response to my message and a GIF from the Hangover movie, welcoming me to Vegas, when I hear a familiar voice a few feet to my side.

Her voice.

"This is the last time I'm going to ask politely. Please, let go of my shoulder, Chaz. I'm not discussing this with you," Bella grinds out through her teeth. A quick scan of her rigid stance tells me she's highly uncomfortable. She grasps the asshole's hand before throwing it off her shoulder, while my brain comes to terms with the fact that she's *actually* here.

How he has the fucking balls to touch her without her permission is beyond me. Every fucking fiber inside me yearns to hurl toward her and pull her away from the man towering over her like a ghoul, before pounding my fist into his bearded jaw. But I keep my feet glued to my spot, listening intently. I can't get involved.

Not yet at least.

Even if my skin is igniting under the surface and my fist is ready at my side, I know how much Bella prides herself in taking care of things on her own, so stepping in like a knight in shining armor would just piss her off more. So, I'll wait.

For now.

"How did you even find me here?" Bella asks incredulously.

The asshole chuckles as if she's just cracked a joke. "As luck would have it, I was sitting a few rows behind you on the same flight." He points to the aircraft I just exited, and I realize Bella was on my flight. "I'm going to the same conference as you, I presume. The West Coast Hardware Engineering Summit?" He leans in toward her, a callous smirk playing on his lips. "Wanna partake in the same fun we had last time?"

Oh, this motherfucker . . . My fist twitches at my side again.

Bella rears away from him as if breathing the same air will poison her lungs. "No, thanks. Once was enough to teach me a lesson."

The jackass shrugs. "Your loss. Anyway, I know you ended up having my kid. I never found you anywhere on social media, but I've asked around."

"That's none of your business. You–"

"She's mine," he drawls, cutting her off. "You and I both know she's mine, and therefore, it very much makes it *my* business."

Bella pulls her shoulders back, looking at him with pure

disdain. "Let me remind you, Chaz, that I went through every hoop to find you–a virtual stranger–four years ago. And when I did, you told me you were married and wanted nothing to do with *it* as long as it didn't involve you." She lifts a brow. "Which is exactly what I did. I moved forward and raised my daughter on my own without *involving you*."

So this is Meera's fucking assblanket of a sperm donor. Just fucking great.

Chaz–he even has a douchey name–softens his stance, trying out a new tactic. "Listen, a lot was going on in my life at that time. I was in a bad marriage, but I thought I could work it out with her–"

"*Work it out with her?*" Bella snorts, mirthlessly. "Right. By picking up an innocent twenty-one-year-old woman at the next conference and telling her you were single. Really seems like you were working out your problems there, Chaz."

Chaz runs his fingers through his dark beard. If he wasn't the scumbag I already know he is, I'd admit he was a decent-looking guy. Currently, however, he reminds me of the gum I peeled off the bottom of my shoe last week. "Look, we made a mistake and unfortunately, you had to bear the brunt of it–"

Yeah, wrong choice of words there, Chaz. If I were you, I'd fucking run.

Bella practically trembles from the adrenaline coursing through her. "The only fucking *mistake* I made was create my beautiful baby girl with *your* DNA. I didn't bear the brunt of anything, because that little girl has been the biggest blessing in my life. For the past four years, I've had more purpose and love than I could have ever imagined. Love that *you* missed out on knowingly. So don't you dare," Bella takes a step forward, looking up at his flushed cheeks, and placing the tip of her finger in the middle of his chest, "say a single word about *my* daughter."

They stare at each other like two lions sizing each other

up before a decided fight. Unfortunately for Chaz, he looks more like the scarred and outcast evil brother to the magnificent Mufasa standing her ground.

And as soon as Bella starts to walk away, Chaz breaks his silence. "I want shared custody and visitation with *my* daughter. I want to see her—"

Fuck!

"Absolutely not." Bella white-knuckles the handle of her carry-on. "I will not have a stranger step into my child's life and confuse her at such an impressionable age . . . especially a stranger who has the moral quotient of an insect. And how would that even work? You live in Texas, and my daughter is well adjusted in her life with me in California."

"I'm moving to the Bay Area in a few weeks, so that won't be a problem."

Bella looks at him like he's absolutely insane. "You can't come into her life after having no connection with her for four years—after not even acknowledging her birth!—and demand to be in it. That's not how this works, Chaz."

"You don't get to tell me how this works and make all the decisions here, you fucking bitch—"

And that's my cue.

I don't even hear the rest of Chaz's statement before my feet are making their way toward Bella. I have no idea what I'm going to do when I get there because my brain seems to have short-circuited. All I know is I need to get to her.

I plaster a smile on my face as fake as the molar I lost in the seventh grade after a lacrosse stick decided to make me its target. "Bella! There you are, baby! I was wondering where you went."

Bella's brows turn down in confusion as she watches me close the distance between us. I can see the wheels turning in her head, trying to figure out how I just manifested out of thin air and what to make of my bizarre outburst. Chaz has a similar look on his face, but his isn't nearly as adorable.

And before she can say another word, giving anything away, I wrap a protective arm around her. Pulling her into my side, I do the only thing that makes sense.

I kiss her.

Chapter Three

BELLA

You know those dreams within dream situations? Sort of like that movie, *Inception*, where it's hard to decipher what's real and what's made up?

That's my current state standing in the Las Vegas airport.

One second I'm ready to pummel my ex whatever he's called—deadbeat baby daddy?—to the ground and break every tooth in his shiny smile, and the next second, my lips are plastered to a gorgeous man wearing a pilot's uniform.

Is this even happening or am I just having a very lucid dream where my cousin's brother-in-law is kissing me in the middle of a busy airport?

I mean, I won't deny having dreams almost of this exact situation where Captain Garrett Meyer has me tied up with a rope on one of these chairs in the gate area, drilling into me from behind with his big . . .

Okay, seriously, what's happening right now?

Where did he even come from?

His lips press against mine before his tongue comes out to caress the seam of my mouth, urging my lips to follow his silent command like good little soldiers. And they do. The little whores that they are open up for him and allow his tongue to find mine. A full-body shiver ghosts down my spine until I sigh into his mouth.

My eyes open at the same time as Garrett's, but his seem to be trying to tell me something, like they're disclosing a secret. That would be nice, because at the moment, I'm feeling pretty damn clueless.

Garrett pulls away and my body immediately mourns the loss of his mouth as I shake out of my daze. "Garr–"

"Sweetheart, where's your ring?" Garrett scoops up my left hand, staring at it with a pronounced frown before giving me a wide-eyed stare.

Sweetheart?

"Wh-what?" I stammer, completely fucking confused.

What exactly is happening here? Why is my brain not catching up?

"Your wedding ring? Did you forget it at home again?" He tucks a strand of my hair behind my ear, his gaze softening over my face. "Baby, this is Vegas. I can't have every drunk asshole gawking at you, thinking they have a chance. I locked you down for a reason." His lips press against the shell of my ear, and if I wasn't on fire before, I feel like I just dove head-first into an inferno. "Because you're mine."

Chaz clears his throat, and it's as if Garrett and I just realize he was even there. Chaz gives Garrett an unimpressed once-over, his jaw tight as if he's assessing a piece of trash. But before he can say anything, Garrett sticks out his hand. "I'm Garrett, Bella's husband. And who might you be?"

My . . . husband?

A part of me wonders if perhaps when I got on the airplane this morning in Oakland, it somehow took me into another universe.

"You're . . ." Chaz seems to go through an array of words in his head, coming up with, "a pilot?"

Garrett looks down at his uniform. "It seems I am! You, sir, deserve a gold star!" Garrett turns toward the large window while I'm still reeling from the knowledge that I somehow got married in the span of an hour and a half. "And that over there," he points, "is called an *airplane*." He articulates the last word as if he's talking to a child.

Chaz lifts his chin with a more pronounced frown while Garrett returns his gaze with a condescending one. Chaz's bored expression finds me again. "I didn't realize you were married."

Me, either.

I clear my throat as Garrett squeezes my waist. "Yes, well . . . it's new. Besides, it's not like I would have a reason to tell you, anyway."

Chaz narrows his eyes on both Garrett and me, and if he can tell we're part of a ruse, he keeps it to himself. "In any case," one of his brows lifts, "we can either do this the easy way, with you agreeing to the terms of a new custody arrangement when I send it your way, or the hard way, with us tied up in court. Your choice, Bella, but my lawyer will be in touch."

With that, he pulls his luggage behind him and disappears into the crowd, leaving me breathless and with my heart at my feet.

Whether he can tell from the way I'm trembling or from whatever he's heard, Garrett faces me and clasps my shoulders, assessing my fallen face with his inky blue eyes. "Are you okay?"

"I . . . I don't know. I'm sort of in shock, I guess. And I'm scared." I look up at him. "How much of that did you hear?"

Garrett scans my face, giving me a guilty look. "Enough, which is why I stepped in. I saw him touch you, and I . . ." His jaw clenches. "I figured he'd leave you alone if I said I was your husband."

"Thank you." I let out a breath, not having enough energy

to assess whether Garrett pretending to be my husband will bite me in the ass later. What if Chaz finds out that I'm not married? Will that hurt me if he decides to make this messy in court? "I can't believe this is happening. I need to talk to a lawyer. He's threatening a custody battle, and I honestly don't know enough to determine if he can actually win it."

My heart hammers inside my chest and my head spins with thoughts of Meera potentially spending time with this virtual stranger. I can't imagine how confusing it will be for her.

I remember how confusing it was for me.

She's asked about her father a couple of times but seemed to accept it when I told her he didn't want to be in our lives. It isn't a conversation I love to recall–her melancholy expression, the way her shoulders sagged–but I also didn't want to lie to her. But if Chaz suddenly comes back into her life, it'll destabilize her.

It'll wreck her, just like it did me.

"Will you come back to visit me soon, Papa?"

My dad looked me straight in the eyes and lied, "Of course, I will, Jingle Bells."

He wouldn't visit soon, but my seven-year-old self still waited for him, looking out the window every day. Sometimes, I thought I saw him at the grocery store, picking up eggs from the dairy aisle. Sometimes, my mind would trick me into thinking he was in the stands at the school pep rally. Sometimes, I'd pretend he tucked me into bed at night.

I waited every day until I was sixteen.

And then, he came back. Miserable and broken beyond repair.

But by then, the damage was done; my wounds were too deep to heal. And when he died a couple of years later from a sudden heart attack, neither Mom nor I could spare more than a single tear.

The very first man I ever trusted had left me and Mom for another woman. And when his life upended with her, and he had a little more than a dime to his name, he begged my mother to take him back—even if it was as a roommate or a house guest.

My mom buried her grief and her broken heart, not because she forgave him, but because of the goodness of her heart. Because she knew she had to stay strong for her only daughter, even if it was forced. She'd made amends with her fate by then—diving head-deep into her job to silence the loneliness—but it wasn't in her nature to turn away a begging man, especially a man she once loved so deeply.

To his credit, my dad tried to bridge the distance between us. I saw him sitting in the stands at my volleyball games. I found the bags of groceries he brought from the store. I even heard his knocks on my door to tell me good night.

I just never answered them.

And now, that would be my daughter's fate.

Sure, she's younger and less jaded than I was, but there is no telling if Chaz will be a permanent fixture in her life. What if he decides to abandon her again after she gets attached to him?

I often wonder if Mom made the right choice by letting my dad back into our lives. On one hand, I gave him a taste of his own medicine by ignoring him while he existed—my broken heart and my immature age made me believe that revenge would somehow cure the pain—on the other, it only shattered me more.

Until today, Chaz has shown us nothing but cowardice and disinterest. He's a useless bag of shit who thinks a tailored suit will hide the ugliness beneath it. He not only cheated on his wife, but he also neglected his responsibilities as a father. He hasn't provided for Meera in any way. Even in the few minutes he just spent threatening me with a custody battle, not once did he ask about her. Not once did I see a single ounce of regret on his face. He has no idea what she looks like or who she is. Hell, he doesn't even know her name!

He thinks he can just insert himself into her life now? Why? Because he's some douchebag executive who's used to having people bend over backward for him and he thinks I'll do the same?

He's out of his goddamn mind.

But it doesn't relieve the twist in my stomach or my short breaths. It doesn't take away the fear that's now settling like an unwanted guest in the back of my mind. What if he has the money and power to take my child away from me?

No court would allow him to take her away completely since I've been the only stable parent she's known, but he could demand she stays with him for parts of the year—especially if he ends up moving near us, like he claims he is.

"Hey, hey." Garrett pulls me out of my daze, grasping my chin and forcing my eyes up. "Look at me and just breathe. Okay? Everything is going to be alright. I'm from a divorced family, and while my parents have a really good relationship, I know that things will be okay for Meera, too. You have to believe that, Bella. The courts will always do what's right for the child in these situations."

Garrett's words only make me feel slightly better. "I know, but . . . you don't understand, Garrett. Chaz has a lot of money. I found out after I slept with him that he's a senior executive for another big company. He not only has the power to get some of the best lawyers on this case, but he could potentially get me fired from my job."

Garrett's brows pinch. "How can he get you fired when you were both consenting adults that night?"

He has a point, but I'm too shaken up to really see it. "I

don't know . . . but he could definitely ruin my reputation. He has clout."

Garrett sighs. "I think the best thing to do is what you said—get some legal advice and see if his side is really something that would be upheld in court."

I nod, not knowing what I'm even nodding to. "I can't lose her, Garrett. Not for a day, not for a week. I can't have her world turned upside down."

Garrett runs his palms over my arms. "You won't. We'll think of something."

As the sounds of the airport come flitting back, drowning out my morose thoughts, I look up at Garrett with more muted surprise than before, as if fully taking in the fact that he's here. "Were you . . .? Did you get off the same flight?"

He grins, the corner of his mouth rising only on one side. For as long as I've known him, I've tried to avoid looking directly at him. Not because he's hard to look at, but because he's *impossible* to look at without gawking.

His face is chiseled, the angles so perfectly symmetrical, you'd think he was carved by Michelangelo himself. His cheekbones sit high, his jaw square, and the edges perfectly visible under what always looks like a five o'clock shadow. His blond hair—longer on top and shorter on the sides—always looks like it's been tousled by hand. Over the years, he's grown it out, compared to the more military-short hair he used to sport.

I like it better this way, not that it matters.

Looking at him, *gawking* at him, desiring him . . . None of it matters, because aside from the fact that I won't give my heart to anyone, I *definitely* won't give it to a playboy pilot like Garrett Meyer—no matter how good-natured and charming he might be.

I'm not slut-shaming, I'm just stating a fact: Garrett Meyer has been around. My cousin, Rani, has been with

Garrett's brother for the past four years, and since Rani and I are more like sisters, I often get invited to their larger family events. And based on everything I've pieced together, Garrett seems to have a reputation of going through women like I do boxes of *Nerds*. Fast.

Rani claims he's changed over the years and that his brothers unfairly give Garrett a hard time about it still, but come on, once a player, always a player. And after the way I was played by Chaz—my only one-night stand *ever*—I refuse to be another notch on someone's belt.

I refuse to be a notch, period. I want the entire damn belt or nothing at all.

And, right now, I'm okay with nothing at all.

None of this is to say Garrett and I aren't friends. We are. He's a genuinely funny and caring person. He's reassured me time and time again that I can reach out to him if I need anything since we live near each other. And, apart from that, he adores Meera.

The sentiment is mutual because she talks about him for days after she's hung out with him. It's clear from every inter-action I've seen them have, whether at family Christmas gatherings or birthday parties, they have a special bond. Though, that's also because my daughter likes bossing people around, and Garrett is content to be at her service. Hence, why she likely had the ridiculous amount of sugar in her system after spending a mere three hours with him when I had a work emergency not too long ago.

"Did you have a good time with Uncle Garrett, Meerkat?" I asked her afterward as I ran a hand through her unruly black hair.

She nodded, holding onto her airplane plushie in bed like it was her lifeline. Her bed was right next to mine in our small, one-bedroom rental, and I knew that no matter how many times I reminded her to stay in her own bed, she'd find her way to mine in the middle of the night. "He's my favorite, Mommy."

I had a feeling my daughter had a little crush, and I couldn't blame her. "He's pretty great, I'll admit that."

She stared at me with her hazel eyes that looked more brown when she was tired. "I want you to marry him, Mommy."

My breath caught in my lungs. She'd spent time with Garrett several times before, but she'd never mentioned something like this. I dismissed it like any other silly comment my almost four-year-old was prone to making. "And I want you to go to sleep, my little love."

But while my daughter might be coddling dreams of Garrett and me being together–shipping us as a married couple–the idea alone made me laugh.

I trust Garrett, one hundred and ten percent. I've called him in a pinch before–like the time a year ago, when I had an appointment I couldn't reschedule, and neither my mom nor the backup sitter I was using at the time was available–and I would call him again to take care of my daughter in the future, too. But that doesn't mean I trust him with *everything*–least of all my heart.

Despite his tall and toned physique, and the way his waist tapers in the center, making his uniform look like it's glued to him. Despite the warmth that envelops me whenever he's around, like the first rays of sunshine after a winter storm. And despite the way my spirit ignites when his smoldering eyes settle on me, so much so that I have both an urge to run and a need to stay.

Despite the number of times I've brought myself to climax to the very vivid thoughts of his face between my legs. And despite the fact that it's him, *always him*, in my most salacious dreams.

Despite *all* that, the only relationship Garrett and I can ever have is as friends.

"I wasn't just on that flight; I was the one who piloted it." He winks. "What did you think of that smooth landing?"

I lift a brow and smile, noticing him eyeing my dimples. "I think the autopilot did a great job."

He throws his head back and laughs. "Touché. Why didn't you tell me you were coming to Vegas? I could have driven you to the airport with me."

I shrug. "I didn't know your schedule or if you were around. I didn't want to burden you."

He shakes his head like I've said the most preposterous thing. "You just don't get it, do you?"

"Get what?"

"You–" He takes a big breath and seems to think better of finishing the thought. "Never mind. Where are you staying?"

"The Encore."

"Come on." Garrett grabs the handle of my carry-on, along with his, tilting his head to urge me to follow him. "I'll share a cab with you. I'm headed in the same direction."

Chapter Four

BELLA

"Hey, Mom. How's it going over there?" I pull my phone out in the hallway, outside the conference room, deciding to take a few minutes to chat with my mom and find out how Meera is doing before heading to the next room for the happy hour event.

Three days of this, and I'm beat. I've walked from one conference room to the next, slept without the little arms around my neck that I miss terribly, and taken enough notes to give myself carpal tunnel. I'm ready to go home tomorrow.

"Hi, sweetie. Oh, it's going good. How is the conference going?"

I think about telling my mom about running into Chaz, but I settle for keeping things to myself for now. There's no one I trust more than my mom, but there's also no need to get her worked up right this second when I don't even know what will happen with his threat anyway. "Good. I'm ready to come home though."

"I can understand. *Ouch!*" my mom cries suddenly. "Meera, *Nani* is not one of your Barbie dolls. I barely have any hair on my head to begin with, and now you insist on ripping out the few strands I have left."

I giggle, knowing my daughter is back to using anyone she can find as her hair model. Aside from a few stuffed toys, she insisted on a hair salon kit for Christmas this year, and from what I can tell, her grandma is her next victim.

"*Nani*, they're Dora dolls, not Barbie dolls. I still need to put the other six clippies in. Now, put on your big girl under-pants and hold still!"

I purse my lips, knowing my mom is probably rolling her eyes but holding as still as possible. No one can escape my little girl's commands. She's tiny but oh-so fierce. "Looks like you both are having a swell ol' time." I snicker. "I should stay a couple of extra days, huh?"

"Don't you dare," my mother scolds. "I'm not sure how long I can survive under this little dictator's rule."

I laugh again, knowing my mother only says that to goad Meera into an argument, but she'd stay longer if I wanted her to because of how much she loves spending time with her. After leaving her job as an emergency room doctor, my mom now has fairly consistent hours at a nearby clinic in the East Bay where I live. Mom even picks Meera up from her preschool sometimes and takes her to her house—the one I grew up in—so I don't have to rush back home.

"Seriously, though, how are you doing, Mom? She's not being too much of a handful, is she?"

"Oh, no. We've had a marvelous time. She did give me some trouble with the fish tacos I made, but—"

"I don't eat fish," my daughter asserts in the background, and I already know what her next words will be—I've heard them every week for the past two months since she made the decision. "I don't eat anything that used to have a brain. I told you that, *Nani*."

"And I told you their brains are so small, they don't count

as brains. You need the B12 vitamin and the omega-3 fatty acids from them," my mother argues back, using her doctor voice, which will have little effect on my little girl.

"I don't like fat acids."

While my daughter and my mom bicker inside my earbud, I watch a crowd of attendees shuffle from the main conference room to another one nearby. And as much as I want to do nothing more than stay on the phone, or better yet, catch the next flight back home, I know my company expects me to network while I'm here. But, God, just the thought of having to plaster on a fake smile and interact with other humans seems so taxing, especially after having done it for the past three days.

As it is, I'm not the most talkative person in the world—I'm not the most social, either. My favorite evening consists of throwing my woolen-socked feet up on the coffee table with one of those hydration masks on my face, while playing *Wordscapes* on my phone and taking swigs out of my box of lemonade-wild cherry *Nerds*. If I'm feeling extra daring, I'll even change it up with sour lemon and amped-apple *Nerds*.

But this . . . having to schmooze and hobnob with people? I'd rather stick my hand inside the garbage disposal and flip on the switch.

Knowing I'll feel guilty if I don't at least go for a little while, I get my mom's attention on the phone. "Hey, Mom? I've gotta go; they're starting the next event. Will you give bossy-pants a kiss for me? And tell her to give you a kiss from me too, since you both deserve one."

"Sounds good. Have fun, sweetheart. Don't worry about a thing here," Mom replies, and I hear a mimicking, "Yeah, don't worry about a thing here," from my baby girl in the background.

God, I miss her.

~

I'M WAITING to order my drink at the bar when I see—no, feel—the heat of an unsettling gaze on my neck. Turning toward the direction, I catch Chaz speaking with a few attendees. Some of them even look familiar from my brief conversation with them over the past couple of days. *Great.*

His icy glare stays on me while he speaks, pretending to smile and nod in time with their conversation. Fucking asshole.

This isn't a mandatory event, and I honestly don't *need* to be here. Sure, the company likes us to socialize and mingle with the other attendees since we're all from similar industries, but this isn't a required event. I could always say I wasn't feeling well and decided to duck out early.

I pull my lips to the side as I think about the pros and cons of my decision, like I do with almost every decision I've made in my life—save for the time I slept with a narcissistic, arrogant asshole at a conference on a whim and ended up pregnant. While the result of that decision isn't one I will ever regret, the person I spent the night with is.

The bartender lifts his eyebrow in my direction, waiting for me to tell him what I want, when I see movement in my periphery. A throat clears behind me. *Shit!*

"Bella."

Before I allow him to say another word—without my attorney present—I make the only decision I can in this situation. Turning the other way to avoid coming in contact with the asshole, I rush toward the other side of the room filled with conference-goers. I follow my instinct, cutting a path through a large group of people chattering with drinks in their hands. I swing my head to get my bearings, spotting the exit to my right.

Thankfully, I don't hear Chaz's voice again, and if he has

any sense of self-preservation, I doubt he'll yell or come after me in this setting. Still, my nerves are shot to hell, and I can't be sure, so without looking over my shoulder to confirm if he's there or not, I rush out of the large conference hall.

My feet still feel like they're on a hamster wheel as I spot the sign indicating the way to the double set of escalators. I jog toward them as fast as I can in my heels, tucking my black purse under my arm. I can feel a bead of sweat line the top of my eyebrows, even as the cool air hits my exposed neck and legs.

I take the escalators down to the casino floor before finally looking over my shoulder, noting that no one familiar is behind me. My heart races under my cream cashmere sweater, and I instinctively raise my hand to my chest in an effort to massage my ribs, taking in long gulps of air. "Shit, shit, shit!"

Once downstairs, I try to read the signs above my head to orient myself again. As with every casino I've visited during my trip, this one is no less grand and impressive—and no less confusing. I recall the massive fountain in an oversized lobby I had passed earlier to get to the escalators. Finding it again, I note the entry into the sprawling casino, currently bustling with patrons.

Every roulette and blackjack table is swarming, while the glittering lights of the slot machines entice players to come take a chance. Every now and then, a huge shout erupts when someone wins big.

My eyes roam, searching for the exit as I pass a few poker tables, when I hear my name. "Bella!"

At first, my shoulders lock and my spine stiffens before I realize the voice isn't the one I was expecting.

I look around, trying to find where the sound came from when my eyes land on the man walking toward me, no longer dressed in his pilot's uniform. Instead, he's now donning a form-fitting gray sweater with a white stripe going across it with dark denims.

His longish, dark blond hair is slightly styled, and his ever-present scruff highlights his angled jaw even more. The sleeves of his sweater are pulled up, revealing not only the sexiest, veiny forearms I've ever seen, but also the softest smattering of blond hair. A silver-banded watch surrounds one of his wrists while a multi-colored beaded bracelet—*Is that the same bracelet Meera made him last Christmas?*—winds itself tightly around the other.

A knot forms in my throat at the sight of him wearing the bracelet my daughter gave him. My eyes rake back over him as I force myself not to blatantly ogle. But, goodness me, how can one man make casual-wear look like something out of a catalog? He gets closer, and my eyes snag on the string of silver around his neck, tucked into the V-collar of his sweater, before my brows pull up in surprise. "Garrett, hi!"

Garrett's smile brightens, competing with his navy-blue gaze, and he slips his hands into his pockets. His brows furrow as he takes me in, and I can only assume he sees the tension lining my features. "Where are you rushing off to? What's wrong?"

"I'm . . ." I huff out a breath, looking over my shoulder again, as if a kidnapper might grab and pull me into an unmarked white van. "I saw Chaz again."

I hadn't run into him this whole time, and stupidly, I was convinced I'd gotten away with not having to see him again. This is a rather large conference after all.

Garrett closes the distance between us, coming to stand a foot away from me. Surprisingly, his presence actually makes me relax, though I suppose I'd feel the same way if I'd spotted any of my friends or family right now. The comfort of finding a familiar face in a crowd of strangers—someone whom I not only know, but also like.

His jaw twitches as if he's grinding his molars. "Did he say something to you again?"

I shake my head, remembering Chaz's glare on me. "I didn't let him. He barely just said my name before I rushed out and came running down here."

Garrett's eyes flit between mine. "Where are you headed now?"

"Back to my hotel." I push my hair over my shoulder. "I might as well pack. I'm going to see if I can get on an earlier flight tomorrow."

Garrett looks over his shoulder, and I follow his gaze toward a few men focused on a poker game, noting one of them to be his twin brother Dean. Garrett turns back to me before sliding his thumb over his lip, seeming to think about his next question. "Do you . . . do you want to grab a drink?"

He must see the hesitation on my face because he amends his question. "As friends, Bells. Nothing more."

I grin, noting the use of my nickname. "So, not as my husband, then?"

"Only if you want me to be," he replies without missing a beat.

Oh, that grin of his . . . It's all sorts of dangerous.

I shake my head, a slow rise of heat pinking my cheeks. My eyes flick to his group of friends. "What about them? Won't they mind you leaving them?"

He doesn't follow my gaze; instead, his navy blues stay pinned on me. "No."

I huff out a breath, my shoulders giving way. It would be nice to just sit down and grab a drink with a friend after so long. How long has it been since I've even had a drink? Months? I don't go out; I don't really even have many friends. When I'm home, I spend most of my time with either Meera or my mom, only changing up my routine to meet with Rani and Melody when our schedules can accommodate it.

Plus, this seems harmless. After all the time I've spent in Garrett's company, and from everything I've seen and heard about him, he's a nice guy—a great guy, really. It doesn't hurt that he's also physically appealing—*very* appealing. As much as I've denied my attraction to him every time Rani or Melody have brought up the subject, I can't deny it to myself.

But, attraction be damned. My heart will go nowhere near him and his deep navy-blue eyes under thickets of long brown lashes—the same ones I can barely look at for more than a few seconds—or his alluring, crooked smile that makes promises I know men like him can never keep.

I nod. "Okay."

Garrett lifts a brow as if he fully expected to have to argue. "Okay?"

"I mean, unless you want me to change my mind?" I hold back my smile, unsuccessfully.

He shakes his head. "Smartass." He tilts his head for me to follow him. "Let's go. I know a really good lounge."

I FEEL tingles in my fingertips and toes as the two margaritas I've already consumed over the past half-hour rush to all parts of my system at the same speed as my blood. I point a flimsy, sweet potato fry at Garrett, licking the salt from the margarita off my lips. "So, that's it? You just went on your first airplane trip at the age of four and knew you wanted to be a pilot?"

Garrett leans back in his chair, taking another sip of his whiskey. "That's it."

"Huh," I muse, impressed with his determination. "I wish I could make up my mind that fast. I'm one of those people who usually weighs out all the options and paths before I decide which one to take. You should see me at a vending machine."

He stares at me for a moment, the dim lighting of the lounge doing nothing to dull his striking features. "Once I find what I'm looking for, I don't waver off course."

I pop the rest of the fry into my mouth, chewing it thoughtfully. My mind tells me there's more to Garrett's declaration, but I'm too tipsy to catch on. Instead, I focus on the part of my brain telling me to make sure I eat. I haven't had alcohol in God knows how long. I'd always been a lightweight, anyway—more than tipsy after two or three drinks max. I need to pace myself and eat enough food to make a nice base in my stomach for the drinks. "And have you?"

Garrett lifts a brow. "Have I what?"

"I mean, aside from becoming a pilot, have you found what you're looking for?"

Garrett puts his drink on the table before pinning me with that unsettling navy swirl. "Yes."

The air in my lungs seems to thin, and I refrain from asking him the next question resting on my tongue. The question that begs to be released: *What?*

Instead, I take another large gulp from my glass, letting the cold liquid quell the heat blanketing my chest before steering the conversation in a safer direction. "Did you have a fun weekend with your brother and friends?"

"They're a crazy bunch, that's for sure. We don't all get to meet up very often, but we keep up almost daily through texts."

I smile. "That sounds nice. Besides Dean, since I already know he lives in Tahoe, where do the rest of them live?"

"Hudson lives in the Bay Area, but he travels a lot as a geologist, and Rohan is actually better friends with Dean. They work at the same fire station together."

I take another sip of my drink. "I don't think I know a geologist. Sounds like a cool job."

"Yeah, he's done really well in the field. He travels a lot, but his daughter is already grown so he has flexibility."

That makes me pause. "He has an adult daughter? He looks really young."

Garrett nods. "Yeah, he became a dad in his teens, but he managed to do a really good job raising her practically on his own and building his career. It wasn't easy, but he doesn't regret a minute of it."

I don't have to say it, but I know exactly how Garrett's friend feels. Raising Meera as a single mom hasn't been easy, but I haven't regretted a second of it. I've been lucky to have my mom nearby, but I've also been bullish about doing things for her by myself for the most part.

Even when Mom asked me and Meera to move in with her—since her house is much bigger than my expensive one-bedroom condo—I refused because I not only wanted my independence, but I also needed to show myself that I could raise my daughter on my own. And I'm proud of the little girl I've raised.

That's not to say it hasn't been tempting to move in with Mom at times. Like when the water heater in my condo broke and it took my landlord a week to fix it. Meera and I had to shower at Mom's house the whole week. And when my landlord finally came by, he made it seem like I'd interrupted his fucking mid-day nap.

Between the fact that the place is small, old, and falling apart, I know one of the things I need to do when I get back is to look for something different. Maybe I'll even find one closer to Meera's preschool. It's time that Meera has her own space and starts sleeping in her own bedroom. As much as I love having her crawl into my bed in the middle of the night, it's a form of independence I want her to learn.

For the next few minutes, Garrett and I talk more about his friends and his job. Garrett tells me more about his family. Even though he comes from a broken family, he's close to both his biological parents. Apparently, his mom lives in Colorado with her husband. His grandma lives with them, and both Garrett and Dean are extremely close to her. I already know Garrett's dad and stepmom since they are Rani's in-laws.

"I don't have any of my grandparents anymore, so you're lucky that you still have her," I say, popping another fry into my mouth and chasing it with a sip of my drink.

"Yeah . . ." Garrett rubs the back of his neck, and I see the concern cover his face. "To be honest, I've been worried about her recently. She's in her late eighties, and she's gone to the hospital a couple of times for pneumonia and other breathing problems over the past year."

I reach out and place my hand over his on the table. "I'm sorry, pilot. I can see she means a lot to you. Maybe you can go spend time with her again soon."

Garrett gives me a small smile but doesn't say more.

Over the next hour—and two more shots that I find myself surprisingly throwing back like I'm some old pro, and another round of drinks—I talk to Garrett about my job as a hardware engineer. I tell him how much I enjoy it, and how I just started leading the current mobile team at work.

"It's not as exciting as flying a plane, but I like the safety and stability of it." I wipe my hand on the napkin in my lap. "It's given me a decent paycheck to provide for Meera."

"And you've done a good fucking job providing for her."

That familiar knot in my throat grates against me. "Financially, yes, but . . . sometimes, I don't know if I'm giving her everything she needs."

This time Garrett grabs my hand on the table, his face serious. "Bells, I've spent time with Meera. She's one hell of a kid. She speaks her mind and knows exactly what she wants. On top of all that, she's brilliant as hell and so mature for her age. If she wasn't getting what she needed, you'd know. You're an amazing mom and she knows it, and so does everyone around you."

"Thanks." I squeeze Garrett's hand as the buzzing in my veins accelerates. "I'm scared, Garrett. I haven't been able to sleep since I've been here. I'm so scared Chaz will ruin the little stability I've built around my daughter."

"I know it's useless to tell you everything will be okay, because you're not going to believe me. But would it help to come up with a plan? Since you like to plan and think through things, do you want to talk through what you need to do after you get home?"

My tongue feels heavy in my mouth and a haze is quickly building around my vision. It's funny how the haze has me focused on things I'd rather not focus on when it comes to Garrett Meyer, like his eyes and his lips. Or the way his Adam's apple bobs when he takes a sip. Or even the ever-present scruffy shadow on his jaw.

And how, in the short time I've actually spent with him alone, he knows me well enough to know that I like to plan things. It's like he knows my love language.

Distracting myself from the overly distracting man in front of me, I eye the full shot of whatever–battery acid?–sitting in front of Garrett.

"Hey!" I reach for it and my speech feels slurred. "Wh–why didn't you take that shot?"

Garrett eyes the battery acid. "For the same reason you shouldn't."

I narrow my eyes at him, pinching the shot glass between my thumb and index finger. "Are you . . . *inspiring* that I'm drunk or something? I'll have you know," my voice sounds loud even to my own ears, "I'm not a drunkard. But if I do drink, I can totally handle my alcohol."

Garrett's palm lays on top of my wrist, stopping me from bringing the shot to my lips. "I would never *inspire* that you were drunk, and even if you were, I wouldn't doubt for a second that you could handle it. But how about you drink that glass of water in front of you first?"

My wrist feels warm under the weight of Garrett's hand. The humming sensation travels up my arm, through my shoulder, and down into my stomach, mixing with the alcohol there and creating a delicious buzz.

"I meant to say 'insinuating.' You were *insinuating* that I was drunk. I just couldn't come up with the word right then."

He lifts his hand off my wrist and I immediately want to snag it back. Too bad my movements wouldn't be fast enough. Pushing the water glass toward me, he urges, "Water."

I groan. "Fine. You're really bossy, you know that?" I pick up the glass of water and take a few sips before putting it down. "There, happy? *Dad?*"

Calling him *Dad* and using that word after so long has melancholy swooping in and settling into my belly along with the acidic alcohol.

"Bells?" Garrett grimaces, probably from seeing the look on my face.

"You know who I deeply dislike, pilot?" It's taking me a little longer to form complete sentences, but I'm still pretty sure I'm not drunk. I don't let Garrett answer. "Dads. *Fucking dads*. They're useless. Most of them, anyway," I press, unzipping my small purse and taking out the little yellow box I'd packed away in there. It's time to take a hit.

Garrett stares at me, but I don't let him lock me into one of his gazes. I've always been good at avoiding his eyes. They're too blue, too deep. *Too dangerous.*

I rip open the flat top, offering him first dibs. "Want some?" When he shakes his head, I shrug before pouring half the small box of lemony rock candy into my mouth. "Suit yourself, *blondie*." I crunch away, feeling a little more like myself.

"I got lucky with one of the good ones, I suppose," Garrett says after a minute.

I nod as slowly as I can without giving myself a head-rush. "Your dad is definitely one of the good ones, pilot. So is your brother, Darian; I'm glad my cousin married him." I lick my lips, tasting the sweetness from my candy still on them. "I bet you'll be a lot like them when you have your own kids."

Garrett stays quiet for a moment before he whispers his reply. I barely hear it over the noise in the lounge. "I hope so."

I go back to eyeing the shot still sitting in front of him. I bet it would taste pretty good washing down this lemon flavor on my tongue. But before I can reach out and snatch it, Garrett throws it down his throat.

I cross my arms over my chest. "Rude."

He shrugs with a smirk. "I guess if you're making bad decisions in Vegas, then I'm making bad decisions in Vegas."

I beam at him. "You're a true friend, G."

A half an hour and another round of drinks later—one where Garrett only lets me take a few more sips like the party-pooper he is—I can officially say, I'm fucking tossed.

Plastered!

Drunk as a skunk!

"What are you laughing at?" Garret's navy blues assess me.

I giggle again, but for the life of me, I can't remember what's so funny. A part of me wants to weep. My life feels upside down and inside out, and I can't figure out why the man in front of me has me feeling so flustered.

He's my friend. *Friend.* He's not someone I ever want to

have any other feelings for besides friendly ones, so why doesn't my body respond to him that way?

I tuck my hair behind my ear to give my hand something to do. "I do need a plan, pilot. Help me come up with a plan."

He nods, his lids heavy over his eyes. "But we're pretty fucking drunk, Bells. Maybe it's not a good idea to come up with plans when we're drunk."

My chest heaves and the water in my eyes from my giggles burns inside my lids, threatening to transform into a wave I've been holding at bay ever since I saw Chaz a couple of days ago. My lips turn downward, and before I can even stop them, the first of what will likely be more tears splashes onto our table. It soaks my cheek, casting a dark haze over the entire room. "I . . . I don't want to lose my baby, pilot."

Garrett scoots his chair closer and before my face can fall, his warm palms capture it, tilting it toward him. His thumbs brush away the tears under my lids and his face comes within inches of mine.

My eyes close on their own and I want . . . I want him to . . .

His voice has my lids rising back up. "Okay, how can I help?"

Snort giggling and crying at the same time, I'm not sure which emotion is stronger in my inebriated state. "Short of marrying me and adopting Meera as your own, I don't think you *can* help me."

Garret's Adam's apple bobs as his face loses all humor. "Then let's start with step one."

Chapter Five

GARRETT

Sometimes what happens in Vegas can stay in Vegas.

Other times . . . not so much.

My eyes snap open as a faint snore fills my eardrum, followed by the gentlest puff of air on my chest. The spot on my skin where her warm breath hits it repeatedly starts to heat, in opposition with the shiver that runs the span of my body.

I turn slightly to take in the mess of dark hair that smells like candy on my pillow. She always smells like sweet lemony candy. Her head lays on my shoulder, her face pressed to the top of my chest. I don't have to look under the covers to know her leg is sprawled over my hip, her calf pressing on my hardened erection. With her arm over my chest, she's holding on to me like some sort of spider monkey.

My wife.

Slowly, as if being replayed at half-speed, with only the highlights turned on, the night flits back to me, and I'm worried my racing heart will wake her up before I can figure out how to handle this situation.

Because one thing is for sure, we have a fucking situation.

My mind flips back on the memory of Bella and me, holding each other up as we first took an Uber to get our marriage license. In my inebriated state, somehow I'd had enough wits about me to do a quick search on my phone and find out the process. Thankfully, the license bureau was still open, and we both pretended to be sober enough to sign the paperwork and take pictures. Then we staggered to the chapel, giggling the entire way, convinced we were on a mission that would be the answer to all her problems.

I remember the receptionist with the multiple piercings in his face and the purple mohawk. He and Bella exchanged tips on hair products—something about bleaches and toners.

I recall scrawling my name on various papers and dropping my license on the floor before picking it up and dropping it again, only to stare at Bella's lips as she giggled at my clumsiness. God, I wanted to kiss those soft lips again. I couldn't wait to kiss them. I couldn't wait to get to the *I do* part.

My hands can still feel the warmth of her face when I held it at the altar before asking her once more. "Are you sure?"

Lids heavy, she said yes. "Kiss me already, pilot."

And I did. Fuck, I *so* did. I might not have been able to feel my legs at that moment, but I definitely felt her lips on mine. Warm and soft, luscious and sweet. I swear, I didn't want to let go.

I don't know how long it took for us to walk back to her hotel, but it was right as we were entering that I remember feeling like I was in a purgatory between fantasy and reality, my senses slowly coming back to me. Maybe it was the fresh air from the walk, or maybe it was the alcohol finally making its way through my liver. My movements felt sluggish, but I distinctly remember getting into the empty elevator and watching Bella sway.

She pulled out her key card, still in the paper insert with

her room number written on it. "Ah! Room 1625." She giggled like she'd just discovered the most amusing thing before taking out another little yellow box of *Nerds* and sloppily pouring half of it into her mouth.

She swayed again, crunching on her candy, and I pulled her to me to hold her steady. My hands laid on her hips as a pang of guilt hit me square in the chest. *What the fuck did we just do? Did we actually get married?*

"Bella—"

She put her index finger on my lips. "You're done for, pilot. You're mine now. Just mine."

"Bells," I mumbled under her finger.

"Blink once if you're mine," she stammered. "Twice if you regret it."

I blinked once.

There was no other answer.

She leaned in to seal me to her with a kiss. "Do you like me, pilot?"

My voice was raspy and, even though she was the only one who would hear it, I whispered, "More than you know."

She nodded, as if my answer was completely expected. "And you like my daughter."

It wasn't a question. "Wholeheartedly."

Her sweet lemony breath wafted over the side of my face. I felt it in my airways. "And now you're my husband."

I tightened my grip on her hips. "It looks that way."

As soon as the elevator doors opened, she pulled me out by my hand. "Then fuck me the way a good husband fucks his new wife."

Jesus Christ.

I followed her to her room, my feet dragging. One foot begged me to turn back and walk the other way, while the other propelled me forward.

The other won.

I watched her—my new bride—undress all the way down to her panties and bra. Beer goggles or not, this woman was a fucking knockout. She was stunning when alcohol sped through my system, and she was breathtaking as my senses came back to me.

A lean figure with the softest of curves I'd ever seen. Her stomach dipped right at the navel, surrounded by miles upon miles of smooth tan skin, like a pristine beach, that had me salivating. The cups of her bra filled out with breasts that I knew would fit perfectly in my hands. Her round hips swayed gently, enticingly. So fucking enticingly.

I walked over to where she stood, her eyes pinned to mine as her thumbs looped on the sides of her lavender-colored panties. For some reason, I knew she'd be wearing purple panties.

Her gaze dropped to my lips as my hands fastened over hers. "Show me how much you want me, pilot."

Fuck, she had no clue, no fucking clue how much I wanted her.

Raising my hands to cradle her face, I took in her heavy lids and bloodshot eyes. "Listen to me, beautiful. There is no world, no fucking planet, no plane of existence where I don't want you. But, tonight . . . tonight isn't the night I take you."

Her mouth turned downward. "Why not?"

"Because even though I know I won't regret this, *you* will tomorrow. And because when I fuck you the first time, I need you to remember every single detail of it."

I stared at her pouty, downturned mouth. Whether I had just rejected the offer of a fucking lifetime or not, I knew I needed to do the right thing—even if the right thing was the hardest thing I'd ever had to do.

Her shoulders sagged but she reluctantly climbed into bed. She had no clue what it took for me to not go back on my word, to be the gentleman I knew I wasn't. She had no fucking clue, and she'd fall asleep thinking I didn't want her.

I hobbled to the minibar, taking out a bottle of water, knowing I only had a few minutes before she passed out and it would be impossible to wake her up. Unscrewing the cap, I made her drink half before going in search of something to quell the hangover that was as certain as the morning when she woke up. Fuck, I needed something myself, too.

I found a travel-sized packet of Tylenol with only two pills in her makeup tote. She needed both of them more than I did. Traipsing back to the bed, I shook her just as she was sinking into the pillow, curled on top of the blankets.

"Go away, pilot," she grumbled. "You're a terrible husband. First, you won't do naughty things to me, and now you won't let me sleep."

I bit back my smile, pulling her up from her curled position on the bed. "Take this and then I'll go."

She reluctantly got up, taking the pills from my hand before I held the bottle of water to her lips again. She took a sip and swallowed, her chocolate-brown eyes peeking out of her lids. "Are you really going to leave?"

I took in the vulnerability on her face. "Do you want me to?"

She licked her lips, not at all trying to be seductive but being so anyway. "I want you to stay." Those chocolate pools slowly flicked back and forth between my eyes. "Please stay with me."

I stared at her for a moment, trying to think of the right thing to do. I should go back to my own hotel and into my own bed, but I wanted to stay. And at three in the morning, my mind couldn't hold on to a single thought past the fact that I was fucking bone tired.

I nodded, pulling off my sweater and throwing my jeans onto the nearby chair. Coaxing her under the comforter, I scooted in behind her and wrapped my arm around her, pulling her back to my chest. The last thing I remember is placing a kiss on her shoulder before tucking my nose into her candy-scented hair and drifting off to sleep.

Somehow, through the middle of the night, we'd ended up in this position—with her draped over me like a blanket—and there was nothing I disliked about it. I'd make wishes on every falling star and toss a million pennies into a well from now until the end of time to wake up like this with her every damn day.

From the bright light peeking in through the curtains, I can tell we've slept in. Though, I'm not sure how long. I'm still thinking about what to say to her, wondering how she'll react when she wakes up, when she mumbles something into my skin, stirring softly. Her lips tickle my side as her calf presses down even farther on the boner I'm barely containing inside my boxer-briefs. I hold back an audible groan.

Bella takes in a sharp breath before pulling away from me. "Ouch. My head." Her hand rushes to capture her forehead before she shifts to the side. She starts to wipe off the drool on the side of her mouth with the back of her hand when she goes completely stock still.

Oh, yeah. Here it comes.

"Wha . . . What?" She eyes me with utter bewilderment, like one would if they woke up next to a wild animal. Her hair is a tangled mess, a few strands sticking to her face. "Garrett?" Her voice is hoarse from drinking too much last night. "What are you . . .?"

I stay quiet, unmoving, as I watch the realization settle into her features. The beginnings of denial wash over her before her eyes widen and her mouth turns downward. "No! No, no, no." She gets up frantically, then grasps her head between her hands. "Oh, God, my head. I feel like I was hit with a sledgehammer."

That wouldn't be too far from the truth with how much she drank.

She assesses me warily before she looks down at her scant clothing. She pulls the blanket back over herself quickly, completely panicked, as if I hadn't gotten an eye-full last night. "Garrett! Please, tell me we didn't."

I swallow, slowly getting up next to her and scooting back against the headrest. I'm a little unsure about how to handle this, seeing as I've never ended up drunk and married to a woman in Vegas before, but I do know that I need to stay calm for her. It would do no good for both of us to freak out. "Didn't what? Didn't sleep together or . . . didn't get married?"

Her face pales and for a second, I'm worried she's going to vomit.

"Bells?"

"No." She shakes her head and her bottom lids pool. "No, this can't be happening."

My chest tightens at the sight of her—a sight I tried to prepare myself for late last night when I started getting my bearings back, but a sight I'm unprepared for still. I lean forward to place a hand on her bare shoulder but she jerks away from me. *Ouch.*

"We didn't sleep together. You asked me to stay, but I didn't touch you." Given her history with Chaz, I know how important it is for her to know that. When her chest still rises and falls like her heart is pounding to break free, I gently prod her to see what she recalls. "What do you remember about last night?"

She shakes her head, like if she denies it, it'll become untrue, but a sob still bubbles up through her throat. "Garrett, please . . . *please* tell me it's not true—" She stops abruptly and scans the room, her head swiveling from the nightstand to the little study table in the corner.

No longer caring about her modesty, she gets out of bed and rushes toward the papers I'd placed on the desk.

"No." She reads the confirmation of our decision last night, her eyes dropping to our joint signatures, before looking back at me with the same bewilderment she woke up with. Her chin quivers as she shakes her head in disbelief. "This can't be happening."

Bella's knees wobble and I'm on my feet, making my way to her before she can crash to the ground. I wrap my arms around her, holding her up as she hangs limply against me, sobbing. "How could I have done this? How could I have been so irresponsible *again*?"

Wow. I know we were both drunk, but it still feels shitty to be lumped in with her waste of space sperm donor.

Once her full-on sobs turn softer, I lean back, cradling her face in my palms. I wipe her tears, laying a gentle kiss on her cheek. She flinches a little, but I don't take it as an insult. "Do you remember *why* we did it?"

She sniffles, nodding. "Because of Chaz and . . . because I got the brilliant idea that if we got married and you adopted Meera, he wouldn't be able to demand custody since you'd legally be her father."

I nod, giving her a meaningful look. "So, what's the problem?"

Her breathing falters for a second and, as expected, her brows fold. She looks at me like I've lost my goddamn mind.

I probably have.

"What do you mean, *what's the problem*? We got *married*, Garrett. *Married!* Do you know how crazy that is? What the hell are we going to do now? What are we going to tell people?" Her eyes widen to large pools of chocolate. "Oh, God . . . What am I going to tell Meera and my mom?"

Not going to lie, my brain has been reeling with many of the same questions, but one of us has to hold it together. I run my hand up and down her arms. "First, I think you need to breathe–"

"*Breathe?*" Her face morphs as if I've said the most preposterous thing. "How the hell are you so calm right now? Why aren't you freaking out with me?"

Because I feel like I've hit the fucking jackpot.

Beat the house.

Struck fucking gold!

I wish I could tell her how much I don't regret a single minute of last night, aside from wishing we'd done it sober. But instead, I keep my cards close to my chest, knowing she'd look at me with an even more crazed look in her eyes–one that wouldn't bode me well–if I said it. "I woke up about an hour ago. I had time to process it."

"And? What have you processed? That we're completely crazy?"

"What we did may have been rash, but we did it for the right reason–"

"The right reason?" she snaps, not letting me finish. "As in you adopting Meera?"

"Yes."

She scoffs, giving me that same glare like she thinks I'm a few cards short of a deck. "I think you're still drunk, pilot." She nods as if agreeing with her own assessment. "That would explain why you still seem to think this was a *good* idea."

"Why? Why isn't it a good idea?" I dip my head lower to catch her eyes. "So we rushed into a decision to get married. So what? I agree we were crazy and drunk, but now that it's happened, why can't we move on to the next step?"

"The next step," she huffs, "as in, moving forward with the adoption?" She backs away, putting distance between us as if she's having a hard time thinking in my arms.

I nod.

"No!" She raises her arms before dropping them back at

her sides. "No, Garrett. That *was,* and still *is,* a terrible idea! Meera may trust you and love you, but that doesn't mean you can adopt her. You might not be a stranger to her like Chaz, but you're not her father, either. Can you imagine how confusing it would be for her if you just became her adoptive dad out of the blue?" She shakes her head. "In my drunk brain it may have sounded like a logical solution, but it's *one hundred percent* the wrong one now."

I won't deny that Bella makes sense. As much as I fucking hate that she does, she has a point. I don't have to have experience raising children to know that telling Meera that I wanted to be her adoptive dad out of the blue would confuse her. It would even confuse the shit out of an older kid, let alone an almost four-year-old.

Bella steps toward me, pulling my hand into hers. "We have to get an annulment, Garrett." She scans my gaze. "This is Vegas; I'm sure this sort of thing happens all the time here."

Fuck.

I nod, shoving down the wistfulness from showing on my expression. "Okay, but I doubt anything official will get done today since it's Sunday."

"Shit! I forgot about that." She runs to the nightstand to grab her purse, pulling out her phone. "Dammit, my battery is low but it's ten-twenty-two. My flight is at four today." She rushes to the closet, pulling out the hotel robe and draping it around herself. Then, she squeezes her temples, talking to herself as she paces. "Okay, okay. I'll get home and research what we need to do to get an annulment, and I'll start the paperwork tomorrow. Maybe I can even talk to the same family lawyer who'll advise me on Meera's case. Wait!" She stops to look at the wall in front of her. "I think Melody's mom is in family law! I need to text Mel and find out."

I walk back to the mattress and perch on it with my

elbow on my knees. Pulling my head between my hands, I rake my hair. She's right. I know she's right. This plan was half-baked under the spell of a shitload of alcohol, and as much as I wish otherwise, we'd be stupid not to do what she's suggesting by annulling it.

Wouldn't we?

Bella flutters around the room, mumbling to herself, seeming to plan out what she's going to do. At one point, she stops and walks to where I'm sitting before kneeling in front of me. She rests her hands on my knees. "This was my fault, G. I'm the one who came up with this dumb idea and got you into this mess."

"Bella—"

"It means a lot to me that you were willing to help me out—whether you were drunk or not—and that you're not freaking out like I am right now. This impacts your life just as much, and I promise I'll do everything in my power to get this fixed as soon as possible. I didn't mean to drag you into my problems like this."

"You didn't drag me into this; I *volunteered*. I was drunk, but not so drunk that I didn't have control over what I was doing. In fact, I'm the one who suggested it in the first place."

Bella squeezes my knees. "You might have suggested it, but I remember enough to know I planted the idea in your head. In any case, why would you even consider doing any of this for me, Garrett? Don't you know how much this would unravel your life to be a husband? To adopt a child?"

"It wouldn't."

"It would!" she insists. "Even if I could look past how an adoption would impact Meera—which I can't, but for the sake of argument, let's pretend—it would completely change your life. It would mean no longer being able to date other people. It could mean being responsible for Meera—physically, emotionally, and financially—and I could never ask you to do that! You have your life to live, and if you wanted to be married, you would have been already."

"You wouldn't have to ask. I would do it, if it helped you with this Chaz situation."

She looks bewildered again. "Why? Why would you do that for me—for us? Why would you be okay with turning your life upside down like that?"

Because there's nothing I wouldn't do for you.

My heart gallops inside my chest as my mind forms a response without hesitation. But my lips keep that truth sealed behind them. I hedge with a middle-ground answer. "Because I'm your friend, and I care about both you and Meera. If staying married and adopting Meera means hurting the chances of that weasley asshole getting joint custody of her, then it doesn't matter to me, even if I have to change my life to do it."

Bella shakes her head. "It wouldn't be the right decision for Meera, and I always have to think about what's right for her first. Maybe you'd help get Chaz off our backs if you were to adopt her, but then what? You and I couldn't be married forever, and how would that work for Meera when we got divorced and you'd already adopted her? She'd be back to being in an unsettled situation."

She continues, "Anyway, I don't even want a boyfriend, let alone a husband . . . And even if I did decide to get married one day," she swings her finger between us, "you and I would be totally wrong for each other."

Jesus. Does she need a searing knife to help her cut me open?

It's as if she's been given an extra dose of truth serum, and she can't stop herself from speaking her mind, even when I haven't asked.

"I mean, you live up in the sky and probably have a thou-sand women throwing themselves at you at any given time.

I'm not oblivious; I've heard your brothers tease you about how many women you've been with. I can't ever imagine you'd want to tie yourself down to just one." She stops to scan my face, probably noting the slight offense I've taken. "I'm not judging you, Garrett. It may seem like it, but I swear, I'm not."

Yeah, it certainly seems like a no-judgment zone over here.

I must be a fucking glutton for punishment, but I try to keep the bite out of my voice. "Go on."

"Well, I live down here—on earth. I like my routines and quiet evenings; I like stability and security. I've only slept with two people in my entire life, and if I was to get into a relationship, I'd need to know it was for the long haul. I'd never be okay with being one of any number of women in anyone's life—"

"Are you implying that I would cheat on you or that being married would be something I would take casually? That I wouldn't or *couldn't* be in a long-term relationship?" My nostrils flare slightly as I rein in my tone, but nothing can be done about the small fissure that's opened up in my chest at her insinuation.

Is that what she thinks about me?

Is that how little she thinks of me?

"No!" She shakes her head for a moment before a cloud of doubt and guilt hangs over her face and her chin drops. "I don't know what I think, G. I guess I don't know you well enough to think one way or the other. I was basing my opinion on hearsay and probably my own insecurities." She lifts her eyes to meet mine briefly before letting them flit back down. "I'm sorry if I made you feel bad."

I swear, I don't know whether to laugh or shake her, but at this moment, the only thing I can do is bury the anger and frustration bubbling inside my chest and grit through my next words. "Bella, I get that you may have heard things about me, and I even get that you've been hurt in the past, but let me make one thing clear—I'm not the guy who hurt you." I say the next line slowly, deliberately, knowing she'll know exactly who I'm referring to. "I'm neither of them." I don't know the whole story about what happened between her and her father, but I gathered enough from her comment last night to know it didn't end well. "I'll never intentionally be that guy."

Bella's face falls and a tear drops to her cheek. "I'm sorry, pilot. I was totally unfair to you when you've done nothing but be nice to me. You've been nothing short of an amazing friend, even when I landed you in this strange position. I'm so sorry, Garrett. I think . . . I'm just broken in ways no one can ever fix. Not even someone as wonderful as you."

I raise my hand to wipe off the tear staining her cheek, coming to terms with the fact that some sins can't be forgotten, even in the heart of Sin City. "If an annulment is how you want to proceed, then go ahead and file it."

She lowers her head, her shoulders hanging low, and nods.

Chapter Six

BELLA

"Alright, girl. You just dragged my pregnant ass into a dress I can no longer fit into to come to dinner and watch the two of you drink wine on a Monday night. You better have a good reason for this." My friend Melody takes a loaf of bread from the basket at the center of our table, picking up her butter knife to spread a dollop of butter on it. "And why did you text me yesterday asking for my mom's number?"

I take in a cleansing breath, giving both Melody and my cousin Rani a shaky smile. They both eye me warily, knowing I wouldn't have called a meeting—taking Rani away from her kids on their visit with her parents here in the East Bay, and Melody from her husband and one-year-old at home—unless it was an emergency. And right now, the way it all stands, with my life toppled on its side by my decision forty-eight hours ago, I'd classify this as an emergency.

"Bells." Rani places a hand on top of mine with a concerned look. "Tell us what's going on, babe. Why do you look like you haven't slept in days?"

I press the tips of my fingers to the spot between my

eyebrows and close my eyes, trying to figure out how I'm going to tell my friends that I've yet again—for the second time in my entire life—made an impulsive decision that could have long-term consequences.

Me! The woman who claims to think things through. The woman who likes routine and stability and surety. I feel like a fucking crock of shit in my own head.

I mean, it's not like I wore the wrong heels and made a fashion faux pas. I got fucking *married* in Vegas to our mutual friend and Rani's brother-in-law! I thought I was past making dumb decisions after sleeping with the biggest douchebag in history, but apparently not! Apparently, I still had one more catastrophic decision left in me.

There's no point in dilly-dallying around it. I just need to let the bomb drop and wait for the shrapnel to come flying back. "Garrett and I got married in Vegas while we were both drunk."

The hum of the restaurant thunders inside my ears. A little girl somewhere behind our table screams bloody murder while a small family chatters boisterously at the table to our right. And though I'm focused on my friends' voices, I hear nothing but silence. Did I even speak or was that all in my head?

I open my eyes, my fingers still pressed to my forehead, totally expecting them to ask me to repeat myself, but instead, I find Rani's mouth slightly agape and the tips of Melody's fingers pressed firmly over her lips as if she's trying to physically restrain herself from speaking. I'm worried that neither one of them are breathing.

I'm not sure how long we all stare at each other, letting my words hang in the air between us before Rani finally pieces a sentence together. "You and Garrett? As in, Darian's brother and my brother-in-law, Garrett?"

I nod slowly. "That's the one."

"You guys got ma—"

"How did you and Garrett even end up in Vegas together at the same time?" Melody interrupts. "You know what? It doesn't matter. The question is, are congratulations in order? And if so, why do you look like you're going to cry?"

I rub my palms over my face, squeezing my eyes shut once again before answering, "No, congratulations are *not* in order. I told him in the morning that I was going to file an annulment."

Rani's expression remains baffled, though her mouth is now stretched into a ridiculous smile. "Holy shit. You and Garrett got married?" Clearly, my cousin didn't hear a single word I just said. "I swear, you've had that wild girl cooped up inside that perfect cage of yours for so long, the second you turn your head, she breaks out, roaring."

"Which is why I keep her locked away in the first place . . . because, *obviously,* she's an idiot," I groan.

It's not a secret to those who know me that I've always been a bit of a perfectionist. A goody-two-shoes, if you will. As a kid, I was the careful type—walking around the puddles while my cousin and friend skipped through them. I liked rules and boundaries because they didn't leave too many questions in terms of right and wrong, permissible and prohibited.

I suppose when the rest of my life seemed lawless—with my parents' marriage in shambles, and my dad doing whatever the hell he was doing with a woman who wasn't my mom— rules kept me sane. Following them made me feel like I was in control of *something*. So, I became adept at burying the wild child within me because she liked to push buttons. She liked to have a drunken night of fun, to hell with the consequences.

And she's the reason I'm in this predicament today.

Rani shakes her head. "I'm not sure I've been this speechless in my entire life. How . . .? How did this even happen?"

I look up at the ceiling. "I swear, I shouldn't be left unsupervised because I clearly end up making stupid-ass deci-sions." I look from Melody to Rani. "I ran into Chaz at the airport."

"Chaz? As in your baby-daddy?" Melody asks with her nose wrinkled in disgust.

I nod. "He sort of ambushed me."

For the next fifteen minutes, I proceed to tell my best friends the entire story—from my fateful run-in with Chaz, his threat to take me to court if I didn't agree to let him have visitation with Meera, and Garrett randomly swooping in, pretending to be my husband, and diffusing the situation between me and Chaz.

Then, I tell them about how I ran into Garrett a couple of days later, and how I proceeded to drink my body weight in alcohol before proposing my brilliant idea for him to marry me, adopt Meera, and make all my problems disappear.

Even recounting it makes me cringe.

"Do you see why I keep the wild child inside me locked up?" I huff out an embarrassed laugh.

"Wow." Rani eyes me curiously. "Do you even remember the ceremony? I assume it's still called a ceremony, even if it's not done in front of a lot of people."

Melody crosses her arms. "I, for one, am pissed I wasn't asked to be a bridesmaid."

I roll my eyes, chuckling. I suppose there's not much else to do but laugh about it all now. "I remember bits and pieces," I answer Rani. "I remember giggling and thinking the entire thing was the most genius solution I'd ever come up with."

I don't mention it, but I also remember walking back hand-in-hand with Garrett. I kept dropping my purse so at one point, he hung it over his shoulder while his firm hand on my hip kept me steady on my feet. I remember our closeness inside the elevator—though, I don't quite remember what we said to each other—and how I dragged him by his hand to my hotel room.

I cringe as I remember what I said to him inside the room. I recalled it soon after I woke up in bed with Garrett the next morning, but I've been shoving the entire drunken exchange under the proverbial rug until now.

God, I totally embarrassed myself, practically begging him to fuck me. I'd like to say it was all fueled by alcohol, but I'd only be lying to myself.

And, yeah, I remember those lips.

Lips that dropped down to mine as his large, warm palms encircled my neck after we exchanged our vows at the altar. Vows I don't recall, but ones I apparently repeated with my husband in mind. My breath caught in my chest as his lips took mine for the second time that weekend, and even in my inebriated state, I felt the tingles travel all the way down to my toes.

I smile to myself at the irony of that kiss—the first one exchanged when he pretended I was his wife and the second when I *actually* became his wife in front of an officiant dressed as Slash from *Guns N' Roses*—complete with a black top hat and sunglasses. Or maybe it really was Slash following his passion for officiating drunken idiots' weddings. I can't be sure anymore. But, when he said the words, "You may now kiss the bride," and strummed the guitar around his neck once for full effect, I remember jumping almost completely out of my skin.

Rani turns to me. "From the smile plastered on your face right now, I'd say you remember a lot more than you're telling us." Her gaze bores into me like she's trying to count the pores on the tip of my nose. "Oh, my God . . . You like him."

I reel back, scoffing. "No, I don't."

"You do. You like him, Bells."

"No. I don't." I argue. But when she makes an incredulous

snort, I decide it's not worth the trouble to change her mind. "Anyway, it doesn't matter whether I like him or not. I've said it before and I'll say it again—I want nothing to do with men. I haven't been able to rely on one my entire life, and I'm not about to start now. I made a mistake in Vegas, and I need to get this marriage annulled on the basis of being intoxicated—and liking or not liking my husband has nothing to do with it."

"Did you sleep with him?" Rani asks, dismissing my assertion.

My face heats again as the memory of taking my clothes off in front of Garrett fills my vision. "No, he knew I wasn't in the right state of mind. Hell, neither of us were."

"I'm just going to come out and ask . . ." Melody sits back in her chair, pulling her box braids forward and patting her small belly. I hold back my smartass retort, wondering when she's ever bitten her tongue or asked for permission before speaking her mind. "Are you blind, Bella?"

I narrow my eyes at her. "What?"

"What I'm asking is how the hell are you not seeing how ridiculously sweet this man is?" At my blank expression, she continues, "He literally married you because he wanted to help you and Meera. Who the fuck does that? And, from what you told us, you're the only one pushing for this annulment."

"Well, he did tell me to go ahead and file it. Anyway, it's the right thing to do, Mel," I argue. "It's not just the right decision for me and Meera; it's right for him, too. Plus, why would I stay married to someone for any reason besides love?"

Melody leans forward again, putting her elbows on the table. "Could you see yourself falling for him?"

I open my mouth before snapping it shut, then reopening it again like a damn fish. I don't want to consider that question. I don't want to consider any questions when it comes to my feelings for Garrett Meyer, because I have none. "What is the point of even talking about this? He's not the type of guy who will ever settle down. He married me because he was drunk, not because he has feelings for me. He might not have said he wanted an annulment specifically, but I know he isn't the type who *wants* to be tied down."

"I've told you this before, but he's changed a lot–" Rani starts.

"*Pssh!*" I wave her off. "He might have, but it would take a lot more than words to convince me, and he doesn't owe me that. We'll get this annulment, and then he is free to do whatever he wants with whoever he wants and I am free to be alone, not worrying about anyone but me and Meera. It's the best decision for all of us."

"Have you considered that perhaps it's *not* the best decision?" Melody tilts her head, inquisitively. "That perhaps it could actually end up being more of a detriment to you right now?"

Both Rani and I give each other a quizzical look before turning to Melody.

"Huh?" I ask. "Why would it be a detriment?"

"Look, I'm not an expert in family law–that's my mom's area of expertise–but I've picked up a few things from hearing about her cases over the years. You should really talk to her, but if you don't settle on a visitation agreement with Chaz outside of court, his lawyer could find an annulment in your public record and use it to slander you as an irresponsible mother."

Both Rani and I have similar gasps before I find my voice. "*An irresponsible mother?* Are you kidding me? Because I made a mistake and am trying to rectify it?"

Melody sighs. "Court battles can get messy, Bells. I'm not saying he *will* do that or that even if he does, it will hold up in court because you've been nothing but a great mom to a well-adjusted, well-cared-for kid for the past four years. But it might be worth considering delaying an annulment until all this blows over. It never hurts to have a clean past record. The last thing you need on top of any of this is for your decisions to be scrutinized under a microscope."

Well, fuck. This was not how I'd expected my evening to end.

"HEY, sweetie. Melody gave me a rundown of your adventurous weekend," Wendy, Melody's mom, chuckles on the phone the next evening, "but how about you tell me in your own words how it all went down and we can go from there?"

I look over Meera's shoulder to make sure she has her snack and paint supplies in front of her before sneaking into my bedroom to chat with Wendy privately. Along with the hair salon kit, I bought Meera a few small canvases for Christmas since she's been super into painting lately. Plus, it keeps her busy for *hours*. "Sure, I can do that, but could you please tell me how I can secure you as my lawyer? I'm happy to call your office and send my information so you can invoice me."

Wendy huffs out a short laugh and it reminds me of how Melody does the same thing when she finds an idea preposterous. "Sweetheart, I am not going to charge you for my time on this. How long have I known you? Fifteen years? Maybe more? You're like a daughter to me, and I don't ask my kids for money. Now, walk me through what happened."

From my mom to my cousin and best friend to now her mother, I consider myself one of the luckiest to have so many strong and caring women all around me.

For the next twenty minutes, I recount my weekend in Vegas with Wendy—minus the part about Garrett and me spending the night in my hotel room—and answer any questions she has for me.

"Well, this Chaz guy hasn't served you with papers yet," she states. "There's a chance that he might not, either. In my experience, when an estranged parent asks to establish a parental relationship and visitation with a child, they usually follow through with papers pretty quickly. Although, you did say he was moving nearby, which could cause a bit of a delay on his part. In either case, I would give it at least two weeks to see what he does."

"And, what about this annulment?" I ask, peeking my head from my bedroom to check on Meera again. "Will having an annulment on my record hurt me in any way if this becomes messy?"

Wendy pauses, thinking about my question for a moment. "Well, it takes six months and one day from the day of filing in the state of California for an annulment to be finalized."

Six months! How am I going to break this news to Garrett that we're going to be married for at least six months?

"What?" My brows fold. "I had no idea it took that long."

Wendy continues, not knowing how frantic I feel internally about the information she just dropped on me. "So, you could file for an annulment, but then you'd be dealing with two separate legal issues—that and the visitation order, if Chaz decides to pursue it. And no, even if the opposing party brought up the fact that you were pursuing an annulment, it really wouldn't hurt your position in court. The court looks for patterns of irresponsible behavior and how that would harm the child. Your marriage this past weekend might have been done while you were intoxicated, but the child was not in any danger because she wasn't even there. So, Chaz or his lawyer really wouldn't have a leg to stand on—"

I huff out a breath of relief. "Okay, good."

"*However*," she continues, and my newly found respite shatters yet again, "it doesn't hurt to wait to file the annulment. A, it would be yet another thing for you to worry about legally, and B, you already made it seem like you were married in front of Chaz, thus he thinks Garrett has an established parental relationship with your daughter–"

"Well, Garrett loves my daughter and she loves him, but I wouldn't call it a parental relationship, because it's not like he is responsible for her day-to-day. We don't live together and we only see each other once in a while."

"Yes," Wendy continues, "but Chaz doesn't know that. In his mind, someone else has already fulfilled the role of a father figure. Now, that won't stop him from his desire for visitation, but it's all about optics and perception. It could make his resolve to pursue joint custody a little weaker in the long term, if you know what I mean."

My stomach twists into a knot as my mind buzzes with all this new information. "So, what you're suggesting is for me to stay married for now because this could benefit the case, even if it's just perception?"

Just the idea of asking Garrett to stay married to me, and not start the annulment process, even for perception's sake, doesn't sit well with me. And even though he told me he'd help me and Meera in any way, I find it hard to ask him to be tied down to me when he's not the type to be tied down at all.

"I'm not telling you that seeking an annulment will hurt your case–it more than likely won't. What I'm saying is, it may be beneficial for you to wait on it until after your custody situation gets resolved. At the very least, you should wait two weeks to file the annulment to see if Chaz serves you papers. But, remember, it'll take six months for the annulment to come to fruition, anyway. At the most, I recommend you wait until this custody and visitation order is finalized."

I'm too afraid to even ask, but I know I have to. "How long could that take?"

Wendy sighs. "It's hard to give you a firm timeline. It could be four to six weeks, or it could be six months."

Adding that up in my head with the six months it would take to finalize the annulment, I say, "So I could be married on paper for six and a half months—if I requested an annulment now—or longer based on how long the custody case takes?"

"Yes."

I close my eyes as my shoulders sag, but I don't vocalize what's on repeat inside my head. *This is a total clusterfuck . . .*

Chapter Seven

BELLA

I PACE FROM ONE END OF MY LIVING ROOM TO THE OTHER for what seems to be the four-hundredth time, but my nerves still feel like they're connected directly to the power outlet. I'd just painted my nails yesterday—my standard black polish—but over the course of the past thirty minutes since Garrett texted me, I've peeled off the polish on both thumbs.

Over the past week, neither Garrett nor I have reached out to each other. He told me before we left Vegas last weekend that he was going to be working all week, and he'd be home on Friday. So, as soon as I got home from the office today, I texted him to see if he wanted to drop by my place so I could give him the updates of what I'd learned after my conversation with Wendy.

He texted me thirty minutes ago to let me know he'd be over soon, and I called my mom to ask if I could drop Meera off at her place so she wouldn't overhear.

Strangely—and yet, unsurprisingly—Mom took the news of Garrett and I drunkenly getting married really well. I was so nervous when I sat her down and told her on Wednesday night, after putting Meera to bed, but instead of telling me how disappointed she was with me, she was more concerned with how I was handling the fact that Chaz claimed he wanted to be in Meera's life after being estranged for so long.

She's surprised me both times when I've given her less-than-ideal news. Even when I told her I was pregnant with Meera, I expected her to be disappointed—for her to tell me I'd really fucked up—but instead, she took the news in stride. I won't say she was happy about it, but she quickly got over her feelings about it and supported me in a way I never expected.

She did the same Wednesday night.

"I know how worried you are. It will really confuse Meera to have this stranger spring up in her life." She grabbed my hand. "But she's young. She might be able to forge a good relationship with him and forgive him for not being in her life this whole time."

I shook my head. "I just don't trust him. He gives me the creeps, Mom. He comes across a certain way when you first meet him—sophisticated and smart—but he's a conniving coward inside. I don't want him near her."

For the millionth time since meeting Chaz, I thought about how I could have ever been enamored with the guy. Even if it was for the duration of a short conference, how could I have not seen through his slicked-back hair and his overpriced Manolos to the person he was blatantly telling me he was—arrogant and self-righteous? And what about his holier-than-thou, upward-turned nose? How the hell did his shallow compliments and his pretense capture my attention enough for me to sleep with him?

I suppose I wanted to be 'real' for one night—to let my inner wild child free and discard the sweltering coat of perfection.

Mom's hand tightened on mine. "I don't want someone like that in Meera's life, either, but if he pursues visitation and custody, the court will likely allow him to start reconciliation therapy with her, like Wendy told you. But I can understand how hard it will be for you."

I looked down at our connected hands. "I don't want him to disappoint her if she gets attached."

I knew I'd given away too much with my words, and Mom was nothing if not astute when it came to me. "Is this about you or about Meera?" When I didn't answer, she continued, "I know what happened with your dad wasn't easy for either of us, but people make mistakes—"

My head snapped up. How could she just call what Dad did a mere mistake, like all it deserved was a slap on the wrist?

"He left us to go live with someone for years, then he came back when it was all over with her. That wasn't a mistake, Mom; it was a decision he made every day for years! Just like it was a decision Chaz made to cheat on his wife and stay out of his daughter's life."

Mom sighed. "I know how betrayed and hurt you feel, and not just for yourself, but for your little girl. I understand that. I felt it once, too."

"How did you get over it? How did you move forward?"

She blinked, giving me a withering smile. "I forgave. I forgave because forgiveness is the only remedy for pain."

"And this huge mistake of a marriage I've gotten myself into? Don't tell me you're not disappointed." It was as if I was insisting on her scolding me.

Mom seemed to think for a moment. She was never one to say more than needed or speak irrationally. Just as I was careful with my decisions, Mom was careful with her words. "Bella, the biggest mistake you could make is to not make any at all. In fact, the times you've made a mistake are the times you've found your greatest treasure. Plus, I've never had to be hard on you . . . you're plenty hard on yourself."

A knock on my door has me jumping out of my thoughts. I smooth my palms over my tights and make sure my tunic sweater covers my ass before traipsing to the door.

As it always happens when I see the hottest pilot to walk the earth, my breath catches in my chest before working its way out. His navy-blue eyes lock on mine, and his plush lips pull up on one corner. My gaze travels from his mussed blond mop to the delectable light-colored scruff on his jaw, to the silver chain around his thick, long neck. It disappears into the rounded collar of his black Henley, which is molded to his sprawling chest and defined abs. Something about the way his hands are tucked into the pockets of his jeans has me thinking the most obscene thoughts.

I snap my gaze back to his face, clearing my throat. "Hi."

His navy blues smolder under long lashes and my chest tightens. "Hi."

I open the door wider in silent invitation and his arm brushes against mine, sending a flurry of goosebumps over my skin before I close the door behind us. He's so tall and his presence is so overstated that he instantly crowds my foyer. I lean my back against the door for a moment, trying to catch my breath.

Honestly, I'm having a hard time remembering why I even asked him to come over.

"Do you want something to drink?" I ask when I finally find my voice again.

Garrett turns to me, shaking his head. "No, I'm good." He sweeps his gaze over my small condo. "Where's Meera?"

I tilt my head in the direction of the sectional and we both take a seat, leaving a good amount of space between us. Thank God and furniture builders everywhere for big couches. "She's at my mom's house. I figured it would give us a chance to speak without her interrupting."

He leans back on the sofa, putting an ankle on his knee, and again, my eyes snag on the way his shirt adheres to his abs, making them look like the tops of Hawaiian rolls, though I'm sure I'd jam my finger if I pressed on one. "Okay."

I slide my palms over my knees, reminding myself of the task at hand. "So, I talked to Melody's mom, who's in family law. She suggested that . . . um, we stay married until this visitation order and potential custody change with Meera gets sorted out."

I study Garrett's face, trying to read his expression. It's inscrutable, besides a small twitch in his lips. "Okay."

"Let me clarify," I continue. "She didn't say we *had* to stay married, but she recommended it based on the fact that an annulment would take six months to be finalized, so it would be yet another thing I'd have to deal with from a legal perspective, and also because if we stay married, Chaz or his lawyer can't slander me in any way for making an irresponsible decision. Plus, it would be better for optics."

"Makes sense."

Well, this is all very agreeable of him. Maybe he doesn't understand exactly what I'm asking here.

"So, I was wondering . . ." My heart thunders inside my ribs and I try to swallow my nerves. "I was wondering if, uh, your offer to stay married to me for a little bit longer was still on the table?"

Garrett stays still, save for a vein on his neck that pulses rhythmically. Jesus, this is not the time to be salivating over his vein like a hungry vampire. Seriously, what the fuck is wrong with me?

When he doesn't say anything for a few moments, I lift my eyes to find him biting his bottom lip, almost like he's trying to bite back a smile. He clears his throat, making his Adam's apple bob, and my eyes find that vein again. Clearly, I've got problems.

"Did you get served papers from Chaz yet?"

I shake my head. "No, and if I don't within another week or so, I'll file the annulment like we discussed. It would take six months for it to be official, but we can continue life the way we have been. Separately. We'd just be married on paper until the annulment finalizes."

Garrett nods contemplatively, but his eyes twinkle in a

way that has me shifting in my seat. I can barely keep my gaze locked with his but that's nothing new. "And if he *does* file a motion to establish parental rights, then you'd like to stay married until visitation and custody are figured out?"

I nod. "It could be six weeks or it could be six months, barring any delays."

"And then you'd file for an annulment after that?"

I nod again. "We'd be legally married for six months from the date of filing, but yeah." I watch as his eyes swing between mine, wondering what's going through his head. I tilt my face down and raise my brows. "So, will you, um . . .?" I take another breath and look around the room before coming back to face him. He has a small smirk on his face, and if I didn't know any better, I'd say the bastard was enjoying my unease. "Will you stay married to me for a little longer?"

Garrett's tongue peeks out, swiping over his bottom lip, and I try to force away the memory of having that lip in my mouth not too long ago. "On one condition."

I squint. "What?"

"I want you and Meera to move in with me."

I'M JUST unbuckling Meera from her carseat in my driveway the following Wednesday when a car pulls up to the house. I help Meera out, grabbing her hand in mine.

"Who's that man, Mommy?"

A man in a white button-down, slacks, and a tie approaches us, and I catch a glimpse of the tan envelope in his hands. I already know what he's going to say before he says it. "Bella Patel?"

"That's me."

He pushes the envelope into my hand. "You've been

served with legal papers." He turns to head back to his car. "Have a nice evening."

My stomach plunges to the floor as I unfasten the clip on the back of the envelope and pull out the papers half-way, mostly out of curiosity. It's not like I need to see them to believe they're real. I already know what they are and who they're from.

Fuck! I thought maybe Chaz would have let it go.

"Come on, Meerkat," I urge Meera. "Let's go inside."

I don't look at the papers again until after I've given Meera a bath and put her to bed, though I can't say my head was totally in my conversation with her this evening. I found myself just nodding while she told me about how her friends Trinity and Nolan pretended to be pilots on the swing set at school, and how Nolan ended up going the highest. Even as I read to her, I barely registered the words, speaking them without any intonation or excitement like I usually do.

I pluck a small box of *Nerds* from the large glass mason jar on the kitchen counter and rip the top. Pouring most of the box into my mouth, I take the envelope to the kitchen table and pull out the papers inside. As expected, Chaz is asking to establish a parental relationship and visitation with Meera. And I know if he's granted that, he'll be able to request joint custody after some time. As per the dates on this document, I'm to show up to court in forty-five days.

With my conversation with Wendy in mind, I text her, letting her know I have the papers in my hand. Her response comes back shortly.

> Wendy: Can you come by my office around
> lunch tomorrow?

Thankfully, my Thursdays aren't usually filled with meetings, so I respond back with a *yes* without needing to look at my work calendar.

I stare at my phone for a moment before scrolling to the name in my messages and recalling our conversation. Before he left my house last Friday evening, Garrett told me to call or text him with my answer.

"Why?" I asked him. "Why do you want us all to live together?"

It didn't make any sense. Why would being married on paper require us to change our lives? What would it even accomplish, besides more confusion for all of us? And how would I even explain it to Meera?

In my last conversation with Wendy, she'd made it clear that I shouldn't tell Meera anything about either situation—the potential visitation request from Chaz or the accidental marriage to Garrett. Her strong recommendation was to keep Meera out of such situations until deemed necessary, because if for any reason Chaz pulled out of the entire ordeal or Garrett and I ended up separating, it would just put undue stress on her. She might be mature for her age, but she's still a little girl who doesn't need to worry about such things.

Garrett's gaze moved from the chevrons on my family room rug to my face. "Because A, it would look weird if that asshole's lawyer looked into us and saw we had two residences and lived separately."

I didn't quite buy his argument and was about to object when he barreled past me. "And, B, this marriage actually helps me, too."

A seed of doubt bloomed inside my gut, but all I could do was narrow my eyes at him. "How so? What would you even get out of it?"

"You're the one who said you'd heard about my reputation as a playboy, commitment-phobe, call it whatever you want." Garrett lifted his chin. "You're not the only one who sees me that way. I'm almost thirty-nine years old, Bells; it's about time I settle down."

I frowned, still not understanding his logic. "But our marriage would be fake. Purely for convenience."

He shrugged. "Yeah, but my colleagues and friends don't need to know that. In fact, I have a gala coming up in two weeks to inaugu-

rate the opening of this new aviation museum. I would love it if you came with me—"

"As your wife?"

"As if I was the love of your life," he confirmed with a playful smirk. "It'll be a great way to show those 'thousands of women who are throwing themselves at me at any given time,'" he put air quotes up with his fingers, "as you pointed out during our last conversation, that I'm off the market, permanently. It'll also shut up all those who think I can't settle down."

I crossed my arms over my chest. "So, let me get this straight. You want to live together, like an actual married couple, and you'll stop seeing other people by officially taking yourself off the market?"

Garrett got off the couch, slipping his hands into his pockets again, and I noticed he was still wearing the beaded bracelet Meera had made him. His jaw stiffened as he focused on me. "Whatever perception you have of me, Bella, you'd be mistaken to think I'd cheapen this marriage—real or fake—by stepping outside of it and disrespecting you. We may not have gotten married conventionally, but we're married nonetheless, and I plan to adhere to the vows I made. And I expect nothing less from you in return."

He'd left me staring after him, under a mist of embarrassment and admiration, as he walked out my door, telling me I needed to think about his offer when and if the time came and Chaz followed through on his threat.

I suppose the time was now.

My hands shake as I click on his name in my text messages and type out my response.

Me: Okay.

His message comes through not even a minute later.

Pilot: Okay :)

Chapter Eight

GARRETT

I GRUNT, MY FACE CONTORTING AS EACH SET OF MUSCLES from my shoulders to my thighs tense, threatening to collapse under the load.

"You got this. Last one."

I flick a glance at Hudson's hands in position to spot me if I need it, before focusing on the barbell extended halfway up. Breathing through my nose, I dig deep for the last of my strength before fully extending my arms. "Fuck."

My biceps and triceps shudder as I lift up on the bench and a trail of sweat streams down my temple, landing on my bare shoulder and chest. I grab my towel, drying myself off, and I feel my phone buzz inside my gym shorts pocket.

"Good set," Hudson says as he walks over to the leg press machine.

I nod, acknowledging my friend, before pulling out my phone. It's rare for both of us to be in town at the same time, given both of our work schedules, but we try to meet up whenever we can. Today, we decided to hit the gym before going to grab drinks later.

"So, did you ever hear back from your new wife?" Hudson snickers, increasing the weights on the leg press before taking a seat on the bench, oblivious to me staring at my phone.

Both my brothers and my friends, Hudson and Rohan, have been informed of the recent developments in my life—namely my accidental marriage to the most unavailable woman on the planet, as well as my recent proposition for her and her daughter to move in with me. Needless to say, I've gotten a shitload of questions and a few wife jokes in our group texts over the past ten days. Thankfully, I've taken up quite a few shifts flying, so I've chalked up my lack of response to having my phone turned off.

I read the message lighting up my screen.

Bells: Okay.

Okay, as in yes. *Okay,* as in she'd been served the papers and was agreeing to my terms. *Okay*, as in she and Meera are going to move in with me. I read it again to make sure I've interpreted it correctly before letting a satisfied grin erupt on my face.

Truth be told, I wasn't expecting this answer. Given how our conversation ended in Vegas—with her basically telling me she trusted me less than she trusted a ripped parachute to carry her safely to the ground—I fully expected her to say no. But I suppose I didn't give her much of a choice, either.

I'd tried playing the nice guy—telling her I was happy to stay in the marriage if that's what she needed when we woke up after our adventurous night. What did it get me? Fucking nothing besides having to endure her confessional, admitting that I was the last person she'd ever marry.

That fucking splintered my heart more than I wanted to admit.

Now, it turns out she *does* need the last person she'd ever marry to stay married to her, and I've decided that I'm either going to have it my way or no way at all—even if I have to bend the truth and color outside the lines to do it.

Because the truth is, I want Bella like I've never wanted a goddamn thing in my life—with every ounce of my soul. And I'll do anything to get her, even if that means making her feel like I have other motivations for being married to her, like my *oh-so-lecherous* history with women. If playing that card up a little was going to sway her decision to stay married to me— if it made her feel like she was returning the favor I was doing her—then I wasn't above using it. So, I did.

Call me devious, call me morally gray.

But the number of guilty fucks I give about it are roughly zero.

Sure, if I could do it all over again, I wish I hadn't fucked around with as many women as I did, but I also won't dwell on it. It fucking sucks that, because of my history with women and Bella's history with men, I'm the last person she'll trust with that fucking organ she holds on to so dearly. But what's life without a little challenge? And if the past four years of my self-imposed chastity hasn't proven that I can take on a fucking challenge and then some—that I'll fucking wait forever if I have to for the one woman who has ever made me feel anything—then I don't know what will.

I get her reluctance. I really do. She fell for an asshole at his word and was fucked over. And while she may not have loved or cared for him, she *had* trusted him enough to spend the night with him. And when that night resulted in something that required his support—or at the very least, his empathy—he told her to get lost.

So, even though I know, without a shadow of a doubt, that Bella feels *something* for me—because real or fake, no one kisses someone the way she kissed me and feels nothing after it—she's too afraid to do anything about it or risk anything for it.

But I suppose she never accounted for the fact that I'd be ready to risk it all for her. Because for me, Bella *stubborn-as-a-fucking-mule* Patel is a sure bet, and I'd wager my goddamn life for her.

> Me: Okay :)

> Me: My friend Hudson and I will help you pack and move.

As expected, her reply comes back almost instantaneously.

> Bells: Whoa! Cool your jets, pilot. You want us to move in with you? What if you moved in with me and Meera?

She clearly hasn't thought this one through, given she's asking me to move into her one-bedroom condo in which she shares her room with her daughter. But if I know this purple-haired pixie, then I know shooting her idea down right away will only hurl me into a whole heap of trouble and she'll just dig her feet in deeper, anyway.

> Me: Meera's preschool and your office are closer to my house. Staying here would cut your commute. Plus, I have two spare bedrooms, so you both will have plenty of space. But . . . if you insist on me moving, then I don't mind us all sharing a bedroom. Your call.

I wait patiently, watching the dots jump on my screen while she types out her reply. If I've learned anything from observing her over the years, it's that she will think through each option, trying to foresee all potential potholes before deciding on the path forward. And sharing a bed with me while being perfectly sober is a pothole too large for her to ignore.

> Bells: I guess it does make more sense if we
> move in with you. I was going to start
> looking for new places since we're starting
> to outgrow ours, anyway. Plus, it isn't in the
> best shape. I suppose I can continue to
> keep looking while we stay with you
> temporarily.

Checkmate!

If I wasn't at the gym with a bunch of strangers, I'd do a fucking victory dance. I swear, the woman makes every goddamn thing a battle.

> Me: Then it's final. We'll come by this
> weekend.

I can practically see her choking on her lemon *Nerds* reading my text. And of course, she doesn't disappoint.

> Bells: You want us to move in this
> weekend!? Like, in three days?

I grin at my phone, thankful she can't see me. She makes it almost too easy to fuck with her.

> Me: No, like in two days. The weekend starts
> on Friday night, wifey.

Meera looks up at me from her spot on my front porch. Her hazel eyes dazzle behind her pink-framed glasses. Today, her usual unruly hair lays on both her shoulders in long plaits as she clutches the airplane plushie I gave her for Christmas between her arm and chest. I've yet to see her without it.

Both her brows are perched high on her head, and she reminds me even more of the beautiful woman standing next to her now than ever before. "Come on, Uncle Garrett! We aren't getting any younger. Are you going to make us stand out here all darn day?"

"Meera!" Bella chides, scrunching her brows down at her. "Where are your manners?"

Like Bella, I was a little worried about Meera's reaction to moving in with me, but my fears of her feeling uncomfortable or confused were short-lived. Apparently, the kid squealed when Bella told her they'd be moving in with me to be closer to her preschool and that she'd be getting a new room.

I chuckle, turning my key into the lock before taking it out and looking back down at her. "I don't know . . . It doesn't seem like you're very excited. Are you sure you even want to see your new room that badly?"

Meera groans, bouncing on her sneakered feet. "I'm sure! I'm *really* sure. Now, let's get this show on the road already!"

Bella starts to scold her again, but I throw my head back and laugh because everything about this kid makes me fucking happy. Unlocking the door, I stand aside and gesture for both of them to go inside. "Well, alright then, Meerkat. Go find your room."

Meera bolts inside, toeing off her shoes at the base of the stairs before climbing them in a rush. Bella shakes her head after her, bending down to place her shoes to the side and feigning exhaustion. "She can be such a handful sometimes." She looks over her shoulder. "Are you sure you want us in your space?"

I come up behind her, placing my mouth at the shell of

her ear and taking a deep inhale of her candy scent. A shudder ghosts down her spine, bouncing against my chest behind her. "I've never been more sure of anything in my whole fucking life."

Her cheeks pinken as a smile blooms on her lips, her red lipstick contrasting against her flawless cappuccino-colored complexion. I get a vision of the same red smudged around my mouth after I've thoroughly devoured her lips, and a spark of heat rushes to my groin, making my dick twitch uncomfortably.

She must see my heated gaze pinned to her mouth because she bites her bottom lip, sucking off a hint of the lip color before clearing her throat. "You didn't have to move your study furniture into the den so she could have her own space, Garrett. It's not like we'll be staying long."

I ignore the challenge in her eyes, goading me to argue. "I want her to feel like she's at home."

Both Meera and Bella have been to my place before, so it's not like it's new to them, but I've redecorated over the past couple of days to make it more suitable for two extra people. Truth be told, I'd started redecorating when I left her house last Friday.

Then today, both Hudson and I hauled most of Bella's boxes here so she could set up her bedroom—right across the hall from mine—the way she likes.

I follow behind Bella as she climbs the stairs, allowing my eyes to travel down to her pert, round ass. It sways gently under her long hair—the purple tips hitting right above it—almost like a hypnotic dance. If an ass could be classified as flawless, this one would be it.

Christ. How am I going to make it with her bouncing that weapon of destruction everywhere while she lives here?

I suppose my only saving grace is that I'll be away a lot for work. That's not to say I won't wake up with a semi every morning wherever I am thinking about that ass bouncing around my dick while I'm ramming into her like a charging bull. Lord knows I've woken up with that same fantasy more times than I can count over the past four fucking years.

I adjust myself as inconspicuously as possible before we hit the landing and my eyes immediately slide over to Meera.

With her plushie in her arms, her mouth hangs agape right outside the door to her new bedroom like she's viewing it through a glass enclosure.

I tuck my hands into my pockets, unable to take my eyes off her while she's unable to take her eyes off her new room.

"What is it, Meerkat?" Bella asks, shuffling toward her daughter. "Why aren't you—" A gasp leaves Bella's mouth when she follows Meera's line of sight into the room, and her head snaps in my direction. She releases my name in a choked whisper, "Garrett."

I look from her to Meera. "Go check it out."

Meera strolls inside gingerly, as if she can't be sure she's not dreaming, with Bella tailing her. I lean my shoulder against the doorframe, watching them take it all in.

I enlisted more than just Hudson to help me get this place ready this week. Thankfully, Dean was able to drive down on short notice as well.

Meera's eyes stroll over the magenta-colored walls and the billowing yellow window coverings to the scene from *Dora the Explorer,* where Dora high-fives her best friend Boots under a massive willow tree. Green fields, a bridge over a small river, and birds flying in the bright blue sky complete the background.

Another gasp leaves Bella's lips as she surveys the new white furniture—the low, full-sized, four-poster bed with Dora bedding next to a lamp with a bright yellow shade sitting atop a white nightstand. "When did you do all this?" Her eyes flit to mine, but I don't miss the pooled emotion in them before they rush off me again.

I leave her question unanswered. It doesn't really matter when or how; the only thing that matters is the look on that hazel-eyed little one's face. And right now, it's a mixture of bewilderment and disbelief.

Meera's toes curl into the plush yellow rug under her bed before she walks to the large white bookshelf, scanning the various books I'd filled the shelves with. She has yet to say a word, but her face speaks volumes for the waves of emotions hitting her all at once.

Pulling out a picture book, Meera climbs into the oversized magenta chair next to the bookshelf. She tucks her plushie to the side before looking down at her book, and I don't miss the slight tremble in her hands.

A frown pulls on her lips, barely visible with her head tilted down. I glance at Bella, silently asking for her guidance or interference. Her eyes are glazed over, but she nods at me, giving me the signal to proceed with my gut, before stepping out of the room.

Stepping over to the chair, I get down on one knee in front of this kid who's determined to make me like children more than I'd ever thought possible. Her chest rises and falls as she white-knuckles the hardback in her hands, and she avoids my eyes just like her mom does.

I tuck my index finger under her chin and lift, my jaw clenching automatically at the sight of emotion free-falling on her cheeks.

This fucking kid will be the death of me.

I clear my throat, using my thumb to wipe a few of her stray tears. "So, what do you think, Meerkat? Like your new room?"

Her eyes bounce between mine behind teary puddles. And before I can say another word, she throws herself around my neck, squeezing me so tightly with her tiny arms that my lungs constrict. A tightness claws inside my throat while my heart balloons in my chest. I rub her back, letting her hold on to me as she says everything she wants to with her silence.

I hear you loud and clear, Meerkat . . . and I hope you can hear me, too.

Chapter Nine

BELLA

I click Meera's bedroom door shut softly, taking a moment to get my thoughts together before I turn and head downstairs.

I saw the look in her eyes today—the one that made her speechless. My daughter . . . the one who always has an opinion and a sassy remark about everything in life, was rendered speechless when she saw her new room.

I stood outside the door, eavesdropping as Garrett knelt in front of her. I heard her gasp as her little arms circled his neck, and I felt the tightness inside my lungs at the vision of their sweet embrace. It left me breathless and confused.

My hand slides down the railing as my thoughts morph from one to another. *This is all temporary.* We discussed it was all temporary, didn't we? So, why does it feel like we're not reading from the same book? He seems to be enraptured in a fiction overflowing with fantasy, while I'm stuck in my own autobiography, in a chapter that reminds me that men have never had a place of trust in my life.

I hear Garrett rinsing dishes in the kitchen. We'd ordered takeout and sat around the coffee table, eating. He doesn't own a dining table—he said he never used it—so it made the most sense for us to sit on the rug and eat in his family room.

He glances at me before reaching for a couple of plastic takeout containers to put into the trash. "Hi."

I swallow, wringing my hands in front of me. "Hi. Um, I just wanted to say thank you."

He puts his hands in his pockets, eyeing me with a soft gaze but doesn't respond.

"Thank you for doing what you did for Meera. She really appreciates it. She's never had a room of her own, and I can tell she absolutely loves it."

"You're welcome."

It's at the tip of my tongue to ask why. Why go through all this effort? Why make us feel so welcomed . . . so at home? Why go through the trouble of making sure Meera loved it here when we'll be moving out shortly, anyway?

When this is all fake.

He even rearranged the furniture in my bedroom. I don't recall there ever being a queen-sized bed in there the last and only time I had a glimpse inside his house when I came to pick Meera up a few weeks ago . . . but there is one now.

It's at the tip of my tongue to urge him to tell me what he's thinking, but as always, my mind—or maybe my heart—holds me back. As always, it tells me not to open up a box I'll never be able to shut again. As always, it tells me that opening any box when it comes to Garrett Meyer would fling me into the deepest, darkest, navy-blue ocean with no life vest in sight.

I give him another smile, watching as his eyes home in on my dimples. I used to be self-conscious about them since they're deep and I'd get a lot of comments from people pointing them out as if I didn't know I had them, but over time, I've come to love them.

"She really likes you and . . ." I don't know why the words

get stuck in my throat. "Well, she doesn't have many men in her life she can count on. So . . ." I look around the kitchen, blinking rapidly before meeting his eyes briefly again. "Thank you."

It's been a long day with moving and getting both Meera and my things put away in our rooms. Maybe that's why I'm feeling emotional, or maybe it's just the exhaustion settling into my shoulders and neck. I'm ready to slide into my new bed with my calf-length socks and drift off to sleep.

I squirm under his gaze as silence settles over us. His gaze is too heavy, too piercing, as if he's watching me under a microscope. I'm just about to turn to go back upstairs and retreat to my room for the night when the rumble of Garrett's voice has me stalling. "I'm not going anywhere, Bells. Marriage papers or not, I'll be right here."

I lick my lips, nodding toward the floor but only halfway believing his sincere words. Isn't that what *anyone* would say in his place? Isn't that what he's supposed to say? "Thank you."

"You might not believe me now, but I'm not like *them*. Don't let two assholes define the rest of us, Bells."

The translucent edges of a tart and impassioned assessment I made in my drunken state about fathers comes back to the forefront of my mind. Neither of us has to say it to know he's referring to my dad.

Garrett leans against the counter behind him, his stance wide. The long sleeves of his shirt bunch around the broadest part of his forearms, revealing long, thick veins curling around it, disappearing into his pockets along with his hands. "I'm scheduled to fly out tomorrow morning."

A soft *oh* leaves my lips.

"I'll be back early Friday morning, probably before the two of you are up."

"Okay." A mix of unexpected feelings swirl inside me. I

don't mind being here in Garrett's house alone with Meera, but I guess I still feel a bit like a stranger or a guest.

Garrett steps forward, closing the distance between us and the waves of heat from his body dance on my skin. He's not even touching me, but I feel like I'm standing next to a furnace. He tips my chin up and his eyes rake over my face, reading me like a book. "This house is just as much yours and Meera's as it is mine. You're welcome into any room and to live the way you please. Feel free to cook or order in." He glances at the counter next to him. "My credit card is right there."

My brows knit. "I have my own credit card, but thank you."

His hands find their way back into his pockets and I can't decide if I liked them better on me. "It's there, nevertheless." He throws a thumb behind him. "Can I show you a couple of things?"

I nod, following him toward his small pantry. He opens the door and my eyes immediately find a large mason jar–similar to the one I have sitting in my room–full of little individual boxes of lemonade-wild-cherry-flavored *Nerds*. "Did you . . .?"

He shrugs. "I figured, you know, in case you ran out of the ones in your room." He points out other items–bags upon bags of Meera's favorite potato chips, boxes of Goldfish crackers, and vegetarian refried beans and tostada shells–but I'm barely able to hear past the humming in my ears. He's literally stocked a pantry full of things I doubt he eats much of, for us.

I point to the last item he'd indicated before he shuts the pantry door. "Vegetarian refried beans? I didn't realize you were vegetarian."

Garrett chuckles. "No, I'm very much a carnivore, but I remember Meera telling me she was, so I bought a few cans."

He winces, looking at me guiltily. "I didn't ask you, but I hope that's okay. I figured they'd be good on top of the tostada shells. I actually don't know if she even likes any real food besides tater tots, chips, and cotton candy ice cream." He laughs louder and that same moisture I was trying to blink away earlier makes another appearance.

I divert my face a little as he moves to the fridge. "Speaking of which . . ." He swings open the freezer door, completely oblivious to my internal melt-down. "Pretty sure we can hunker down for the end of the world and survive on these, don't you think?"

I take a quick peek inside, seeing the freezer packed to the brim with tater tots and ice cream. Swallowing the thickness building in my throat, I shove down a sob trying to wriggle its way free. Nodding, I pray for my voice to sound steady. "She'll love this. Thank you."

I turn just in time to catch the stupid tear from falling onto my cheek. I don't think I can even manage standing here a minute longer without becoming a useless puddle on the floor. It's only been ten minutes, but my chest feels the emotional toll of years. "I'm pretty tired; I think I'll head to bed now." I give him a wobbly smile over my shoulder. "Goodnight, pilot. Safe travels tomorrow."

"Goodnight, Bells."

~

I RUN a hand through Meera's dark tangles, watching her eyes flutter shut. Ever since she was a baby, she's liked me rubbing her head to put her to sleep. Some things don't change, and I quite prefer it that way, in this case.

Her eyes flip open as she stares at me in the dim glow of the lamp near her bed. "Do you like it here, Mommy? At Uncle Garrett's house?"

My hand stops its caress in her hair as I take in the hope-fulness in her face. In just three days of living here, I'm seeing changes in her I hadn't expected quite so soon. For one, she no longer crawls into my bed in the middle of the night to sleep, preferring to sleep in her beautiful new room. And, for another, she just seems . . . happier.

I'd always thought my daughter was a happy kid—a mix of sassy and silly—but it's as if the past three days have unfurled something I didn't know even existed inside her. A longing for something I hadn't quite realized she had.

I place a kiss on her forehead. "I do like it here. Do you?"

She yawns, snuggling her airplane plushie closer to her chest. "Yeah. Uncle Garrett's my favorite." She grins mischievously at me. "Don't tell him that, though. I like telling him that Uncle Dean or Uncle Darian are my favorite."

I tickle her tummy and she wiggles, giggling. "Oh yeah? That doesn't seem very nice of you."

She giggles some more. "I like it when he gets jealous and then he spends more time with me."

An unexpected pang hits the center of my chest as I process the meaning behind her words. Maybe I'm just over-thinking it, but I've come to learn that as vocal and upfront as my daughter is, I still have to read between the lines when she hasn't processed her own emotions. I can't say it doesn't worry me that she's so attached to him.

"Meerkat, I don't think you'd have to make him feel jealous for him to spend time with you. He likes spending time with you, and he cares about you."

She nods. "I like spending time with him, too."

Still thinking about her words, I give her another kiss before tucking her in and turning off her lamp. I slip out of her room before walking down the corridor and down the staircase to make myself a cup of tea.

I'd left my phone next to the tea kettle, so as the water is boiling, I flip it over to check for messages, seeing one from Garrett. My mouth turns upward at the image of a sunset taken from the cockpit.

> Garrett: It was too beautiful to not capture.
> Hope you and that spunky Meerkat are
> settling in.

The message seems to have been sent about an hour ago, so I respond, hoping he doesn't think I've ignored him.

> Me: Those clouds and all that color. It looks
> like it's been painted. It's simply magnificent.

Realizing I hadn't answered the second part of his text to me, I send him another message.

> Me: You've officially trained my kid to sleep
> in her own bed. :) She refuses to leave her
> room as soon as she gets home. Good
> night, pilot.

I pour a cup of tea for myself and am about to go check the front door to make sure it's locked and close the blinds in the living room when a movement outside the window grabs my attention.

I watch from one of the slats in the window to see what made the bushes near the fence shake when I see a little white furry head pop out.

Sliding on my slippers, I walk out to the patio, closing the door behind me. The chilly February breeze runs through my robe, sending a shudder through my body, but I turn on my phone's flashlight to guide me around the side of the house.

A scampering noise, along with a soft *meow* lets me know that my hunch was right. I crouch down, pointing the light more toward the grass and not at the cat, whose body is tucked behind the bushes.

Leaning closer but not moving from my spot, I notice one of its shiny black eyes staring back at me from behind some branches, but in the low lighting, I can't quite tell any more about the state of the creature.

She—though, I can't be sure if it's a male or female—meows at me, and while a part of my brain warns me to be cautious since I don't know if it has diseases, the bigger part only cares about her safety and the flicker of fear and emotion in that one eye.

Even without a whole lot of movement, I can see enough of her white fur to know she's breathing fast. And it's when I hear a mimicked meow along with hers, almost in a sing-song, that I know she's not alone.

A shuffle in the bushes has another tiny head poking out from under her. A much tinier head.

"Hi, Momma," I whisper, staying in my spot. "How long have you been here?"

At my words, the cat seems to decide she's had enough. She quickly grabs her kitten around the neck and scurries off behind the bushes. And with it being so late, and my body feeling more tired than I have in a long while, I decide to leave her and her little one alone.

I'm still wondering about where the rest of her litter might be—I can't imagine she only had one—when I come back into the house. I grab my cup of tea and pad up the stairs, feeling the vibration of my phone in my hand as a text comes in.

Garrett: Good night, wifey.

BELLA

"Girl, I swear, this kid eats like there's going to be a world hunger crisis tomorrow and he won't get fed," Melody announces, repositioning her son, Nelson, in her arms as he wiggles around her chest, grabbing a hold of her breast with his mouth. His little pinkish fingers gently scratch at her collar as he finds his rhythm, while his bright red curls—much like his dad's—blaze against her rich black skin. The kid is so flipping cute, he gets attention wherever he goes. "I need to wean him off my boob, like stat."

"I honestly don't know how you're managing being pregnant and breastfeeding still," Rani states, leaning in closer to her camera. "I couldn't go past a couple of months breastfeeding Avya."

"Where is that little cutie pie of yours?" Melody asks.

Rani looks past her screen for a second before focusing back on us. "Darian's putting her down to bed. She was so fussy and clingy today. She barely let me get any work done, so as soon as Dar got home, I told him he was in charge of both kids tonight."

"Atta girl!" Melody exclaims. "I'm handing this little monster off to Liam as soon as he gets done eating."

Both Rani and Melody have one-year-olds–Rani's little girl, Avya, being only a few months older than Nelson. And while a decent part of me misses Meera being so little, I definitely don't miss my boobs being in a constant state of discomfort while I breastfed for the few months that I did.

I sneeze, reaching for the box of tissues on my nightstand. My head has been ringing since I woke up this morning, but right now, it feels like there are fire alarms blaring inside it. I've been drinking hot tea all day, but the fire inside my throat refuses to quench. Now everything just feels worse–the chills, the headache, the body ache–like I've been at the wrong end of Mike Tyson's uppercut. I should have canceled this call with my friends today, but I thought I could pull through.

"Excuse me," I say, wiping my nose with a tissue.

Both my friends *bless me* at the same time before Rani speaks. Her eyes flash with excitement, and she rubs her hands together as if she's waiting to open a well-wrapped present. "Alright, Bells, spill! We have way too much to catch up on, and Mel and I need the deets."

"For real. I'm totally living vicariously through you. While you're having Vegas sexcapades and accidental marriages, I'm sniffing for poopy diapers and getting the room ready for baby number two."

A warmth settles over my skin, weighing a few hundred pounds, and I shift on my bed. It takes all the energy in me to argue. "There was no sexcapade."

"Not yet, anyway," Melody retorts quickly. "But you know it's just a matter of time. That husband of yours is going to deliver on his vows and then some. I mean, look at the way he moved you guys into his house like *The Flash*! The guy knows exactly what he's doing."

My brain feels too foggy to argue with her, to remind her for the tenth time since Garrett had us move in with him, that this arrangement is fake. It's for the sake of optics when I go against Chaz in court in five weeks. This entire marriage is a sham—all so I don't have to deal with too many legal issues all at once. Garrett is sweet to play into it—he did say he wanted to change his image with his colleagues too, so I know he gets something out of it—but we're both just playing roles, nonetheless.

Honestly, I think both my friends just like the idea of me being swept off my feet in some fantastical romance. They want me to have a fairytale love, something that changes my jaded view of men in general. Too bad that's not going to happen when the entire relationship is based on a farce.

Rani giggles. She'd messaged Melody and me earlier this week to say we needed an emergency FaceTime meeting to talk about my life updates. "So, how has it been living with him? Does Meera like it?"

I slowly reach for my water bottle and take a sip, pushing through the pain of swallowing. Hopefully rehydrating will get me over this little bug quickly, but right now, I feel like I'm directly connected to a heater. "Well, he left Saturday morning, after moving us in the day before. He doesn't get back until tomorrow morning, so we actually haven't lived with him much." I sneeze again, rubbing my nose with my tissue. "Meera's finally sleeping through the whole night in her own bed, though, and it's been nice having a shorter commute."

Even today, I didn't have to call Mom to pick Meera up from school when I was running late, because just that extra fifteen minutes gave me enough time to wrap up at the office and make my way to her.

She chatted my ear off in the car about her performance

tomorrow with her friends, Trinity and Nolan—apparently, they've been practicing all week.

And as soon as she went to bed, I went outside to check on the new furry family that recently moved into the bushes. At least, I'm pretty sure it's recent because I don't think Garrett knows about them.

Sure enough, like the past two evenings, momma cat and her kitten were huddled in a small burrow they'd created along the side of Garrett's house. This time, I noticed a small dead bird inside it, but I couldn't get close enough to see much more.

And even though I was already feeling like shit, I couldn't let them go another night without water or shelter of some kind. I went to Garrett's garage and found an empty cardboard box, placing a couple of what looked to be old towels inside. I brought it out, along with a bowl of milk, and left it near Winky and Brown Sugar. It's the name I'd given the mom—who definitely only had one eye and a badly mangled ear—and her light brown and white baby girl.

Winky still doesn't trust me—she has no idea how much I understand that—but I figured my friendship offering might at least make her more amenable to the idea.

"Honey, you don't look so good." Melody frowns. "You looked a little pale earlier, but I thought maybe it was just my screen. Are you feeling okay?"

I wave, half-heartedly. "It's probably just a little cold or a symptom of being overtired. Meera has a preschool performance tomorrow—they're putting on a nursery rhyme concert. I took on helping the school with creating the stage backdrops and props, so I probably just exhausted myself with that and working all week."

"I think you need to get some rest, Bells," Rani insists. "We can reschedule our chat."

I nod, wishing I could stay on with them, but knowing

that if I don't get some rest, I'm not going to be able to thwart whatever this is and miss Meera's performance. She's been working so hard on it, and I can't disappoint her by being absent. "Okay, let's reschedule. I think I'm going to pass out."

"Do you have a temperature?" Rani eyes me on the screen as if she can measure my body temperature by just staring at me. "I feel like you have a temperature. Can you check?"

I shake my head. "No, I'm fine." I cough and it nearly crushes my ribs. "I just need to sleep it off."

"Bells—"

"I'm going to click off now. Love you guys."

I don't have it in me to argue or discuss any more, even though I know Rani is just saying it out of concern for me. Even if I have a bit of a temperature, it's probably from exhaustion or maybe a little cold. I don't have the luxury of being sicker than that—not when I have to take care of my little girl, go to work, and get things done for the court hearing. I need sleep and the longer I stay awake, the worse I'll get.

The girls blow me a last-second air kiss before I click off my screen. Since my feet are sweltering, I pull off the socks I always wear to sleep and drop my head to the soft pillow behind me.

God knows how many hours I sleep because before I know it, I'm rushing to the toilet just in time to cough up the contents of my stomach.

Chapter Eleven

GARRETT

I CLICK THE BUTTON TO LOCK MY TRUCK BEFORE ROLLING my luggage in through the front door. I usually park my truck in the garage, but since opening and closing it would make too much ruckus at almost four in the morning, I decided to just park it in the front.

The house is dark, save for a few automatic nightlights I'd recently added to make sure little feet could find their way, even in the dark, if they needed to. I've been wondering how my wife and her daughter were faring in the house this week. We've only chatted briefly through text, and I've been excited about seeing them all week.

I take a deep breath, relishing a new scent that hadn't been there when I left the house—the scent of candy and fruit—before picking up my luggage by the handle and climbing the stairs as quietly as I can.

I'm just about to enter my room when I hear Bella groan from across the hall. My brows pinch and I shuffle closer to her door, leaning my ear against it. There's another unmistakable groan and then a rumbling cough. *Shit.*

I leave my luggage in the hallway and turn the knob to her

room without knocking. If she's sleeping, I don't want to wake her up, but I need to check on her. Whatever is going on with her, it doesn't sound good.

My eyes wander around the room. She's not in her bed, but there's a light turned on in her bathroom where I hear her cough again.

"Bella?" I softly knock on the door but get no response. My gut tells me if she was okay, she would have responded. "Bells, are you alright?"

Nothing but another God-awful cough.

I turn the knob with my heart rate elevated, not giving a shit about right or wrong. If she's in a state of undress . . . well, it's not like I haven't seen it before. But I'm unprepared for what I see when I open it.

Bella is curled up around the base of the toilet, her palms in a prayer position under her head and eyes shut tight. Her tangled dark hair with its purple tips is in a halo around her and a deep frown pulls her lips down. I can't be sure if she's sleeping, but I know she has no clue I'm here.

"Fuck." I reach for her, kneeling on the floor next to her. As soon as my hand curls under her neck, Bella jolts. "Shh, shh. Baby, it's me," I whisper near her ear. I quickly scan the area for the rancid smell. I definitely smell the distinct odor of vomit, but I can't see it, though her pajama shirt seems to be wet.

"Pilot?" Bella groans, coughing again. "What . . . what's–"

"Shh. It's okay. I'm here, sweetheart." I touch the back of my hand to her forehead. "You're burning up."

I quickly pull her against the wall and turn the tap to draw up a lukewarm bath. I already know when I take her temperature, it's going to be off the charts. Bella's head wobbles against the wall. "I'm fine, G."

I kneel next to her again, tucking her hair behind her ear. Along with her cheeks, even the tops of her ears are bright red. *How long has she been this fucking sick? Why the hell didn't she call me?*

"I'm going to go grab a thermometer and some ibuprofen. I'll be right back."

"Just a little cold. Need to sleep," she mumbles almost incoherently behind me as I rush to the medicine cabinet in my bathroom. "Meera's performance . . ."

Just a little cold? She clearly hasn't seen herself in the mirror. She looks like hell, and this is definitely not a little cold. If my hunch is right, based on the cough, her listlessness, and her heated skin, this is the flu.

I get back to her bathroom and find her sprawled on the floor again. She couldn't even hold herself up against the wall where I left her because she has no energy. Just the sight of her so sick has my chest collapsing on itself.

I kneel to check her temperature with an ear thermometer. One-hundred-two-point-six. *Shit.* I wrap my palms around her face and she lets her head hang in my hands. "Baby, I need you to take this medicine, and then I'm going to get you in the tub, okay?"

Her eyes open a little and she tries to steady them on me unsuccessfully. "I threw up."

I nod. "It's okay."

I press the pills to her lips and she barely opens her mouth enough for them to slip in, keeping her eyes shut. Then, I press the cup of water against her lips, urging her to drink a few sips and swallow the pills.

I survey the bathtub quickly, seeing that it's full enough to get her in. My mind toggles between what to do and whether I should let her climb in there on her own and watch to make sure she stays steady or get in there with her. It doesn't take but a few seconds for me to make my decision, given that the girl can barely keep herself upright against a wall.

I quickly take off my uniform, hanging it on the towel

rack. I strip down to my boxer-briefs and lower myself down to her again and clasp the hem of her pajama top. I eye her for permission. "Lift your arms for me, sweetheart."

She does so without a fuss, which is a further sign of the state she's in. The same headstrong woman who's argued with me at every turn since we got married doesn't have the fortitude to fight me on this.

She didn't have on a bra underneath, so once her shirt is off, I do the same with her sleep shorts, pulling them off along with her panties. Even sick as a dog, she's absolutely beautiful. And the sight of her lithe, long legs and delicate curves should not be turning my dick to stone—at least, not at this particular moment—but clearly, he doesn't give a shit how sick she is. The selfish bastard is all-too-ready to jump into action.

Lifting her to her feet, I pull her to me. She lays her head on my collarbone with her arms draped around my neck and presses her warm body against mine. Working fast, I turn her around, putting one arm under her knees and the other under her back before lifting her, bridal-style.

The irony of picking up my accidental bride like this for the first time to cross this unusual threshold isn't lost on me. I suppose everything between us over the course of the past few weeks has been fortuitous and unforeseen, hasn't it? I'll just file this away as yet another unexpected first, along with *the first time I claimed someone as my wife at an airport* and *the first time I actually married her while intoxicated*.

I step into the tub with her, lowering us into the lukewarm water. Her arms tighten around my neck and I hold her to me, kissing her temple. "It's okay. I've got you, baby."

After coughing a couple of times, she relaxes into me while I use a towel to run the water over her arms and legs. Bella's eyes open a minute or two later, and she watches me with a careful but tired gaze, her familiar bright chocolaty browns sunken in like endless dark caves. She raises them and our eyes connect momentarily, and something passes between us in the silence, punctuated only by the sloshing of the water.

Something buried long ago but something that aches to fracture the surface, like the bulb of a daffodil planted in the dead of winter, ready to bloom at the precipice of spring.

I don't take it lightly, knowing how difficult it is for this ridiculously stubborn woman to give someone her trust, especially someone like me. I don't take it lightly that she's finally–*fucking finally!*–allowing her eyes to linger on me for more than a mere second without darting them away as if the sheer sight of me will freeze her in place.

She licks her dry lips, heaving out a shallow breath, and I feel her fingers brush the nape of my neck. "Thank you."

"I wish I was here earlier," I respond, feeling like shit that she was this sick and had no one here for her.

"You're here now." Her body sags against me, another frown pulling down her lips. "I won't be able to go to Meera's performance in the morning."

I heard her say something about this performance earlier. But, unfortunately, I agree. She's in no shape to go. "You need to rest. Plus, you don't want to get her sick."

She nods reluctantly. "I wanted pictures of her first performance."

I scrub the wet towel over her back gently. "You'll still have them." Her eyes shift to mine in question, and I place another kiss on her temple. "I'll be there to take them for you."

"Garr–" Bella's mouth curves down again.

I give her a quick shake of my head. Her voice is hoarse and her body screams for rest. This isn't the time for her to spend her energy needlessly thanking me.

We remain in the water for a few minutes longer before a

shiver passes through her, goosebumps wafting over her skin. Her jaw tightens against the cold.

Taking that as my cue, I quickly get her out of the tub, drying her off while she unsuccessfully tries to close her legs and cross her arms over her breasts.

Apparently, she's feeling modest all of a sudden, and if I wasn't still so worried about her health, I'd laugh at the preposterousness of it. I'd also probably be punched firmly in the jaw, but that's not something I want to linger on. I suppose her sudden bashfulness is a good sign her fever has reduced, at least temporarily, and she's feeling more like herself.

Once she's fully dry, Bella points me to her drawer and I pull out a new pair of underwear and pajamas, helping her dress and get into bed. Once she seems settled, I shuffle over to the bathroom to take off my wet boxers and wrap a towel around me.

Coming back into the room, I lean down to tuck her hair behind her ear and pull a light sheet over her instead of the thick blanket that's rumpled at the foot of her bed. I'm just about to head back to my room when I feel her fingers wrap around my wrist. She searches my eyes like she did in the bathtub, and I swear I can see the tiniest fissures in the shut-ters she always has closed.

"You probably caught whatever I have by now," she croaks.

I keep my face close to hers, my eyes finding it hard to move off her entirely too luscious lips, the fanned half-circle of her lush lashes, and those fucking adorable inden-tations inside her cheeks where her dimples reside. "Probably."

"You're probably going to get sick soon."

My lips twitch with a smile trying to get loose. "Probably."

She hesitates for a moment. "I probably shouldn't be alone tonight." Her eyes widen in surprise.

The beating inside my chest accelerates. "Probably not recommended."

She tucks her bottom lip in between her teeth, seeming to think for a moment. "Pilot?"

I place my thumb on her chin and pull her lip out of its grasp. "I wasn't going to leave you alone, Bells. I was just going to grab some pajama bottoms and then come back here."

A tiny relieved smile touches her lips before I leave her to get some pants on, praying that the damn-near steel pipe under my towel softens by the time I come back, though I know it's already a foregone conclusion that it won't.

Her raspy breaths find my ears as I amble back into her room. Climbing into bed, I scoot in behind her as a sense of déjà vu drifts through my senses. It wasn't long ago she asked me for something similar, but unlike in Vegas, this time I leave a good amount of space between us.

We were both not entirely of discerning minds that night, but today, I am. And as much as I want to hold her, to nuzzle my nose in her candy-scented hair and take a step forward, the last thing I want to do is cross a barrier that will throw us two steps back.

Sure, I undressed and bathed her. I washed and redressed her. I had her defenseless and exposed inside my arms. But this feels . . . different. Forbidden.

I'm just drifting off to sleep, my eyelids heavy from flying all night, when Bella's rasp penetrates the approaching haze. "Thank you, G."

"You don't need to keep thanking me, Bells," I mumble.

She shifts, groaning as she turns to face me, and even though I'm not looking at her, I can feel the heat of her molten eyes on me. "Why?"

I keep my eyes closed, contemplating her question. At first thought, it seems simple enough, but given the woman laying in bed with me is anything but simple, I know the question isn't what it seems. "Are you ready for that answer?"

She's quiet for so long, I assume she's fallen asleep, but then her hand crosses the chasm and finds mine in the dark. She entangles our fingers together and my heart skips a beat. She pulls our clasped hands to her soft lips, brushing them over my knuckles, and whispers words that keep me awake until the light streams in through her window. Mumbled words that she probably won't even remember when she awakes. "I don't think I'll ever be ready for you, pilot . . . but I'm learning that it doesn't really matter."

Chapter Twelve

GARRETT

"WHAT'S THAT?" MEERA POINTS TO THE PACKAGE IN MY hands from her perch on the counter next to me. Her hair is tamed in a loose braid that's not quite as neat as when her mother does it, but I was quite proud of my work, given I had very few women with long hair in my life growing up. One quick tutorial on Youtube and I'm quite the hairdresser now, if I do say so myself.

"Gnocchi." I open the package after seasoning the carrots and celery that Meera helped me chop using her kid's knife and pouring vegetable broth into the heavy pot. I don't cook much, so I called Grams this morning, asking for a quick and easy recipe that I could follow step-by-step. So far, it seems to be turning out like she explained it. "They're potato pasta."

Meera's nose wrinkles, pushing up her glasses to above her eyebrows. "Do they have any chicken in them?"

I chuckle, tapping her nose with my index. "No, silly Meerkat, they're vegetarian. In fact, I'm going to make two versions of this soup—one for you and one for the rest of us. I'll add the chicken after I take out a bowl of it for you. Deal?"

She grins. "Deal!"

"You think your mom will like it?" I ask, gently putting the gnocchi into the liquid and turning up the heat.

Bella hasn't come out of her room in almost three days. I've taken her tea and saltine crackers, chicken broth, and toast, but she's only taken a few bites of almost everything. Her fever finally seemed to have broken last night, but she's stayed in bed all day and I gave her some meds for her cough.

I haven't slept in her room since the first night, nor have we talked more about the questions she's too afraid to receive answers for. But I suppose that can be blamed on the fact that she can barely get out a few words before hacking.

Meera nods enthusiastically before putting her index finger on her chin and tapping it dramatically. "You know what I think?" I don't answer because I know she'll tell me. "I think this'll taste better if we add ice cream to it. Mommy loves cotton candy ice cream."

Pretty sure the kid's talking about herself.

I glance at her, giving her my most dubious look. "Sure about that, kid? Ice cream in soup doesn't sound like the best plan."

The resident drama queen folds her little arms across her chest, turning up the theatrics. "Well, neither does *potato* pasta, Uncle Garrett, but I didn't say nothin'."

I laugh like I always do in this kid's presence. "You have a point there, Meerkat. I'll tell you what? If your mom eats a little bit of this soup, then you can ask her if she wants ice cream afterward."

"Okay." She leans over to get a whiff of the soup. "Mmm. It smells good. I bet *Nani* will like it."

"I hope so, but if your grandma is anything like your mom, she's going to be a tough nut to crack."

Apparently, Bella texted her mother sometime over the past

two days to tell her that she was sick. Bella's mother promptly messaged me to ask if she could come over to see her daughter, and of course, I wasn't going to say no. This is as much Bella's house as it is mine. So, I invited her mother for dinner tonight.

Meera giggles with her hand on her mouth. "I'm going to tell *Nani* you called her a nut."

I wince. "You wouldn't. It's the first time I'm meeting your grandma. Don't you want me to make a good impression?"

"No!" Meera giggles harder, bouncing her legs off the cabinets, and I place a protective hand on her knee to make sure she doesn't fall.

A knock on the door has both our heads turning in that direction. I lower the heat under the pot and pull Meera off the counter and onto her feet. I give her my most serious glare, knowing the kid will take me about as seriously as a pop-up toy. "Behave, Meerkat."

My 'mother-in-law' greets us, holding a brown paper bag in both her hands and a smile the size of Texas peeking out from behind it. "Hello, hello!"

I've met her before a couple of times—once at Darian and Rani's wedding—but this is the first time I've actually had a one-on-one encounter. And though she's said no more than two words so far, I can already tell we're going to get along just fine.

"Hi! Come on in." I open the door wider as she makes her way in. "It's good to see you again, Jaya."

"*Nani*-pants!" Meera wraps her arms around her grandmother's legs before she can respond to me. "Do you like our new house?"

My mother-in-law gives me an admonishing look. It's amazing how much the simple expression reminds me so much of her daughter. She leans closer to me, ensuring Meera won't hear. "I will not have any son-in-law of mine calling me by my first name; you can call me Mom."

I barely have a moment to process the fact that she seems to have plainly accepted this marriage before she's handing me the paper bag as if we've had this exchange a million times.

She bends down to address Meera next, tucking a few wayward strands from her braid behind her ear. "Well, I just got here, didn't I? How can I decide if I like your new house if I haven't seen it yet? And, what is this *Nani*-pants you've started calling me lately?"

Meera giggles again, pulling her grandma's hand forward. "I could always call you a nut instead!"

Jesus. This kid is going to have me in fucking hot water before I even have a single conversation with her grandma.

Thankfully, Meera doesn't explain herself any further, and Jaya—er, Mom?—doesn't seem to notice.

"*Nani*-pants. Come on! Let me show you my new room!"

Jaya looks to me for permission as she's dragged behind an ecstatic Meera toward the stairs. I nod with a polite smile. Truth is, I no longer make decisions in this house, not that I mind my new mother-in-law having a look around, anyway.

"Mommy's sleeping, so you need to use your inside voice, *Nani*. No yelling," Meera warns her grandma seriously. Her eyebrows lift in punctuation as if she's not fucking around, and I can do nothing but bite my cheek to hold back another laugh. "You got it?"

Jaya looks back over her shoulder at me incredulously, like she can't believe the way her granddaughter is commanding her, but I just shrug because I'd rather be kicked in the balls than voice an objection to my stepdaughter. Grandma is on her own with this one.

And . . .

Holy. Fucking. Shit.

My. Stepdaughter.

Yeah, that's a realization that just slammed into me like an eighteen-wheeler carrying a ton of bricks.

Meera is my stepdaughter.

Not that it changes how I feel about her—I adore her with the same amount of my heart as I do her mother, meaning all of it—but I guess the word does take a bit of getting used to. But I'll just add that to the list of other words I'm getting used to, like *wife* and *mother-in-law*.

Meera and my mother-in-law make it back down the stairs a few minutes later as I'm putting the soup into bowls for us. I have a tray of sliced and toasted garlic bread, too.

Jaya comes to stand next to me, reaching into the paper bag she brought and taking out a box of salad and what looks like apple pie. She glances to the side to see that Meera is busy with her hair salon kit before turning to me. "You're very sweet to decorate Meera's room like that, Garrett."

I offer a quick smile, feeling a bit out of sorts. "It isn't a big deal."

"Oh, but I think it is." She eyes me quizzically, and I try not to wither under her piercing stare. Jesus. The woman might only be an inch or two over five feet, but everything about her—from her perfectly coiffed hair and discerning gaze, to her sparkling diamond bracelet, to the way she gets right to the point—speaks of a woman with control, focus, and an IQ higher than Einstein. She'd do well in the CIA if her doctor gig didn't work out. "Correct me if I'm wrong, but you don't strike me as the type of man to marry a woman on a whim and redecorate a bedroom in your home for her daughter."

I know this is a trick question and that either answer will give her exactly what she wants to hear. I go with the easiest: the truth. "I'm not."

My mother-in-law lifts an eyebrow, a smile playing on her

lips. "I thought as much." She takes the bowls of soup to the coffee table in the family room, returning for the salad. "And I'm sure my daughter hasn't made any part of this adventure easy."

I just grin in response. She clearly knows her daughter well. "She wouldn't be who she is if she was going to make things easy, and I wouldn't lo–" I snap my mouth shut.

What the fuck? Did the CIA mother-in-law drug me with fucking truth serum?

Bella's mom keeps her widened gaze on me and then smiles knowingly, taking a seat on the couch with her plate of salad. She slides a spoon toward Meera, who's sitting at the end of the coffee table on her booster seat, indicating for her to eat.

I clear my throat, making a note to purchase a breakfast table and chairs for the breakfast nook. "I'm just going to see if Bella wants any soup."

I don't wait for Jaya's response, needing to create a little distance from her all-too-knowing chuckle at my back as I carry the soup up the stairs to Bella's room.

I lightly tap on Bella's door, and when I don't hear anything, I swing it ajar and slide inside. The shower seems to be running in her bathroom–a good sign that she's feeling better–so I leave the tray of food on her nightstand in case she feels like eating it in bed after she comes out.

Jaya has already served me a plate of salad when I return downstairs. "How is she?"

"She's in the shower, so that seems like progress." I sit on the sofa opposite her and pour a little oil and vinegar over my salad.

"The cough might linger for a bit but hopefully, the worst is over. I'll check on her before I leave." Jaya stirs the soup in her hands before taking a sip, looking intently into her bowl. "This is delicious, by the way."

"Thanks. It's my grams' recipe."

My mother-in-law smiles warmly. "I hope I get to meet her someday, then."

"I'd love for all three of you to meet her. She's pretty great."

During the rest of dinner, Jaya asks me about my job, informing me that Meera often tells her she'll become a pilot when she grows up, too. I ask her about her work and if she misses working in the ER.

"Oh, goodness, no." She wipes her mouth with a napkin. "The ER was a nightmare on the best of days, as you can imagine. But, for years," she shrugs, leaning back into her seat, "with everything going on in our personal lives . . . the ER was a needed distraction."

I assume she's referring to Bella's dad. "You mean with Bella's father?"

Jaya sighs. "It's a huge regret of mine . . . leaving Bella alone like that during her formidable years."

She watches Meera multitask, eating her soup and continuing to color, before bringing her eyes back to the bowl in front of her. "Bella's father left when she was around seven, and the shock of it all—finding out he'd not only been cheating on me, but that he'd fallen in love with another woman and wanted to leave us to be with her—created a void inside me that I tried to fill with work. So, while I was there to make sure Bella was fed and taken care of physically . . . I wasn't there for her emotionally."

She chuckles without humor. "I actually suppressed any emotion about it for a while and just continued living somewhat robotically for years." She glances at me. "If it wasn't for Rani, Bella would have been completely alone. The two of them were like sisters—they still are, as you know. They both had their own experience with trauma and gave each other the best support they could at their age."

Part of me wants to delve into this deeper with Bella herself, but my curiosity gets the better of me. "So, Bella never saw her dad again after he left?"

Jaya shakes her head before leaning over to place the bowl on the coffee table. "He actually came back when she was sixteen. Apparently, the woman he was with had left him for someone else." She glances at me. "Karma has a way, I suppose. But, by then, it was nine years too late. Bella and I had forged a life without him. I know she harbored a lot of resentment toward him for a while, and I couldn't blame her. He left when she needed him the most and when he came back, she had already moved on. She no longer wanted or needed him; she no longer trusted him."

I stir around a green olive on my salad plate, distractedly. How shitty must it have been for Bella to have no one to talk to besides her cousin for all those years? For her to have waited day in and day out for her dad to come back?

While Meera is also being raised without a father, at least she never knew him. At least she never got attached to him. It's not an ideal situation either way, but at least she hasn't known any differently. I can completely understand Bella's concern about Chaz wanting to come back into Meera's life, toppling the peace and security Bella has worked so hard to provide for Meera.

I'm taken out of my thoughts when Jaya speaks again. "So, as you can imagine, between the abandonment she felt at a young age and the distrust she formed with that Chaz idiot . . . she doesn't let people in very easily."

"Who doesn't let people in very easily?"

We all turn our heads to find a freshly showered and dressed Bella at the foot of the stairs, holding her bowl of soup in hand, regarding us with lifted brows.

Chapter Thirteen

BELLA

"Mommy!" Meera jumps out of her booster chair with her arms stretched wide, almost knocking over the bowl of soup in front of her. Thankfully, Garrett steadies her bowl in time. She barrels into my legs, wrapping her small arms around my hip. "Are you feeling better?"

"I still have a little cough, but I'm feeling a lot better." Holding my bowl in one hand, I push some of her wispy hair off her face with the other. I know she didn't braid her hair herself, so I'm assuming it was either my mom or Garrett.

She takes my hand and drags me to the couch. "Did Uncle Garrett show you the pictures from my performance?" She scoots herself onto the couch next to my mom. "I did so good, Mommy. Trinity and Nolan even said so, and you know they never lie." Her eyebrows lift and she shakes her head seriously, as if the thought of her friends lying is unthinkable.

I take a seat next to her before looking at Garrett, who's been eyeing me quietly from the other couch. His gaze assesses me softly, as if he's trying to catalog that I'm really okay. I rub my daughter's back. "I did see them, my little meerkat. Uncle Garrett sent them to me, and you looked like you were having so much fun."

"I did!" Meera eyes my half-eaten soup. It was delicious, but my appetite is still coming back. "Want to eat some ice cream?" She wiggles her brows. "It might make you feel even better."

My mom reaches out to place the back of her hand on my forehead, halting my response. "Give your mom another day or so before she starts heavier foods, Meera." She assesses my tonsils with her first two fingers and thumb, feeling them before addressing me. "Lots of water, keep yourself hydrated, and lots of rest. You should probably skip work tomorrow."

I smile at her. "Yes, Dr. Patel."

Mom gets up and splays her arms out in Meera's direction. "Come on, Meerkat. Let's give you a bath, huh? Maybe we can read one of your new books during bedtime."

My daughter promptly climbs into her grandma's arms, even at my protest. I've told my mom to let her walk, but she insists on carrying Meera, saying that she won't be little for too much longer.

Mom looks at Garrett before climbing the stairs with my daughter in tow. "Thank you for the lovely dinner, Garrett. You're quite the exceptional cook; your grams would be proud."

Garrett picks up the bowls from the table, smiling at my mom and my eyes get pinned to his lips. "You're welcome."

He carries the dishes to the kitchen as my mom and Meera disappear into her bedroom upstairs, and I follow him with the last of the plates and utensils.

He places the dishes in the sink before turning around to lean against it. He presses the heels of his palms on the counter and examines me. "Feeling better?"

I nod, taking a step in his direction to slightly close the distance between us. Strangely, it isn't a calculated move. It's as if my body just wants his nearness, like a beachgoer looking for a sunny spot to bask in. "Thank you for the soup. It was delicious."

Garrett smiles. "I'm glad you liked it. Though, you should know that I almost tried a new recipe, courtesy of Chef Meera. She wanted me to add a scoop of cotton candy ice cream to it."

I giggle. "Well, I appreciate you not making me your guinea pig for that one. That girl would eat ice cream for all three meals if I allowed it."

My smile wanes slightly as I recall the way he took care of me on Friday night. I've already cringed about a hundred times in the privacy of my own room, thinking about the fact that he saw me sprawled out on my bathroom floor, and then he had to help me take off my vomit-covered shirt to get me into the bathtub. And though I should be more embarrassed about Garrett seeing me completely naked in the state I was in, I'm more embarrassed that he had to take care of me after flying all night and being tired himself.

Yet I wouldn't have wanted it to be anyone else.

It's a realization I never thought I'd come to, but no matter how many times I played the entire night over in my fever-induced haze, one thing was clear—Garrett was the only one I wanted to take care of me. And even as my disoriented mind recognized him in the bathroom with me, a part of me kept wondering if I'd wished him, willed him, into existence.

His gentle words and his firm touch sent shivers down my body that I know weren't caused by my feverish state. It was an intimate moment I can't imagine having spent with anyone else, and if it wasn't for him getting home at the right time, who knows how long I would have laid there in my own filth. Probably until Meera found me that way on the floor the next morning, and that would have scared her so badly.

It's why I didn't want him to leave me after he put me to bed.

The truth is, as much as I know this marriage is fake—vows taken for the purposes of fulfilling a need—my feelings are . . . mixed. Feelings I never wanted to have for this man. But feelings I can't help but catch when he shows me a freezer full of tater tots and ice cream for my daughter or when he drops everything to make sure he attends her school event so I can have pictures of it. Feelings that I know I need to rein in, because feelings are what will get me into boiling water.

Deep, navy-colored boiling water, reflecting the most sinful smile a man could ever have.

A smile I've been the recipient of—like many other women before me—but one I'm desperately trying not to melt me . . . or my panties.

I keep asking myself what his angle is. Why does he insist on going so far with this whole charade? Is any of it sincere or is he just really that into this role-play? I feel like I might have asked him the same question Friday night, though I can't be sure since my recollection of what I actually said versus what I was thinking and feeling seem befuddled. And if I did indeed ask him why, then I definitely can't recall his response.

But no matter how much I want to believe his actions are just for show, no one could be that great an actor. Could they?

I don't doubt for a second that he loves Meera whole-heartedly. The fact that he painted the walls in his extra bedroom, added Dora decals, and got matching furniture and bedding says as much.

And I've concluded that he cares for me, too. If the fact that he married me on a drunken whim, didn't freak out the next day or ask for an annulment—like I did—and took care of me all Friday night while I could barely manage to keep my head up isn't enough evidence of his dedication to our friendship, then I don't know what is.

This man standing in front of me has a soft spot for me and my daughter. I don't know why, and I don't understand what we could have done to deserve it, but one thing is clear—Garrett Meyer is true to his word, and I am forever grateful for it. He said he was my friend and would help me however I needed it, and he has.

I can't say I've ever had such friendship with anyone besides my cousin and best friend, and now that I've found it, I don't think I ever want to lose it.

"G?" I lick my chapped bottom lip, trying to come up with the right words. "I know you told me not to thank you, but honestly, I . . . I don't know what else to say. The way you took care of everything this weekend, the way you checked on me and kept Meera entertained—"

"Bells," Garrett interrupts, using my name as a way to stop me from continuing. Why does this man never let me thank him properly?

I cough against the back of my hand and hold the other up to tell him to let me speak. "It means a lot to me, Garrett, so please, just let me thank you."

Garrett sighs, his shoulders slumping slightly in defeat. "You're welcome."

I look around the kitchen, not having the strength to hold his gaze. "She's right, you know?" At Garrett's puzzled look, I continue, "My mom. I didn't hear everything she said to you, but I got the gist of it. It wasn't hard to figure out she was talking about me . . . about my, uh, issues." I chuckle mirthlessly. "I *do* have a hard time letting people in, and I'm aware of the walls I've erected around me to keep everyone but a handful of people out. And it's not often that someone new makes a crack or has that wall crumbling down enough to get through . . ." I find his eyes, assessing me gently, before I swallow. My heart sprints inside my chest as my walls come down enough for me to admit something I've never admitted aloud to anyone before. "But you have."

Garrett pushes off the counter, traipsing toward me and my body immediately goes on high alert. His palms encircle my neck before his thumb glides gently along my jaw, his eyes holding mine. "I don't take that lightly, Bells. I don't take any of this lightly."

"You're a good friend, Garrett." My words seem to cool the growing heat between us—drenching us both with cold water—and I watch as Garrett's mouth turns downward slightly. I honestly don't know whose benefit I said it for—mine or his—but my throat feels raw as the words bubble up through it, and I can't seem to unravel the knot that's twisting up my insides. I can't even understand why the damn knot is there in the first place.

What are these confusing feelings? Where are they coming from? Am I just trying to dredge up more than there is behind his kindness and getting emotionally attached because, for better or worse, I've never had a man show me this sort of compassion before? Am I so impoverished that I'll try to find deeper meanings behind his acts of goodwill?

Get a hold of yourself, Bella. You've never meant that much to any man.

"Bells—"

Garrett interrupts my internal conflict, but I speak over him. "I promise we'll be out of your hair soon, G. I wholeheartedly appreciate everything you've done for us—we'll never forget it—but you have your life to live and you can't do that stuck in limbo like this with me forever."

"Bella, listen—"

I shake my head, encircling my hands around his wrists, feeling the bracelet Meera made him under my palm. "I already know what you're going to say, pilot. That we're welcome here as long as we want. That you're barely even home, so it's fine. And I truly appreciate all that, but the court date is in less than five weeks. Unfortunately, Chaz will likely establish some sort of visitation with Meera if he really wants it, even if Wendy and I fight against it. So, as soon as I know which way this is going to go, I'll file for an annulment and we'll move into a new place." Garrett's jaw tightens but I continue, speeding through to finish what I want to say, "I actually started looking for places nearby last week."

Garrett slides his hands off me, taking a step back, and every cell in my body begs me to pull him back. It's a wonder how quickly my body has veered off its conditioning to the cold and loneliness I've nurtured for so long. Somehow, it perceives these moments of warmth—where Garrett's hands are on me and where his warm gaze assesses me—will last forever.

They won't, though.

They never do.

My heart and mind are well-versed in thriving inside the cold loneliness. It would be best if my body got back on track as well.

Despite the constant warmth radiating off him like solar flares, it'll take a lot to melt this glacier.

Despite the wounded look that flashed across his face a second ago, Garrett relents. "As you wish, Bells."

I nod. "But don't worry, I haven't forgotten my side of the bargain. I'll accompany you to any work event as your wife if it helps you reinvent yourself." Garrett raises his chin in response but keeps his emotions guarded. "I haven't forgotten about the gala this weekend."

"But if you're feeling under the weather—"

I wave my hand, cutting him off, "Don't be silly. I'll be all better by then. I'm almost there now. I'll go shopping this week and get something gala-worthy so I'll be ready to play your doting wife."

Garrett leans over to grab the credit card he left on the counter before he went to work last week. "Please use this to buy yourself whatever you'd like."

"Gar–"

"Bella." His firm tone leaves no room for argument, and for a reason I can't quite understand, it sends a thrill down my spine. Up until now, I'd only been the recipient of Garrett's cajoling tone–somewhat soft and insistent–but this. . . Just the way he says my name has my full attention, and I can't help wanting to piss him off a little bit more, just to see how far he'll go with it. "Take the card and, for once in your life, don't argue with me. Buy the dress on it."

I bite my lip, grasping the card between my fingers. I don't mean to say the next thing with any insinuation or heat. I don't mean to caress his face with my gaze under the thicket of my lashes, but I do, nonetheless, feeling the tiniest bit of electricity buzz between us. "Is there anything you'd like to see me wear?"

His Adam's apple bobs as he swallows, absorbing the current from my body to his. His voice sounds rough around each syllable. "Nothing . . . comes to mind."

And as I walk back upstairs with his card in my hand and the tingling sensation of his gaze at my back, his words tumble inside my head.

Nothing . . . comes to mind. Nothing, comes to mind.

Why do I get the feeling he said them knowing full well they'd elicit a double entendre?

Chapter Fourteen

BELLA

Melody: Please tell me you're wearing that
lacy lilac thong with the bows on the sides I
like so much.

MY NOSE WRINKLES AS I READ THE TEXT FROM MY BEST
friend. She can be so weird.

Me: Firstly, it's disturbing that you've been
through my underwear drawer and
cataloged my things, and secondly, why the
hell would I wear something you like?

I go back to pinning my hair on one side and patting
down the little wisps with a touch of gel. The other side of
my hair is loosely curled so my purple tips lay neatly over my
bare shoulder. My makeup is minimally done, aside from my
red lips, and I've spritzed on my favorite perfume.

I trail my eyes down my figure, wrapped in the new gold
dress I begrudgingly bought yesterday using Garrett's card.
The A-line shape accentuates my curves, draping all the way
to the ground in a flowy material that cinches at my waist,

but that's not the reason I bought the dress—though it does make me feel like royalty. I bought it especially for its heart-shaped, strapless bustier and the split all the way up my thigh. I can't remember the last time I felt so sexy.

I almost decided to forego Garrett's firm command and not purchase the dress on his card. But then I imagined having to tell him I didn't and the look of disappointment on his face was too much, so I clenched my teeth and found myself something priced mid-range.

I also bought a new pair of shoes and a clutch using my own card. But as far as I'm concerned, what he doesn't know can't disappoint him.

My phone buzzes again while I'm applying another coat of red lipstick. I've caught Garrett's eyes on my lips before, especially when I've worn this shade, so I know he'll approve. And because I've just caught myself having that stray thought in regard to his approval, I quickly distract myself by picking up my phone.

> Melody: Because I have good taste, that's why.

> Rani: @Melody, this is just one of your various disconcerting behaviors, aside from describing Nelson's poop to an unwelcome level of detail. I've seen you look through my underwear drawer as well, and I have to agree with @Bella . . . it's a complete invasion of privacy.

Melody: Bitch, you watched my OBGYN jam-pack his hand all the way up my hoo-ha during one of my prenatal exams. I'm pretty sure if someone had handed you a bag of popcorn, you would have eaten that shit as if you were watching the world's most riveting on-stage performance. So, let's not even start on the whole 'invasion of privacy' shit. I'm pretty sure you won that competition.

Rani: I had my eyes closed the whole time!

Melody: Girl, please. I saw you squint your curious little eyes open like a pervert.

I laugh at the text exchange between my best friend and cousin. I swear they can keep going like this for hours, and if anyone was to read their messages without understanding the deep love between them, they'd think all they did was bicker.

But that's how we've always talked to each other—freely and without judgment—knowing that everything we say, even if it might come out rough around the edges, is said with the respect and love we have for one another.

Rani: Fine! I took a little peek for the sake of curiosity and science! Sue me!

Melody: I'll get my mom right on that. And for the record, Nelson's poops are fascinating.

Me: @Rani, do you get the feeling that we're being distracted by the underwear inspector between us?

Rani: Yes, yes, I do.

> Melody: Oh hush, Cinderella. Now, show us
> what you're wearing to the ball. I can't wait
> to find out what that gorgeous husband of
> yours will be peeling off you later before you
> boink his head off.

I roll my eyes, though it's too late to throw the thought of boinking my husband out of my mind. In a matter of five seconds—only a few seconds longer than it takes me to roll my eyes at Melody's absurd comment—I've already envisioned my husband tearing the thin piece of light purple fabric between my legs and ramming his thick cock inside me.

Shit. I need to apply another layer of deodorant.

It's not that I've never had these lecherous thoughts about Garrett before, because I have—a multitude of times, and in various states of undress. I mean, I can hardly be blamed. The man incinerates panties wherever he flies with little more than a smile, and mine aren't fire-proof. It's just that these intrusive and inconvenient thoughts seem to be happening on the regular lately.

I quickly try to clear my head, reminding myself of the same thing I've said every time I've had the thoughts—that they're only occurring because I haven't been laid in ages. Four years to be exact.

Four years, where I haven't felt anything besides my own hand and my vibrator between my legs. Four years that I haven't been touched in any carnal way at all.

And at this very moment, four years feels like a lifetime ago.

And while I've only been with two men in my life—an on-and-off again college boyfriend and . . . well, the douchebag I'll be seeing in court in the not-too-distant future—I know for a fact that whoever I end up spending my life with—*if* I spend my life with anyone at all—will thoroughly enjoy my healthy sexual appetite. An appetite that wouldn't shy away from trying something new. Because while I've only had sex a few times, what I had never satiated my need for all-consuming, passionate—if not a little rough—sex.

A need to be fucked thoroughly and repeatedly until I can't see straight.

Perhaps it's that wild girl inside me, who's had me by my proverbial balls these days, but denying my attraction to my husband seems to be futile.

Opening the little box of *Nerds* sitting on my nightstand, I pour half into my mouth, letting the lemony flavor coat my tongue and simmer down my sex-laden brain. *So fucking good.*

Then, after checking to make sure my teeth look clean, I angle my phone and take a picture of myself in the floor-length mirror before sending it to my friends. Their *oohs* and *aahs* vibrate against my hand as I place my phone and the half-eaten box of candy into my black clutch and slip on my new heels. I'm praying they don't pinch my feet too much tonight.

I'm not sure what to expect at this gala. I know it's for the opening of a brand-new aviation museum, and from what I understand, Garrett has been advising the committee working on it, ensuring its success. But other than that—and the fact that there will be dinner and dancing involved—I have little additional information. And with my long hours at work this week and Garrett flying out most of Tuesday to Thursday, I haven't had a chance to ask much about it, either.

Garrett said he'd pick me up after dropping Meera at my mom's for the night, but I haven't heard the garage open yet, though I suppose it's still early enough that we'll have plenty of time to get there.

Flicking the light off in my room, I take in a calming breath before shutting my door behind me. I've felt short of breath and jittery all day. I know this is just an event that he's asked me to accompany him to, but for some reason, I can't help feeling nervous about it, as if I need to make sure I don't mess this up for him in any way.

Maybe it's just the fact that this is the first event I'm going to with him as his wife, or perhaps it's the jitters from not knowing how to act or what to say when I meet his colleagues. Will they be able to see right through our act? Will they—especially the ones who have experience being married—immediately know that Garrett and I are nothing but underwhelming actors who'll never see the lights of a real stage?

It's been nearly a month since we got married, but so far, we haven't had to behave as a married couple. Everyone who knows we're married knows the terms in which we did it, and thank god, they haven't expected us to act any differently. But tonight, our performance skills will be put to the test, and that makes me nervous as hell.

But anxiety be damned, I owe him my end of our bargain.

Garrett told a few people at his work that he recently got married and confessed to me that word traveled fast. People he didn't even know were sending him congratulatory messages, which means I won't be able to let my guard down at all during the gala.

It's fine, though. I mean, how difficult could it be? We're friends—as made clear by Garrett, himself—and comfortable around each other. The man cleansed me of my own vomit, for crying out loud. We'll mingle and dance, pretending to be irrefutably in love for a few hours, and then we'll come back home, laughing about the whole thing.

Easy-peasy.

My heels *click* on the hardwood stairs as I make my way down, my hand gently resting on the banister. I'm halfway down when I hear the garage door opening. Garrett must be back from dropping off Meera.

I take another quick breath, my stomach flipping over in

anticipation. I haven't seen him much all day, even all week, so the prospect of seeing him in a tux has me feeling . . . *something*. The man has a way of inciting the most lustful thoughts inside me in just his casual wear, so I can only imagine how fucking depraved he's going to make me feel wearing a tuxedo.

Garrett's footsteps resound on the floor as I get to the bottom of the stairs, and he halts in place as our eyes connect.

Dear God Almighty, I was not prepared.

My gaze swallows him up hungrily, from his styled-back hair to the barely-there stubble on his angled jaw, contrasting perfectly with his elegant black bow tie. His suit wraps around him like it was stitched on him directly, and he looks both salacious and dapper at the exact same time.

I suppose I shouldn't be surprised. My husband looks impressive wearing simple pajamas any given night, so it shouldn't be shocking that he looks downright lethal in a tux.

My hand tightens over the banister, and I shove down a sudden, unfamiliar urge to pull him by the lapels and place my nose directly under his jaw to inhale him like a potent drug. I'm positive that the way he smells will either place me in a trance or knock me out, dead.

"You look . . . impossibly beautiful, Bells." The gravel in his voice fills the space between us, and I can't help but blush.

"Thank you. You look incredible, too," I stammer and then hear my next words in a breathy whisper, all too late to stop them from leaving my mouth. "But you always look incredible."

Garrett stares at me as I take an audible breath with my admission. *God, please let him not have heard that last part . . .* My cheeks flame, and I try to cover up my verbal diarrhea by waving my hand holding my clutch over my dress. "Um, I hope this isn't too much."

He takes the steps to cover the distance between us before coming to stop in front of me. I'm still on the last step, so while I have to look up at him, it's not quite as much as usual. His gaze wafts over my lips before he licks his own. Then, seeming to regain his sense of purpose, he pulls something out of his pocket, and I finally unpin my eyes from his lips to glance at the black velvet box in his hand.

My eyes widen as he flips the box open, and I spot the most beautiful emerald-cut diamond winking in the light. A gasp sputters out of me, but otherwise, I'm left speechless. "Garrett . . ."

Pulling the ring out of the box, Garrett places the box back in his pocket before lifting my hand off the banister. Both our eyes land on my small hand inside his large one, and I relish the slide of his thumb across my knuckles. It sends a flurry of goosebumps across my arm, tingling all the way to the base of my spine.

Garrett's gaze turns soft and vulnerable—thoughtful—as he strokes my hand with his thumb again, and I wish to high heaven that I could hear what he's thinking.

There's no questioning the weight of this moment, the silent conversation we seem to be having. Even if we're both aware this marriage is a sham, this moment between us doesn't feel as though it is.

Similar to a few moments over the past few weeks.

But why?

What are these goddamn feelings that I keep having . . . that I keep fighting?

Our heads rise and our eyes connect while so much hangs in the air between us. The air that's simply not enough to fill my lungs, but almost too much to let me breathe. The air that has me ascending higher with each moment I spend in his proximity.

What is this tightness inside my ribs?

Why can't I fucking *breathe?*

My hand twitches inside his embrace. Not because it doesn't want to be there, but because all I can think about is wrapping my hands around his jaw and pulling his lips to mine. All I can imagine is breaking down my walls and letting go of my reservations to jump into his arms.

But would he even want that?

Would that completely torch our friendship?

Isn't that crossing the bounds of this charade?

Before I can get out of my head long enough to decide what I want to do, Garrett clears his throat. The vibration of his words and the sexy lilt of his voice rolls down through my sternum, pooling inside my belly. "Real or fake, I'm well aware I don't deserve you, Bells. I know, given what you think about me, you'd never purposely *want* to be in this position. But I want you to know that even if you're counting the days until we go our separate ways, I'm not."

My brows furrow and my mouth opens and closes, and I seem to have lost my voice. I want to tell him that's not true. That, over the past few weeks, I've done nothing but question my previous opinions about him as a hedonistic playboy and a commitment-phobe. That I've seen more commitment from him over the past few days and weeks as a friend and a caretaker than I have from any other man in my life.

That I no longer can even make sense of what I feel for him.

That I do, indeed, *feel* for him, but I just don't know if I can or should. Because putting my heart on the line feels a lot like placing it inside a guillotine without knowing the exact verdict—whether he would chop it in half or not—and the fear of putting it out there overwhelms my sense of self-preservation.

But the words seem to be stuck somewhere between my brain and my mouth.

His thumb slides over my ring finger. "So, until then, I'd like you to wear this whenever we're in public. It's my grandmother's—"

"Garrett." I pull my hand out of his grasp, no longer able to hold myself back. Letting my purse, my inhibitions, and my self-preservation fall to the floor, I do exactly what I envisioned earlier. I wrap my hands around the sides of his neck and lay my lips firmly against his.

My eyes close on their own accord, and for a moment, neither of us moves. Then, slowly—ever so cautiously—I tilt my head and swipe my tongue over his lips, encouraging Garrett to open his mouth. He stays relatively still, letting me figure out my next move, and my tongue delves deeper into his mouth tentatively before I pull back slightly to pull his bottom lip between my teeth.

Gently, ever so softly.

It's a cautious exploration, a tender embarkation. And though I've tasted his lips before, it still feels completely uncharted. His lips are soft and plump; the most perfectly kissable lips a man can have.

The scruff around his mouth scratches the tip of my nose and a wave of lust vibrates inside my core.

The kiss only lasts a few seconds, but the groan that wrestles out of his throat has me freezing. My eyes fly open with its sound, as if I just realized how far I've taken what was supposed to be just a kiss to shut him up. A reaction to his overwhelming sweetness.

My hands have slid to the back of his neck, my fingers are tangled in the hair at the nape of his neck, my breath skimming over his lips rhythmically.

Jesus, have I ruined everything? Have I pulled him into the same confusion I've been reeling in? What am I doing?

"I'm sorr—"

"Don't you dare finish that sentence," he croaks, his navy-blue eyes swirling with a warning and a plea.

I lay my forehead against his while my heart hammers inside my throat. We both look down between us at the ring still in his grasp, and I put my questions, my apology, and any further conversation of this exchange between us aside. What's done is done, I suppose, and as with many moments shared with this man, I never seem to have my wits about me.

"I'll take good care of it, pilot," I whisper as I splay out my left hand so he can slide the ring over my ring finger. It's only a bit loose, but not enough that I'm worried I'll lose it. My other thumb strokes the stubble over his jaw before I look back into his deep navy blues, temporarily taking off the life vest that keeps me afloat around him. "I may not have chosen to be in this position, pilot," I cup his jaw with my left hand, savoring the beautiful sparkle and weight of our vows around my finger, "but for the time that we're together, I'll willingly choose you every single day."

Chapter Fifteen

BELLA

WE CLIMB THE STAIRS OUTSIDE THE NEW MUSEUM BUILDING after handing the car keys to the valet, and I watch the various other couples next to us do the same—some speaking in hushed tones, while others giggle amongst themselves. Even under the long coats protecting them from the late-February Bay Area wind, everyone is dressed to the nines.

Through the entire drive here, Garrett was particularly quiet, and I can't say it didn't unnerve me. He usually has this big personality—a presence that can't be ignored—so when he's quiet, it's incredibly unsettling.

I can only assume it was the kiss that was taking over his thoughts. Another impulsive decision on my part, but one I keep playing over and over again in my head, especially his warm lips, his heady scent, and the way his skin felt under my fingertips.

I want to regret my spontaneous decision. I wish I could even voice a sincere apology for making him feel uncomfortable and blurring the lines of our friendship, but I can't seem to find the words.

God, why can't I get any of these feelings untangled?

As if sensing my internal turmoil, I feel the warmth of Garrett's hand over mine as we climb the last step together. What I hadn't noticed in his house—probably because my eyes were clouded in a haze of emotion—that I noticed in the car when his hand was wrapped around the steering wheel is the gold band around his left hand ring finger. The same hand he also wears the beaded bracelet Meera gave him.

With my hand inside of his, I can't help but like the feel of it against my skin. It makes me feel strangely possessive of him, as if a simple ring is all I needed to proclaim my ownership of him. As if somehow the rings on both of our fingers legitimized everything we'd done.

"Get out of your head, Bells," he says, pulling the door open for us as we enter the museum. He's using that same stern tone, the one I've recently noticed sends a flood of tingles over my skin. The one I want to press on a little more and find out how commanding he can really be.

We get inside and he helps take off my coat, handing both his and mine to the man standing at the coat check, before I turn to him. My head tilts up as I look into his eyes with a newfound and mischievous rebellion. "Get out of *my* head? I could say the same for you, Mr. *Quiet and Reserved*. You were nothing but withdrawn and . . . and unapproachable through the entire drive here."

"Unapproachable?" His brow lifts, but I see the twitch on his lips.

I nod. "Yes, unapproachable. Aloof."

We stare into each other's eyes, and I swear, he leans forward just a tad. "Bells, I—"

"Garrett! Good to see you here!" A hand lays on Garrett's shoulder, and he turns to look at the intruder.

I pull away from him, but Garrett keeps his hand clasped over mine in a relentless lock. He reaches out to shake the hand of the very attractive gentleman in front of us, though I don't miss the irritation in his expression. "David. Good to see you, too."

The man's pale green eyes twinkle at him before he turns his curious gaze toward me. "And who might this be?"

Garrett unclasps his hand from mine before sliding it behind me to grasp my waist. He pulls me to his side, and I can't help but notice the way his jaw grinds as his eyes bore into this David person. "This is my *wife*, Bella." Garrett enunciates my title with enough fervor that if he'd written it, it would be underlined about a dozen times. "We were just about to go find our table."

"Sure! I'm sure I'll see you in there. I'm sitting at the same table as the other chief pilots." David turns his attention to wink at me, and Garrett stiffens at my side. "Bella. A beautiful name for a beautiful woman. I do hope we meet again."

I give him a tight smile. He's clearly accustomed to women falling for his flashy smile and gratuitous compliments. "Nice to meet you, David."

And before more can be said, I don't know if it's me who pulls Garrett or the other way around, but we're heading toward the entrance to the hall, our hands still locked at our sides.

We find our table and Garrett pulls out my chair before sitting next to me. As soon as he's seated, he clasps our hands together and rests them on his thigh. He's been holding me, touching me all night, and I have to wonder how much of this is for show. Did our kiss earlier perpetuate all this touching, or is this for the benefit of everyone else?

In some ways I feel even more confused than I was before, but as I look around at the guests taking seats at our table—some of whom Garrett seems to know—I settle on the decision that it is all for show.

Because why would it be real? How could it be real?

"Who was that David guy, by the way?" I murmur, leaning

into Garrett's ear. He turns his head ever so slightly and his scruff gently slides against my lips, almost making me forget the rest of my sentence. "I felt like you both had history."

Garrett keeps his eyes on the stage, where various people busy themselves doing last-minute sound checks and whatever else goes into ensuring the person taking the podium can be seen and heard. "He used to be a captain, like me—a colleague of mine. But he brown-nosed and hob-nobbed his way into the right circles and became chief pilot without enough experience. And he likes to throw that in my face any chance he gets." Garrett shrugs. "So aside from the fact that he blatantly flirted with my wife, he also seems oblivious to the fact that I have little respect for his undeserving title. I don't like people who pretend to be anything they're not."

My eyes follow Garrett's gaze toward the stage, and I momentarily mull over his words. He doesn't like people who pretend to be anything they're not, but . . . aren't we doing that exact thing? Isn't *he* doing that exact thing?

A few people sitting at our table start conversations with Garrett, and he introduces me as his wife. I smile genuinely back at them, getting more comfortable in my role. As the speeches begin, I look around, admiring the beautifully decorated hall with its large chandeliers, enormous bouquets, and strategically placed airplane ice structures. I'm just about to turn back to the stage when my eyes land on someone who brings my heart to a complete halt.

My vision blurs, and I instinctively place my other hand against the pit forming in my stomach. Snapping my head back toward the conversation at my table, I whisper, "Shit!" hoping to be as quiet as possible..

Garrett is mid-sentence with someone when he turns his puzzled gaze in my direction, clearly having heard me. Then, as if he'd been tracking exactly what I'd been doing this whole time, he turns his head in the direction I was facing when I saw the ghost in the first place.

His hand tightens around mine, and I'm positive it'll lose circulation if he doesn't ease up on it soon. "Fuck," he mumbles before his lips thin into a straight line, his jaw working so hard the vein in his temple throbs visibly. "What the fuck is *he* doing here?"

And as if the speaker on stage has heard his question, he leans into the microphone with a smile. "I'd now like to welcome a few key players whose companies are revolutionizing the aviation hardware space. Please welcome to the stage, Mr. Charles Gallaway from Techware Hardware, and Ms. Breana Thompson from AVA Technologies."

The speaker continues over the applause as Chaz makes his way to the front, but my ears ring so badly that I'm almost tempted to shove my index fingers into them. I only hear bits and pieces of the rest of the speech as Chaz takes the podium, looking all-too-proud and self-important as words like 'transforming aircraft WiFi technology' and 'avionics upgrades' stir up the crowd further.

Of course, he would be working for an aviation hardware company. *Of course*, it would only be my wishful thinking that would have me believing that I didn't have to see him until our meeting at the courthouse.

And then, as if I've somehow summoned his gaze, Chaz looks right at me as he continues on to finish his speech. And whether anyone else notices it or not, I don't miss the small crooked smile that pulls up his lips from under his beard.

My fucking blood runs cold.

Why the fuck can't I get away from this guy?

Jolting me out of my stupor, Garrett rounds his arm over my shoulders, pulling me into him before placing a soft kiss at my temple. "Do you want to leave?"

My brows furrow. *Leave?* We just got here. We haven't

even had dinner or danced, haven't met all those people who needed to see Garrett as a married man, and now he wants to leave? I shake my head, looking into his beautiful eyes that resonate the same hint of anger I feel inside, surely for the man still standing at the podium.

My voice quivers, betraying my resolution. "No."

"Are you sure? We can go right now, Bells."

"No. This was part of our deal–"

"I don't give a shit about our deal." Garrett's eyes hold mine.

I glance over at Chaz with contempt. "Still, no. Even if I want to, I won't let that asshole run me out of another event. Fuck him."

Garrett's lips rise. "That's my girl. And as for running you out? He could give it his best fucking shot but he'd have to go through me. I won't let him near you, Bells."

The expression on his face is both threatening and severe, but my body only feels the warmth that's ever-present in his proximity. It washes over me, and I give in to the feeling over-taking all my senses once more–a feeling I can no longer rein in around this man.

God, he looks insurmountably handsome in his tux, with his hair styled so neatly. My on-paper-only husband.

Before I know what I'm doing yet again, I lean in and place a chaste kiss on his lips. "I know, pilot. Thank you," I whisper over them.

"What have I told you about thanking me?" He keeps me from moving away by clutching me a little tighter.

I squint at him, our faces mere millimeters apart. "And what are you going to do to stop me, pilot?"

His jaw works again as his irises take on the color of a starless evening sky. "Let's get one thing clear, sweetheart . . ." His warm breath wafts over my still-tingling lips. "I don't give a rat's ass who's watching us or where we are, but if you test me any more, I'll take you over my knee, right here, right now."

His words hit me right between my thighs, and I shift in my seat to squelch the need. My eyes widen slightly as I swallow the drool I'm sure would leak out if I wasn't careful.

The prospect of Garrett spanking me, turning my ass red as he fingers me, fucks me . . . I'm sweltering with the thought. My mind gets carried away with deliciously lewd images while I force my mouth not to hang agape. I'm sure he can see the color seep into my cheeks, but a soft 'excuse me,' spoken by a server behind me pulls me out of my stupor.

Garrett and I pull apart as our dinner is placed in front of us, but my mind is still reeling with his filthy insinuation. Having forgotten all about the asshole on stage, I slide a quick glance at Garrett's face. He seems to be studying the food in front of him, but I don't miss the way his lips have turned slightly upward. Unlike me, who's constantly second-guessing my actions around him, my husband seems to be completely in control of himself and deliberate with his behavior.

So, I know I've royally fucked up when the night ends with a drastic shift in his warmth—moving me from my sunny spot on the beach to a cold, reclusive desert.

Chapter Sixteen

BELLA

I DIDN'T REALIZE GARRETT WAS GOING TO GIVE A SPEECH, too.

He looks incredible on stage, his impressive presence illuminated by the backdrop. I'm already smiling—having forgotten about the dessert in front of me—in response to something he's said to make the audience laugh, when he looks over at me and winks. That same warm feeling rolls down to my stomach.

He's just on his way off the stage and back to his seat next to me when someone calls to him. I watch as the two men shake hands and then Garrett gestures for the other man to follow him. When they approach, I note the man's salt-and-pepper hair and sharp, assessing gray eyes. He's probably in his late fifties, early sixties.

"Bella, I'd like you to meet Pete Overland, the CEO of *Blue Breeze Airlines*. He's not only my boss but has been a long-time mentor as well. He's also played a huge role in the establishment of this museum."

I get out of my seat as an applause erupts for whoever is on stage now. Quickly wiping my hand on my napkin, I jut it out to introduce myself to Garrett's CEO. "Bella Patel. So nice to meet you."

Pete shakes my hand, his eyes crinkling at the corners with his smile. "*Mrs. Meyer*, from what I hear! I believe a formal congratulations is in order."

"Thank you so much." I smile back, glancing from him to Garrett and back again.

Pete lets my hand go and turns to Garrett, slapping him on the shoulder in the way men do. "You did well for yourself, son! I can't say I ever thought of you as the type to settle down, given your penchant for charming the ladies, but I'm glad you have and with such a beautiful woman as your wife here."

I lift an eyebrow at Garrett and then offer him a knowing smile. I can't say that a reminder of his past as a womanizer doesn't bother me, but isn't that what I'm here to help him reinvent? Isn't that why I'm even at this gala? So his colleagues can see him more as a family man than the reputation that seems to follow him around.

"Sometimes you spend all your life trying to find the right woman, Pete," Garrett states, with his eyes locked on mine. "And then, you spend the rest of your life convincing her to stay."

Gosh, if I didn't know we were playing a part in this entire charade, I'd be a puddle on the floor right now. The man has a way with words.

Pete chuckles. "Well, that ring on her finger says you won't have to convince her much more." I fiddle my ring with my thumb as Pete continues, "Anyway, what I wanted to tell you is that Brooke has been dying to meet your lovely wife ever since I told her you got married."

Garrett looks around at the crowd. "I haven't seen her today. Did she not accompany you?"

Pete places his hand in his pants pocket. "Our daughter,

Kylie, just had her second baby a couple of weeks early last night, and Brooke flew out to Pittsburgh this morning to see her."

"I hope mom and baby are doing well," I say, grateful for the change of subject.

Pete leans back on his heels a little. "Brooke has been keeping me well informed, and from what I'm told, they're both doing fine. I'll visit once they're all settled back at home."

"Well, congratulations on becoming a grandfather again, Pete." Garrett squeezes Pete's shoulder.

"Thank you. I feel blessed." Pete pats Garrett's hand on his shoulder before turning to me. "Now, as I was saying, Brooke really wants to meet you. Has Garrett told you about the St. Patrick's Day party at our house in a few weeks?" I look at Garrett, but he seems to be focused on Pete at the moment. "We host a gathering on the weekend after St. Patrick's Day every year and invite our close friends and colleagues. Brooke specifically asked me to extend an invite to you both. The only requirement is that you wear something green."

Garrett must see the hesitation on my face and chimes in. So far, we'd only agreed to me coming to this one gala with him, so I'm sure he's thinking it would be too much for me to attend another event. "Thank you, Pete. We'll look at our calendar and see if that would be possible—"

"Oh, but I insist that you at least try; otherwise, Brooke will really have my head for it," Pete urges.

Knowing that Garrett just started working for this new airline not too long ago, and how important networking and work relationships are from my own work experience, I decide to make the decision for us. It'll be a week before the court hearing with Chaz, but Garrett and I will still be married and living together. I promised that I'd help him establish his new reputation at work, and this will hopefully seal the deal for him . . . until we're no longer together that is, but I'm not going to churn on that thought right now.

"Please tell Brooke we'll be there, Pete." I smile, meeting Garrett's knotted brows with what I hope is a reassuring look. "I can't wait to meet her."

"Oh good!" Pete rubs his hands together as if he's excited by the prospect of seeing us again, when music filters in through the speakers and the announcer on stage invites all the guests to the dance floor. "Well, congratulations again, you two." Pete turns to Garrett. "I think it's time you take your new bride dancing, captain!"

Garrett gives his CEO a casual salute, watching him head back to his table for a moment before turning toward me. He moves a step closer, grasping my hand in his. "Dance with me?"

I grin, looking up at him. "Okay, but I'll warn you, I have two left feet. And with these new heels pinching me all night, I'm probably not going to last long."

He looks down at my feet. "You could take them off."

I wrinkle my nose. "And dance barefoot? What if the floor is dirty or someone spills their drink on it and I step in it? Or what if someone steps on my foot?"

"You really don't shy away from overthinking, do you, wifey?"

I bat him on the chest with my free hand. "Oh, hush."

"I could carry you. Swing you around in my arms."

A laugh bubbles out of me as I imagine the ludicrous sight of Garrett swaying with me, *literally,* in his arms on the dance floor. "Right, and that wouldn't be crazy."

He starts pulling me toward the dance floor with my smaller hand enclosed inside his much larger one. "I'd say we've crossed the lines of what might be considered crazy, don't you?"

I giggle behind him. "Touché."

I scan the crowd for Chaz as Garrett and I make our way to the center of the room. I'm sure the asshole is still around somewhere but thankfully, nowhere I can see him. We're just about to reach the dance floor, where other couples are swaying gently to an Adele song, when someone calls out to Garrett from our right.

We both look over to see a woman standing up from her seat. She only glances at me before lifting her hand up to wave at Garrett. I note his fingers tightening over mine slightly, giving me a clue as to who she might be. I can only assume she's someone from his past.

"Ally." Garrett gives her a curt nod.

"Glad to see you again, Garrett. I felt like our time in Vegas was cut short."

A stab of pain like I've been hit in the gut has me turning to look at my husband, but I'm surprised by the unamused look on his face. *Their time in Vegas?* Does she mean the same time both Garrett and I were there? Did he hook up with her that weekend after he kissed me in the airport?

But even if he did, why should that bother me? It's not like I had any claim on him then—it's not even like I have any real claim on him now, besides a piece of paper legalizing a marriage we went into intoxicated, and one we're headed to annul. He didn't owe me any loyalty then and he doesn't really owe me any now.

"You mean the few minutes we spoke on a flight that both you and I were working on?" Garrett asks her, lifting his brow. He doesn't let her answer before he turns to me. "Bella, this is Ally, one of the FAs—er, flight attendants—who also works for *Blue Breeze*. Ally?" He doesn't even look at her when he addresses her, keeping his eyes fixed on me. "This is my beautiful wife, Bella."

"*Wife?*" Ally stammers, finally regarding me. "I didn't realize you were married."

"I am. Very happily so. Now, if you'll excuse us, we were just on our way to the dance floor." With his arm now wrapped around my waist, Garrett walks us to the dance floor, not sparing another glance at Ally.

I swear, I was not prepared in the least to navigate this gala. From the strange conversation with that David guy right when we entered, to being blindsided by my douchebag baby-daddy, to meeting one of the women from my husband's past—who clearly still seems to be pining for him—I'm dodging grenades like I'm in battle.

And I must say, I'm doing a fucking phenomenal job of it!

I promised Garrett I'd be at this gala with him—that I'd hold up my side of the bargain—and that's exactly what I'm doing. And even if that stab of jealousy pierced my insides, his swift response definitely pulled me out of any mistaken notions I could have veered into. Anyway, what choice do I have but to believe him?

Once I wrap my arms around Garrett's neck, he pulls me into him with a strong hand on my waist, eliminating whatever space was left between us. The movement has my lips landing at the bottom of his jaw and this time, I do what I'd imagined doing earlier—I take in a deep inhale, letting his delicious woodsy cologne send goosebumps down my spine, curling my toes inside my all-too-uncomfortable heels.

His low voice vibrates over the shell of my ear, practically making me pant and sending electricity coursing through me. "Remember what I told you the day we got married?" He doesn't wait for me to answer. "That I'd never intentionally hurt you."

I nod, feeling the weight of his arms around me and his intoxicating stubble on my lips.

"Remember what I said to you that day at your apartment, when I asked you to move in with me? That I'd never make you look or feel like a fool because of me."

My chest tightens. "I do."

His hand lifts my chin to look up at him. "Good, because I wouldn't. And just so you don't start overthinking things," he smiles when he feels me pinch the back of his neck, "she means nothing to me. Just a blip in my past."

A little thought crosses my mind, wondering if I'll also just be a *blip in his past* after this is all over, but of course, I shove the insecurity away to worry about later. I also don't show how that thought has melancholy sweeping through my insides, creating a solid weight in my chest. Instead, I play with the hair on his nape. "You don't have to explain it to me, pilot. I understand."

"But I want to." His mesmerizing eyes have me entranced. "In the past, I might not have been the most committed guy in the universe—"

My lips twitch. "Seems like an understatement."

"But ever since you, ever since Meera . . ." He trails off without finishing his sentence. "Bella, I'd never do that to you."

Hopefully the low lighting will keep my glassy eyes and lonely soul veiled. Ruse or not, I believe him when he says he'd never do something to hurt me intentionally. I trust him when he says he's not like the other men from my past. And perhaps that's the crux of the situation.

I trust him.

Not just with Meera, but with me, too. So much so that I moved into his home, allowed him to take care of me when I was at my most vulnerable, and let him start chipping away at the ice around my heart. And because of that—because of his relentless smiles and his warm touch—I'm losing my sense of reality and possibly my mind.

"G?"

Garrett pulls his bottom lip into his mouth, letting it go slowly, and I all but groan out loud, only slightly registering the song changing and John Legend crooning out his lyrics to *Conversations in the Dark*. It seems befitting for this moment and, dare I say, for us. "Yeah?"

"I want . . ." My heart thrashes against my ribs, and I'm sure he can feel it slamming over his chest. I close my eyes, not able to withstand seeing the expression on his face. "I want you to . . . I need–"

And before I can finish, Garrett's mouth crashes down on mine.

Chapter Seventeen

BELLA

I'M MOMENTARILY STRUCK SILENT—MY BODY, MY MIND, MY heart—and everything seems to stop. The crowd around us disappears as John Legend's voice fades somewhere in the distance. I'm not even sure we're still standing on the dance floor anymore. We might have traveled to outer space, and I wouldn't really know it. I wouldn't even care.

Garrett's tongue delves into my mouth, parting my lips as if he's done it a hundred times. His tongue has no intention of asking for permission. It's on a mission, and come hell or high water, nothing will stop it. His hands cradle my neck, tilting my head in the angle he wants it so his tongue can swirl further in. I'm putty in his hands, completely at his mercy and completely oblivious to this very public display.

He pulls back to suck on my upper lip as his tongue slides into my mouth. My pulse goes haywire, electrifying my blood when he tugs me closer, eliminating even the iota of space between us.

A groan escapes from Garrett's throat, undulating through my ribs, all the way down to my very wet center. My thighs clench involuntarily, trying to give myself some sort of relief from the building need between them.

If the kiss we shared earlier this evening—the exploratory, sweet exchange—was a sample of the way Garrett kisses, then I definitely sampled the wrong dessert because this . . . this is hot lava cake with the finest molten chocolate oozing out the center, while that was just a bite of something sweet.

This is the kind of kiss that makes your knees wobble and your nipples harden inside your dress.

The kind of kiss that makes butterflies soar inside your belly and stars dance at the corners of your vision.

The kind of kiss that makes you feel indecent for watching but glued to the sight, nonetheless.

My brain whirls as my hands tighten behind him, and I pull up on my toes to give in to his silent commands.

"Garrett," I whisper.

And, as if he's pleased with my ability to take orders, his kiss turns rougher. It wasn't soft to begin with, but as his teeth graze over my lips, pulling my bottom one between them, my body practically vibrates like a stringed instrument in his hands.

God, I wish we weren't on this dance floor right now because I'd climb him like the sequoia tree of a man he is and grind him with everything I have.

I'm practically dripping through my thong as it is because my husband is one hell of a kisser, and I'd give up my ticket into heaven just to keep his lips on me.

"Your fucking dimples, that damn smile," he growls into my neck before softly biting the skin of my bare shoulder. "And that fucking red lipstick . . . You drive me insane, Bella."

Does he mean that or is this still part of us pretending?

Does he realize no one can hear him over this music?

Did he feel the intensity and emotion in that kiss as much as I did or was it simply just good chemistry?

As much as I try to shove the buzz-kill questions aside and enjoy this moment, they keep sneaking in like roaches to filth.

God, my overactive brain! I wish I could turn it off, but no matter what I do, I can't help but wonder if my husband really got carried away like I did or if this is still all for show.

It has to be all for show, right? Because as much as I want to let my imagination soar with possibilities of more—something real—with the man in my arms, I can't deny the premise for why we're both here. A temporary arrangement. A means to an end. A few papers binding us legally.

I surmise, however—based on the very hefty erection digging into my belly—that perhaps it could be both. That, from a purely physiological sense, he might indeed be affected by this—his body reacting to a hot kiss—but it could also be for show.

"Good insane or bad insane?"

"*Terrible* insane." He releases a shuddering breath into my hair and I smile, dropping my forehead to his shoulder.

I chuckle softly, swaying in his arms. "Then you might want to get that head of yours checked."

He shakes his head, laying another kiss under my ear. "No. I'm quite fond of my condition."

We've garnered quite a few raised eyebrows in the crowd because of our overt display, and I assure myself that it's a good thing—it's exactly why I'm here. Now, anyone who knows about Garrett's newlywed status will also see how happy he is.

A win-win.

As the song ends—and the pinching in my toes gets to be unbearable—I feel Garrett's eyes on me. And even though my lips feel swollen from his kisses, I lean up to place another soft kiss on his mouth. "I saw a few people eyeing you earlier. I think they were looking to get a little bit of your time."

"I'm not looking to give my time to anyone else."

God, the man is so confusing. The way he's looking at me, the way we kissed, the circles he's making on my waist with his thumb. Circles no one else can see. Circles that don't belong in this ruse. Circles that have my mind spinning. Is he still acting or is any of this . . .?

No. Of course, it's not real.

My heart is just an idiot.

I put my hands on his chest. "How about this? I'm going to head to the restroom, and I'll see you back at our table in a few minutes. Until then, why don't you mingle? You worked hard to be a part of this night, so you should be able to talk about it with the others."

His brows turn down. "What if that asshole follows you?"

"He won't," I answer, knowing he's asking about Chaz. Instinctively, I turn to look for him, as if I'll find him right over my shoulder. I turn back to Garrett. "I looked around for him earlier and didn't see him anywhere. I bet he left. Anyway, it's not like he can come into the ladies' room with me."

Garrett seems to mull on that for a minute before finally giving me a nod. "I'll see you back at our table in a few."

Separating from him, I head to the ladies' room to do my business. After exiting the bathroom, I take a quick glance around inside the ballroom, finding Garrett laughing heartily with some other attendees. Someone else approaches him, patting his shoulder, and the two shake hands and fall into another conversation.

I'm not sure how long we'll be here, and I don't want to rush Garrett. Figuring it's a good time as any, I decide to get some fresh air outside. Maybe it'll help cool down my still-heated skin. Nothing can be done for my still-throbbing center, though I did clean myself up the best I could.

I stop off at a bench on my way out to take my painful feet out of my heels. My toes are numb, my pinky chafing from its continuous slide against the inside of my shoe. Carrying my heels—no longer concerned with how gross the floor might be—I walk toward the coat check.

Since I only plan to get a quick breath of air, it'll be too complicated to stand in line and ask for my coat, only to return it a few minutes later. Instead, I push the large doors to the building and make my way outside. A full body tremble goes through me as my feet hit the cold concrete, while the chilly breeze against my bare thigh—courtesy of the long slit in my dress—and shoulders have my teeth chattering. But, God, how I needed this fresh air.

I find a secluded corner and lean my back against the wall, wishing I'd snagged the half-eaten box of *Nerds* from my purse before I came out here. I place my heels beside me and frown up at the dark sky, following the flickering lights of an airplane thousands of feet in the air.

Thoughts of the entire night play like a slideshow in my head.

I kissed Garrett. Outside the boundaries of our arrangement, in the privacy of his home, where no one else was watching—I kissed him.

Sure, it was in response to the sweet words he said to me, the ring he placed on my finger, and the vulnerability etched all over his features, but I did it, nonetheless.

Another unplanned and uncontrolled reaction to the unexpected man who is now my husband.

I look down at the large stone on my finger, moving it around with my thumb again. It wiggles left and right, picking up the transient light coming from various areas around the building. He could have given me any cheap ring that looked real enough for tonight. He could have bought a simple band or not given me a ring at all. But he chose to give me his grandmother's. *Why?*

Could it be that Garrett has developed feelings for me like I have for him—unexpectedly . . . unconsciously?

I laugh out loud at the thought, the chirp of my voice drifting into the silent night. "Yeah, right. Don't be an idiot, Bella."

"Bella?"

My smile drops as my spine stiffens at the familiar voice, and I find myself wishing I hadn't chosen this barely-lit corner. Feet shuffle over the concrete toward me and my breathing accelerates when the man I've been avoiding all night finds a spot in front of me.

"I'm pretty sure there are rules about us speaking without our attorneys present, so if I were you, I'd walk right back to the shit hole you came out of." I snap my head to the side, staring off into the distance instead of at his greased-up beard and flashy suit.

Chaz snickers, making my jaw tighten. "I heard your voice and couldn't miss the opportunity to come see the mother of my child, now could I?"

My head snaps back toward him at the way he said 'my child,' knowing he's goading me. "A child whose name you don't even know, you disingenuous piece of shit."

Chaz casually puts his hands in his pockets, as if he's listening to a meaningless mouse squeak rather than someone he'll be battling in court. "It doesn't matter whether I know her name. We'll be spending plenty of time in the future for me to get to know her better."

His gaze trails down the length of me lecherously, as if he's trying to recall what I look like underneath my dress, and an overwhelming urge to kick him in the balls courses through me. At least I'll have enough flexibility to do so, given one of my legs is damn-near unrestrained.

"I did want to chat with you about parenting styles and . . ." His eyes linger on my bare shoulders, then sweep down to my thigh. I quickly pull my dress to cover it, chiding myself internally for not getting my coat from the coat check. "Values."

I squint, keeping myself from snarling. "Excuse me?"

His lips turn up mockingly. "I won't allow my daughter to become a slut like her mother. Sleeping with random men at conferences and looking like trash with her tits spilling out of an obscene dress at a distinguished event. You're a cheap whore and a–"

But before he can finish his sentence, Chaz is slammed and pinned to the wall next to me, pulling at the hand firmly around his neck. "Try and finish that sentence, motherfucker," Garrett growls dangerously, his voice so sharp, it could cut metal.

"Garrett!" I grasp his arm as a trembling Chaz tries to pull him off. "Let him go."

"This piece of shit has no idea who he's fucking with." Garrett sneers, his furious eyes boring into Chaz.

"G, please," I beg. "Please, just look at me."

Garrett's gaze finally detaches from Chaz and turns to me, but his hand doesn't relent. I've never seen this side of my husband. And even though that gaze is soft when it lands on me, the lines etched on his face are anything but.

I speak softly in Garrett's ear, though my voice shakes from the adrenaline coursing through my veins. "I don't know how he could use this in court. He clearly just wanted to goad me." I'm surprised to see Chaz is still struggling to get out of Garrett's hold. "Please, G, think about Meera."

That seems to get his complete attention. Garrett's fingers unfurl off Chaz's throat, and Chaz coughs, sucking in air. I wouldn't be surprised if he wet his pants with the way he scurries away the second he's released, like the douchebag wimp that he is.

Both Garrett and I watch for a second before his hands grasp my head and the rage in his eyes subsides. He walks me backward to the cold concrete wall, but the warmth of his hands is all I can focus on. "Are you okay? Did he do anything to you?"

I shake my head, still breathing hard. "No. Just talked a lot of shit."

Garrett's nostrils flare. "What were you doing out here, anyway? You said you were just going to the restroom. I was looking for you."

I shift my gaze off his face. "Just getting some air."

"Why?"

Bringing my eyes back to him, I encircle my hands over his wrists. Neither a hair is out of place on his head nor is his breathing labored, which is a feat given the events over the past few minutes. He's still as devastatingly handsome as ever.

"I just . . . needed a breather. You know, after that performance between us earlier." I swallow, watching Garrett's brows turn down right along with his mouth. "It just got to me."

His jaw locks as he seems to consider my words before a look of simple defeat washes over his features. But before I can ask him if I've said something wrong, he turns to walk back inside. "Let's go home."

THE RIDE back home happens in almost utter silence. Even when I asked if I could turn up the heating, Garrett just mumbled an incoherent response, then flicked on the seat warmer without taking his eyes off the road.

I don't know if it was the altercation with Chaz or something I said, but this curt and standoffish Garrett isn't the one I know.

I clear my throat, wiggling in my seat. "G, is everything okay?"

Garrett's gaze stays locked on the road as if he hasn't heard a single word I've said, but I don't miss the slight slump in his shoulders.

"I'm sorry about the Chaz thing," I stammer, trying to fill the silence. "I didn't know he was out there, and I'm sorry I didn't tell you I was going outside."

Nothing. He says nothing in response, making my stomach knot. I slide my hands under my thighs to give myself something to do while I breathe in the suffocating air of . . . confusion and guilt.

A minute or two later, Garrett pulls into his driveway and puts the car into park before he slinks back in his seat, resting his head on the headrest behind him. His eyes stay fixed on the garage door in front of us, but he doesn't utter a single word.

Where is the guy who warms up every space he walks into? The man whose smiles are as bright as the moon shining in the sky tonight.

Because this man . . .? This man is not him.

My throat closes up as my gaze trails down his forlorn profile. Without realizing it until after I've done it, I reach over and grab the hand resting on his thigh, as if touching him will pull him back to me somehow.

But his fingers don't curl around mine the way they did all night, and my heart twists painfully inside my ribs. "Please," I whisper, a pit growing in my stomach. "Talk to me, G."

It's when the air between us couldn't feel any heavier that Garrett finally turns to me, but his eyes lack their usual luster and shine. Instead, what I see in them breaks me right down the middle.

His throat bobs before he speaks. "I remember the first day I met you." His voice sounds thick and gravelly. "You were standing with Rani and Melody outside of Darian's school, waiting for the kayaking tournament to begin. You were wearing this lavender-colored tank top with white shorts and a white, open button-down shirt over it."

My breath falters and I squeeze his hand, not entirely sure who I'm comforting.

"I remember the way the purple tips of your hair waved in the wind. You pulled them to the side and placed an elastic around them, but there were still some wisps that flew loose on the other side." He takes a breath and I hold mine. "I remember this because, even though you looked so incredibly sad that day, I thought you were the most beautiful woman I'd ever seen.

"And ever since then—at every event and every gathering—the only person I've looked for is *you*. The only person I've thought about, pined for, and lost my mind over is *you*. Forget looking at someone else, Bella; I haven't even *touched* another woman in four years—"

He pauses when he hears my soft inhale or maybe it's my heart thudding rampantly inside my chest. "So, you wonder if everything is okay?" He squints at me incredulously. "No, Bella, *nothing* is okay, because nothing I've done until now, not one fucking ounce of it, has convinced you that *this* . . ." he points between us, "has never been a performance for me."

He unbuckles his seatbelt and pulls on the door handle just as my world starts to spin. Every thought inside my head collides with another, vying for attention, yet I can't hold on to a single one.

I grab his hand right before he exits, staring at him with wide eyes as flashes of the day we met—the same day I told my friends I was pregnant—flit through my memories. I remember it clearly—the confusion and sheer weight of those days when everything seemed to be out of my control. When I felt like I was in a pinball machine, bouncing off its barriers and walls without a single say in the direction I wanted to go.

But that's not the only thing I remember from that day.

I remember looking into the eyes of a man with a pull so strong, I felt like I was taking on an ocean wave. A man with sun-kissed hair and a smile to match, who made me want to run away while I desperately wanted to run to him.

And though I smiled back at him, it wilted under the weight of my reality. I remember wondering who I was kidding. A man like him wouldn't want *me*—not when he found out how my life was about to change.

And it's not like I could hold that against him, could I? It didn't take a genius to see that the man had his pick of the lot. Why on earth would he choose a single mother, whose life would soon revolve around dirty diapers and baby food, over someone who could dedicate every smile only to him? That didn't seem fair, and I felt that on his behalf.

Was I wrong to?

Garrett holds my gaze, surely waiting for me to say something—*anything*—but neither my mind nor my voice seems to be functioning at the moment. I take in a shaky breath, trying to find the words, but the somber resignation settling on his face—as if he's making peace with my silence—has any words halting on my tongue.

But even with the pain etched over every curve on his face, there's a tenderness that never leaves his eyes. A tenderness that I've become accustomed to over our time together. A tenderness that he seems to reserve just for me.

He pulls his hand from mine, placing a foot on his driveway as he makes his way out of the car but stalls, looking over his shoulder to say a few more words that shatter me even as they heal me before he heads into the house.

"I can't convince you anymore, Bella. I can't lay my heart and soul out there any more than I already have. You have them both. Do with them as you wish."

Chapter Eighteen

GARRETT

GRAMS' HONEY-COLORED EYES GLEAM BACK AT ME THROUGH my phone screen, though the bags under them seem to be getting worse each time we speak. My gut twists, knowing that she's not the same grandma I had even last week when we FaceTimed. She's deteriorating day by day.

Her short blonde hair—the same color as mine, though hers has been dyed to match her natural locks—is perfectly styled. With her favorite pearls—the ones Grandpa got for her on one of their anniversaries—sitting over the round floral neck of her blouse, you'd think she was headed to church. Except, I know she's not; my grandpa was the more religious one.

"Is it me or do you seem to get more beautiful each time I see you?" I ask her, knowing it'll have the wrinkles around her eyes crinkling.

She purses her lips like she always does when she's holding back her smiles. "Oh, you hush." Her voice is raspy and deep from her recent bout with another bad cold. Each time she gets sick, I worry she'll end up at the hospital again. "You and your brother are such flirts. Now," she coughs into her pristine white handkerchief with the white lace—I've seen her carry a version of it my whole life, "when am I going to see your bride? You know I don't have much time, Garrett."

I smile through the intense ache inside my heart. "Do the dramatics increase with age, Grams? What is all this nonsense about not having enough time? You've been repeating it every time we're on the phone."

"Garrett Colton Meyer," my grandma's wheeze decreases the sternness she's trying for in her tone, "I may be your best friend, but I will not sit here and have my acting skills criticized!"

I laugh, throwing my head back against the headrest. Grams—and as she rightly mentioned, my best friend aside from my brothers—has always had a way of getting a surprised laugh out of me. No matter what she's going through in life, she's always given others a reason to laugh and smile, to take life a little less seriously.

Since we were children, Dean and I have referred to Grams as our best friend. We loved our grandfather as well, but Grams was the one who knew us best. She's the one who acted more like one of us than an adult.

I have hundreds of memories of her playing baseball with us in the backyard, teaching us how to fly kites, and hauling us to her lake house a couple of hours away for a weekend filled with fishing and canoeing. We'd stay up watching scary movies and playing foosball. She was even the one who got us our first pack of beer and a box of condoms when we turned seventeen. Nothing was off-limits in terms of conversation, especially her most favorite topic—our love lives.

Which is why it's not surprising that she's asking to meet Bella, because even if she knows this marriage was orchestrated on a whim like the rest of my family, she's known my truth for the past four years.

A truth I finally got off my chest last weekend to the woman at the center of this story.

"I could never dream of insulting your acting skills, Grams. As far as Bella is concerned . . ." I take my free hand off the steering wheel and glide it through my hair before sliding my eyes to my left and looking out my window.

After getting in late last night, I left for Tahoe early with the hopes of avoiding my wife this morning. I'd flown out the morning after the gala, so while we both were able to avoid the morning-after conversation, five days later, I'm still not sure where we stand.

So, after visiting with my dad and my stepmother, and swinging by to see my niece and nephew at Darian's house, I decided to come to the pool hall early before giving my grandmother a call from the car.

My mind replays the entire night from last weekend, and everything inside me tells me to turn around and head back to her—to force her to read me my fucking fate. But I told her the ball was in her court, and I intend to wait for her to lob it back to me or forfeit the game.

It doesn't mean I haven't thought about her incessantly for the past few excruciatingly slow days.

To say she surprised me with that first kiss last weekend would be an understatement. I knew things were getting more blurry between us, but that my words would affect her that much . . .? I hadn't expected that, and if I'm being honest, I didn't really know how to interpret it, either. I recall driving to the gala in a surprise- and confusion-mixed haze.

She'd thrown back my words about being friends enough times that I was convinced that's all she'd ever want from me. But then her soft lips landed on mine, tentative and unsure, and I just knew.

She was lying to herself as much as she was to me.

Throughout the night, I found myself barely able to stay

inside my skin. It was all I could do to not peel that bewitching golden dress off her body with my teeth. Everything about her, from head to toe, made me feel feral–like a wild animal guarding what was his–and I knew I couldn't keep the ruse up any longer. I was at the summit, the fucking height of my patience and restraint, and I wasn't going to last much longer.

And when I ravaged that beautiful mouth of hers, I could have sworn she felt it, too–that same ferocity, that same wild craving. At least that's what her hooded eyes told me. It's what her subdued whimper and her short pants against my lips told me. It's even what her arched back and pebbled nipples against my chest told me.

That she felt it, too. That I wasn't completely alone in this.

That is . . . until she told me it was all a *performance*.

Like the abrupt and cacophonous interruption to a beautiful melody, a fucking ice-cold bucket of water dumped on you when your body was just warming up, my thoughts came to a sputtering stop at her words.

I couldn't do it anymore. I couldn't keep it in and live a lie, not when I knew–tentatively after our first kiss that night, and irrevocably after the second one–that she was living a lie, too. So, I did what any exasperated person in my situation would do; I obliterated her dreams of going to Broadway.

And since I haven't heard from her besides the short text exchange between us yesterday–that she surprisingly initiated–I can only assume she's overthinking everything.

> Bells: I found an interesting list of yours in the kitchen drawer.

My lips had twitched reading the message after I landed at JFK.

> Me: Oh?

Bells: A list appropriately titled, 'Garrett's
Bucket List.'

Me: I didn't realize you were so interested in
my drawers.

*She'd conveniently ignored my double meaning, sending me
another text a few moments later.*

Bells: 'Bake a cake from scratch.' 'Get a
tarot reading.' Surely, these can't be the
most challenging things on your list.

*I'd looked out the cockpit windshield and mulled over the response
before I hit send.*

Me: I crossed off the most challenging thing
from that bucket list last weekend.

I waited a few minutes—and then all night—for a response
to that text, knowing she read it before I realized I wasn't
going to get one.

Grams' coughing brings me back to the present, and I
realize I've been looking out the window, lost in my thoughts
for longer than intended. I internally cringe at the violence of
it. Her face flushes and the phone in her hand shakes before
she puts it down, and all I see is the ceiling.

"Grams?"

She comes back on a few moments later when her
coughing fit ceases. "Tell me what happened, Garrett? Did
she wear the ring you gave her?"

"Grams, have you been to the doctor recently? I don't feel
like you're over that cold. Where's Mom?" I try to search
behind her for my mom, as if she'll just appear out of
nowhere since I'm looking for her, but Grams' entire head is
covering the screen.

Grams takes a sip of something from her cup, making the camera shake again before she comes back. "Oh, stop your fussing. It's just the last of that nasty cold. Your mom and Douglas went out for groceries and to refill my prescriptions. They do enough for me as it is, those sweet souls." She clears her throat, seeming to give me another stern look. "Now, stop evading the subject, and tell me what happened."

Knowing my grandma would be relentless now that she knows something is up with me and Bella, I take another glance at the clock. I have about ten minutes before I need to go meet everyone. It's enough time for me to give her a shortened version of the night, though I leave out the part where I pinned Chaz against the wall because there's no point in making her worry.

"I think you did the right thing by telling her, dear boy," Grams concludes when I've finished.

I slide my tongue over my bottom lip, pulling it in between my teeth as I mull over the same thought for the millionth time this week. "Did I, though? Maybe all I did was make her run even farther away from me. Maybe I just need to get it through my head that she doesn't want me. That this has always been for the sake of this pretense for her."

"I don't think you believe that to be true."

I swallow, looking out the window again and seeing my two brothers, Darian and Dean, laughing as they enter the pool hall together. "It doesn't matter what I believe, Grams. In fact, I don't even know what to believe anymore."

"From everything you've told me about this beautiful but scared woman, it seems she's been hurt quite badly. Some people are able to process abandonment and not lose their foundation of trust. They can go on to trust others, build relationships as usual, and put their heart on the line again. But some aren't. We're all different in that way, aren't we? The abandonment she felt when she was at a critical juncture in her life—not once, but twice—is so strong that she can't recognize love, even when it stares her in the face."

She pauses, taking a sip from her cup. To my relief, her color seems to have come back slightly.

"So, what should I do?"

Grams fixes her gaze on me. "Stick around. Don't abandon her like the others have. Especially not after finally giving her the truth to deal with."

TAPPING the cue ball with my pool stick at a thirty-degree angle, I watch as the solid purple four ball rolls gently into the pocket, before setting my eyes on the eight ball.

"Show off," Dean bellows from his perch on the barstool before taking a sip of his beer.

"It doesn't count as showing off when it's so fucking easy to kick your ass, I could do it with my eyes closed," I jeer back. Talking shit to my brothers is one of the finer joys in life.

"Oh, fuck you. You got lucky with the break I made right at the beginning. If I hadn't scratched on that last play, you'd have nothing to gloat about. You're probably used to it, though—not being able to gloat when I'm around—seeing as I'm the better-looking twin."

Calling the pocket near me, I lob the eight ball off the back of the table and track it all the way in, winning the game for me and Darian, then give Dean a smug smirk.

Darian clasps my shoulder. "Let's get a round of beers and sit for a bit. I'm fucking beat."

Hudson waves down our waitress and orders us another round of beers before we all take a seat around the table. He drove into Tahoe earlier this morning for some business as well, so it worked out for us to all meet today. "Fuck, if you're asking for a beer, you must have had a rough night. I haven't seen you drink anything but water, ever."

"Or milk," Dean chimes in with a shit-eating smirk. It's been an ongoing joke between the three of us since we were younger. Karine, Darian's mom and our stepmom, would always mix chocolate into his glass of milk to make him drink it because he hated the taste of plain milk. "Preferably in a sippy cup, with chocolate mixed in."

Darian flips Dean off, making us all chuckle. He runs a hand over his face. "Fuck. I don't remember Arman being this fussy. I'd put him down to bed, and he'd just fucking sleep. But Avya . . .? The girl still wakes up at least three times a night."

The waitress drops off our beers, and Dean takes a pull from his bottle. "Is this more about Avya not sleeping, or you not getting laid because you guys are so tired?"

Darian takes a sip of his beer. "Both."

"She'll grow out of it," Hudson chimes in, and I can only assume he's talking about his daughter, Madison, who is now almost twenty-five. "Soon enough she'll be out of the house, dating jackasses you'll want to strangle."

Darian groans. "Fuck. I'm going to lock her up and throw away the fucking key."

I pat him on the back. "Good luck with that, brother."

Dean gives me a questioning nod. "So, shortcake, how's the marriage of convenience going? Have you finally consummated it? I'd assume they call it a marriage of convenience because it's *convenient* to have sex whenever you want."

While the other guys squint at Dean with a *what-the-fuck* expression, I roll my eyes, first for the nickname and then for the rest of his comment.

I'm literally an inch shorter than my six-foot-three twin, but he rubs it in every chance he gets. Aside from our blue eyes and blond hair, we don't share many other features. He's had his hair shoulder-length, which he sometimes keeps in a half bun on top of his head, while I've always had shorter hair. Where my jaw is more square and my cheekbones are higher, his narrower face makes him look a few years younger than our thirty-nine years. And aside from all of our feature differences, our personalities are completely different, with him never taking life too seriously, sometimes even to his detriment.

"That is *not* why they call it a marriage of convenience. The presumption is that a normal marriage entails convenient sex as well." I keep my tone flat.

His eyes get slightly hazy. "You lost me at *presumption*."

I shake my head, holding back my smile. The guy is as smart as a whip, but he has a way of being self-deprecating and acting dumb for the sake of keeping the mood light. He's always used humor to deflect attention off him. I take a sip from my beer, keeping my eyes connected to my brother. He can read me better than anyone else. "It's fine."

His brows lift slightly, hearing my unspoken words clearly. "Something went down between you guys, didn't it?"

Hudson's confused gaze meets my face before looking at Dean and then Darian. I don't blame him for feeling like he's missed a conversation—my brothers and I have always just had a way of understanding each other without actually speaking. "Wait, I thought he just said everything was fine. What do you mean something went down between them?"

Dean shrugs before everyone's gaze lands back on me. I slide my tongue over my teeth. "I told her."

They're all quiet for a long minute, processing my words. They've all known. Fuck, everyone has known almost since I have. Though, interestingly, I've never explicitly told them. We've never even had a conversation about it, which is not surprising, given none of us are overly emotional.

Dean gives me a knowing look and I hold his gaze for a second, silently confirming everything.

"Fuck." Hudson puts his beer bottle down on the table before we all watch a new group of guys set up the billiard table using the triangle rack to center the balls in their starting position. Hudson looks back at me. "Everything?"

I nod, not taking my eyes off the guy about to make the first break.

"How'd she take it?" Hudson's brow lifts.

"I don't know. I didn't stay long enough to find out."

A loud *crack* sounds as the cue ball makes contact with the others, inciting a number of softer cracking sounds as all the balls hit each other and scatter on the table.

Darian twists his bottle on the table, staring at it intently, and I realize he hasn't said a word during this entire conversation. He lifts his head, meeting my eyes as if he could feel my stare.

"You already fucking knew," I accuse.

Darian winces. "I might have overheard a bit of the conversation between Rani, Melody, and Bella while they were all on FaceTime a couple of days ago."

"Well?"

Darian shrugs. "I just heard part of Bella's side of the story, but not what Rani or Melody had to say because I was actually on my way out. So, I don't know much more."

I squint at him. "And Rani didn't tell you?"

He shakes his head. "I can't infiltrate that bond; it's fucking Fort Knox."

I can't argue with that. He's done the same for me, as well. He's known I have feelings for Bella for some time but has done me the favor of not telling his wife.

Dean finally speaks. "You need to talk to her."

I scoff. "As far as I'm concerned, I've said everything I needed to, everything I could have."

"Well, then you need to be there to hear her response. Has she even tried to reach out to you since?"

I think of the short text exchange between us, the one where my last message is still sitting on *Read*. "Yeah, but—"

"So don't be an idiot. That was probably her way of breaking the ice. Women are complicated like that."

I chuckle. "You'd know. Care to tell us about your current relationship status?"

I know I'm deflecting, but I need the conversation taken off me for a moment so I can process what both he and Grams seem to be saying—that I need to go see her, that I need to talk to her. It's all I've been wanting to do all fucking week, anyway.

My brother runs a hand over his neck. "No. This isn't about me."

"Oh, shit. Is this about Mala?" Hudson asks him. "What's happening on that front?"

My brother gets off the barstool abruptly. He winks at the bartender headed our way, presumably to ask if we want another round of drinks, and it doesn't take a genius to see the crack in his facade. He hides it well under that ever-present and mischievous grin. He's been fucking lost ever since his best friend—and the woman who everyone at this table knows would be the only one who truly made him happy—moved away a year ago. He was dating his on-again, off-again girlfriend, Jessie, until then, but from what I know, he hasn't been back with her since.

I'm about to ask him where things stand between him and Mala, and if there's more to that story, when my phone buzzes inside my pocket.

> Bells: Want to know the first item on my
> bucket list?

I swallow against my dry throat, despite having had an entire beer.

Me: Yes.

Bells: 'Tell the pilot I haven't stopped thinking about over the past four years how I really feel about him. In person.'

Chapter Nineteen

BELLA

AFTER PARKING THE CAR IN THE DRIVEWAY, I WALK OVER to the side of the house to check on Winky and Brown Sugar. Just like over the past few days, I only see Brown Sugar, huddled in the back corner of the box. She lifts her head to acknowledge me but snuggles back into her blanket with a mewl.

I know Winky's been back based on the fresh meat I've seen in the box—I'm positive one was a mouse carcass—but I haven't seen her in a while. Still, I find it a good sign that she seems to trust this place—and me, perhaps—enough to leave her baby here on her own.

I don't know why that makes me feel so relieved, but it does.

It's been a couple of weeks of getting to know the two of them, and while Meera had seen the mom and baby walking around, I only recently showed her the box I put out for them with the towels. I suppose I wanted to let my new furry friends settle in without too much additional excitement. For the past few days, Meera and I have even put out some food for them and changed their bedding. I'm still hesitant to pet them, and from what I can tell, that seems to work just fine for Winky and her daughter.

While I feel like the trust is finally building between us, Winky still regards me with hesitation. But I don't take offense to her apprehension. It takes her time to trust someone, and if anyone can understand that, it's me.

I know I should tell Garrett, or call animal control, or do something but keep the two strays from hanging around the house. Given the interesting array of meat Winky seems to drag back with her, it's only a matter of time before we have other animals coming around to inspect. But I can't seem to find the heart to do anything about it yet.

Maybe because I feel her, *know her*, at a deeper level than anyone else. Maybe we're just two broken pieces of the same soul. Life hasn't turned out the way she expected, but she's making it work and fighting for herself and her baby girl every day.

A part of me wants to tell her that it's all going to be alright, that things will work out . . . but I'm not even sure I believe that myself.

I pad back in through the garage door at Garrett's house before pulling my phone from my back pocket. I still don't have a reply to my last message.

Maybe I'm too late.

Five nights. Five nights of seeing his sullen expression, his deepened frown, and his averted gaze behind my eyelids each time I tried to sleep. Five nights of feeling like I was carrying an Everest-sized boulder inside my stomach, the jagged fragments of which scraped against my throat. Five nights of typing out a novel-length message, only to delete it a few minutes later.

Three days after the gala—feeling like I was just performing tasks on autopilot, jumping at my phone the moment it buzzed, and oscillating between a state of belief and disbelief—I put Meera to bed and sent out an S.O.S.

Melody blinked at me through my laptop screen—rapidly, and with an all too smug expression. Her onyx-colored eyes seemed to sparkle off the light in her room. "Four years. The poor man has waited four fuc—er, freaking years." She looked to her side before turning back to me and Rani on the screen. "Sorry, now that Nelson is trying to speak, I'm trying to be good about not using profanity. I don't want him picking up Mom's foul mouth . . . not yet, at least." She grinned devilishly.

I gave her a half-hearted smile, my gaze drifting to the water-color picture of an airplane Meera painted recently. It had a wing close to the cockpit and one on the other side toward the back of the plane. I also noted the happy-faced pilot in the cockpit window, and the two passengers—both with black hair, but one with purple tips—smiling from their windows in the middle of the plane. "It's not like he's the only one, you know."

Moments later, when I noticed the silence around me, I looked back up at my screen, wondering if maybe my FaceTime call had dropped. Instead, I saw my friends staring at me, giving me a sense of déjà vu from the time I told them I'd spontaneously married our mutual pilot-friend in Vegas.

"What?" My gaze flipped between both of them on the screen.

"I knew it!" Rani's eyes widened as her words rippled the silence between us.

"Someone please mark this moment down as an important date in history," Melody chimed in. "The day Bella finally admitted what we've all known for years."

"I knew you liked him!" Rani started again. "All that crap about him not being your type—"

"Girl, please. You weren't fooling anyone . . . except maybe your-self. You know why?" Melody wrapped her arms around her chest, tilting her head. I knew she wasn't waiting for an answer, and it was

her typical tell-it-like-it-is pose—one I didn't care for but knew I had to endure, just the same. "Because you've been a fool."

"I—" I tried to cut in, feeling ambushed. Wasn't this supposed to be my S.O.S? What was I thinking calling up the two people who would never let me just wallow in my self-pity?

"Don't even try to deny it anymore. You just admitted you've been waiting four years for him, just as he has been for you. Now, spill. What have you been waiting for? Why allow your vag to dry up in the California drought?"

"I just—" I took in a heavy breath, running my fingers over my brows. "Yes, okay? Yes, I've liked him for a long time. And yes, I've been denying it to everyone, especially to myself. It's not that I was waiting for him from the first day we met or anything, but the more I started to get to know him, the more that attraction grew. And, if I'm being honest, he's the only man I've thought about in that way for a long time." I shifted in my seat. "But you guys know how skeptical I am of men in general. I mean, if my dad couldn't stay with a woman who gave him every bit of her love and support, then how could I ever expect that for myself?"

"Because every story is different, Bells," Rani said softly. "Because you're not your mom, and Garrett's not your dad. He's not Chaz, either."

I nodded. "I never thought someone who could have anyone he wanted would ever want me, and if he did, he wouldn't want me for more than a night or two."

"I remember what you said to me one time. It's stuck with me. You said you refused to watch a sunset with someone, not knowing if they'd be around for the sunrise."

I pressed my lips together, feeling the tingle at the tip of my nose and a heave of emotion forming inside my chest. "Sometimes . . . some-times I feel so alone. Not because you both aren't there for me. You are, and so are my mom and Meera. And I love you all so much. But there are still times I wish . . . I wish I could have more. Someone of my own. Someone who sees the nutcase I am and still chooses me."

"You do," Melody pressed. "Don't you see? You do have a man who sees the nutcase you are, and chooses you despite it."

"You're beautiful inside and out, Bells," Rani added. "As much as you focus on your flaws and what you think are your shortcomings, Garret has only focused on you."

A tear rolled down my cheek just as I snorted with a laugh. "What if I ruined everything? What if I'm too late, and he's realized I had way more baggage than he could handle?"

Melody chortled. "Have you seen the man's biceps? He'll be able to handle your baggage just fine. Don't wait any longer. Don't think anymore. Let your heart lead, Bells. Call him."

"Tell him how you feel, sis," Rani joined in. "He deserves it. You deserve it."

I'VE GOT my arms wrapped around my knees on my bed, a small empty box of *Nerds* lying next to me, and I'm picking at a string of yarn on the top of my woolen sock when I hear the door open and close downstairs. My pulse instantly spikes, and I look toward my closed door as if it'll open at any moment.

Garrett's footsteps resound on the stairs and I swear, I hear them stop in front of my door before they keep moving. And just as my heart had jumped at his arrival, it thuds back into place with the *click* of his bedroom door.

I turn in place, putting my covered feet on the rug below me and grasping the edge of my bed with my fists. My knees bounce as I worry my bottom lip between my teeth.

He never responded.

Maybe he's done responding. Maybe we're done before we even truly began.

I don't know when I made it to my door, but I find my palm on the knob, staring down at my hand. The air stalls in my lungs as I pull my door open and pad across the hall to wait in front of his door. I'm not sure what I'm expecting while I mentally tell my heart to cease its thundering.

My brows pull in when, before my knuckles have even made contact with his door, it opens. A part of me wonders if my thudding heart somehow leapt out and slammed against it, but those thoughts vanish as my eyes trail up the most delectable washboard abs, stalling there to then run back down the softest happy trail I've ever seen. It disappears into the elastic of dark gray sweatpants. And though I force my eyes back up his bare torso, I don't miss the outline of a rather large and promising-looking coc–

"Bells."

My eyes dash up to meet Garrett's blues, and I'm both embarrassed and annoyed. I was sort of hoping to peruse my way up on my own time. "Hi."

Garrett blinks, only a hint of a smile playing on his lips. "Is everything okay?" He leans forward, poking his head to look down the hallway toward Meera's room, and notices that it's wide open. "Where's Meera?"

"Sleeping over with my mom," I stammer, not understanding why heat travels to my cheeks.

"Oh, okay."

I take a breath, my chest rising and falling as I search for the words I'm looking for–all the words I've wanted to say out loud for both our benefit–but end up with, "I'm sorry." My face falls and I clasp my hands in front of me. "I'm sorry I didn't see it . . . I'm sorry I didn't know before." My eyes glaze over as I meet his gaze on me.

His face gives nothing away. "Do you see . . . do you know me now?

My eyes well and I shake my head. "It was never a question of *seeing* you, pilot. You're like the sun; I couldn't miss your light, your warmth, or your pull, even with my eyes closed. I just couldn't look directly at you. Do you know what I mean?"

He stays quiet, his hand still grasping the door.

My chin quivers. "Have you ever forced yourself out of a beautiful dream, pilot? Even when everything is perfect in it, and you were sleeping soundly with a smile playing on your lips?" I don't wait for him to answer. "I have. Every time I dreamt of you."

"Why?" he whispers.

"Because I didn't want to dream if I couldn't have the reality. Because I didn't think it could be a reality. Because I knew you'd break my heart—I believed it in my soul." The gravel in my voice pierces the air between us, and Garrett takes a step forward.

His warm palm curves around my jaw and neck. "And now?"

I tilt my head back to look at him, noticing how close his face is to mine. So close that our breaths intermingle. "And now, I realize all that self-inflicted torture, all that denial, was useless because, drunk or not, I was yours the second you kissed me on that altar, Garrett."

My chest finally feels lighter after voicing my truth and laying my soul bare, just like he did days ago. "So, I guess what I'm asking you, pilot, is . . . will you forgive me for not seeing you before? Because now that I have, there's no one else I'd rather see."

Chapter Twenty

BELLA

GARRETT'S EYES BLAZE LIKE FIRE ENTRAPPED IN COAL before his mouth drops over mine, and I immediately wrap my arms around his neck. His hands lower to my waist, tightening as they pull me further into him. His tongue finds my eagerly awaiting one, tangling and rubbing against it.

We moan into each other, my hardened nipples grazing against my sleep tank and his wide chest. His lips, his tongue, his hands are pure sin and indulgence—ones I can no longer deny myself. His tongue slides against mine again as his hands drop to my ass, finding the bottom of my cheeks under my shorts.

He palms my ass before squeezing my cheeks, swallowing my soft groan. "Fuck."

His erection digs into my belly, and he hoists me up so I can wrap my legs around his naked torso. He turns us, walking toward his bed before one of his hands slides to my front. His thumb presses against my wet center, and I moan into his mouth, rubbing my swollen nub against his thumb.

"Garrett," I whimper, before delving back into his mouth.

I suck on his tongue hungrily as my body erupts with goosebumps.

"Tell me all this is mine. This pussy . . ." He circles his thumb around my nub again, and I mewl, closing my eyes tightly as my body ramps up with a kind of need I've never felt before. His mouth drops to my breast, sucking my nipple through my shirt, and I buck against him, arching my back. "These fucking nipples ready to shred through that shirt." His mouth trails back up my chest, biting my neck, then my jaw, before coming back to my mouth. "These lips. Tell me they're all mine."

"Everything is yours," I breathe, grinding against him, feeling the head of his erection in the sweetest spot under my entrance. "But if you don't fuck me right now, pilot, I'm going to come all over your sweats." I grasp his head between my hands, holding his heated gaze. "And don't you dare take it easy on me."

Garrett chuckles before dropping me onto his bed unceremoniously. Pulling up on his knees, he positions me in between his legs. The silver chain around his neck gleams as his fingers grasp the bottom of my tank, bunching it before sliding it up. "As you wish, wifey. Now, lift your arms up for me."

I do as he asks, thinking he's going to pull my shirt off, but Garrett only slides it up my torso. My body feels like it's on fire, even as the cool air wafts over my skin, and my hair fans out in a halo around my head. His eyes track his movement as he slowly pulls my shirt over my breasts, licking his lips like a beast over his kill before he takes in my puckered nipples.

He slides the shirt farther up, flipping it so I'm getting ready to take it off, when he suddenly stops, leaving the thin material over my face. My lashes flutter against it as I breathe through my mouth.

I wiggle in place with my arms still above my head. "Garr—"

"Shh," he chides, letting me know that pulling the shirt off me isn't an option. His fingers tweak my nipples hard, and I buck and moan, not finding enough purchase above me. "I've waited four long years, beautiful. There's no way I'm going to be done with you in four minutes. Now, lay back and relax for me."

My heart beats furiously against my ribs, my skin peppered in goosebumps, as I try to make out the outline of him through my shirt.

His fingers play with my nipples some more, oscillating between gentle and hard as a pool of my want collects inside my thin panties.

"Oh, God. Please, Garrett." A full-body tremble ghosts through me, and I take in gulps of air, trying to decrease my heart rate. It's no use, though.

His mouth drops to my nipple and his warm tongue laps over my almost painful skin. Without being able to see much, the rest of my senses feel heightened, right along with my libido. He works my other nipple between his fingers while he pulls one into his mouth between his teeth—biting and sucking, over and over, until I'm panting and squirming.

"Please, pilot. I'm going to—"

"Don't you fucking dare." His low command has me momentarily freezing in place before I'm heaving again. *Good God, how I love when he uses that voice.* "You come when I let you."

Garrett's mouth makes its way to my other nipple, spending time in the valley between my breasts, before he pushes them together and laps at my warm skin. His mouth travels from one nipple to the other repeatedly, until I'm practically coming undone, squirming and writhing with need.

My only solace is that he's now lowered enough over me that I've wrapped my legs around his back, locking my socked feet together, rocking and grinding against his hard dick. Though he's still keeping it at enough of a distance that I can't completely get off.

Ugh!

I'm almost in tears when he bites my nipple, sending another zing down to my center. It's as if he's punishing me by giving himself to me, only to keep himself just far enough away.

I suppose this was partly my doing.

I did ask him not to take it easy on me.

My arms trail down, pulling the fabric over my face slightly so I can see him, but Garrett quickly lifts it back up. "Arms up, Bella. Don't make me ask again."

I chuckle, breathing in through my nose and sensing the slight scent of detergent mixed with something else through my shirt–something a little more pungent and heady. *Me*. My juices, waiting to be lapped up by the frustrating man above me.

And because I love poking this bear of mine so much, I can't help but challenge him, "And what if I do?"

Before I can figure out what's happening, Garrett turns me around roughly so my face is in the mattress and pulls my waist so my ass is in the air. I have just enough time to turn my head to the side–still inside my tank top–and gain my bearings before he pulled down my shorts and panties in one go and slapped my ass. *Hard*.

I yelp as the sting registers on my skin, clenching my center instinctually.

Seconds later, he does it again on the other side. "That's what happens if you do."

"Oh, God," I moan, bearing my chest down against the bed and trying to catch my breath. I clutch the cover in my fists, feeling my wetness trickle down my thigh. If the sharp smacking sound is anything to go by, I can only imagine what his handprint must look like on my bare ass.

"Want to test me again, sweetheart?"

Yes.

But instead of answering him, I lower my arm and Garrett chuckles. I can only imagine him shaking his head.

He slaps the same ass cheek again and I groan, fisting the blanket where my hand now lays and waving my ass in the air.

More.

Who is this woman inside me? When did the wild child decide to come out and play when I do such a good job keeping her behind lock and key?

I have no idea where Garrett is or how absolutely lewd I must look in this position, but I'm beyond caring. I've waited long enough–played it cool, kept things safe. What did it get me besides an emptiness that follows me around like my shadow? *Nothing.*

"Fuck, who knew?" he mumbles to himself as he takes a palmful of my ass. "Who knew how beautiful the tinge of pink would look on this ass? You like being spanked, baby?" His warm hand caresses my stinging cheek before I feel his lips and tongue on them. "Well, I'm just the man to do it."

And just like he did with my nipples, his tongue laps at my ass cheeks, soothing the burn. I mewl as his long, adept fingers travel between my legs to rub over my wet center.

I'm all too wrapped up in the feel of his tongue on my cheeks and his finger playing with my clit when his mouth slides down my ass. I'm not even sure what he's doing since I have little visibility, but soon enough, I feel his lips underneath me. His tongue finds my folds as his palms wrap around my ass cheeks. My legs straddle his head and I lower my center to him when he pulls me against his lips.

"Oh, God! Garrett," I whimper, feeling his warm tongue gliding over my folds.

He plunges into me ferociously, sucking my right fold and then my left, pulling each into his mouth and against his tongue before lapping my center. "You're fucking delicious. I swear, I want to die with my nose and my mouth inside this pussy."

I clench unintentionally as another loud moan elicits from my throat, my climax building between my thighs, making them tremble. I pull my bottom lip under my teeth as Garrett sways my hip over his mouth, eating me out with the vigor and need of a hungry animal.

"Oh! Oh my God!" I scream. "Garrett!"

He doesn't let up. And as if he knows exactly what I need, he slaps my ass before soothing it with his palm. The twinge of pain mixed with the exhilaration of pleasure has me flying, arms up, on this joyride.

My eyes roll back in my head and a strangled sound leaves my mouth. My body flushes with heat and darkness descends against the edges of my vision as my orgasm surges through me like an awakened geyser.

I don't know how long it takes me to travel back to the present, but soon enough, I'm turned around, my shirt thrown off me, looking at my devilishly smug husband.

His lips glisten with the evidence of my desire, and he languidly swipes his tongue against them like he's licking whipped cream from an overfilled latte.

While I'm still barely able to breathe, he looks only slightly unruffled, his blond hair mussed to perfection.

His already ruinous smile turns absolutely deadly. "If my mouth finds you this delicious, then my cock is going to devour you."

Chapter Twenty-One

GARRETT

I TAKE IN MY WIFE'S DEVASTATINGLY BEAUTIFUL FORM, STILL writhing on the sheets in front of me. Finally, for the first time in what feels like centuries, I can admire it, touch it, and kiss it without feeling like I'm bound in chains.

She's so disarming, it should be unlawful.

Her luscious tan skin—currently flushed and glistening with a sheen of sweat—wrapped around the most alluring curves. Her heaving chest, full breasts that make me feel fucking animalistic, and her doe-like eyes seeking me from behind her long lashes.

She wants to look away like she always does—I've come to expect it. But as we both breathe in time, speaking through the silence, she surprises me by holding my gaze. And when the slightest smile blooms on those pouty lips and those dimples dig into her beautiful cheeks, it's all I can do to not lunge at her like a lust-stricken madman. Fuck, those dimples make me feel maniacal. How can the sweetest feature be so damn sexy?

Not able to endure standing a moment longer, I crawl back over her, hovering atop my elbows on either side of her head. My eyes take in her flawless face, lingering on her parted lips. "First, I need you to kiss me, and then I need you to tell me how you want to be fucked."

Her soft hands slide over my stomach, sending a shudder rolling down my body. Her thumbs circle my pebbled nipples before creeping over the sides of my neck to cup my head. She lifts up and I meet her halfway, my tongue immediately demanding entrance into her mouth.

Her taste, her scent, her touch—it's all so intoxicating. My hard-on bears down on her center, rioting to be let free, and I groan into her mouth to release a little pressure.

She kisses me with abandon, her soft moans and lemony taste making me feel unleashed. Fucking heaven and earth, the stars and the goddamn sky—that's what she tastes like. Like having something unattainable against your lips.

My mind conjures up the image of her at my door earlier this evening. Nervous even as she found her nerves. It's not lost on me how hard she made me work—fuck, I've lived through every fleeting eye contact, every unsaid word, every time my hands wanted to reach out and touch her but couldn't—but it's also not lost on me how hard it must have been for her to finally surrender to our connection. To *us*.

This wild attraction goes so far beyond just physical chemistry. So, when she came to my room to admit defeat? I was all too happy to capture that white flag.

She writhes under me as our lips find a rhythm. Her hands tighten over my shoulders, her little black-painted nails biting into my skin while her back arches so her pelvis meets mine in time with our lips. My baby wants more, and I couldn't be more ready to give her exactly that.

Fuck, she surprised me with her reaction to me slapping her ass.

Though, I suppose it shouldn't have caught me off guard, either. Not when I'd seen the curious glint that stirred in her irises when I threatened to take her over my knee at the gala. Her eyes lit up like there were fireworks behind them. She'd pictured exactly what I'd said and liked the visual.

But her reaction tonight—her guttural moans as she acquiesced to the pleasure and pain—was unexpected.

It also turned my dick to stone.

I pull away from her lips to take a breath before giving her a peck, and then another, before bringing my mouth closer to her ear. "Tell me what you need, wife."

I feel the tiny shudder my whisper spurs in her. Her feet slide up the sides of my thighs and she hooks her toes on the waistband of my sweats and boxers, keeping her eyes on me as she pulls my pants down. I lift to let her. When my pants are around my calves, I tug them off, letting them land somewhere on the ground.

She runs her hand down my stomach, stopping to rub her fingertips along my happy trail, making my dick jump, before wrapping her fingers around my shaft. Her thumb rubs over the slit on my throbbing head, massaging the pearls of liquid gathered there while keeping her eyes on my face to gauge my reaction. She won't have to guess too hard with the way I release a hard breath through my nose.

"*You*," she whispers. "I need you, in every single way."

I lean forward, keeping my weight on one elbow while I pull the drawer to my nightstand open and reach for the new box of condoms I'd recently purchased. Pulling it out of the drawer, I rip the top and wiggle out a packet before bringing it to my lips. I tear it open with my teeth, keeping my eyes locked on the whiskey-colored ones staring back at me. As if she's heard my silent command, her free hand slides up my torso to pull out the condom from the wrapper before she rolls it over my thick shaft.

We breathe into each other as she guides me to her entrance, lifting her knees and opening herself up wider. She's wet and ready for me, like she's been waiting the same centuries I have. I don't give her any other warning before I impale her heat as far as my cock can go, and she screams as her hips jump with the arch of her back. She's so goddamn tight, I'm nearly ready to explode.

"*Fuuuck*," I hiss, grasping her hip hard enough that I know I'll leave a bruise. Her fingernails dig into my biceps, leaving their mark on me just the same. Keeping her pinned against me, I dip my head to the place between her neck and shoulder, biting her skin gently. Jesus, I want to mark her skin wherever she'll let me. "Fuck, you feel so good . . . So wet and so tight."

My hips start rocking against her before she widens her legs some more to accommodate my girth, letting me delve deeper. One of her hands settles on the back of my head, pulling at the hair at my nape, while the other tightens around the bed cover. I grab the back of her thigh and pull it forward, making us both groan at how that tiny shift has us almost at the brink of release.

I rocket into her, my balls slapping against her wet skin, while my cock deepens its exploration. *In and out.* A *slap, slap, slap* mixed with the sounds of our pants and the bump of my headboard hitting the wall behind it. I fuck her like my life depends on it, feeling her walls tighten further around me. Her breasts bounce against my chest, her neck and chest covered with a delicious flush as my eyes take her all in. I won't dare fucking blink for fear of missing even a second of the beauty underneath me.

The way her eyes close, succumbing to the pleasure . . . The way her mouth opens with a silent *oh,* and how her chest heaves with each breath.

She's a fucking sight.

And all fucking mine for the taking.

"I'm close, pilot. I'm so close."

I lift slightly, pulling my hand off the back of her thigh and circling her clit with my thumb. She moans at the contact. "Let go, Bella. Come on my cock, baby."

"Garrett . . ." Her head tosses from one side to another, her hips meeting my thrusts.

I feel her clench down on my shaft, my thumb moving in circles over her perfect, swollen little nub, when I decide to up the ante and pinch it between my index and thumb. Bella yelps, her eyes rolling back in her head again, as she seizes up below me. I don't need her to tell me to know she's coming based on the way she's pulsing around me and the sound of her throaty moan. It's so loud, I'm positive we'll be hearing from the neighbors in the morning.

"Garr," she pants, taking in lungfuls of air. "I'm . . . I–"

I don't let her finish. Lowering my head to hers, I cover her mouth with mine, entangling our tongues once more, swallowing her sexy whimpers. I drive into her, slamming into her tight center, and burying myself to the hilt with each thrust. "Fuck, fuck, fuck! You're everything, Bells."

The cadence of our bodies slamming together becomes erratic as I piston into her harder, taking from it everything I need, everything I've ever fucking wanted. With each drive and thrust into her, I make a vow—one I'd made years ago, and then again at the altar.

Her.

It will always only be her.

A few more overwhelming lunges inside her and my orgasm pummels through me with the speed of a fucking tornado, eradicating all thought in its path. My balls tighten right along with my hands on her, and I groan out my release, unloading inside her like a broken dam. I keep my eyes on hers the whole time, forcing her to see exactly what she does to me.

She has me in the palm of her soft little hand.

All I want to do is collapse on her, staying buried in her warm heat and her candy scent, but I force myself to pull out before getting back on my feet. I eye her spent form on my bed, wondering if I'm dreaming.

"Don't move," I order as I shuffle to my bathroom to pull off my condom and clean myself up.

I get back with a warm rag for her, watching as she gets up in my bed. She juts her hand out, indicating for me to give her the cloth. "Thank you. I should probably just get cleaned up in the bathroom."

I pull the rag back and tilt my chin at her. "Lay back. I'm not done with you."

Her brows dip but she smiles as she lays back on the pillow behind her, pulling her hands over her face like she's embarrassed. "Oh, my God. Are you seriously going to clean me up?"

I kneel at the foot of the bed and pull her toward me by the backs of her calves. She squeals before getting up on her elbows and eyeing me from between her bent open legs, where my face is once again in line with her beautiful, and still glistening, pussy.

I run the warm rag over her, wiping down her folds and being careful over her center, listening to the soft moan that slips from her lips. I run the wet cloth over the sides of her thighs and under her bottom, making sure to clean her the way she might do herself.

A fresh scatter of goosebumps erupt over her damp thighs and stomach as I watch her throw her head back, her toes curling at the edge of the bed. And right when she's about to lift her head back up to face me, I dip my mouth down and lick right up her center, from her entrance to her clit.

"Garrett!" Bella thrusts her hand out as her hip jumps into my awaiting mouth. She shakes her head. "I can't. I can't again!"

Putting the rag on the floor, I place my palms on the inside of her thighs before sucking her clit and then circling the tip of my tongue around it. I murmur directly against her skin so she can feel the vibration of my mouth over her sensitive skin. "I'm pretty sure this pussy disagrees."

Her hand goes into my hair, pulling it so hard, I'm sure she's going to take a chunk out. "Please."

I lap at her once more before lifting my head, knowing I've put her on a tightrope where it's her decision if she wants to stay on or jump off. "Please yes, or please no?"

She shakes her head, her back lifted off the bed and her core driving into my mouth. Her head says no but the rest of her body screams yes.

"Words, baby; I need your words." I lick and suck her folds into my mouth, pulling them gently as I move from one to the other. I pay additional attention to my laps over her entrance, swirling my tongue and teasing her until she's whimpering.

Her hand tightens in my hair, the bottom of her palm pushing my head and guiding me to where she needs me. "How is this even possible?" she cries. "God, what are you doing to me?"

I place the tips of my first two fingers into her entrance, going only knuckle-deep, and Bella mewls. One of her hands glides up to her breast and she plays with it, making my cock bounce again for round two. "Making sure you remember who you belong to."

I circle my fingers into her, going a little deeper as I flick her needy little nub with my tongue. The sounds of my laps and licks mix with her whimpers and they fill the room before she's moaning again outright. "Garrett. Oh, God!"

I push my two fingers in all the way before pulling my mouth off her. "Yes or no, wifey? I need an answer."

She doesn't answer, moaning and arching simultaneously,

so when I start to pull my fingers out of her, she directs the fire in her eyes right at my face. "Don't you dare, pilot! I will strangle you in your sleep if you don't finish what you just started."

I smirk. "So, that's a yes, then?"

"Yes! Yes, dammit! Now make me come," she growls.

I laugh into her wet center, my shoulders shaking against the edge of the bed. God, she is so perfect.

She widens her legs again, something I'm realizing is her way of telling me she wants more, and I shove my fingers into her all the way. She cries out in ecstasy, the sound of her euphoria vibrating against the walls, and I suck on her clit again.

It only takes a few more good pulls into my mouth and some thrusts into her heat before Bella comes completely undone. I lap at her juices, making sure to get every drop until her pulsing gets shallower, along with her pants.

When I lift back to my feet, my wife's eyes are closed, her face lying against the side of an arm above her head. Her hair is a mess of black and purple, while her body shimmers from head to toe. She looks completely spent, as if she just finished a race . . .

In some ways, I suppose she has.

But what she doesn't know is, I have no plans for us to take part in a race. I'm in this for the long haul—a marathon, through and through.

Chapter Twenty-Two

GARRETT

I still remember the first time I flew an aircraft on my own. The exhilaration of doing something so monumental that every moment before it felt inconsequential. The ascent into the open sky, my pulse thumping against my neck, and every cell inside my body buzzing with a charge I'd never felt before. I remember thinking that was it; that I'd never be able to recreate a moment like that again.

Until tonight.

I stare at her face lying next to me in bed, the cover around the middle of her torso and her arm between us. Her eyes are closed, but I know she's not sleeping. "Bells."

Her lids lift and she finds my eyes.

I put my index on her temple before tucking some hair behind her ear. If I know my wife, her brain is running a mile a minute. "Tell me what's happening in that head of yours."

She swallows and a frown tugs her mouth downward. "I've been stuck in the 'what-ifs' for so long that my mind is accustomed to buzzing with them."

I link our hands together and she scoots closer so our faces are next to each other on the same pillow. "Like?"

Bella licks her lips. "What if this is a dream? What if whatever this is fades? What if you decide you can't handle me anymore or that you've had enough?"

Her gaze flickers away like she's finding it hard to look at me again, and I tug on our linked hands, pulling her attention back. I place a kiss on the back of her knuckles. "Anything else?"

"What if I'm not enough for you, pilot?" she whispers. "When I was younger, it was just me and Mom. It didn't come easy, but I eventually made peace with my broken heart—with the man I loved more than anyone else on the planet leaving us because he was selfish enough to and because we weren't enough for him. For the past four years, it's been me and Meera. She hasn't felt loss the same way I have, and I . . ." Her eyes bounce between mine. "I don't want her to feel that same loss. I don't want her to fall in love with you and have that taken away from her. Because, Garrett?" She inhales a shaky breath and her eyes glisten. "You make it all too easy."

My next breath catches in my lungs but I don't break our eye contact.

"If someone like me—someone who refused to fall for your smiles and your charm—can't resist thinking about you every second of every day, then how can I ask that of a little girl who is head over heels for you already?" Her brows pinch as she looks at our hands. "Those are the 'what-ifs' scrambled inside my head. I don't take a whole lot of risks, and I don't let a whole lot of people in. I like my routines and simple pleasures." Her eyes find mine again. "But with you . . . I feel like I'm risking it all."

I wrap my hands around her head, letting her know with the intensity of my touch and my gaze, with everything in my being, that I don't take a single word she said for granted. I know the kind of trust she's telling me she wants to put in me. I hear her vulnerability, loud and clear. She's serving up her heart on a platter for me, and I'll worship it with everything I have. "There's no risk when it's a sure thing, sweetheart. *We* are a sure thing. And as for your 'what-ifs,' let me counter them with one of my own. What if this is it? You and me. Are you willing to risk not finding out?"

She shakes her head. "It's why I'm here, pilot. The risk of not finding out seemed to outweigh everything."

I grasp her chin, pulling her mouth to mine hungrily, feeling my chest ignite with a warmth I've never felt for anyone before. She kisses me back, sliding her leg over my torso so she's now straddling my once again growing arousal. Her beautiful breasts rub against my chest and I cup her ass, sliding her bare front against my dick.

Bella breathes against me. "Garrett."

I cup her face again, foregoing my aching hard-on to get something through her stubborn head. "I'll work my whole fucking life to chase away your 'what-ifs,' baby."

Bella kisses me again, her tongue plundering inside in response to my plea, her long hair like a curtain around us. Her hips start to rock over me, her juicy lower lips sliding and gliding over my thickening hard-on. She pulls away from my mouth before her short fingernails scrape down my chest.

She watches her hands as they roam over me when they come to a sudden stop. She squints down at her discovery before her eyes widen. She brings her face closer to the left side of my chest, the area that usually stays hidden under my bicep. "I didn't know you had a tattoo."

I run my palms over the sides of her smooth torso, feeling the dip of her waist under my skin. "Just one."

She studies it and a gasp tumbles out of her lips when she deciphers it. *I.XXVII.* "One-twenty-seven." She rises, finding my eyes with a question in hers, even though she knows the answer. "January twenty-seventh."

I nod.

"When did you . . .?" Her face is a mix of disbelief and wonder, but I don't miss the slight tremble in her chin when her eyes pool.

"The night after."

"You believed in us that much?"

My hands still on her hips. "I hoped for us the day I met you, but I believed in us the day I married you. I believed in *us* enough to tattoo it next to my heart."

Bella stares at me in simple disbelief before a tear breaks the dam and tumbles onto her cheek. I lift my thumb up to wipe it and she grasps my hand, kissing the center of my palm. "You make it so easy, pilot."

Her lips brush over the ring on my finger before she lowers and kisses the spot where our wedding night is forever marked on my skin. Her lips trail over to my chest and then to my nipple. She kisses and sucks, getting a low groan from me before she licks and sucks her way to my neck.

Her hands tangle in my hair as her hips rock over my erection. The girl knows how to move in such a way, I feel like I'll combust right under her. She bites my neck, squeezing her fists inside my long strands, and I grab her hips, pushing her down onto me. My erection wants to slide inside her wet heat so fucking bad, I can barely see straight.

Her mouth trails up to my ear, grasping my lobe between her teeth, pulling and sucking while my hands tighten around her.

"Bells," I grit out her name in warning. I swear she's intent on seeing me embarrass myself by coming on my own stomach.

Her mouth finds mine again, kissing me hard, and my hands travel over her back to tangle in her hair. Her long, thick hair—that's just as soft and silky—reminds me of waves under twilight, gleaming against the moon. I wrap a thick heap of it around my fist and feel her press down harder on my dick before she moans into my mouth.

When we're both hungrier, she lifts back up, showing me her flawless flat stomach and the rise and fall of her tits as she sucks in each breath. She arches and throws her head back so I feel the ends of her hair grazing my thighs.

She's grinding down on my arousal, and I'll let her take whatever pleasure she wants for a bit, but if she's thinking I'll let her come just by sliding around, then she's in for a rude awakening.

I want her orgasm either on my tongue or with my cock buried deep inside her, and nothing else will do. "You get five more seconds, and then I need that pussy of yours to swallow my cock. Understand?"

Her head lifts back up and there's a heat like I've never seen in her eyes. "Do you know how crazy I get when you use that tone with me?"

I swirl my thumb over the swollen nub peeking at me from where she sits. Lifting it back up with her juices glistening off it, I suck it off my finger, watching her. "Good. I'm glad we're finally seeing eye-to-eye in this marriage."

She pinches my thigh teasingly, but I can't feel anything with her shifting around on my shaft. "Times up, wifey."

Bella smiles as she gets up on her knees and lifts her hips off me. When she has my length in her soft palm, she directs it under her entrance, and I hold my breath in anticipation for her to slam down on me. But thankfully, at least one other neuron is firing inside my brain. "Wait. Fuck." I reach over to my nightstand. "Let me—"

"No, Garrett." Her eyes are stuck to mine. "I believe you when you tell me it's been four years. And you know—or *should* know—that I haven't been with anyone since Meera was born. I don't want anything between us."

I release a breath, realizing how big of a moment this is

for her. Not only is she giving me her trust, but the last time—as much as I fucking hate thinking about her douchebag one-night stand while I'm seconds from being balls-deep inside her—she had sex with someone, whether it was with or without a condom is beyond my knowledge, she ended up in a situation that caused her to shut the barely open door of her heart completely. "Are you sure?"

She nods. "I'm on birth control."

I bring my hand back to her hips and relish in her beauty. She looks so fucking hot, hovering over me with my cock in her tight grasp. With her eyes pinned to mine, she starts to swallow me, inch by excruciating inch, until I'm completely sheathed in her. We moan together and my eyes flutter shut as the sensation of her warmth takes over me in the most exquisite way. "Fuck, baby. You fucking kill me."

When she's seated over me, she circles her hips and my fingers dig into them in response. I'd always prided myself in my ability to hold back an orgasm for a decent amount of time—enough to let my partner get off at least twice, or even three times—but right now, I honestly feel like a goddamn inexperienced teenager, ready to come seconds after plunging inside a woman.

A minute later, Bella's hands find a spot on my chest and she starts to slide up and down my shaft, riding me in earnest. I feel her juices trail down to my balls as her inner walls clamp down on my erection.

Soon, she's slamming down on me with her hands supported on my thighs. "Garrett! God!"

I lift up and pull her body closer to me with my hands on her ass. The angle makes us both groan, and Bella finds her rhythm again. Her breasts bounce around my chin, and I lower my head to grab her nipple with my mouth, sucking and teasing. I move over to her neck and lick the sheen covering her skin before sucking it, too.

"Garrett! I'm so close."

Pulling away from her, I look down to see the way her thick and swollen lower lips suck up my cock. *Fuck, I'm going to come.* The feeling builds so fast and so powerfully that I'm not going to be able to hold on. The sight of her devouring me loosens every hold I have on myself. In a last-ditch effort to make her come with me, I rasp out, "Look down, baby. Look at how fucking hot this looks."

She does and her fingers tighten over my shoulders. She screams with her head thrown back, her walls pulsing around me as I come right along with her. I pull her into me by her ass, burying myself even deeper inside her, flooding her with my cum.

We heave in big breaths, draped around each other, before I carry her to my shower. She's completely exhausted, so instead of taking her once more against the shower wall like I'd planned to, I lather her with soap and wash her off.

Once we're both dried and ready to get back into bed, she finds the socks she was wearing and slips back into them, completely nude save for her feet. I pull her into me and Bella closes the distance between us, tightening her grip around me. She whispers into my neck, "You're written across my heart too, pilot."

Chapter Twenty-Three

BELLA

MY EYES FLUTTER OPEN WITH THE LIGHT COMING IN through the window in Garrett's room, and I take stock of my position. My face is on his chest, over the tattoo of our wedding date, and my forearm is draped around his waist. I trail my gaze over his gorgeous physique, lingering on the patch of hair I've recently become fascinated with—his happy trail running under the waistband of his boxer-briefs.

I wonder why I find it so specifically sexy when every part of this man is so alluring? Perhaps it's the softness of the hair against the hard ridges of his abs. Or maybe it's the fact that it merges with an area I got *very* familiar with last night.

I smile as the memories of the night dance inside my head—memories I'll be revisiting any time I spend alone. His fingers gripping my hips, the zing on my skin after he slapped my ass, his lips around my nipples, and the rasp in his voice when he whispered in my ear.

One thing is for sure—my husband knows how to deliver on his filthy promises, and I'm all too eager to be on the receiving end.

Garrett's face is turned away from me, his arms curved above his head, and for a moment I stay still, listening to the strong heart inside his chest. His rhythmic breathing tempts me to go back to sleep, but I reluctantly pull away—my body sore from the full workout—recalling all the things I have to get done this morning.

Thankfully, Mom is taking Meera to school, and I don't have to physically go into work since it's an optional work-from-home Friday for my company, though I still have a couple of meetings I need to attend.

I also have a video call with Wendy in the afternoon to talk about the case. We're supposed to go over any evidence she's collected against Chaz that may help us in court and the personal character references I turned in a few days ago. If we have time, we might also start developing my testimony and discuss how to answer any questions the judge might ask.

Even though we still have three weeks until the court date, a restlessness makes my stomach twist. To be honest, my anxiety hasn't relented ever since I got served those papers, but I've tried to keep myself busy and not dwell on it too much.

I'm not naive, though. I know that if I'm preparing as thoroughly as possible on my side, then so is Chaz—and there's a good chance he'll get what he wants.

I'm trying to come to terms with what Wendy has said to me several times—barring unforeseen circumstances, the court will likely grant Chaz reconnection therapy with Meera so he can start to have regular visits with her.

But I haven't given up hope that sometime before the date, he'll pull out of this entire ordeal because it's either bored him or he finds it all too burdensome.

I find my tank top and shorts on the floor and press my feet into the carpet so I don't make too much noise while I'm getting dressed. Rubbing the sleep from my eyes, I find the clock on Garrett's nightstand. Six-twenty-two. I don't think I slept more than four hours, but another look at the man sleeping peacefully on the bed tells me I'd better get used to it.

And because I just can't help myself, I lean over to run my fingers through his blonde mop. The corners of his eyes twitch, but he just takes a deep inhale without stirring much more. I almost place a kiss on those cushiony lips, but I also know it's a rare chance for him to sleep in and that would definitely wake him up. Most days he's out of the house and on his way to the airport before the first rays of the sun. So, as tempting as he looks right now, I really just need to get out of here.

After brushing my teeth, putting my hair into a messy bun at the top of my head, and wiping my face with a wet towel, I tie a robe over my pajamas and pad downstairs in search of coffee.

Once I've turned the coffee machine on, I get out a bowl and find the box of cat food I'd bought recently in the pantry. I shake out some food and fill up another bowl of water. Managing both things in my hands and opening the front door, I trudge down the patio steps, to the side of the house in search of Winky and Brown Sugar.

As if she's expecting me, Winky peeks out of the box, assessing me with her no-nonsense, one-eyed gaze. But instead of leaving the breakfast out for them like I usually do, I kneel down next to it, relaxing my shoulders and speaking softly.

"Come on, Momma. We're friends now, wouldn't you say?" I tilt my head at the food and fresh water. "I've got breakfast for you. All you have to do is come say hi."

Brown Sugar peeps out the side of her mother's torso,

eyeing me with curiosity. And while she has enough appre-hension for humans, I'm glad to see it's not at the same level as her mother's. A bulb inside my head sheds light on the correlation between mine and Winky's life, but I stay focused on my furry friends.

Brown Sugar has definitely gotten bigger over the past couple of weeks. Her khaki-colored fur still looks disheveled, like her mother's, but she looks as healthy as a stray can without knowing for sure. At least she isn't hurt or injured in any way, so that's a relief.

I shake the bowl of food, and Brown Sugar's eyes widen slightly before she meows. She takes a tentative step forward, giving her mom a lingering glance, before scampering toward me on hurried feet. Her bushy tail gives a quick whack to the air before she sniffs at the bowl. And as sure as I am that she's focused on nibbling the pellets inside, I also know she's got one eye trained on me.

I don't try to initiate contact, crouching down right where I am. I lift my head toward Winky, urging her to come closer. Her eye bounces between her kitten and me before she finally decides the food is too tempting to miss and parades over to the bowl, digging into her meal.

Holding back my smile as if it would catch their attention and make them retreat, I watch the cats eat for a few minutes. It's only when both their heads pop up at the rustle of grass behind me and then quickly scamper away to their box that I realize someone is standing there.

I get back on my feet, turning to find Garrett giving me a curious look. He's wearing a gray T-shirt over his pajamas and slippers, but his hair is still as messy as when I left him in bed. I have to control the urge to leap into his arms and shove my nose into his delicious scent.

His eyes travel from me to the box at the corner of the house to the partially-empty bowls lying near my feet before coming back to my face in question. The side of his mouth pulls up in an adorable crooked smirk once he's processed the scene. "I see you've made some friends and have asked them to move in?"

I wince. "I hope you're not mad. I saw Winky and her daughter Brown Sugar in those bushes one day," I point to said bushes, "and I thought they'd leave, but they seemed to keep coming back. I figured I'd give them a warm place to sleep until they found another place to go."

This time Garrett's lips twitch like he's holding back a smile. "Winky and Brown Sugar? You've named them?"

I nod, looking over at Winky, who's now scrutinizing the man next to me with the same untrusting expression she gave me the first time around. "Look at her, G. She's clearly been in some sort of accident or brawl. And I don't know where the rest of her litter is. It's just the two of them . . . like me and Meera."

Garrett's navy blues linger on mine before his hands cup my face, and I inch closer to him to eliminate the space between us. I grasp his wrists and look at his serious face.

"It's not just you and Meera, Bells. I'll keep saying it until I lose my voice, but it's never going to be just you and Meera."

"I know, I just meant–"

He shakes his head. "After everything over the past week, after last night . . . Get it through your head, beautiful. I'm right fucking here, and I always will be."

I get up on my toes and place a kiss on my husband's frown. He doesn't return my kiss, and I know he's holding my misspoken words against me. "Some habits die hard, pilot, but I swear to you, I'm trying. I see you for everything you are, and . . ." I smile, knowing the rest of my sentence will just rile him up more, but not being able to help loving this sight of him annoyed with me because he's so fucking sexy, "I couldn't have dreamed of fake-marrying someone better."

His gaze hardens and he grabs me around my waist, pulling me to him. A thrill rushes through me. "Nothing about this . . . *nothing* about us is fake."

I giggle, placing a kiss on his jaw as butterflies take flight inside my belly. "I know, my pilot."

I feel some of the tension release from his shoulders and circle my arms around his neck, pulling his face back to mine. I kiss his mouth and this time, I don't stop until he gives in. His hands tighten on my waist and he deepens our kiss, tangling his tongue with mine. We both groan softly into one another, and I feel his hardened erection against me.

I pull back with a heavy breath. "If you're planning to do any of the dirty things that look on your face is promising, just know that I need to be fed and coffee'd first."

Garrett chuckles, the sound of his voice traveling down to the achy apex between my thighs. If we don't head back inside right this second, I'm positive I'll let him have his way with me right here in the cold.

Leaving the bowls where they are and the cats to carry on, I pull Garrett into the house. We barely close the door before he has me up against the back of it. His mouth travels from my neck to my mouth, kissing me hungrily, while his hand finds its way under my robe, his thumb flicking my hard nipple over my tank top. *Jesus, this man has the keys to my body.*

He pulls away before leaving another peck on my swollen lips. His brow rises and he gives me a meaningful and lecherous smirk. "Let's first get you fed and caffeinated . . . and then I'll get fed."

～

Meera walks into the house like a cyclone out for destruction, throwing her little backpack onto the ground, along with her Dora the Explorer lunch bag. "Mommy! Guess what?"

"What?" I ask, though I look up and smile at my mom right behind her. "Hey, Mom. Thanks for helping with her last night and today."

My mom lifts her arms, indicating for me to give her a hug, but she doesn't come inside the house. "Oh, it was nothing. I'm working in the clinic all this weekend, so I'm glad I had the day off yesterday and could help."

I pull back after embracing her. "Won't you come inside? I can make chai or one of those Bloody Marys you like so much." I wink at her.

She squints at me. "I don't like them *that* much, so stop making me feel like a lush." She leans her head in, and I assume she's looking for Garrett before she clears her throat. "I need to get going. I'm going to watch the new Bollywood flick in the theater with um," her eyes get shifty, making my head tilt in confusion, "a friend."

I blink at her. My mother is a terrible liar and an even worse actor. "A *friend?*"

"Yes." She leans in again before running her hands over her pants unnecessarily. "So, I heard Garrett left Tahoe early last night."

"Mommy! Guess what?" Meera yells again, pulling my dress and looking up at me.

"Give me two minutes, Meerkat. I'll talk to you after I say bye to *Nani.* Did you thank her for taking care of you last night?"

Meera stomps back out to the patio and gives my mom a hug. "Thanks, *Nani*-pants, but can you not cook fish when I'm over next time?"

My mother gives me an astounded look, like she can't

believe the words out of her granddaughter's mouth, and somehow, I'm to blame for it. "Now I'm not allowed to cook meat in my own house? I swear, this daughter of yours is such a tyrant."

I laugh as Meera giggles, placing a kiss on the back of her grandmother's hand and skipping inside.

"So?" My mom raises a brow. "Garrett came home early last night?"

I give her a blank look, feigning disapproval. "Let me guess; Darian told Rani, and Rani told her mom, and of course, the first thing your sister did was call you."

My mom wraps her arms around her chest. "I will never reveal the identity of my assets."

"Mom, you're not in the CIA." I roll my eyes. "And don't think I didn't hear you dodge the question earlier. Who is this friend you're going to the movies with? Why are you being shady?"

My mom tilts her head up. "If you won't tell me what happened between you and Garrett, then I won't tell you about my widowed radiologist friend."

My mouth drops right as my mom realizes how much she's given away. "Arthur? You're going to the movies with *Arthur?*"

On occasion, over the past month, Mom has slipped in Arthur's name as the new, older radiologist who recently started working with her. I hadn't thought anything of it . . . until now.

My mom abruptly turns, waving behind her. "Not saying a word." She turns back as soon as she gets to her car. "Unless you want to tell me if anything happened between you and Garrett."

I give my mother a mischievous grin, knowing that, over the years, we've gotten to a place where we're more like friends than typical mother-daughters, where boundaries need to be respected. "Mom, if I told you what happened between me and Garrett, you'd need more than one of your favorite Bloody Marys."

I don't have to say much more because my mom quickly gets into her car and drives off, leaving me in a fit of giggles behind her.

Chapter Twenty-Four

GARRETT

"HI UNCLE GARRETT!" MEERA COMES BARRELING AT ME full speed, and I lean down just in time to grab her under the arms and raise her over my head while she giggles. Her hair swings up and she sticks out her arms like she's flying above me. I've missed this bossy little squirt over the past few days. "Can you throw me on the couch like this again? That was so much fun!"

"Uh." I sneak a quick glance at Bella, who is just coming back into the house. I assume she was saying bye to her mom. I was hoping she hadn't heard us, but the look on her face says she has and she's not impressed. "What do you mean, silly meerkat?" I feign incredulity as I gently put her back down on her feet. "I would *never* throw you on the couch like that!"

"Uh-huh." Bella blinks once, but her pursed lips indicate she's hiding a smile.

"Yes, you would, Uncle Garrett! Remember last week, when you threw me like an airplane onto the sofa, and–"

"Okay, okay, Meerkat," I cut in, then clear my throat, trying to figure out how not to get my ass kicked by the woman staring daggers at me with her arms crossed over her chest and her eyebrow lifted. I flash her a withering smile before I focus on her blabber-mouth daughter. "You've clearly had a long day at school. Why don't you tell us about it."

"Oh yeah! Guess what, Mommy?" Meera's eyes widen under her pink glasses as she makes her way to Bella, and I'm thankful for the change in subject. She wraps her little arms around her mom's thighs and looks up, not waiting for Bella to respond. "Ms. Loveland brought her cat to school, and we all got to play with him! Well, she had to keep him in a different room because Nolan and Blakely are allergic, but me and Trinity got to play with him. His name is Fluffsters, and he's *soo* cute! Just like Brown Sugar and Winky." As if just realizing I'm in the room, Meera turns to me. "Uncle Garrett, did Mommy show you our new pets?"

"She did." I look from her to Bella, who now has the same guilty look on her face I did moments ago. I'd rather her have that look than me—especially if I have to explain playing human airplane with Meera last week.

"Well, I'm so glad you got a chance to play with Fluffsters, but Winky and Brown Sugar are not our pets." Bella glances at me. "They're stray cats, and most of the time strays don't want to be indoors, especially if they've gotten used to being outdoors."

Meera juts out her bottom lip, bowing her head as her brows fold down. "Aww. I thought they'd like us by now, and maybe they'd want to live at home with us. I wanted them to sleep in my Dora bed."

Bella lifts her daughter's chin. "You're a big girl now, remember? You don't need anyone else to sleep in the same bed as you. Plus, this is Uncle Garrett's house; we aren't going to be here forever and he might not even want pets."

Not here forever? Oh, that's right. We haven't talked about our particular living situation, or how I plan to have them here for as long as we *all* plan to be here together. I suppose that conversation was forgotten somewhere between the multiple orgasms last night.

"But, Mommy, pets are different." Meera looks at me hopefully, and I already fucking know that no matter the fact that I, myself, am allergic to cats, I'll fucking say yes to whatever it is she wants. "Uncle Garrett, you like cats, don't you? Maybe . . . maybe we can have one for a little while?"

"I do like cats."

"Meerkat," Bella brings Meera's attention back to her, stroking her fingers through her daughter's hair, "pets aren't something you have for a little while and then forget about them. It's a big decision to have one, and then when you do, you have to take care of them for the rest of their lives."

When Meera's shoulders slump, I find myself saying something I wouldn't have ever given into if not for the two women in front of me to whom I've lost my heart—and my mind. "How about we see if the two cats outside want to become indoor cats?"

Bella's mouth opens to protest as Meera squeals, "Really?" She runs over to me and puts her hands in mine, swinging from them. "You want to adopt them?"

"Garrett—" Bella starts.

I shrug. "It's more a question of, do *they* want to adopt *us*? Let's see if we can urge them to come inside on their own. Maybe we can put a bowl of food out in front of that window and leave it open for a few hours to see if they want to come inside and explore. I have a feeling they'll tell us pretty quickly if they like it or hate it."

"But what if they have diseases?" Bella argues.

"Let's see if they even want to stay. If they do, then we'll take them to a vet."

"Omigosh! Omigosh!" Meera hops on her feet.

I take a deep breath before turning to Bella and holding

her eyes while speaking to Meera. "But only if your mom is okay with our new living situation going forward, though. All of us, here in this house, without an end date."

Bella stares back at me, emotion and disbelief swirling in her eyes before she seems to finally find her voice. "Are . . . are you being serious right now?"

I lift my head, my eyes hooding on their own. "I've been serious since day one."

As Bella and I have a silent exchange—one where I know she's overthinking all the 'what-ifs,' while I'm responding to each one with a firm stance on where I want us headed together—Meera continues to jump up and down.

Whether she's comprehended the secondary conversation happening between Bella and me—one where I've asked them to move in with me permanently—is unclear, but she continues squealing with an ear-to-ear grin that could rival the lights of Vegas. "Mommy, please say yes. Please, please, please!"

Bella looks to the side, shaking her head in defeat, but smiles. She looks back at me and I see something shift in her gaze. Perhaps it's been there longer than I've noticed it, but today, right now, it's taken the stage, front and center. An emotion I'm too afraid to hope for, fearing I'm reading it wrong, but one I know I've felt for quite some time. Her hands lift in the air and then drop to her sides. "I guess you two have it all figured out so . . . yes."

I PEEK at the opened window from my spot in the kitchen. The house feels mildly cooler with the early March evening breeze, and if I listen closely against the hum of the heating and the rustle of the trees, I can make out the squeaky meow of one of the cats outside.

Meera helped me put a bowl of cat food on the windowsill before she went to bed. She was on her best behavior—doing everything her mom told her to do without a single reminder—after Bella agreed to let us try to domesticate the cats. We shook the bowl of food, and Meera called to the cats, as if they'd understood their newly given names. And while one of them gave us a leery stare, I'm not sure they understood our request.

I'm rinsing off some dishes and putting them in the dishwasher when I hear the footsteps of someone I've become quite accustomed to in my house. I turn over my shoulder to watch as Bella hops up onto the counter behind me.

Her socked feet—a soft, pink-colored pair with lavender polka-dots—cross in front of the cabinet below her. My eyes trail up her toned legs that disappear into those tiny sleep shorts she always wears. She has on a new light blue tank top—an outfit I'm quite fond of—revealing the points of her pebbled nipples poking out from under it. She must have changed into her pajamas after putting Meera to bed.

My eyes flick to the opened box of her favorite lemony candy in her hand. She lifts it to her lips and tilts her head back. Her long hair, currently in a ponytail, touches her lower back as she empties the box into her mouth. I listen to the crunch of the little rocks between her teeth before she licks her lips, watching me curiously.

Not able to withstand the distance between us any longer—especially since we've had to play it cool in front of Meera all evening—I wipe my hand on a towel and amble over to her. Pressing her knees apart and pulling her closer to the edge so her center aligns with my growing hard-on, I bring my face close to hers. Her lemony breath fans over my lips and I lick my own, almost like I can taste the candy on them.

We stare at each other for a few heated seconds before

Bella wraps her fingers around the hem of my shirt. "You want us to live with you."

It's not a question, but my fingers tighten on her ass in response.

Her hands flatten on my chest, and she drags them up to my shoulder before cupping my neck. She watches her movement, and I can see her mind working behind her eyes—questioning, deliberating, circling. "What else do you want?"

"For you to forget that we got married in Vegas under false pretenses," I respond softly. "I'll marry you a hundred more times if it'll make you believe this is real." I pull her left hand off my neck and press my grandmother's ring against her finger. A surge of possessiveness toward her comes over me, almost unbearably, whenever I see her wear it. "I want you to know that *this* is yours in every way."

Her sweet breath fans my lips as she whispers, "I do."

"Good."

"Pilot?" She pulls me by the hem of my shirt as if we're not close enough.

"Yes," I rasp.

"I want to live with you. I like living with you."

I softly nuzzle the tip of my nose over her cheek and feel a shudder go through her. "Good."

"Pilot?" She sighs.

"Hmm?"

"Please, for the love of God, just kiss me."

Closing the distance between our faces, I pull her lips to my mouth and slide my tongue inside. Her arms and legs wrap around me as we deepen the kiss, and my hands move along the sides of her torso, heating her up with my touch. I flick both her nipples with my thumbs and Bella moans softly, grinding her core against me needily.

I break our kiss to drag my face down to her neck while my hand slides into her shorts. I find her satiny folds and glide my middle finger in between them, covering it with her juices. She's delectably wet and my mouth waters in anticipation of tasting her until she can't take it anymore.

"Get on your knees on the counter, facing me. Grab the cabinet handles behind you."

Bella doesn't question me, doing exactly as I've asked. I help her get into position, making sure she clasps her hands around the handles before I pull down her shorts and panties. She shifts from one knee to the other, helping me take them off.

Her bare center stares back at me and my nostrils flare in anticipation. I glide my palms over the smooth outside of her thighs before I make my way to the middle of her. I circle my thumb around her entrance and Bella hisses, sucking her bottom lip into her mouth.

I pin my eyes to her, every cell kindling inside my veins. "Spread your knees."

She does as I ask, and I rub her wet center. I switch to my index and middle, dipping them into her so they're halfway inside. Bella moans and her juices run down my hand.

Fuuuck.

Lowering myself so I'm at eye-level with her center, I lap up her tight nub with my fingers still inside her.

Bella's breathing picks up as she grinds out my name, "Garrett."

"I want you to ride my fingers and my face. Got it? Hold on to the handles behind you."

I swirl my tongue over her clit and slide it back down to where my fingers are inside her, while I push them in deeper before taking them out, fucking her like I would with my dick. Meanwhile, my actual dick screams inside my pants, raging to be let out and to get in on the action.

"Harder, Garrett. More." Bella grinds down on my hand

and my mouth. "God, it's so *good* . . ." she moans, stretching out the word.

I lick her with more vigor, tasting every ounce I can get of her nectar on my greedy tongue while a droplet of her juice runs down my wrist. Just watching it increases my thirst for her. I suck on her clit—the sounds of my lips against her skin mingle with the sounds of Bella's moans. At one point, she even lets out a cry before she snaps her mouth shut, groaning and breathing hard when she realizes we still have a little girl upstairs who could wake up with the commotion.

I jackhammer my fingers into Bella as she thrusts her hips against them, taking from me whatever she needs.

"Please. More, please." Her voice is urgent and longing, and I feel her clench around my knuckles. She's so damn close, she grinds her jaw, trying to keep her moans from slipping out.

Sucking her clit harder, I decide to help her get there. My girl doesn't shy away from a little pain, and as surprised as I was to see her naughtier side come out last night—one that she definitely keeps well hidden—I'm grateful I'm the one who gets to see it.

Using my front teeth, I gently bite down on her clit, and Bella practically jumps against me, her breasts bouncing inside her tank top.

"Oh, God! Yes!" Her hips gyrate on my mouth erratically, and I alternate between sucking and biting until she's pulsing around my mouth. Her head hits the cabinet behind her as she comes on my mouth, her swollen nub practically vibrating on my tongue.

I ease up the pressure from my fingers but keep lapping and licking her sweet slit, not wasting a single drop.

When the last of her pulses drain from her body, I gently pull my fingers out of her. Lifting back up to meet her face—

to-face, I take in her flushed face and the sheen covering her forehead, and give her my smuggest smirk.

Her hooded gaze lingers on my glistening lips, and I place the fingers covered in her juices on her lips. "Be a good girl and suck."

She opens her mouth, pulls in my fingers and sucks them in kind. Her warm tongue rolls around them as her cheeks hollow out, and fuck, I think I'm going to come in my pants.

I'm one second away from asking her to get on her knees so I can rock in and out of that sexy mouth of hers when we both jump from a clattering sound in the living room.

Bella's face pales. "Meera?"

I quickly help her down from the counter, and Bella pulls up her shorts and panties before we investigate where the sound came from. Thankfully, it's not Meera.

Our eyes land on the bushy brown tail behind the leg of the table before two glittering eyes stare back at us. The kitten—the one I believe has been baptized Brown Sugar, or is it Sugar Ray?—meows once, either in greeting or warning before she examines the cat food spread out on the floor, ignoring the turned-over bowl lying next to it.

I flit my gaze around the area but don't notice the one-eyed cat anywhere, so perhaps the kitten is starting to find her independence.

She nibbles the kibble for a few minutes under our gaze before she examines the back of the couch in front of her. Pouncing on it with silent feet, she brings up a paw to rub her eyes and then licks her wrist, keeping one eye on Bella and me standing there, gawking at her.

She finally settles down on the couch like she's the one who paid for it, and I catch Bella's part-relieved, part-startled expression. "It might be too soon to tell but . . . it looks like we've been adopted."

Chapter Twenty-Five

BELLA

I'VE PLAYED BY THE RULES MY ENTIRE LIFE.

I've colored inside the lines; I've avoided puddles.

Because I got myself into trouble whenever I didn't.

And as I watch my husband, standing on his bare feet—feet so beautiful they do things to my girly parts and make me question my sanity—wearing nothing but his pajama bottoms while placing avocado mash, sliced radishes, and a sunny-side-up egg on sourdough bread to make me breakfast . . . I know with utter confidence that I'm in big trouble.

The kind of trouble where I've called in sick to work because he's been flying for the past three days and leaves again tomorrow morning, and I can't fathom not spending the entire day wrapped around him.

The kind of trouble where my words feel garbled inside my head, and even more so on their way out of my mouth whenever he's close.

The kind of trouble where his eyes on me make the rest of the world disappear, like I'm caught in a navy-blue vortex that I'm happy to never find my way out of.

The kind where every step forward is a step toward that

sunlight and a leap away from the thunderous clouds that have followed me relentlessly for so long.

Garrett glances up at me, catching me staring, and my eyes flick to his hands. Hands that were on me at least eight times last night; hands that gifted me eight orgasms over the course of the five extra hours we stayed up well past our bedtime.

I take a sip of my coffee, letting it mingle with the warmth that's taken over my chest over the past few weeks. All that sun. "I've never had avocado toast with radishes before."

Garrett shuffles to my spot against the counter and picks up the toast from the plate between us. He brings it to my lips and I take a bite, keeping my eyes on his smoldering ones.

The smooth and salty taste of the avocado and sourdough mixed with the spicy crunch of the radish is beyond what I'd expected. I hum in agreement, swiping the crumbs off my bottom lip with my tongue, before Garrett lowers his head and pulls me in for a kiss.

"So fucking delicious," he rasps before he saunters to the coffee pot.

Thankfully, Mom was able to take Meera to school today and will be keeping her overnight so Garrett and I can have some private time. She's been tight-lipped about Arthur–and whatever is happening between them–but I'm also not pushing her to tell me. She will on her own time.

I can't imagine Mom has been with a man after Dad died, so if she's found a friend or something more with Arthur, then all I can hope is that she's happy. I've always made it a point to support her with finding love again.

I haven't always taken my own advice, but one could argue I've never felt that sort of chemistry with anyone before.

That is, until . . .

I take a sip from my cup, watching Garrett fill his own. "So, that bucket list of yours . . .?"

Leaning against the counter, Garrett lifts the cup to his mouth and watches me from the other side of the kitchen.

"You've never baked a cake?"

He shrugs. "My mom or grandma would always bake them for me, or I'd just pick one up at the bakery. I've never had a reason to make one myself. Dean was always the baker, using sugar to charm the girls." He gives me a gleaming toothy grin. "I was more of a fish and grill sort of guy."

"You definitely know how to use that fishing rod to hook the ladies," I tease him, even as a tinge of jealousy burns inside my chest. I hate the idea of his hands having been on anyone else, even though I know how ludicrous that sounds.

He pads over to me, as if knowing I need him closer. Putting our cups on the counter, he lifts my chin as his thumb caresses my jaw. "The only fish I care about is the one who broke my damn fishing line. The one with unending dimples and soft brown eyes. The one I'm so crazy about, I had to use the net of a marriage proposal to capture her, and I don't ever plan on letting her go."

I slide my hand up his bare chest, lingering on the tattoo of our wedding date. I pull him by the neck into a kiss and then lean back with a grin. "I'm pretty sure I'm the one who proposed."

"Details." He presses his lips to mine again.

I giggle. "Anyway, it's just unacceptable that you don't know how to make a cake. We're going to have to change that because everyone should do it at least once."

His eyes trace my face before settling on my lips again. "Yeah? And who's going to teach me?"

"Me, of course. We can make one this evening and have it for dessert."

"Okay." He takes his cup and goes back to stand across from me again.

"Oh!" I blurt, remembering the woman I met years ago when Melody, Rani, and I went out. I bet the rides have started back up, and I'm sure Miss Cressida is all set up in her tent. She told me she'd never leave since it was the easiest money she made working there. "And as for the other item on your list, I know the perfect place to take you to get a tarot reading—the Berkeley carnival. Let's go check it out today, and then we'll come back and make that cake."

He takes a sip of his coffee and my hungry eyes flit to the little divot under his neck and his collarbone. Has a divot and a collarbone ever been so sexy? And that sparse hair covering the tops of his pecs with the silver chain hanging over it. Have I ever been this enamored with a male body before?

"You're an everyday genie, making my wishes come true." His voice pulls my eyes back to his face.

Not able to stand the distance between us, I leave my coffee and toast on the counter and pad over to him, getting up on my toes to kiss his lips. "Genies usually grant three wishes, you know."

He licks his lips as if he's licking up the taste of me and nods. "They sure do." He tilts his head toward the drawer where his list lies. "You might want to read the third item on there."

My brows dip. "Did you add another one to it? I just read the list a couple of days ago."

A devilish grin takes over his face, reminding me of a hunter assessing his prey with satisfied consideration, and I get the feeling I'm not going to love his third request. "Just remember, you're the one who said you owe me three wishes."

God, what have I gotten myself into? My gut tells me I might have spoken too soon, but I walk back to the drawer, lifting the list and reading the third item. It's scrawled in a different color pen than the others.

Yup, definitely spoke too soon.

I huff out a short laugh, turning back to him. "You can't be serious."

The asshole just takes another sip of his coffee before lifting his brow. "How convenient that we could cross off two items at one carnival."

"What?" I look back down and read the item again. "But how are we going to do this? Garrett, we're not teenagers anymore." Though the number of orgasms I've had since sleeping with my husband would argue that perhaps, I'm still a horny teen. "What if we get caught? This is . . . " I shake my head while Garrett watches my internal dilemma happen out loud. The good girl in me is actively warring with the wild child, who's telling me to let loose and have fun for once! "This is crazy. I'm a . . . I'm a mom. Would we even have enough time to . . .? And what if someone sees us? What if we get *arrested*?" I look up at him. "We could get arrested for this, couldn't we?"

"Are you finished with your overthinking?"

"G, pick something else. I'm not into public," I wave my hand in his direction for no better reason than to give myself time to process it and come up with a word, "displays."

He strolls over to me, all long legs inside his checkered pajamas. All bare feet and flexing abs. Ugh! Why does he always have to be so damn distracting?

"Are you reneging, wifey?" He frowns in disappointment. "Didn't think you were the type . . ."

Oh, this infuriating man. Why does it feel like he somehow always gets what he wants, all while making it seem like it's my decision?

I intake a fast breath, shaking my head. "Fine! But if we get arrested . . ."

He lowers his head to whisper in my ear, "Then I'll make jail time worthwhile for you." He thumbs my lips before leaning down to place a kiss on them. "Now get ready. We have a bucket list to get through today."

I watch the muscles in his back flex as he heads up the stairs, wondering for the umpteenth time how this man has managed to make my life feel both chaotic and complete at the same time.

And while the safe-loving, rule-following, overthinking girl inside me swallows her panic as she looks down at the third item on his list, the reckless girl inside me—the one who's been dying to come out for years—flashes an unrestrained and undeniable grin.

3. Fuck my wife on a Ferris wheel.

Yeah, Garrett Meyer is trouble with a capital T . . . but knowing that he's all mine might be the kind of trouble I'd like to have around all my life.

I GLANCE over at Garrett sitting next to me. His face reveals nothing to convey whether he's buying any of this, but knowing how polite and charming he is in general, I would never expect him to insult a person or experience. Especially not one he put on his own bucket list.

Miss Cressida has her eyes closed on the other side of the table, murmuring what I can only assume is some sort of chant or affirmation while I look around the familiar tent—purple drapes and crystals hang from the coned ceiling, swaying gently with a breeze I can't find the source of. A few flameless candles line all sides of the tent, along with painted skeleton heads.

On the table in front of us lies a burning incense stick, an array of stones organized in a circular fashion, and a deck of tarot cards. Based on the way the corners are frayed, I gather they're the same ones she used on me when I came here with Melody and Rani years ago.

I only remember bits and pieces of my own reading now. The part that stands out the most is when I turned over the last card—the one called *The Empress,* which had indicated my future. I recall the way Cressida had taken in a lungful of air and lifted both her dark, penciled-in and pierced brows. She'd held my eyes as if she was trying to press upon me how fateful the card had been, and I remember the way I'd rolled my eyes internally.

"Something huge is about to take place in your near future, my friend. Someone new, someone you'll love even more than yourself—the way a mother loves her child—is about to enter your life."

It was the beginning of my last year in college, and the only thing on my mind—besides blowing off some steam with my friends at a carnival and eating my weight in sugar—was lining up a job right after graduation. It was all that I'd worked my ass off for.

So, when I processed what Cressida was saying as she went on about how *The Empress* represented pregnancy and fertility, I exchanged glances with Rani and Melody and guffawed right in her face.

I mean, what a load of bull, right?

Right . . .

Garrett pulls my hand into his and brings it to his thigh while we wait for Cressida to open her eyes. I play with his wedding ring and smile when I glance at Meera's bracelet he's still wearing.

I'd asked him on the way over here why he'd put this item on his bucket list when he seemed rather skeptical of it, and he'd chuckled, saying he tended to challenge his own beliefs. And when I'd asked him how baking a cake was challenging his belief, he'd given me a side glance and said, "I don't *believe* in measuring stuff when it comes to cooking. It's unnatural."

Cressida opens her eyes before gently crossing her arms on the table, making her numerous bangles jingle. Both her hands and wrists are strewn with intricate tattoos, rings, and bangles, but it's not just her arms that are covered in tattoos and jewelry. There's an intricate rose inked over her bare shoulder and neck, and at least five gems sparkle from various locations on her face.

"Thank you for being here, my friends." She looks at me with recognition in her eyes. "I gather *The Empress* was right. How has motherhood been for you?"

My eyes widen at her impeccable memory, given that I haven't seen her in years and she's likely seen hundreds of people since then. I'm not only impressed by her recall, but by her confidence in her craft and abilities.

"It's been incredible, thank you for asking." I look over to see a quizzical look on Garrett's face before turning back to Cressida. "How did you know?"

Her sea-green eyes—a vivid contrast against her dark hair and brows—pick up the traces of light illuminating off the candles in the tent. "You're here, aren't you? I would venture to guess you wouldn't bring along your," her gaze drops to my ring finger and then to the gold band on Garrett's, "husband if *The Empress* hadn't been correct."

I offer her a smile. "I've told my husband a little about you, and he wanted to do a reading with you." I leave off the part about him challenging his beliefs and this being a bucket list item and all that. "We're both excited to see what his future holds."

Garrett introduces himself to Cressida, and she nods with a kind smile.

She waves over the deck of cards in front of her, looking at me. "As you know, the future can't be read without examining your past and your present. So, if you're ready, Garrett, let's get started."

She shuffles the deck in an intricate way, cutting it into thirds and then choosing to place one pile over the other, and doing it all over again until she seems satisfied. She spreads the cards face-down in an arc in front of Garrett, who watches her with quiet interest.

Cressida keeps her focus on Garrett. "Now remember, tarot cards will never be able to tell you exactly what will happen in the future. You make your own choices, but they can bring to light what is happening in the present and give you some insight for the future. The tarot works on your energy and the reader's intuition. Bring forth the energy you want before you choose the three cards. Remember, take your time before choosing—see if a specific card calls to you—and leave them face-down in front of you."

For his part, Garrett keeps his face neutral. If he is dubious, he's keeping his cards close to his chest. *Pun intended.*

He surveys the deck in front of him before pulling out three cards, and Cressida moves the rest of the deck aside, displaying his cards side-by-side.

She points to the first one. "This card will represent your past and offer an indication of what led you to this point." She turns the card and claps softly while both Garrett and I lean in to examine a rather unimpressive-looking picture of a bunch of sticks in front of a mountain. "Ah! I actually like seeing this card, and sure enough, it's faced correctly—toward you and not reversed. This is called the *Eight of Wands,* and it represents movement, speed, and travel." Her eyes crinkle at the corners. "I suspect your job has some travel in it, and perhaps the two of you had a whirlwind romance?"

Garrett and I look at each other with restrained surprise before he tells her he's a pilot and the two of us mumble our agreement for the whirlwind romance. I suspect, like me, he's also on the fence about how much of this is hocus-pocus versus just a great shot in the dark.

Garrett tightens his hand on mine and I squeeze it back.

Cressida flips over the middle card, representing Garrett's present, which has *The Lovers* written on the bottom of it and is also facing toward Garrett. "Well, this is no surprise at all, now is it?" she exclaims with an ear-to-ear smile. "*The Lovers* represents a blooming relationship. Most of the time this is romantic in nature, and looking at the two of you, I'd say that is what this represents for you. But this card also represents a choice. The choice that you, Garrett, have made in choosing your wife." She nods toward me. "The choice that you make every day when you choose her."

Garrett's gaze smolders as it meets mine, bouncing between my eyes. It's so intense that I swear, if Cressida wasn't in the room, we'd have our clothes off right now. He says a million words with that gaze, but he settles with, "I do choose her, every single day."

Cressida clears her throat to get our attention. "And for the last card here, that represents your future . . ." She flips it over and her smile falters at a multi-colored card with a picture of a wolf and a dog howling at a yellow moon. "*The Moon.*"

I see her shoulders slump slightly. "Well, this is interesting. *The Moon* represents a dark night—a period of difficulty and uncertainty. It may even come with unexpected turmoil. And while the moonlight itself can guide that uncertainty away, you must follow your intuition," she turns to me as if her words are also meant for me, "and believe that you'll get through it."

Garrett's brow furrows before his lips lift into a smile. "Difficulty and uncertainty?" He speaks to Cressida but turns to look at me, lifting the back of my hand to his lips. "With the amount of difficulty and uncertainty this woman has put me through already, I'm pretty sure I can handle anything in our future."

I give him a feigned dirty look, wrinkling my nose at him for his backhanded compliment, but I can't help giggling, knowing he's right. I haven't made it easy.

Cressida smiles but it doesn't reach her eyes like the last time. "I'm glad to hear that, and I wish you all the luck in the universe."

We're just on our way out after having thanked Cressida when she stops us, pulling a card from a small plastic bin against a wall of the tent. It's one for *The Lovers*. She hands it to me with a reassuring smile. "I know this reading was for your husband, but I have a feeling you'll need it more than him."

I look down at it with a frown, wondering why she thinks I'm the one who will need it more.

"Keep it with you to remind yourself of what you have when times get difficult. Remember that you are stronger than the forces against you, and that when it's true and meant to be, it will always find a way, no matter what challenges lie in its path."

And while Garrett sets his eyes on the next item on his list as we exit the mysterious purple tent, mine haven't moved off the card in my hand.

Chapter Twenty-Six

BELLA

I LEAVE ONE MORE LINGERING LOOK ON THE CARD BEFORE placing it at the bottom of my purse while walking alongside Garrett. My stomach tightens as I think about Cressida's words, but I remind myself that none of this is real. It's all for fun—or it was supposed to be, anyway—and no silly card can determine fate.

Garrett's hand shifts to my lower back as he directs us toward the enormous Ferris wheel at the center of the carnival.

The man is focused, that's for sure. Once he decides he's going to do something, come hell or high water, he's going to do it.

We get in line and my heart goes from a jog to an all-out sprint as my anxiety spikes. In an attempt to calm myself, I pull out my trusty box of rock candy and empty some into my mouth, crunching it vigorously.

While each bucket seems well-enclosed—with glass compartments with half-walls that would likely hide any nefarious activity happening inside—I'm scared we're still going to get caught. What if the ride operator calls us out on the loudspeaker? *Oh, God.*

Garrett's palms wrap around my face as he focuses on me, not giving a damn about anyone else near us in line. "Do you trust me, sweetheart?"

I nod in his hold. "This is just outside my comfort zone."

He's outside my comfort zone. And yet . . .

"I've got you." He rubs the tops of my cheeks with his thumb so affectionately, my rushing heartbeat settles into a casual stroll. "I've always got you. But just say the word and we can turn back right now. I will never force you to do something you don't want to do."

And just like that, I want to.

Just like that, I want to do so much more.

Say so much more.

"Garrett?" Oh, fuck. I can't even stop the words at this point as Garrett's inquisitive eyes assess mine. "I'm in lo–"

"Tickets."

Both Garrett and I blink out of our haze and turn toward the lanky man with thick dark curls, holding out his hand. For a second, I'm so confused, it takes me a moment to realize where I'm standing and that we've actually made it to the front of the line.

It seems Garrett is also taken aback because it takes him a second to process what the operator has asked before he pulls the tickets from his back pocket.

He keeps his hand firmly locked on mine as we're ushered over to a gondola. Another young girl with a similar uniform to the curly-haired operator ensures we're both settled into our seats before locking the swaying compartment's double doors.

Garrett watches me from his seat across from me with his head tilted back, giving me a chance to figure out my next step.

Just as the ride starts, I swallow my nerves and make my way over to him. Ignoring the natural wobble of the enclosed compartment and the creaking of the wheel as it ascends toward the sky, I straddle his lap.

He releases a breath as his hands clasp behind my back, and I casually look through the window behind him to survey our surroundings. And while I see another couple in the gondola next to us, I can't make out anything through the scratched windows. I settle my thumping heart with the assurance that if I can't really see them, then they won't be able to really see us, either.

Garrett's hands stroll up my back before one tightens under my jaw. "Are you sure?"

I nod, grinding down on his already thickening erection before lowering my mouth to his. I don't know how many turns this thing will do, but I recall rushing past a sign that said six and a half minutes. While I didn't get a chance to read it at length, I'm going to take my chances in thinking that's how long we have.

Garrett's mouth works against mine before my fingers make their way to his hair. I relax into his touch and his lips, fluttering my eyes closed, and when his mouth opens, my tongue finds its way in. I moan my appreciation of his taste, the feeling of him all around me.

My body starts to tingle, my toes curling inside my white sneakers as my hips roll over his lap, kneading his substantial girth.

Knowing what we were going to be doing, I'd worn a thigh-length flowy yellow dress with my jean jacket. I slide my hand down to rub Garrett through his jeans, and he takes in a sharp breath, pumping his hips into my hand.

"I want you," I whisper against his lips.

So far, he's given me a few moments to get settled with this idea, but he takes control the second the words are out of my mouth. His hand finds its way under my dress and to my dampening center. He shoves aside the thin lace and glides his middle finger in between my folds.

He pulls away from my lips and watches me with hooded lids. "You're already soaking and ready for me."

I unzip his pants and he lifts us to pull his pants and boxer-briefs down over his thighs. I work fast as the Ferris wheel climbs to the top, fisting Garrett's erection and stroking it.

"Jesus Christ," he mumbles as the softest flush takes over his neck. His Adam's apple bobs and his jaw hardens, watching me work him. "You have no idea what you do to me."

I lick up his neck, taking his earlobe into my mouth and sucking it before I slide his mushroom tip in between my heat. My head falls back, making me gasp at the sensation—soft and silky against wet and ready.

My nipples tighten inside my dress as my stomach contracts with anticipation. I need him like my heart needs to beat, like my lungs need air.

Garrett's hand slides up my dress, finding my bare breasts, and his eyes darken. "Fuck, you're so hot," he murmurs into my neck as his tongue sweeps over my heating skin.

I guide his tip into my entrance, and we both hiss as he penetrates my barrier. Pressing down against him, I start to inch my way down his shaft, taking his entire length inside me. My walls immediately clasp around him and Garrett groans. His hands come back to my hips as mine find their hold on his shoulders.

I pull off him almost completely before thrusting him back into me once, twice, and another time. My body feels like it's attached to a jumper cable as electricity courses through me. I stroke his silken hard shaft with my sex as I ride him, circling my hips as I come down on his lap.

The scent of us—his woodsy cologne mixed with a scent uniquely him and a scent I recognize as my own lust—permeates the air around us, making me feel delirious.

My stormy eyes find his calm blues, and a wave of something deep passes between us—an emotion so clear and so massive that it threatens to suffocate me from within. It's on the tip of my tongue and at the edge of my consciousness, ready to be free.

Garrett guides me up and down his shaft and I press my mouth to his, kissing him with everything I have. The sounds of our bodies thrusting against each other, mixed with our groans and heavy breaths, silence the world. Nothing and no one else exists in this little piece of serenity. Nothing and no one else matters.

Except for the man inside my arms.

The one I've waited for all this time.

"I love you," I whisper against his lips with my eyes closed. "I'm so in love with you, Garrett Meyer."

His hands cup my face as I accelerate my rhythm, reopening my eyes to find his gaze locked on mine, acknowledging the heft of my words.

There was nothing else left to do but to tell him. That he's the only one I've ever given my heart to and the only one it'll ever belong to.

Sweet fucking surrender.

It's a sensation like no other and a yearning clawing out through my every pore.

My chest starts to rise and fall with each breath as my core tightens around him, trying to milk him with each pull and every thrust. My walls are stretched around him in a perfect balance of pain and pleasure as he penetrates my senses and my wet center slides against him, drawing him in deeper.

Garrett's thumb finds my center, circling over my swollen

nub. His gaze seems unsteady, his nostrils flared, and his jaw tight. It's an expression I've become familiar with over the course of every intimate moment. He's close, and I'm right there with him.

"Give it to me, Bella. I need you to come on my cock right the fuck now."

It takes me two more thrusts, feeling the silky skin of his hardness inside me, hitting that sweet spot at the end of my channel. My body gives in, my back arching and my walls clenching as I succumb to the buzzing inside my core. I scream with my head thrown back as I undulate over him clumsily while tremors flutter across my skin.

My climax seems to last forever, making me pulse and quake as I moan through to the end. Garrett pummels me from below in a quick, steady blitz. My ass bounces on his lap as he tries to keep me pinned until his roar fills the small compartment. A warmth shoots up inside me, coating my ovaries before he lays his forehead on my shoulder.

We both gulp in lungfuls of air when I feel his lips on my neck. My eyes find his, and while I don't know how long it's been exactly, I can feel the wheel slowing down. I try to move off his lap but Garrett presses his fingers into my sides, holding me in place.

"There's not a single person on the planet for me besides you, baby. And every day that I think I couldn't love you more, I wake up to find out how wrong I am."

I crash against him again, my lips trembling as I hold back a sob bubbling through my throat, my lids barricading the emotion ready to spill over. I brush my mouth against his, showing him through my kiss everything I feel for him.

"Take me home, pilot."

～

I GIGGLE when the icing tickles my skin. "You're crazy, you know that?"

Garrett has his face in between my legs in bed and a cone of buttercream icing in one hand. After stopping at the grocery store to get the essentials after the carnival, we made chocolate cake from scratch. Surprisingly–or maybe not so surprisingly–Garrett was a natural. Then, we iced it using homemade buttercream icing.

And since there was some left over, what better way to use it than Garrett's brilliant idea of licking it off my lady bits?

He zigzags some icing on the outside of one of my folds, being careful not to get it near my entrance, before he lowers his mouth to lick it off.

I whimper when the softness of his lips and the scrape of his stubble meet my most sensitive skin and the sides of my thighs. He sucks on my fold, humming his appreciation, while his tongue moves back and forth, licking up every bit of the sugary confection.

I wiggle and squirm, squeezing the pillow behind me and arching into his adept mouth.

When he's done licking one side, he pops off–literally making that noise as he releases me from his mouth–one side and regards me with a heated gaze. "No one can blame me for wanting a little dessert before bed."

I pull my bottom lip into my mouth and watch him. His tousled blond hair sticks up around his head from my fingers being in it earlier. His long lashes flutter as he concentrates on covering my other fold, licking his lips as if he doesn't want to waste even a drop.

God, how could I have been missing this all these years? With him, no less.

His mouth lowers again and he proceeds to do the same thing with the other side of my sex. I tangle my fingers in his hair again, and Garrett goes to town, licking, sucking, slurping me until I'm gasping for air. Putting the icing cone aside, he inserts his first two fingers into my opening, and I jump to his mouth.

At this point, he's licked off all the icing and now his tongue is flat against my center, tasting me from bottom to top as he plunges his fingers inside me. I clench my eyes shut as a wave of lust rolls through me, and Garrett groans, the vibration of his voice rippling against my skin. I grind into his mouth unabashedly, almost pulling his head toward me to get what I need. His tongue swirls around my clit while his fingers curl against my walls, and I can feel myself get closer to the edge of release. He laps at me like he's been hungry for centuries.

Between the friction of his fingers and the caress of his tongue and lips, it takes no time before I'm screaming his name with a flash of white behind my eyelids. I roll my hips into his mouth a few more times, and Garrett doesn't let up until I'm nothing but a heap of flesh on the mattress. My usually restless brain feels like it's gone on vacation and doesn't plan to be back until next year.

Garrett moves back up my body, laying on top of me as he pulls me in for a kiss. I love the weight of him on me—solid and taut. I lazily scratch his back with my nails—something I've noticed he likes a lot—as I taste myself mixed with a touch of the buttercream flavor on his tongue.

He rolls off to lie next to me, before running his fingers through my hair and pulling on one of my purple ends. "You taste better than the cake or icing."

I snort. "Yeah, right. I just tasted myself on you and it was . . . interesting, but I wouldn't say better than the cake."

He shakes his head. "That's where you're wrong. See, anyone can make that cake, and sure it's sweet, but you . . .?" His hand travels down my stomach to the sensitive flesh in between my thighs. He swirls his middle finger around my swollen nub again before bringing it back to his mouth. "You're sweeter than any cake, and I'm the only one who gets to taste you."

"What about you?" I find the bulge straining through his pajama pants. "When do I get to taste you?"

"As much as I want to see my cock sliding through those pouty lips, I think we should get some sleep." He flicks his gaze to the clock on his nightstand. "It's nearly midnight."

I nod but a frown pulls at my lips. "And you have to get some rest before you fly out tomorrow morning."

He taps my nose. "I do, and you can't skip another day of work. I'll be back Saturday before you and Meera wake up."

I wrap my arm around him and he pulls me into his neck. "I'm going to miss you."

"I'll send you pictures of every sunset."

I look up at him and place a kiss on his jaw, loving the way his scruff feels on my lips. "I want you in them."

He brushes my hair back with his hand and my eyelids get heavier with his touch. "What do you think about driving to Tahoe this weekend to go see everyone?"

I smile into his skin. "I haven't seen Rani and her kids in forever, and I know Meera misses them, too." I look back at him. "But will it be weird? You know, with us being real and all now?"

Garrett chuckles, shaking his head with a sigh and tucking my head back under his neck. "Oh, my dear bullheaded wife. When will you ever realize that we were never anything but real?"

Chapter Twenty-Seven

GARRETT

I look down at my phone to read the message she sent me hours ago. Her response to the last sunset I sent her yesterday from Florida.

Bells: Come home to me. I miss you.

I hadn't gotten it until I landed at SFO early this morning, and I was too afraid to reply, thinking I'd wake her up. But I swear, that text was the only reason I sped home as fast as I could.

Picking up my suitcase to take it up the stairs, I put my keys inside the bowl next to the door. I'm barely up three steps when a movement catches my eye. I walk back down, making sure not to scare off our new family member after glancing at the half-open window.

Bella purchased a few items for the cats last week, including a small cat tree with a built-in compartment that the cats can hide in. And although I have yet to see Winky, Bella messaged me this week, telling me Winky made her way inside as well and snooped around for a bit.

I find two bright green eyes staring back at me from the opening in the cat condo. Brown Sugar paws the air as if she's trying to swat an invisible fly, and I decide it's as good a time as any to say hello properly. Thankfully, I'd taken my allergy meds before heading home so I'm not feeling the itchiness I would generally feel around cats.

Whispering to her in my most soothing voice and not looking at her directly, I inch closer and kneel in front of her little cat house. Bringing my hand closer to her, I wait for her to sniff it or give me an indication to let me pet her. Surprisingly, she moves her nose toward the backs of my fingers, sniffing and evaluating.

Just when I think she's either going to jump out of her house or retreat back inside, another head pokes out, startling me. I hadn't seen Winky's one eye, given I hadn't turned on the lights in the living room. And while she doesn't sniff my hand, giving me the same greeting as her daughter, at least she doesn't look at me with the same wariness as before.

I suppose I've learned a thing or two about winning over skittish moms.

I leave the cats alone, knowing one or both will likely go in and out of the house throughout the day and that making them into true house cats will take several weeks.

I'm just taking off my uniform inside my closet—ready to slip into Bella's room and into her bed until Meera wakes up and I have to sneak back to my room—when there's a soft knock on my bedroom door.

I poke my head out of my closet to see Bella in her skintight tank top, short shorts, and her woolen socks. Our eyes collide as soon as she closes my door and she instantly runs across the room. I've just managed to take off my uniform pants and am in nothing but my boxer-briefs when I open my arms and she launches herself at me.

She wraps her arms around my neck and her legs around

my back, and I place my hands on her ass, kissing up her neck and grabbing her earlobe with my teeth. Her hair is a curtain around our heads as she hugs me like she hasn't seen me in a decade.

I walk her to my bed, holding her like she's the most precious thing in the world and kissing her like she's my lifeline.

"I love you," she whispers.

"I know," I rasp.

Within seconds, we've shed every piece of clothing and I'm buried deep inside her, my balls slapping against the bottom of her mound, my hand covering her mouth, reminding her to stay quiet. My bed creaks with our weight while my body feels slick against hers.

We're desperate for each other, all lips and limbs, with nothing but each other locked inside our senses. Fuck, I love this girl. So fucking much, I can't think, I can't breathe . . . I can't live without her.

We come together with restrained moans, tightening our holds on each other before slowly coming down off our high, like a drug leaving our system.

We're breathing hard and facing each other when I lift to look at my door. Relief courses through me, seeing that it's locked, and I collapse back on my pillow, breathing hard.

Bella giggles but keeps her voice low. "You know, it's a little late for you to check the door at this point. She could have walked in and been traumatized for life if she'd seen us."

I run my palm over my face, chuckling softly. "Fuck. I'm not good at this, am I? Being any sort of parent figure in her life."

Bella gets quiet, and I open my eyes to see her regarding me tenderly. "I'd lost faith in a lot of things after my dad left . . . And then with everything that happened with Chaz . . . well, you already know how I felt about men and their role in mine and Meera's life. I didn't think we needed them."

She pulls my hand to her lips and lays a kiss in the middle of my palm. "But you changed all that for us, G. You made me believe again. Meera hasn't had a father figure–or even a grandfather for that matter–in her life. She's not just lucky to have *someone* like you, she's lucky to have *you*–specifically you. You've been more of a father to her than I ever expected, and no one could replace you. So, no, you're not good at this; you're incredible."

I tuck her hair behind her ear, letting her words resonate inside me. They mean more than she could ever know. We stare at each other for a long moment, like we seem to do often. "When do you think we should tell her about us?"

"Well, to be honest, I think she already suspects something is going on between us because I was talking to Melody and Rani a couple of days ago. I thought Meera was watching Dora; I didn't think she had her ears tuned into our conversation, but I should have known better."

"Uh-oh." I can guess where this is going. That little eavesdropper is always tuned into the things she shouldn't be listening to.

Bella squeezes her eyes shut, cringing. "I was telling them about the um . . . Ferris wheel–"

My eyes widen and I remember to keep my volume low. "What? Wait–"

Bella puts her hand on my chest. "Before you freak out, remember that Meera is too little to understand *that*, but she found out we'd spent the day at the carnival alone."

"Shit." I frown.

"Yeah, so that didn't go well, and she was almost in tears. I tried to explain to her why we went to the carnival without her."

"What did you tell her?" Fuck. I feel like shit for not

taking her with us because we totally should have. It would have been such a great little family outing.

Family.

Because Meera is nothing short of being my own.

"I took her out for ice cream after dinner that night and told her we had wanted to see a friend who worked at the carnival. I explained we only took one ride because we didn't want to enjoy the carnival without her and that we'd be coming back. It seemed to make her feel better, but she definitely suspected something between us."

"Yeah? Because we went on the Ferris wheel together?" The corner of my mouth rises in a crooked smile as the memory flits back to the forefront of my brain.

"I guess for a little girl like her, going to the carnival and riding the Ferris wheel with a boy has a more romantic connotation." Bella side-eyes me. "And we'll always keep it that way, because she will never ever want to know what really happened in there."

I wince. "She'll never see a Ferris wheel in the same way."

"No, she won't." Bella laughs softly before her expression turns thoughtful. "Though, I don't think she would be very happy if she found out we got married without her, either. And while I'd never expected to be married, I can't imagine ever having a wedding without her there. You know?" I nod as she continues, "Wendy had advised me not to tell Meera about the circumstances of our Vegas wedding because we wanted an annulment and it would have become a source of confusion for Meera."

I clear my throat, wanting to make sure she gets her facts straight. "*You* wanted an annulment; I just wanted *you*."

Bella rolls her eyes, throwing my own retort from earlier back to me. "Details."

I gently glide my fingers along her bicep as a thought stirs in my mind. "What if . . .?" My heart starts a trot inside my chest, and I clear my throat again. "What if we did it again?"

Bella's eyes ping-pong between mine. "Did what? Get married . . .?"

I nod, watching her expression carefully. "Would you marry me again? You know, after the court stuff is settled? No Vegas, no drunken vows, no charades. Just our truths."

I want to marry her with our families cheering us on, sharing the happiest day of our lives—my grams dressed in one of her fancy and frilly dresses she complains she never gets to wear enough—and forget the entire Vegas ordeal.

Bella's gaze caresses my face tenderly. "I'll marry you a hundred more times, my pilot."

"Grams, I want you to meet Bella and Meera." I wave to both my girls to get next to me in the camera so my grandma can see them.

I decided to video call Grams right before we left for Tahoe since I hadn't had a chance to catch up with her this week, and I knew I wouldn't have much time over the weekend, either.

Bella and Meera lean over me from both sides on the sofa, waving and saying hi to my grandma.

She beams back at us, and I'm happy to see her looking healthier than the last time we saw each other on video call. "Well, aren't you both a sight for sore eyes. I've been telling my Garrett that he's purposely hiding you from me."

I've been texting with Mom and Douglas regularly, as well as checking up on Grams, because I know if I leave it up to her, she'll never tell me exactly how she's feeling. Most of the time I just get a bunch of hand waving, halting me from asking more in-depth questions.

Thankfully, she hasn't had another stay at the hospital, but Grams' immune system has gotten weaker with time, and after her last stint with pneumonia, her lungs definitely took a bit of a hit.

"We don't want to be hidden anymore." Bella smiles up at me, the corners of her eyes lifting before she turns back to the camera. "I wish we could have met you in person for the first time."

"Oh, same here, dear. I've been told I give the best hugs in the family, so it would have been nice to give you a hug in person. Perhaps you both can fly over here with Garrett soon."

"We would love that!" Bella looks at Meera, who's being unusually quiet. "Right, Meerkat?"

Meera nods enthusiastically, giving up her bout of temporary shyness. "I'm going to be a pilot when I grow up, Grams."

A warmth creeps up inside me, and I see it reflected in my grandma's face at the sound of Meera calling her Grams. The kid has a way of winning anyone over.

"Well, that would be nice, wouldn't it? We need more women pilots in aviation," Grams responds.

I circle my arm over Meera's shoulders and squeeze her. My words are directed at Grams, but I smile down at the sassy little diva. "I'm going to take her to the aviation museum one of these days so she can see what the inside of a cockpit looks like and learn a little more."

Meera raises her index finger as if she's about to make a point, and one of her brows lifts accordingly. *Seriously, where does she come up with these dramatics? "After* you take me to the carnival." She looks at my grandma incredulously while my grandma looks as though she's never met a more interesting girl in her life. "Can you believe they went on a Ferris wheel without me, Grams? I've loved the Ferris wheel my *whole entire life!*"

Her whole entire *four years* of life, yes.

"Well, that doesn't seem very fair," Grams laments. "Sometimes you can see the best rainbows from that high up."

Meera gleams and then pouts again. "I love rainbows!" She turns to Bella. "Mommy, did you guys see a rainbow that day, too?"

"No, thankfully, we didn't, so you didn't miss much." Bella clears her throat and gives a pointed look to Meera. "But, you know, the last time I tried to get you on a Ferris wheel, you nearly cleared the carnival out with your screams because you were so scared."

Meera wraps her arms around herself, giving her mother an insulted look. "Mommy, that was when I was having my terrible threes. I'm bigger now."

"You're absolutely right," Bella concedes. "I apologize."

My grandma turns to look behind her on the camera, and I see my mom and Douglas appear on the screen. "Oh, there you are, Douglas and Jolene! Come say hi. I'm just talking to Garrett, Bella, and darling little Meera."

Grams hands over the phone to my mom and stepdad, and Mom immediately launches into telling Bella and Meera how beautiful they are. "Oh, Garrett has told me so much about you, Bella! We are so excited to meet you," she addresses Meera next, "and you too, Meera!"

Bella's face flushes, and I can tell for the first time she seems a little nervous. "Thank you. I can't wait to meet you both, either."

I know my mom well enough to know that when she gets that lilt in her voice, she's already thinking a mile a minute about the future. She's already hounded me a hundred times about letting her throw us a wedding party on the ranch that she and Douglas own in Colorado, and I've had to put the brakes on, telling her Bella and I are taking things slow. I'm sure Bella wouldn't mind my mother throwing a party, but I also know her first priority is the upcoming court date. Once that's all behind us, we can figure out another date for the wedding and a party.

As my mom continues chatting with Bella and Meera—not letting Douglas say much more than a few words—I get a gnawing feeling to remind her that Meera doesn't know about mine and Bella's current situation. A feeling to interrupt her before she blurts something that'll get us into a sticky situation.

I'm trying to figure out how to remind her without being obvious when I realize I'm already too late.

"I mean, you and Garrett make such a beautiful couple. I am just so thrilled to—"

"Mom," I cut in as Bella's face pales and she glances at Meera.

We both know that, while the kid may only be four, she's as sharp as a whip.

Realizing her mistake, my mom snaps her mouth shut, then mouths an 'I'm sorry' directed at me but for all of us to see . . . including Meera.

Yeah, thanks, Mom.

Meera's expression turns from confusion to a face-splitting smile as her eyes bounce between me and Bella. She jumps off the sofa, squealing like she just found out she got front-row tickets to a Nick Jonas concert.

"Mommy, are you Uncle Garrett's girlfriend now?! Is that why you went on the Ferris wheel? Did you kiss him?"

Bella's smile wobbles as she figures out how to address Meera's question grenades. "I . . . I suppose I am, sweetie. And um, yes," she gives me a secretive glance, "I suppose we did kiss on the Ferris wheel."

I bite the insides of my cheeks, trying but failing not to respond. "Just a peck though, because anything more would have been very unladylike of her."

The daggers Bella throws me with her eyes could stir the dead back to life.

Totally worth it, though.

Chapter Twenty-Eight

BELLA

Karine, Garrett's stepmom, takes a sip of wine from her glass, looking out at the backyard along with Rani and me. "He's a natural, isn't he?"

We're sitting on Darian's deck, watching the three brothers horse around, laughing with the kids. It's a little glimpse into their own childhood—three hellions who were as thick as thieves. Though, I get the sense that Darian was probably the most well-behaved of the bunch. Dean and Garrett on the other hand . . .? Yeah, not so much.

"Yes." I don't even have to ask her to clarify what she means. We're both watching my husband lift up my daughter with one arm so she can hand-walk across the monkey bars behind Rani's son, Arman. It's probably the twelfth time Meera has demanded he carry her, and he's done it with a huge grin on his face.

Garrett takes a swig from the beer bottle in his other hand before laughing at something that either Dean or Darian has said. As if he can feel my eyes on him, he turns to lock his gaze with mine and gives me one of his toothy, panty-dropping grins.

I sigh, smiling back.

He's perfect.

"Have you both talked about having more kids?" Karine's eyes gleam under the March sun before a light breeze has us all pulling our blankets around us a little tighter.

"Karine!" Rani leans over me to look at her mother-in-law incredulously. "They just made things official. Give them a br–"

"I know. I know." Karine lifts her hands in surrender. "But a mother can hope, right?" She looks at me. "Whether or not I gave birth to Garrett and Dean, I've never thought of them as any different than my Darian. They are all my boys. And I want you to know that even if Meera isn't my flesh and blood, I consider her mine, too . . . the same as Arman and Avya."

I reach for her hand, squeezing it in mine. "Thank you, Karine. That means a lot to me."

It's rare to find a family dynamic quite like the Meyers', where everyone–parents and step-parents, included–balances respect and affection for one another and genuinely likes each other.

Garrett and Dean's parents separated when the boys were quite young, but they made it a point to stay amicable. And when Marvin married Karine, she brought her strong sense of family values to the mix–accepting Garrett and Dean like her own.

"So, don't think I'm trying to put pressure on you, sweetheart." She tilts her head in the direction of the guys. "You see how close they are? It's a bond like no other. Your little girl should have a brother or sister of her own to feel that same love and connection."

"Karine . . ." Rani scolds her again.

But I don't mind Karine being candid with me; I get what she's saying. Seeing Garrett's relationship with his brothers, and the way he plays with, protects, and loves Meera like she's his own. . . I can't say the thought of having more children with him hasn't crossed my mind, either.

Having siblings is something I never experienced myself. While Rani and I were always close growing up, especially after Rani's late sister eloped with Darian when Rani was really young—which is a story on its own—it wasn't the same. We didn't live together; we weren't raised by the same parents or shared similar physical traits.

My mind wanders with images of what mine and Garrett's child might look like. Would he or she have my tan skin or his beautiful blue eyes? Would they have my dimples or his flashy smile? Would I see a reflection of Meera in them, too?

Meera's giggles float back to our ears, right before she hugs Garrett with one of her all-consuming bear hugs, and my mouth forms into a smile all on its own.

One thing is for sure, whatever our future children look like, they'll have the most incredible father.

"So?" Rani lifts a brow toward me while adding a few more items to the charcuterie board. "How are you feeling about the upcoming court case? Two more weeks, right?"

We're standing in her and Darian's kitchen while Darian, Dean, and Garrett hang out in the living room. Karine and Marvin left a couple of hours ago with the promise to come back tomorrow to say bye to us before we head back home.

I groan. "I just want it to all be behind us, you know? I can't stand the thought of that scumbag being in my little girl's life, but I also know I can't do much more than I'm already doing."

"I understand that," she says as a loud eruption of laughter commences between the guys, trailing over to the kitchen. "If Chaz does end up getting visitation with Meera, how are you going to break the news to her?" Rani's expression turns worried. "I can't imagine how confusing it will be for her."

I sigh, pinching the bridge of my nose. "I'm sure there's guidance on how best to do that. I just . . . I can only think about one thing at a time, you know what I mean?"

"Oh, honey, I don't mean to stress you out more than you already are." She places a hand on my forearm. "I'm just so glad you have Garrett in your life and you're not dealing with all this alone. I see how happy you are, Bells. I've never seen you so in love before."

I blush as the tension in my shoulders releases, thinking how he came barreling into my life all those weeks ago in the Vegas airport and turned it upside down and inside out with one startling and scorching kiss.

That one kiss sealed our fate forever.

"He wants to do it right." I think about our conversation from this morning. At Rani's quizzical expression, I clarify, "The wedding and vows. He wants us to redo them with our family and friends there."

Rani's mouth drops, her eyes widening to saucers. "Are you serious?" She doesn't wait for me to confirm. "Oh, my God. I am so excited. When? Where? Do you need any help?"

I giggle. "Settle down, tiger. One thing at a time, remember? Though, I think it'll be pretty soon after the court stuff is finalized."

Rani squeezes my arm. "I am so freaking excited, Bells. I can't wait to see you in a wedding dress." She fans her eyes with her hand. "God, I'm getting emotional already."

I pull my cousin into a hug. "I love you, sis. If I ever saw myself getting married—not that I ever really did—I always knew you'd be a part of it."

She squeezes me back. "I love you, too, and I am beyond happy for you."

A few moments later, once the emotions have settled, she asks, "Weren't you telling me and Melody on our last call that you have a party you're attending with Garrett at his boss's house next weekend?"

I nod. "Yeah, he has this St. Patrick's Day party that he invited us to. Apparently, he and Garrett go way back, so we're committed to going."

"Well, that'll be fun." She places some crackers on the cheese board. "I'm so glad to see that married life is going so well for you, babe."

I smile in earnest. "Yeah. It's—"

"Incredible, other-worldly," a deep voice that sounds a lot like my husband's proclaims from behind me. He kisses my neck, wrapping his arms around my stomach. "It helps that Garrett is a god in bed and has a superhuman di—"

I turn around, placing a hand on his mouth, giggling as I push him out of the kitchen while Rani wrinkles her nose. "Out of here, pilot. I wasn't even talking about you."

Garrett's eyes darken as he backs me up to the wall, out of anyone's line of sight. "If it was about our married life, then it had better only been me you were talking about, wifey. I don't want another man's name on this pouty little mouth."

I tilt my head up, getting that daring look in my eyes. "Possessive much?"

He nods slowly. "Yeah. Possessive, selfish, greedy, hungry. I'm all of those things when it comes to you."

I wrap my arms around his neck. "Yeah? And what if I was talking about someone else?"

Garrett's nostrils flare. "Then I'd say you're due for another spanking, Mrs. Meyer."

I lift on my toes to reach his ear. "Is that a promise, Mr. Meyer?"

God, the thought of his handprints on my ass, the zing of pain and pleasure that will roll up my body. I must be maniacal and depraved for wanting to find an excuse to get out of joining the others in the living room to have my husband make good on his word.

In fact, if it wouldn't have looked so suspicious, I'd drag him to our room upstairs right this second. I'd kneel in front of his hard-as-stone erection, paying homage to it until he erupted inside my mouth.

Garrett squeezes my ass, just as I palm the bulge at the front of his pants. "Bella."

"Mommy!" I hear Meera yell, and we both release each other abruptly as if we've been scorched. "Rani *masi,* have you seen my mommy?"

"She'll be back soon, honey." I hear my cousin reply. "I think Mommy and Uncle Garrett decided to have a quick, uh, *workout.*"

I turn to walk back toward Meera when Garrett's hand clasps around my wrist. His eyes reflect a fire that's anything but snuffed. "You better believe we'll be resuming this later."

I give him a look that says he doesn't need to tell me twice before heading back to find Meera.

"Oh, Jesus. Fuck!" Garrett hisses. "Goddamn, you're good at that."

I hum, looking up at him from my perch between his legs. Thankfully, I remembered to snag a small cushion from our guest bed and placed it under my knees before I started.

I have my mouth wrapped around one of Garrett's balls and am rolling it on my tongue, while he mumbles something incoherent. His back leans against a wall behind him, and he has his legs spread out in front with me in the middle.

I have never felt more powerful as I do now, with him so lustfully delirious and at my complete mercy.

I stroke his long, thick cock while I move my mouth to his other ball, doing to it what I just did to the other–sucking and rolling it on my tongue, then popping off and doing it all over again. All the while pumping his silken rod in my fist.

"Oh, fuck, yeah," Garrett whispers as his breaths pick up.

I shift on my knees, using my pointed tongue to whirl around his mushroom head, tasting the bead of precum on top. I love the taste of him. I suck on his tip, passing over it again and again with my tongue, thoroughly massaging it until he's practically about to explode.

"Put me all the way inside your mouth, baby."

I lower my mouth over his girth, visualizing how it must look to him to see it completely stretched over him. Keeping my hand at his base, I bob my head up and down his length. I flatten my tongue to get him deeper inside until his tip hits the back of my throat, and I suppress my gag reflex.

Garrett wraps his fist around my ponytail possessively, guiding my head and driving into my mouth. "I want you choking on my cock, smearing that red lipstick all over it." He draws out and then pushes back in. "That's it, sweetheart. Keep doing just that. Let me fuck your mo–" He hisses abruptly, "Oh, fuck."

I pump him, hollowing out my mouth as I continue to suck and lick, feeling my own sex clench with desire. My thong feels uncomfortable against my wet skin as a wave of my juices drench it.

I moan over Garrett's erection, and he pumps his hips faster into my mouth. "You ready to swallow me down, baby?"

I hum my agreement, wrapping my hands around him and squeezing his firm ass. It's taut with all the tension vibrating through his body. The sound of my mouth working over his thickness mingles with his low grunts as I milk him for everything he has.

Within seconds, his entire body stiffens and a gush of salty liquid cascades onto my tongue. I swallow it all, slowing my hand strokes.

Garrett looks utterly spent, yet still so ridiculously gorgeous as he peers down at me with hooded eyes. He helps me to my feet and brings his hands to cup my neck. "Fuck, I love you so much. I want to marry you."

I chuckle softly. "Yeah?"

"Yeah."

I brush my lips against his. "Well, if you get up the courage to ask me, I might just say yes."

Chapter Twenty-Nine

BELLA

The sounds and smells of food being mixed in their bowl has Brown Sugar appearing inside the kitchen from around the corner. She sits in attention, watching my movements carefully as I spoon out the last bits of her wet food to mix into the dry cat food.

"Is someone hungry?" I murmur, and her head tilts just a little as if she were trying to read my lips. "Where's your momma?"

I look up from the bowl to see if I can find my ever-elusive momma cat. I know she's inside the house because, over this past week, I've closed the window in the evening so she can't get out.

I had to open it back up after an hour or so the first day when I heard Winky meowing and scratching at the glass, but each day after that, she allowed me to close it for longer. Last night I had it closed all night and opened it this morning, and I plan to do the same tonight.

Thankfully, Brown Sugar seems to have adjusted for the most part. She's still a little skittish with loud noises and comes out to inspect things in her own time, but otherwise, she's adjusting and even lets us pet her.

Winky, on the other hand . . . She's a whole different animal. Though, I do take it as a positive that both cats allowed us to take them to the vet this week. Okay, so maybe I'm using the word 'allowed' loosely, but they didn't put up as much of a fight as I expected when I put them in the pet carrier. That didn't mean they didn't vocalize their disdain, meowing through the entire drive there and back.

But at least they're both up to date on their shots and have been treated for fleas. And it's no secret that they both look healthier and just overall better.

I lower the two bowls to the ground, knowing Winky will eat when she's ready, before inspecting myself once more in the mirror.

Per the instruction on the invitation from Garrett's boss to wear green, I'm wearing a solid-colored, ruffle-hemmed dress that lays at my thighs with a deep V-neck. It makes me feel extra feminine, though I can't say I love how the purple tips of my hair contrasts with it.

I'm not going to change my signature hair color for one evening, though.

I pick up the gold chandelier earrings from the table I'd placed them on when I came downstairs and thread them through my earlobes. So, aside from the tall gold heels I plan to wear, I'm ready to go.

Garrett was in the shower when Mom came to pick up Meera fifteen minutes ago, so I'm sure he's ready by now.

His footsteps on the top of the stairs tell me I'm right.

My breath gets caught in my lungs as I watch him roll up the sleeves of his green button-down, brandishing his veiny forearms and those long fingers I love so much. And, as usual, he's wearing his bulky watch on one wrist and his favorite beaded bracelet on the other, along with his gold ring on his fourth finger.

"Hi." His eyes home in on me. "You look stunning."

"Thank you," I respond, looking down at my dress again. Somehow his piercing eyes always make me feel exposed, and I have to take a moment away from them to find my bearings. "You do, too."

He ambles over, towering above me. "A part of me just wants to slide that dress off you, bury my face inside that endless cleavage while I bury my cock even deeper inside you, and forget any other commitment for the night."

My face heats as my mind conjures up the image. "A part of me wants that, too–"

"Good." Garrett starts pulling me toward the couch.

I giggle, urging him back. "But we promised Pete we'd be there." At Garrett's frustrated huff, I continue with a coy smile, "How about I don't take this dress off until you take it off me tonight?"

His jaw ticks as he thinks about my offer. "How about you take off your underwear and at least give that to me to hold?"

My brows rise. "And go commando?"

He nods, his eyes swirling with carnal desire. "I like the idea of being the only one to know you're completely bare under that dress for me. That all I'd have to do is pull you into a room, flip it over your ass, and sink inside you without a single thing in the way."

I keep my eyes on him as I raise my dress to my hips, hooking my thumbs on the sides of my thong. Garrett's breathing accelerates as I pull my thong down until it drops to my feet, and he kneels to pick up his prize.

Stuffing the tiny fabric inside his pocket, he raises my dress and brazenly places his nose on my exposed sex, inhaling me like he's taking a whiff of dinner on an empty stomach.

"Fucking heaven," he rasps.

Bringing my heels to my feet, he lifts one, silently urging me to slide in.

I try to protest, placing my hand on his shoulder for balance. "You don't have to–"

"Shh." He focuses on his task, buckling my shoe in place and moving to the next one with a slide of his fingertips at the back of my ankle. "I want to."

This man. How does he go from being lecherous one moment, to a gentleman the next without so much as a blink? I swear, I am always reeling from a state of whiplash whenever I'm with him.

And though we sit in comfortable silence through the car ride there, with Garrett's fingers threaded through mine, my mind is anything but quiet.

Sometimes I feel like I'm bubbling over with emotion for him, but other times, I wonder if he's even real.

Could this really be real? Could any man be this thoughtful and dedicated? Especially a man who, by his own admission, has never been so with anyone else before me.

My fingers hover over the side of my thigh, waiting to pinch myself awake, but I pull them back. Because if this is a dream, I want it to last longer.

I want it to last forever.

"Oh goodness, me! You are just as lovely as Pete said you were," Brooke proclaims, keeping my hand in between her warm ones. Her short black bob is tucked neatly behind her ears, which sparkle with two-carat emeralds that match the color of her blouse. She looks over at Garrett. "You did well for yourself, Garrett. How did you manage to snag her?"

Garrett looks pointedly back at her. "I got her drunk in Vegas and married her before she could think better of it."

Both Pete and Brooke throw their heads back, laughing heartily. Brooke's eyes glimmer with mirth. "You are such a kidder. You're the last person on the planet who would need to get someone drunk to marry you, Garrett." Her smile turns to me. "Well, whatever the real story is, I'm sure it's special. One thing is for sure, Bella; this man will always keep you laughing." She pulls back and loops her arm around her husband's. "And that is the key to a happy marriage."

Pete leans toward Garrett with a hand on the side of his mouth, like he's letting him in on a secret, even though he's loud enough for both Brooke and me to hear. "Well, that and doing the dishes every night, protecting her from spiders, and not getting her birthday confused with our anniversary."

Brooke playfully smacks her husband's bicep with the back of her hand. "Oh, stop it. Last I recall, I was the one you were asking to get rid of that spider."

"Did you see how big it was? I'm pretty sure it was a female spider, too. I figured I'd have you squash her since you ladies all seem to have an unspoken understanding amongst yourselves. I didn't think she'd hold it against you as much."

We all chuckle, standing under the string lights in their backyard and enjoying the soft breeze and the drinks in our hands. Another couple joins the group, introducing themselves to me and Garrett before carrying on a new conversation with Pete and Brooke.

I look around at the beautifully decorated backyard with St. Patrick's Day decor and an array of food laid out on both sides. There's even a waitstaff mingling around, offering various green-colored cocktails—two of which I've already consumed and am feeling rather nice and loose from—and Irish beer on large platters to the hundred or so guests chit-chatting in small groups.

Breaking away from his conversation, Garrett presses his mouth to my ear. "Hungry?"

I nod. "A little. You?"

"Just for that bare pussy."

I shudder as heat collects in my cheeks, and I bite my lip, trying to hold myself together. Meanwhile, Garrett goes back to the conversation he was having as if he'd never left it.

After a few minutes, I leave Garrett to chat with some new acquaintances and head over to the hors d'oeuvres table. I know all too well what happens when I drink on an empty stomach, and I'd like to keep my wits about me this time.

I'm just placing what looks to be like a smoked salmon and mandarin orange canapé on my plate when the light-hearted notes of some women laughing flutter into my ears.

I'm still focused on picking out the next hors d'oeuvres to put on my plate when my hand halts over some stuffed cherry tomatoes.

"So, did you hear Captain Garrett Meyer got married?" one of the women asks. It's clear from her tone that she finds Garrett getting married amusing. "I mean, can you even imagine him settling down?"

I glance up, seeing three women chatting around a bar table nearby, oblivious to my eavesdropping. There's a beautiful and put-together brunette, who looks familiar—I'm almost certain she's the same woman who spoke to Garrett at the gala. I recall her seeming stunned when he told her he was married.

The brunette giggles, but there's an underlying wickedness to her laugh. "No, I definitely cannot."

"Ally, didn't you guys . . .?" another asks, leaving her last words to interpretation.

The hair at the back of my neck rises, but I swallow through the jealousy trying to taint my vision. I already knew Garrett had a colorful past—it's what kept my heart guarded around him in the first place. But knowing is different from seeing, and now that I've seen, I have a sudden urge to stab something.

"Yeah, I mean, it was just sex. You know I couldn't develop feelings for him because of . . ." She tilts her head in the general direction of where a group of men are mingling, but I have no idea what she means. "Plus, it's not like I was the only one. I'd venture to guess he dipped his cock inside almost every flight attendant by the time I left that airline."

One of them sighs. "Well, you still got fucked over, didn't you? It took you, what, almost four years to finally be in a better place with *you-know-who*? Did you even tell him who it was?"

What the hell are they talking about, and who is 'you-know-who?'

Ally twists the cocktail glass in front of her. "Just recently, yeah."

Huh?

The other one purses her lips. "Anyway, guys like Garrett don't change. And even if, by some miracle, he *did*, how long could it really last? We all know how hard marriage is." At this, Ally mumbles something I can't quite hear before the other woman continues, "It's a long term commitment. And while I don't know the guy well, he's hardly the type to be there for someone when times get tough."

At this, bimbo-brunette—a.k.a, Ally—chimes in, "No, definitely not. Some men are marriage material, while others are fuckboys. And I've always known which category Garrett falls into."

The reverberation of the anger rising inside me feels almost uncontainable, like the percussion of an enormous gong hit with so much force that it stifles all other sounds nearby. I'm practically coming out of my skin as my molars grind inside my mouth.

How fucking dare they? How fucking dare they even speak his name when they know nothing about him? The man has more devotion and commitment at the tip of his pinky finger than they do in their entire body. Fucking skank-ass bitches!

And that over-Botoxed brunette bitch, Ally? She's just jealous because he didn't marry her! She's jealous that he barely even acknowledged her presence, even when she tried to imply they had a recent tryst in Vegas. I still remember how her face fell when he rectified her misunderstanding by putting her in her place.

But I need to cool it.

I can't lose my shit and embarrass Garrett like that.

I've almost convinced myself to walk away, to ignore the stupid women who have nothing better to do than be bitter about men they pine over, when one of them asks, "Has anyone seen what his wife looks like?"

Ally snorts. "Unfortunately, yes. Let's just say he down-graded, *big* time. For one, the woman has *purple hair*, like some sort of comic book character. And two, she had this stupid smile on her face the entire time I watched them dance. Like Garrett was the reason the sky was blue. What an idiot."

The other women laugh and one of them says, "Bless her heart. She's in for a rude awakening."

I don't even know what propels my feet forward—possibly the alcohol mixing with my newfound rage. One minute I'm standing over the appetizers, looking to figure out if I can fit the crab cakes on my plate, along with the nachos, and the next minute, I'm closing the distance between me and the mean girls' table.

Their shock at my approach registers seconds before I pick up a cocktail from their table and empty the contents on blowjob-brunette's lap. "You're right." I sneer. "Garrett *is* the reason my sky is blue. Unfortunately, yours is looking a bit dank and stormy at the moment."

The other two ladies gasp, getting out of their seats while it takes the brunette a second to even register what just happened and why her overpriced white silk skirt is now stained green. I'm not surprised, though. All that dick she sucked over the years probably gave her permanent brain damage.

Ugh, and now, I've lost my appetite.

I walk away with my spine straight—the wild child in me proudly raising her head at my ability to both shut Ally up and not draw any attention to myself. In fact, besides her bitchy friends and a couple of waitstaff, no one seems to have noticed.

Well, no one except a handsome man with tinsel hair and blue eyes, set in astonishment in my direction as he tracks me strutting toward him. Suffice it to say, he might not have heard the conversation, but he definitely saw my reaction.

I don't even let him speak. Grabbing Garrett's hand, I drag him behind me, my *comic book purple* tips flying in the breeze. "You know how you promised to peel this dress off me and fuck me into oblivion? Well, I'm going to need you to deliver on that, right this second, pilot."

Chapter Thirty

BELLA

I feel frantic.

Frenzied, delirious, and a little tipsy as I pull Garrett toward Pete's house, hoping to not run into anyone on our way there.

I'm in such a lustful delirium, I only barely register Ally screeching gritted words to a brown-haired man in a white shirt before she storms off through the gate.

Good riddance.

Towing Garrett behind me as we enter the house, I open a door, realizing it's a garage. I continue, practically running to another door on the right. I twist the knob, finding it open. *Oh good, it's a bathroom.*

I close the door behind us and shove Garrett's back against it, reaching up to cover his mouth with mine. My hands tremble as I start to unbuckle his belt.

"Fuck, if I knew dumping a cocktail on someone would turn you on this much, I'd have made all sorts of drinks and offered myself to you every day," he mumbles under my lips, his smile evident.

His hands dip down to my waist, wrapping around both

sides, as I shove my chest into his. God, I need him inside me. Right now.

"Bells," Garrett says, his hand tightening to get my attention.

I don't respond; instead, I pull his head forward to deepen our kiss, urging him to open his mouth. He does, letting me explore with my tongue. Letting me suck and tangle his tongue with mine.

"I want you."

"I can see that," he states before pulling away from my mouth. "Bells, baby, slow down–"

I shake my head, panting. "I don't want to talk about it, pilot. Just know, they were bitches. Awful, terrible bitches, and I couldn't stand there and let them spew their bullshit about you." I look at the door urgently. "We don't have that much time. Other people will want to use the restroom."

His large palms cup my face as a smirk plays on his lips. "You defended my honor?"

Clearly, he's in no rush, given he ignores my *hurry-the-fuck-up-and-screw-me* because *others-will-want-the-restroom* argument.

I jab my index finger into his chest. "You're damn right I did. And I always will."

He leans down to press his mouth to mine. "Goddamn, you're cute. The way you looked when you turned around after pouring that drink on her . . . You had fire in your eyes." He tugs on my hair. "Like my very own rabid, purple-tailed unicorn."

My finger presses harder into his chest. "I'm not sure if that was a compliment, but if you don't fuck me right this second, so help me God, I will throw you out and do it myself!"

Garrett's eyes immediately darken to an almost onyx

color. He points his chin at something behind me. "Get your ass up on that counter."

He doesn't have to ask me twice. I practically jump on the vanity behind me.

His eyes scroll up my legs, halting at my heaving chest, admiring my cleavage, before stopping again at my lips. "Slide that dress up your thighs and open your legs for me. Show me what's mine."

I do as he asks, my body heating up underneath the dress. I open my legs brazenly and Garrett licks his lips, getting an eyeful of my bare sex.

"Run your fingers through that wet center." When I do, my head falls back and I take a deep breath. "Swirl them around your little clit. Get it nice and swollen for me."

I pleasure myself with my fingers as a tingle starts up inside my core. My entrance grows wet, dripping my juices over my fingers and I hiss in response. I pinch my folds and circle my clit over and over.

"That's it. Keep doing that." Garrett's hand wraps around his hard-on under his pants before he drops to his knees.

I'm just about to press my fingers into my entrance when he tugs them aside, replacing them with his mouth.

I moan at the contact—his hot, wet tongue at my entrance, suckling me. It only takes him a few swirls of his flat tongue around my clit before I'm arching my back and coming fervently. My body pulses as my walls contract and a tidal wave of need flows into Garrett's mouth.

He drinks me up like a parched plant in the desert, holding me steady with a hand pressed over my belly.

And as soon as I'm done, he pulls up to his feet. "Get down and face the mirror."

God, that voice and that commanding tone.

He helps me down and I turn toward the mirror, taking in my appearance for the first time since we left the house.

I look exactly like I feel, frenzied and crazed. My hair is tangled on one side–though, I'm not sure how it got that way–my cheeks are flushed, and my lips look bee-stung.

Garrett taps the inside of my thigh with the back of his hand. "Spread wider for me, sweetheart."

When I do, he drops his pants, pulling out his hefty length. And while I can only see him from his waist up in the mirror, the way he's looking down at my ass gives me a good idea of what he might be doing. I see his forearm tense as he strokes himself, and then I feel his tip glide through my wet center.

I wrap my hands around the faucet, preparing myself to take his entire length, when a knock on the bathroom door has us both locking our eyes in the mirror.

But we're too far gone to care.

I'm considering saying something when there's another knock, but right as I find my voice, Garrett delves inside me with a low grunt in one powerful thrust.

My voice gets stuck inside my throat and I remind myself to breathe, even as my opening feels stretched to the max. And right when I think I'm finally getting comfortable, Garrett pulls almost all the way out, then sinks back in.

My mouth falls open with a silent scream as he does it over and over, drilling me from behind with his fingertips digging into my waist.

I look up to see the same crazed look in his eyes that's currently in mine, loving the sheen of sweat above his brows.

His low growl has my attention as he rubs his palm over one of my ass cheeks. "Is this mine?"

I heave in a breath. "Yes."

He pulls out and shoves himself deeper inside me, hitting my G-spot. "Is this mine?"

I drop my head, tightening my grip around the faucet. *Fuck, how am I going to explain it if this faucet pops off?* "Yes."

And then his thumb circles over my most private hole. *Oh, God. Oh, no. Please don't ask if–*

"Is this mine?"

My widened eyes lock with his in the mirror and he awaits my response, unrelentingly plundering into me. I nod as a slight tinge of fear rolls up my throat. "Y-yes."

He smirks and just when I think he's going to explore that uncharted area, his palm comes down hard on my ass. I hiss, holding back another scream.

At this point, I have no idea who can hear us or whether they've given up waiting for this bathroom. Because, frankly, I don't give a shit.

As my body ramps up to an impossible height, I breathe through gritted teeth. "I'm going to come, Gar–"

But before I can even finish my sentence, another climax steals my breath, coursing through me like a torrent. With the blood rushing against my ears, I barely hear Garrett's throaty groan, but I know he's coming when I feel him flood my insides.

I practically collapse over the sink, ready to fall asleep right here, when Garrett curls over me, kissing my temple. "I love you, my rabid little unicorn."

His words have an image of blowjob-brunette's stunned expression floating to my forethought, and it's all I can do to not howl in laughter.

My entire body shakes as a laugh ripples through me.

Before we know it, both Garrett and I are holding our stomachs, him leaning his back against the wall and me wiping my tears with my other hand.

Bless her heart, that green stain is never going to come out.

BY SOME SHEER MIRACLE, Garrett and I are able to leave the restroom unseen. I'm not even going to lie and say I didn't have to work hard to put myself back together. After a few slides of my fingers into my hair to get the knots out and touching up my lipstick, I thanked the lord above when I found one of those sample perfume sticks in my clutch. Because not only do I look like I was banged all the way to Sunday, but I smell like it, too.

Somehow, my husband doesn't seem to share my problem. He neither looks nor smells freshly fucked. In fact, I'd go as far as to say the slight tinge of color on his cheeks and his slightly ruffled hair makes him look better! The big jerk!

A group of well-dressed men yell for Garrett, waving him to join them as soon as they see us. And with my stomach growling loud enough to clear the party, I give Garrett a quick kiss, letting him know I'll be at the hors d'oeuvres table and will bring him back something.

Dammit, the tray with the smoked salmon canapés is empty. Those bitches not only ruined my night, but they kept me away from the good appetizers, too.

Loading up my plate with a couple of potstickers and what looks like caramelized onion flatbread, I'm just turning back to find Garrett when a throat clears at my side.

Goddammit! Why won't anyone just let me eat in peace today?

I don't usually get hangry, but I imagine this is what it feels like.

I turn around to face the vaguely familiar man. His pale green eyes aren't quite as striking today as the first time we met. Perhaps because they're being drowned out by the sea of green around us or perhaps because blue is more my color.

If I'm correct, he also seems to be wearing the same white shirt with four-leaf clovers on it as the man who was speaking to an irate Ally before she stomped out earlier.

"Bella, am I right?"

I'd already decided I didn't like him at the gala based on the condescending tone he took with Garrett, so I have no reason to play nice. Clearly, I'm on a roll tonight. "*Daniel.*"

"Uh, *David*," he corrects and I force my lips not to twitch. "Wow, you look even more beautiful in green than you did in the golden number you wore at the gala."

I look past his shoulder, seeing Garrett's back arch as he howls with laughter at something one of his friends has said. God, he is impossibly gorgeous.

Smiling through my disdain for the guy keeping me from joining my husband, I slide my gaze back to him. "Great memory; I barely recall what I wore that evening."

"Oh, I remember everything." His eyes trail down to my cleavage. "But you're the type to leave an impression."

I'm two seconds from *leaving an impression* of my fist on this guy's nose. He picked the wrong night to mess with me. I'm amped up on adrenaline, a couple of strong cocktails, and an open vendetta against anyone who so much as breathes in my husband's direction the wrong way.

And this guy's breath reeks of contempt.

Still, I'm not in the mood to make yet another scene tonight—one was already over my quota—and I try to slide past him. "Then it would behoove you to *remember* I'm married," I mumble the next part, though not entirely trying to stay under my breath. I just want to make my point clear for him to stay away from me. "To a man who isn't a scumbag like you."

I've taken a few steps when the arrogant asshole turns around, snickering.

Because what do arrogant assholes need most in life? The last word.

"Open your eyes, *princess*. Your *husband* is hardly the embodiment of morality."

I whirl around, even as my brain tells me to walk away.

What the fuck does that even mean, and why does it feel like everyone is out for Garrett tonight? "At least my husband doesn't hit on married women."

The asshole has the audacity to find a casual stance, tucking his hands into his pockets, while my spine stiffens. And then he laughs, though there's nothing sincere about the sound. "He must really have you fooled." His eyes slide to look at the empty table that Ally and her friends were sitting at earlier. "But if you think Garrett Meyer is above fucking around with married women, then you're the one who's purposely choosing to be in the dark."

I reel back, giving him another disdainful look. "You don't know anything—"

"Oh, but I do," he huffs. "Because your husband is culpable for my marriage ending four years ago." He looks off over my shoulder before finding my astonished eyes. "You see, I was once married to the woman you doused with that cocktail. That is, until your *saint* of a husband decided he didn't give a shit about anything but getting his dick wet."

No.

No, there must be a mistake. A misunderstanding.

Garrett would never do that.

Before I can piece everything together and ask him anything more, David turns and walks away into the crowd.

I don't know how long I've been standing at the same spot because it's only when a familiar hand wraps around my waist that I jolt out of my haze.

"Everything okay?" Garrett's soft eyes assess my face.

It feels like there's glass stuck inside my chest. "Um, yeah. Fine."

His face screws up, studying me as if he's trying to read between the lines of my words. "Are you sure?"

I nod, but a frown pulls my mouth downward. "I actually

don't feel so good all of a sudden. Would it be okay if we head back? I'm sorry, I know you wanted–"

"Of course we can head back." Garrett cups my face. "I don't give a shit about anything but you. Let's get out of here."

～

'B*UT IF YOU* think Garrett Meyer *is above fucking around with married women, then you're the one who's purposely choosing to be in the dark.*'

My stomach turns and I take in a deep breath, pushing the button on the passenger door to roll down the window.

Garrett's gaze swivels in my direction. "Sweetheart, are you okay? Do you need me to pull over?"

No, I need you to tell me that that asshole was lying. That you would never do anything to play the part in ruining someone's marriage. That you're exactly who I know you to be–kind, generous, loving, and loyal.

I shake my head. "No, I'm just . . ."

Garrett watches the road ahead. "You have a lot on your plate, Bells. Next week's court date, a demanding job, and having to do everything on your own for Meera since I'm barely home to help."

My brows fold and I look at him. How could this man–a man who feels responsible for me and my daughter, a man who doesn't owe us a thing but continues to give us more of him–be capable of ripping someone's marriage apart?

Why is two plus two not adding up to four?

Garrett grasps my hand, bringing it to his thigh. "Take it easy on yourself. It'll all work out. You have one of the best lawyers on your side."

God, he has no clue.

And he wouldn't because I haven't said a word to him.

Why? Because, frankly, I'm trying to wrap my head around if I actually should be upset about something he did in his past or if I just need to let this go.

There's no way I can deny what he did was shitty. Especially given how adamant he was about our vows and faithfulness to each other, even when we got married under false pretenses.

And I have no doubt in my mind he would never step out on me—I know that inside my bones, inside my marrow. He loves me and Meera too much to ruin it.

Not once have I felt like he's given me anything less than the love he says he feels for me. Not once have I felt like he wasn't one hundred percent devoted to me. Not once have I seen anything but sincerity oozing from his pores.

So, if he was responsible for dissolving someone's marriage, I know at my core, he wouldn't ever do that again. And he'd never do that to us.

Then should I hold a mistake he made years ago against him now, when he's made all these strides to change? Should I question his faithfulness and loyalty toward me when I just went to bat for him and my gut says he doesn't deserve that.

That sounds pretty fucking unfair to start voicing my concerns or doubts or whatever these are when I haven't even thought them through.

But a thought keeps nagging at my brain.

Why didn't he tell me?

Why not give me that piece of himself when I've told him so much about me—my history with heartbreak, my history with unreliable men?

Because he thought you'd close up again after everything he's done to bring you closer.

Because, from the very beginning, you've branded him as a player and a womanizer, and he's had to work hard to prove you wrong.

Because telling you something like that would have thrown you backward into that guarded cage you preferred for so long.

I stare out the window, letting the cool breeze waft over my skin and distract me from my thoughts. I feel like I'm on a seesaw, vacillating between what I know of the man I love—what I've experienced firsthand—and a version of him I've only heard about. A version that existed prior to us, prior to what he says was before me entirely.

But which one do I believe?

Who do I trust? The recently pieced-back together organ inside my chest, urging me to take him at his word and his actions, or my ever-suspecting brain, telling me maybe, just maybe, I don't know my husband as well as I thought I did?

Chapter Thirty-One

BELLA

Eight-fifty-one AM.

I look back down at my phone for what feels like the hundredth time. Where is everyone? Did I get the date wrong? Did I get the damn address to the courthouse wrong?

No, I've already verified both, and I even talked to Wendy last night. So, where is she when we have less than ten minutes before this hearing?

Where is *he*?

My arms and legs are trembling. All kidding aside, my body feels like I'm going to have an anxiety attack, and the only person I need right now is him.

I've paced the entire length of this long, stark, granite-tiled hallway for the past hour. And after my two-mile run early this morning to shake off the jitters, I'm clocking about twenty-thousand steps.

I look back toward the arched hallway entrance, set in between two huge, white marble pillars, to see if maybe I can see either my lawyer or my husband walking in, but it's empty.

"Where the hell are you guys?" My voice echoes against the arched ceiling.

He told me to wake him up when I got up this morning, but truth be told, my head's been a mess about everything this entire week—this custody hearing, the stuff David said last weekend . . . *us*.

We haven't spoken much since the party, and it's not for his lack of trying. He's asked me several times if something was wrong, but I've just waved it off each time, making an excuse of being tired. And even when he flew out mid-week, I kept our daily conversations to a minimum.

I know it's not fair to him. I can see myself from the outside looking in and can objectively say I'm not being fair to him, but I'm also the type who takes a little time to unpack and analyze things. And this *thing* was definitely a lot to unpack.

How does one process the fact that the man they love selfishly played the part in breaking up someone's home?

Whether Ally and her husband were happy, whether she played just as much a part in ruining her own marriage, I hate that Garrett was involved.

But it doesn't change the fact that I still need to talk to him—he deserves that much from me.

It's just, every time I get the nerve to, I feel like it'll shatter this beautiful reality we've built. A reality where we're happy and in love. A reality where he's my husband and an incredible father figure to my daughter. A reality where we laugh and make love.

A reality where he's my family.

But maybe what I've been thinking is a beautiful reality is actually not as flawless as it appears. Maybe those flaws run skin-deep, or maybe they're spread throughout our marrow.

I'm just shit-scared to find out.

Still, the only way to move forward is to actually *move—to* take a fucking step. And the only way to do that is to talk to him.

So, as soon as this hearing is over, that's what I plan to do.

Because whatever his reasons were for doing what he did, I need to get this weight off my chest. I can't hold it inside me any longer—it hurts too damn much and I know he can feel it, too.

He can feel the distance stretching between us in the form of short hugs where there used to be long embraces, pecks on the cheek where there used to be ravenous kisses, and silence, where there used to be endless whispered conversations in the dark.

But right now, I can't think about any of it.

All I need is for him to be here.

Having waited long enough, I pull out my phone to call him when I hear the sharp clicking of heels come down the hall. Relief washes over me when I look up to see Wendy approaching, rolling in faster than the actual storm clouds eviscerating the sunshine outside.

She looks so much like Melody today—rather, Melody looks so much like her—I almost do a double take to make sure it's not actually my best friend.

Both Rani and Melody sent me good luck messages this morning, and my mom hugged me extra tight when I dropped Meera off at her place. I told them all I'd call them as soon as I was done here.

And as much as I appreciated their reassuring words, the only person I need to see in my corner right now is the man who's always rushing in to protect me.

Before Wendy closes the distance between us, I quickly send Garrett a text message.

> Me: Hey, are you on your way? I know things have been weird between us this past week and we need to talk, but I need you by my side today, pilot. Please, tell me you're on your way.

"Hey! I was just—"

"I'm sorry for being late, Bella, but something came up this morning," Wendy cuts me off. "It's about the case."

My eyes widen as my heart races at breakneck speed. I turn my phone's ringer off and place it inside my purse. "About the case? Is everything—"

"I don't have time to discuss everything." Wendy moves past me, opening the doors to the courtroom. I follow behind her on wobbly knees, past the bailiff standing next to the doors. I give another glance over my shoulder to see if maybe Garrett is here, but I don't see him anywhere. "I found some interesting information last night."

"Wh-what?" I whisper as I follow her to the defendant's table.

I'd already seen Chaz and his lawyer walk in. It didn't help my anxiety when he sneered at me behind her back, as if he could smell my fear, while his lawyer ignored me like I was filth on her four-inch Manolo Blahniks.

I only have a second to take in the surroundings of a small courtroom with the judge's bench at the front, stationed higher than the two tables facing it—the defendant's and the prosecution's, where Chaz and his attorney are speaking in hushed voices. There's another bailiff standing next to the judge's door. Aside from the smaller size, it looks exactly like the courtrooms I've seen on TV.

Wendy motions for me to sit next to her, taking out a folder from her bag. "I didn't want to call and tell you last night and get your hopes up, but—"

"All rise!" the bailiff in between the bench and our tables

announces as we all stagger to our feet. My mind is still whirring with this so-called 'interesting information' Wendy has found, of which I am yet to know more about. "Court is now in session. The Honorable Judge Matthew Garcia presiding."

Once the judge has taken his seat and we've made our introductions, I take mine next to Wendy again.

Judge Garcia rustles some papers on his desk. "Okay, I believe I have the plaintiff's motion and the defendant's cross-motion. So," he looks at Chaz's attorney, "Ms. Stevens, whenever you're ready, you can begin."

"Excuse me, Your Honor?" Wendy stands, garnering looks from both Chaz and his lawyer. "I have new evidence I was not able to formally submit to you earlier which may have bearing on the outcome of this case." She continues as my opposition's attorney tries not to look flabbergasted, "Unfortunately, the chain of verification took until this morning and it was too late to submit it to you prior."

"I object, Your Honor." Chaz's attorney stands. "Any evidence gathered now could be considered prejudicial."

Judge Garcia does not seem amused. "Objection overruled." He looks at Wendy. "Please approach the bench, Ms. Mallory."

My breathing spikes as I watch Wendy waltz up to the bench, wondering what the hell she's found that is going to have an impact on the decision for this case.

She walks back to the table and her ebony eyes crinkle just the tiniest bit at me.

"Ms. Mallory, have you provided a copy of this to the plaintiff?" the judge asks, reading through the file Wendy handed him without giving anything away in his expression.

Wendy snags a separate copy of the same file from our desk and struts toward the opposing counsel's table before returning to her seat.

A small amount of whispering from the prosecution's desk travels over to us, but I'm still so frozen, I can barely gather the nerve to ask Wendy what the hell is going on. I look behind me once more to see if maybe, just maybe, Garrett has made it in, but I can already feel the disappointment before my eyes find rows of empty jury seats. I can't even take a peek at my phone to see if maybe he's tried to contact me because there's a strict no-cell phone policy inside the courtroom.

God, where is he?

How could he not be here on one of the most important days of our lives? It's the reason we even got married in the first place! The reason was sort of unfounded when we both got our bearings back and our drunken heads cleared, but still.

'Guys like Garrett don't change . . . he's hardly the type to be there for someone when times get tough.'

My stomach turns, thinking about the nasty words Ally and her friends said that night. My gut tells me something is wrong—really wrong—but my stupid, distrustful brain and those insecurities I've worked so hard to overcome start an unrelenting whisper.

You already knew you weren't good enough to keep him. You've never given a man enough of a reason to stay, so why would this one be any different?

What did you expect with how hot and cold you've been with him all week?

He probably lost interest in you.

He's not here on this important day because you're not important enough. Get it through your needy-ass brain.

My frown deepens, and I feel a sudden rush of emotion wash over me, but I blink back the tears before they make me look like some unstable parent on a day where that's the last thing I need.

Judge Garcia regards the prosecution. "What do you have to say to this, Ms. Stevens?"

Chaz and his attorney's whispers seem to get a tad harsher before she looks at the judge. "Your Honor, since this is new information I wasn't aware of, I'd like to ask for a few minutes to talk with my client."

The judge raps his gavel on his desk. "Let's take a fifteen-minute recess. Meet back here at nine-thirty."

I follow behind Wendy as we rush back into the hall. "What is happening, Wendy? Clue me in here. I'm freaking out!"

Wendy grabs my hands, looking at me with the type of calm that only someone who was like a mother to me would provide. "I didn't want to tell you before because I didn't want to get your hopes up, and I needed the time this morning to get the state of Texas to verify the documents."

"Okay . . ."

"Chaz has a prior sexual offense in the state of Texas. It's an old misdemeanor—"

"What?!" I practically scream. "Are you serious?"

Oh my God! Not only is he the biggest piece of shit I've ever met—and unfortunately, slept with—but he's also a sex offender? Is this for fucking real?

"Shh . . ." Wendy scolds me, looking around. "I'm sure Chaz is having to do a lot of explaining very quickly to his lawyer."

Does this mean the case will be dismissed? I mean, how could any court allow a previous sex offender to have visitation or custody of a minor?

"How could she have missed this information?" I ask, astonished. This is a pretty big fucking deal, isn't it?

Wendy shrugs. "Attorneys are people, just like everyone else. He probably didn't tell her because he didn't think it mattered since it's been long enough that he hasn't had to register as a sex offender."

My brows furrow. *"Doesn't it matter?* Can the court *actually* allow him to move forward with this case?"

She grimaces. "Not unless he proves he doesn't pose a risk to Meera, and that requires a hefty list of hurdles for him to cross—potential psychological evaluations, parental fit evaluations, et cetera."

We're just about to go back in to recommence the hearing when I pull my phone back out to glance at the screen. Still no messages from Garrett. I swallow the same emotion that was building earlier as I type out another message.

Me: Where are you, G?

I don't have the time to wait around for his response as I follow Wendy back to our table, but I send up a prayer, hoping he's okay.

Because this isn't like him.

Maybe you don't know what he's really like.

Maybe the time you've spent together wasn't enough.

God, when will my brain's internal crusade against my heart end?

"All rise!" The familiar introduction to the hearing restarting has my palms sweating. I massage them in my lap as soon as we're seated and wait for Chaz's lawyer to speak.

"Your Honor," she says, looking agitated, "given the lengthy process to prove that he would be a fit parent, my client has decided to withdraw the motion for visitation or guardianship of any kind."

My eyes widen to saucers as a hefty breath leaves me. *What?* I look toward Wendy, who gives me a huge smile that indicates I had heard correctly. I barely register Wendy's request to the judge that Chaz relinquishes all his parental rights, Chaz's lawyer's acceptance to formally submit the paperwork, or the judge's dismissal of the court. All I can think about is that we won!

We fucking won!

Wendy pulls me into a hug as tears burn my lids. "Congratulations, sweetheart. We did it."

My nose tingles as tears drop to my cheeks. "I can't believe it," I whisper. "I can't believe I don't have to put my baby through any of that confusion. Thank you, Wendy."

She cups my face, wiping my cheeks with her thumbs. "Of course. Now go call that crazy daughter of mine and tell her the good news. She's been nagging me all week about it."

I nod, getting out of my seat and heading toward the exit, still reeling from the past hour. I search the empty hallway once more, and as much as this event should feel like a cause for celebration, all I feel is utter disappointment.

Chapter Thirty-Two

GARRETT

My eyes flutter open, falling on the empty side of my bed where there's still an indentation of her. A sweep of my hand tells me she's been gone for quite some time.

I turn onto my back, taking the blanket with me, and stare up at the ceiling. A roll of thunder creates a warning in the sky, and I see both the cats bolt under the bed.

It's rare weather for this area—gloom blocking out all the sunshine.

'Ah, but you see the most heartwarming rainbows after the most heartbreaking storms.'

A flimsy smile finds my lips, recalling what Grams always says—her and her love for rainbows.

My tentative smile is short-lived as I recall my brief conversation with Bella last night before she headed up to bed . . . without asking if I wanted to join her like she usually does whenever I'm home.

I told her to wake me up no matter how early she needed to leave because I wanted to assure her, kiss her, and hold her before this huge day.

Clearly, she forgot.

I press my fingertips to my bare chest, trying to rub away the nagging pressure that's been there ever since we left Pete's house last weekend.

Something is off.

I don't know what it is, but I feel it in my gut that I'm right.

One minute she was jumping me inside a bathroom, high off her badassery after putting Ally in her place—though I have no idea what the woman even said to deserve getting a drink thrown in her lap—and the next minute, she was looking out the window in my truck, lost in her own world.

It felt like I came to the party with one girl and left with someone completely different. And even though I keep wracking my brain to see if I missed a vital clue, I can't seem to find anything that would give me a better idea.

I plan to meet her at the courthouse and be there throughout the hearing. I wouldn't miss this day for the world—it's a day we're going to move on from, no matter how it pans out. And no matter how much it doesn't feel like it right now, I know she's going to need me.

We've been off all week. Even before I flew out mid-week, Bella seemed preoccupied and distant. I figured it was the stress of the upcoming hearing, so besides asking her if everything was okay, I didn't push.

Should I have?

Even when I tried to comfort her, she was withdrawn, as if she was somewhere else.

The question is, where? Where in her overworking mind did she disappear off to?

Getting out of bed, I shuffle to the shower after taking a peek at the time. Seven-forty-five. The hearing starts at nine, and knowing her, she didn't eat before she left. I make a quick decision to pick up some coffee and pastries on my way, in case I catch her before she goes in. I also make a mental note to stuff a couple of those damn boxes of *Nerds* in my pocket, too. I have a feeling she'll need the sugar-high.

I've just put on a new pair of boxer-briefs when I decide to pick up the phone and check for any messages from her. The last two messages are ones I sent of sunsets from Arizona and Nebraska.

They're both still sitting on *Read*, awaiting a response.

Even when we spoke on the phone throughout the week, it felt forced, like she was trying to create mental distance between us, along with the physical distance we already had.

A part of me wants to call or text her again since we didn't get much talking done last night after I got home, but I also don't want to stress her out in any way, especially not today.

Fuck, maybe I'm just over-analyzing this like some prepubescent schoolgirl wondering why her middle school crush won't talk to her.

Maybe it's as simple as the fact that she's got a lot on her mind and this—her silent request for space and time—is how she's dealing with it.

And if space and time are what she needs, then I won't force her to talk to me. Even if the alarm bells inside my head are urging me to do the opposite.

My thoughts stay with me through my drive to the nearest coffee shop, where I pick us up pastries and lattes, all the way to the courthouse downtown.

I jump out of the car with the cardboard tray of drinks and paper bag in hand, wincing as I look at my watch. Fucking traffic was brutal, no thanks to the impending storm, and I've barely got five minutes to spare before she's due inside.

I'm rushing toward the door, wondering which wing of the building she's in, when my phone buzzes with a text. It's probably her wondering where the hell I am.

I maneuver the items in my hands to free up one and pull

my phone out of my pocket. As soon as I do, my phone rings with an incoming call from my mom.

"Mom, I'll call you later. I can't talk right–"

"It's Grams." My mom's wobbly voice comes through the phone, along with a sniffle. "Garrett, sweetheart–"

Every fucking hair on my body stands on end and my already sour gut rolls like the dark clouds above.

I'm going to be sick . . .

I halt on the spot, already knowing I'm going to loathe the answer to my question. "What is it, Mom? What's wrong with Grams?"

My mom's sobs spear me like razor-sharp knives.

"Mom!" I yell, garnering looks from a few people on the concrete steps to the courthouse. I can feel a quiver starting in my hands, shaking the tray of coffees. "What–"

"Sh–she had some sort of respiratory distress, and when Douglas and I got back from our walk this morning, we found her collapsed on her bathroom floor. I–I just spoke to her when we woke up, Garrett. She was . . . she was *fine!*"

My chest feels like it's ready to rip open. "Where is she now?"

Mom is sobbing so much, Douglas has to take over the line. "Son, we're at the hospital. But . . . it doesn't look good." He takes a deep breath and I can hear how worried he is. "The doctor just told us that they're doing everything they can, but she's not responding to treatment. And . . ."

I'm already running back toward my truck, shoving the entire tray of coffee into a nearby garbage can. "What?"

Fuck! What more?

"She has an advance directive for a DNI."

Grams, what did you do?

"What? What does that mean?"

I hear Mom sniffling and sobbing near him when Douglas

answers somberly, "It means they can't intubate her, even if that's the only way to save her."

"No!" My ears buzz and full-body trembles threaten to have me collapsing on this damn concrete parking lot. "No! Why would she—"

"Garrett," Douglas continues, "I'm sure I don't need to tell you this, but you need to get here soon, son."

The knot stuck in my throat barely lets me speak. "I'm coming." The rest of my sentence cracks just like my heart. "Tell her to hang on. Just tell her—"

That I fucking love her.

That I'll be lost without her.

That I'm not ready for her to go.

I try to inhale as much oxygen as I can, but I can't get my head around anything.

"I know, son. I know. We'll see you soon."

My tires squeal as I back out of the parking spot, throwing my phone onto the seat next to me. A wave of tears rush to my eyes as I turn out of the courthouse and book it onto the access road.

She has an advance directive? What the fuck?

Why didn't I know this? Why wouldn't she have talked to me about it? Didn't we fucking talk about *everything*? Didn't she tell me once that no conversation was out of bounds between us? So, why didn't she tell me?

Because you would have thrown a fit. Because she didn't want your input in what she wanted for her life.

"You're going to be fine, Grams," I state with as much confidence as I can muster in my empty car. "You're going to make it."

We're not even going to have to worry about this stupid advance directive shit because it'll be a moot point. Though, I am definitely going to try my fucking hardest to get her to reverse it as soon as she's better.

I look at the clock. Nine-oh-six. The hearing has probably begun, so it doesn't make sense to call and interrupt Bella to tell her why I can't make it—it'll only stress her out even more. Plus, there's a high probability she's not even supposed to look at her phone during the hearing. I'll just have to message her later.

Fuck!

I'm not sure how fast I'm driving, but nothing seems to be registering at the moment. Not the swaying trees as heavy winds throttle them, terrorizing their roots, and not the sinister clouds threatening to strike.

Nothing registers but the slamming of my heart inside my ribs.

All my thoughts are with the woman struggling for her life in a hospital bed. A woman who, in all regards, is another mother to me and my best fucking friend.

My jaw clenches as a vision of Grams holding my hand while a nurse stitched up my forehead from a fall I took at Grams' lake house comes fluttering to the surface. Her soothing smile and her warm hand were the only things I could focus on to not tear up and let the nurse see what a little fucking wuss I was.

Images and memories flood my brain as my vision starts to blur, and I blink rapidly to stay focused on the road. To stay focused on getting to her as fast as I can.

The way she folded her white lace handkerchief into a perfect square, tucking it into the purse she always seemed to be carrying with her, even around the house.

The way she circled her lips with the same shade of lipstick she's used for as long as I can remember—blush pink.

The way her eyes would settle on me and those same lips would turn up into a smile, the wrinkles around them making her look even more beautiful.

My ears buzz, creating some sort of charged fence around

the thoughts swimming in my head. And like the weather outside, there's no sunshine to be found anywhere. I try to squelch the feeling that this storm won't bring about any of her precious fucking rainbows.

I pinch the corners of my eyes, trying to talk myself out of the emotion building in my chest, telling myself the same thing. *She's going to make it. I know she's going to make it.*

I'm lost in my thoughts when the buzzing of my phone catches my attention. I see the name on the screen but can't voice a greeting when I pick up.

"You on your way?" Dean sounds both frantic and hoarse.

"Yeah."

He's silent on the line, but I can hear the noise of an engine humming, letting me know he's in his car, too. "She's going to be fine, G."

"I know."

"She fucking has to be!" He chokes on a sob. "Fuck! I'll see you there."

I hang up without a word, taking the next exit.

There's never been a day I haven't wanted to be up in the sky. Not a single day that I haven't wanted to be inside an airplane. No matter when I've gotten on one, I've always looked forward to my destination.

And even though I want to get to her at the speed of light, I'm not looking forward to boarding a plane today.

Bells: Hey, are you on your way? I know things have been weird between us this past week and we need to talk, but I need you by my side today, pilot. Please, tell me you're on your way.

Bells: Where are you, G?

> Me: Hey. I'm sorry I wasn't with you in court today. I got some unexpected news and had to rush to the airport. I'm on a flight now, on my way to see Grams. She's in the hospital.

SHE LOOKS ASLEEP.

Her skin lacks the color and luster it usually has, and if I didn't know better, I'd say her chest just rose with a breath. I'd say her hands twitched at her sides. I'd even say her eyelids fluttered, as if she was preparing to open them to smile at the rain pitter-pattering on the window pane.

If I didn't know better, I'd say she was still alive.

I prayed so damn hard for the storm to pass, but it just followed me to Colorado. It shouldn't be surprising, I suppose, that she'd leave this earth on a rainy day. Perhaps the heavens even planned for it to celebrate her welcome.

Because everyone knew how much Grams loved the rain.

She loved it almost as much as she loved rainbows.

She used to tell me that, unlike other people, gloomy clouds made her feel hopeful, like there was impending sunshine within reach. Like she knew she'd soon get a glimpse of her favorite thing in the entire world—a rainbow.

If there was ever rain or a storm, we all knew where we'd find Grams right after it passed—on the blue Adirondack chair on Mom's covered porch. She'd sit there for hours, knitting or reading one of her favorite romance novels.

The woman had an obsession with historical romance.

I still remember picking one of them up from her nightstand, opening it up to a chapter with one of her million sticky notes, and reading through a rather graphic sex scene.

Feeling both aroused and disturbed, I recall I immediately wished I hadn't read it.

No matter how close we were, no grandson needed to see words like 'substantial pecker' and 'welcoming sodden tunnel' highlighted in their grandmother's books.

I grasp her hand, my thumb rolling over her creased knuckles. I swallow the thickness coating my throat. "Grams." Even her name comes out as a hoarse and broken whisper. "I'm trying not to be mad at you. But," my chin wobbles as the mist in my eyes cloud my vision and I blink rapidly to clear it, "it's hard, you know?"

One of my tears drops onto the mattress under her, seeping into the fabric, just like she seeped into mine from the moment she held me in her arms.

"You were supposed to stick around a little longer. I wasn't asking for tens of years, though I'm sure you would have only looked more beautiful in that time."

An image of her playfully smacking me with the back of her hand has my mouth lifting in a wobbling smile. She might have pretended otherwise, but I knew she always loved being told how beautiful she was.

A sob bubbles through me as I take in her stiff form and hold back my questions and accusations. Why didn't she want to be resuscitated? Why didn't she want the doctors to do everything they could? Why couldn't she have fought just a little harder?

But I know I'm not being fair. It would only hurt her more to know how much I was trying to balance my understanding with my anger. Anger at the situation, anger at myself for not getting here sooner, anger at her.

All my life she waited for me to find someone, and now that I had, she couldn't wait just a little longer to meet her?

"You promised me a dance . . ." Her frail and cold hand feels almost weightless inside mine. I would have been holding these hands, swaying with her to the music at my and Bella's wedding.

I swallow, but the thickness in my throat refuses to ease.

Not once have I regretted marrying Bella. Not once have I wished I hadn't done it on that crazy night in Vegas.

But today . . . today I wish I'd taken my vows with my best friend as my witness.

I place a trembling kiss on her cheek, apologizing for a mistake I didn't know I was making at that time. "I love you, beautiful." I clench my jaw against the emotion seizing my ribs. "I hope you're dancing in a pillow of clouds and sliding down your favorite rainbows. Heaven has no idea how much more fun the party just got with you there."

Chapter Thirty-Three

BELLA

I click the red *End* button on my phone for the third time after hearing my call go to his voicemail yet again.

What is going on?

Is he okay?

Maybe I should just leave a message. He needs to know I'm concerned that I can't get in touch with him.

Maybe he's just over your shit.

Maybe he's avoiding you like you avoided him all week.

Maybe this is the beginning of the end.

My chest aches. Despite the fact that I got the best news in the courtroom, it feels like there's a nail being pounded against it relentlessly.

Does he want to end it? Is that why he's not picking up when I call or answering my messages? I know he definitely saw them. They're currently sitting on *Read,* but I haven't received a reply.

We've come too far, fought too hard, and loved too deeply to just leave things this way. He said what we had was real; he said he was all-in. So would one week of us being on different pages emotionally really be enough to shake everything we've built?

He also promised he'd be there for me today . . .

Something just doesn't feel right.

In fact, something feels really wrong. Like there's a heaviness in the air that has nothing to do with the storm that's been building all morning. Like when it finally rains, it's going to shatter windows and flood the streets.

I'm just about to dial his number again from my car and leave him a voicemail when my phone rings in my hand.

"Hey!" I muster up as much enthusiasm as I can, but it's taking everything I've got.

"Hey! I hear congratulations are in order. Holy shit, girl, you did it!" Melody's cheerful voice lifts a little bit of the weight in my chest.

"It was all your mom. Seriously, she's amazing."

Melody snorts. "That she is but, girl, we don't need to stroke her ego. She already knows she's a badass. I am so happy for you. I heard you guys also got that douche bucket to forfeit any future rights to Meera. You can finally move on, Bells."

"Yeah. Thanks."

God, this weather is getting worse by the second. I should really head home instead of sit here inside my car and wait for . . . something.

"Bells? What's wrong? Why do you sound like your cat died?" She winces audibly as soon as she says it. "Sorry, wrong idiom. I'm still getting used to the fact that you now have cats. What I meant to say is, I don't get the sense you're happy."

I rub my forehead. "Something is wrong, Mel. I can feel it." I intake a heavy breath as if it's my last and the pricks of tears invade my eyes. "Garrett wasn't at the hearing today–"

"What?" Melody shares my surprise. "But why wouldn't he

be there? He loves you. He knows how important this day was for you—you, him, and Meera."

I pinch the bridge of my nose. "That's what I don't understand. We've been a little distant this past week—more because of me—but I wouldn't take him as the type to just not show up, you know?"

You also didn't take your dad as the type to just not show up, either.

"Wait, what was causing you to be distant last week? Did you guys get into a fight?"

I sigh. "No, nothing like that. I found out—"

An incoming phone call from Rani has my words halting on my tongue. She's probably wondering how things went at the hearing.

"Mel, I'm getting a call from Rani. Can I call you a little later?"

"Absolutely, boo. Call me any time. All I have going on today is having my nipples sucked by one of the guys I live with."

My nose wrinkles when I realize she's talking about her husband. *Eew.* "Yeah, T.M.I., weirdo."

I pick up Rani's call, shoving away images of Melody and her nipples. That woman really needs to come with a warning sign.

"Hey. I was going to call you. We won! Chaz dropped the entire case." Again I muster up more excitement than I feel.

Evidently, Rani must be feeling the same gloom I am because her voice sounds anything but genuinely cheerful. "That's great, sis! I'm so happy for you."

"Rani?" My chest constricts, knowing that my usually upbeat cousin doesn't ever need a reason to feign happiness. "What's wrong?"

Rani's quiet for a moment, and all I can hear is the roar of my blood rushing through my ears. "Bells . . . Garrett's grandma just died."

I feel like I've just been shoved right in the ribs and all the air in my lungs has been forced out. "What?!"

"I don't know if he and Dean even know yet. Last I heard, they were on a flight to Colorado, trying to get there as fast as they could to see her. I'm assuming they'll be landing in the next hour and hear the news."

"Oh, my God." My mind works a million miles an hour while my heart breaks for Garrett. I know how much he loves his grandma. "I'll call you later, Rani."

I hang up with my cousin, turn the key to start my car, and call the only person who can help me with everything right now.

"Mom? I need you to take care of Meera for me for another few days. There's been an emergency."

"You awake, Mom?" the nurse asked as I turned my groggy eyes toward her. *"This little one is hungry and ready to spend some time with her momma."*

I smiled naturally, even if my body felt like it had been struck by a mack truck. What the hell was I thinking when I said no to that epidural? *Evidently, at the time, I was thinking if I was going to raise this baby on my own—minus the support of my incredible mother, of course—then I needed to prove to myself that I could give birth without the help of modern medicine, too.*

Yeah, insert eye roll because I was screaming for that shit by the twelfth hour of labor, when I was only eight centimeters dilated. But by then, it was too late because apparently, Ms. Meera was already crowning.

She didn't take too much time after that, but the girl broke my vagina in the process for sure. I had enough stitches up my hoo-ha to feel like a Raggedy Ann doll.

The nurse placed her in my arms, and I took in my baby's thick, dark curls. I wondered if she would always have curly hair. I studied her face but couldn't quite tell the color of her glassy eyes. Right now they looked like a mix of green and brown, but maybe all mixed-race babies had eyes like that.

Her father's eyes are hazel. *I winced with the thought. I hated the fact that she would have anything resembling him. But I guess that was part of my karma to pay—see the asshole reflected in my sweet baby girl's face for the rest of my life.*

I'd work night and day to give her the life and love she deserved as both her mother and father. I had a good example of how to do that already from my own mom.

I pulled open my hospital gown and brought her face up to my breast and she immediately knew what to do, turning to capture my nipple in her tiny pink mouth, suckling like she was an expert. God, I love her already. *I would do anything for her.*

I whispered my love to her and rubbed her blotchy little forehead. The nurses had said the discolorations would fade soon enough.

Mom had a shift in the ER today, so I knew she'd only come by in the afternoon. I'd insisted that she not take more time off just to wait around for me in the hospital after I had Meera yesterday. If anything, I'd need her more when I got back home, so I much preferred her taking a few days off then.

"Bella?" The nurse knocked on my door. "There's someone here to see you. He says he's a friend."

My forehead creased. A guy is here to see me? *I was expecting Rani and Melody in the next couple of hours, but not a guy.* I wonder if it's someone from work . . .

"Did he say his name?"

The nurse—a woman, maybe only a few years older than me—gave me a coy smile. "He's quite the looker, I must say. Definitely didn't have a ring on his finger, either."

I blinked at her. I'm pretty sure I didn't ask for his description and marital status.

"Oh!" She giggled, realizing I was still waiting for his name. "He said his name was Garrett Meyer."

My heart thudded in my chest, and I wondered if Meera could feel it against her mouth. Garrett's here? As in, at the hospital, knowing I'd just had a baby? Why?

I wasn't blind or unfeeling. Far from it.

I knew there was a strange pull between us. I'd felt it the day we met during a sporting event at Darian's outdoor sports school all those months ago. Those eyes of his, bluer than the river we were all standing near.

But I also knew better.

A girl like me, knocked up and carrying a random man's child, wouldn't be the type someone like him would want. He was gorgeous in the most classically handsome way—those all-American good looks. Blond hair and blue eyes with a smile that could have butterflies soaring, even when all you wanted to do was swat them back down.

The last thing he wanted was my kind of baggage when he could get whoever he looked at. And from what I'd found out over the past few months from his brothers teasing him or Rani making a comment here or there, he did. He got whoever he wanted, however much he wanted them. And, apparently, Garrett has a trail as long as the road from here to South Carolina of broken hearts behind him.

And if anyone knew anything about me, they'd know my heart was one thing I protected like a dragon guarding its treasure.

I looked down at my newborn. I'd protect her the same way because hearts weren't meant to be broken; they were meant to be cherished. And I'd never let anyone break hers the way my father had broken mine.

I smiled at the nurse still awaiting my response before adjusting the sheet around me to cover Meera up. "Tell him to come in."

Seconds later, the man I'd thought about on more than one occasion was standing in the same entrance the nurse had left, holding a beautiful bouquet. His eyes glimmered over it, and I quickly averted my gaze to look down at the baby in my arms, trying to hide from his stare.

Those eyes were dangerous.

He placed the flowers on a nearby counter. "Congratulations."

"Thank you." I cleared my throat and smiled. "You didn't have to bring anything."

His eyes dipped down to the bundle now wiggling inside my arms. Apparently, she'd had enough to eat.

Trying to be discreet and not flash him my boob, I lifted Meera and placed her upright, gently patting her back to burp her. The nurses and my mom showed me how to do it yesterday. Apparently, if I didn't get a good burp out of her, she was likely to spit up or have a tummy ache.

Garrett put his hands inside his pockets, watching me while a wave of exhaustion rolled through me. I guess waking up to feed this little thing almost every three hours last night and still dealing with the uncomfortable stitches was wearing on me.

He eyed my face. "Can I, uh . . .? Can I help in any way?"

I weighed my decision. I always weighed my decisions.

He was here. Without me having asked him to be, he had made the effort. My friends hadn't shown up yet, but he was here before them. He must have asked them where I'd had the baby.

So, whether I was going to involve my heart with him—which I wasn't—I couldn't deny I trusted him, either. I trusted him, even with my newborn baby. "Do you know how to burp a baby?"

Garrett shrugged, taking a squirt of the hand sanitizer next to me and scrubbing his hands as if he already knew I was going to hand her over. "How hard could it be? I got the hang of it from watching you."

I made a gesture for him to pick her up, and all the air rushed out of my lungs when I saw her in his hands. This tiny swaddled thing in the strong and capable arms of this large man. It was a mental image

I'm sure I'd revisit again, because it was not only beautiful, it was a complete turn-on.

He took a seat next to me and sat her on his lap, supporting her head as if he'd held a million babies before, all while patting her back at the same time.

"What's this beauty's name?" His voice shook me from my stupor.

"Meera. Meera Isabella Patel."

He nodded, leaning down to place a kiss on her head. "It's a perfect name for her, but I think I'm going to call her Meerkat."

THE MEMORY COMES BARRELING as I take a seat on the flight. I'm shocked it wasn't delayed or canceled altogether due to the weather, but I'm grateful for the small miracle.

I unzip my purse, trying to search for my box of lemon *Nerds* to help me through take off, when my fingers find the hard edge of a thick, glossy paper. Before I know it, I've forgotten about the candy entirely and am pulling out the card Cressida gave me at the carnival.

The Lovers.

'Keep it with you to remind yourself of what you have when times get difficult. Remember that you are stronger than the forces against you, and that when it's true and meant to be, it will always find a way, no matter what challenges lie in its path.'

My breath halts on an inhale. Is this the difficult time she alluded to?

I look at the card depicting a man and woman standing underneath a tree, remembering that conversation when Cressida spoke to Garrett but kept giving me knowing glances.

'This card also represents a choice. The choice that you, Garrett, have made in choosing your wife. The choice that you make every day when you choose her.'

'I do choose her, every single day,' he'd responded.

And, he has. He always has.

He's been there almost since day one for me after I had Meera. I may not have talked to him often after that, but in my heart, I knew I could rely on him if I needed it. And somehow, any time I did, he was always there.

I purse my lips, even as my chin wobbles and tears spring to my eyes for what feels like the hundredth time today.

To hell with his past, to hell with what David or Ally said. To hell with weighing out the wrong and right. The only fucking thing I care about is *today*. *His present*. Which is exactly what this card represents.

I love this man with the force of a million suns—enough to wipe away all the gloom and rain in the sky. And now, it's time for me to show him exactly that. To return the love he gave me before I even knew what it was.

Chapter Thirty-Four

GARRETT

My Dear Garrett,

If you're reading this letter, I've made some sort of dramatic exit and haven't had the chance to tell you a few things in person.

You always did say I had a flair for the dramatics.

Well, I hope however it happened, it wasn't a boring event, like going to sleep and never waking up. With all due respect to those who have passed that way, it seems a little anticlimactic after having lived such an exuberant life.

And the life I lived was anything but mundane—from marrying the man of my dreams, to raising his children, and then watching my grandsons grow up. I've had a vivacious life I wouldn't trade a second of.

Wiping my cheek with the back of my hand, I heave in a breath. It takes everything in me to keep reading without falling to pieces right here in her bedroom.

> You, my handsome boy, made my life even more gratifying. You made me smile and laugh every time we spoke. You kept me feeling young, never hiding anything from me. It was one of the things I loved most about our relationship—our ability to talk about anything and everything without judgment.
>
> And as much as you think I'm responsible for the candor between us, it was really you who put in the work.
>
> Because since you were a little boy, you've never shied away from putting in the work. Whether it was to get into the junior baseball league, to become a pilot—and now a captain—or to get the girl you've been waiting for all these years.
>
> You set your immense heart on something, and then you work like hell until you get it.
>
> It was the same for the friendship we shared. No matter how busy you were or where you were flying off to, you never forgot to call to tell me you loved me or lie to me about how beautiful I was.

I huff out a blubbery laugh, sniffling.

I didn't lie to you, Grams. You were always beautiful.

It was a pleasure to watch you grow into such an incredible young man, but know that I'll continue to watch you from wherever I am. In fact, I'll continue to send you reminders that I'm watching you. Just look up at the sky after a rainy day, because I promise you, I'll be there.

So, wipe those tears, young man. This is not the time to cry; it's the time to celebrate. Celebrate your best friend's life. Celebrate my legacy, because no one is prouder than me that you were a a part of it.

And though my only regret is to not have danced with you at your wedding, I wish you a lifetime of dancing with your beautiful bride.

Don't ever stop working for her, Garrett. The most valuable treasure is found inside the deepest caves. Don't settle until it's yours.

I love you, my sweet boy. We'll see each other again one day a long time from now because I need you to live as full a life as I did. Whenever you are ready to come see me, though, can you bring me up that blush pink shade of lipstick I love so much? I'm pretty sure I'll have used mine up by then.

Cheerio,
Grams

With my elbows on my knees, I place a shaky fist in the middle of my ribs, trying to rub out the tightness that's made a home there. While Dean helps Douglas figure out the next steps—notifying our family, writing an obituary, and making funeral arrangements—I feel like I'm stuck, like a plastic bag tangled on a tree branch, flying helplessly in a high-speed wind. Dean's always been the type to throw himself into work when he's in pain, not me.

I'm the type to shut down. Shut the fuck down like the power cord has been pulled.

She's gone.

I just can't seem to wrap my head around it. I just talked to her this week. She was gushing about how she could feel the crackle and electricity in the air, like a storm was coming.

Yeah, a storm definitely made landfall.

I scan the words in her letter again, looking at her loopy handwriting. Was she sitting at the letter desk in the corner of her room when she wrote it or on the chair on Mom's patio?

I should have called her more. I should have visited more. I should have insisted that she see the doctor more. Maybe then this wouldn't have happened. Maybe then we could have gotten a few more years.

I hear the door open behind me but I don't turn around. It's probably Mom, trying to get me to come out and eat something since I've been in here for hours. We've already had more visitors at the house than I would have expected, though, really, I shouldn't be surprised. Grams had friends everywhere.

Folding the letter back into the envelope that was on her

nightstand for me, I sniffle and get up from my perch on her bed. I can't sit here forever; I need to be there for Mom and Dean, too. I turn around to follow my mom out, but it's not her standing there.

I'm struck silent, able to only swallow my emotion but not to get a word out. And even if I tried, they'd come out cracked.

She came.

She's here, as if she heard my fucking whisper to the universe that I needed her.

As if knowing exactly what I need, Bella crosses the length of the room and when she's no more than a couple of feet away, I open my arms. Bella catapults herself into me, wrapping herself around me like she's protecting me with her body. Her hands find my hair and she tucks her face into my neck, and I tighten my hold around her, sitting on the chair near the window.

Her face lifts and I see the tears lining her cheeks. She didn't know Grams well, but she knew what she meant to me. So her tears may not be for my grandmother as much as they are for my loss.

"I'm sorry," she croaks before placing a kiss on my cheek. She wipes the wetness under my lids with her thumb. "I'm so sorry, G."

I nod. "I didn't think you'd–"

She doesn't let me finish the rest of my sentence, sealing my mouth with hers in a kiss that's both an admonishment and an apology. "I couldn't be–*wouldn't be*–anywhere else but here with you." She grimaces like she's hurt. "Do you think so little of my love for you, pilot?"

I shake my head. "No, sweetheart, that's not what I meant. The weather is shitty, and I didn't think you'd be able to get here so soon."

"I would have driven here if I had to. All I could think about was getting to you."

Our foreheads meet and I grab her hands in the middle of us. "I miss her, Bells."

Bella nods silently. She knows I don't need any verbal reassurances right now. All I need is her here.

"I knew I wouldn't have her forever, but I guess I thought we had a bit more time." I chuckle mirthlessly. "I suppose she could have lived years more, and I still would have said the same thing." I look into Bella's soft gaze. "But that was the thing about her, Bells. She never made you want to let go."

Bella's chin wobbles. "You took after her in so many ways, Garrett. Your heart, your charm, your humor." She looks over at a picture of my grandparents on Gram's letter desk. "You have a way of seeping into someone's soul so they can't fathom being without you." Her eyes come back to me. "You're like her in that way, too."

This girl . . . She has no idea how much I needed to hear those words.

I kiss her, but not our usual frantic kisses where everything around us blurs and the need to consume each other takes over. This kiss is a melody of words, a symphony of endearments. It's soft, but not subtle—and exactly what I need to steady me on this disorienting day.

She pulls away all too quickly. "Do you want a little more time alone?"

I shake my head, getting up with her still latched around me before she places her feet on the ground. I sweep another look around Grams' room, feeling her presence in every nook and cranny.

My heart still has no intention of letting her go, and I have no intention of hurrying it along. Right now, I can't imagine not missing my best friend forever.

I'm following behind Bella, my fingers entangled in hers

when I pull on them, stopping her before she opens the door. "What happened at the hearing? Did you get my messages this morning?"

Her expression is perplexed. "No, I didn't get any messages from you."

I'm sure my face has the same puzzlement as hers. I pull out my phone from my pocket, realizing I'd turned it on airplane mode after sending her the message, and I've been so wrapped up in everything from the second we landed that I never checked to see if Bella even messaged me back.

Bella watches as I turn it back on, and we notice the message delivery failure notification ping in our text thread. Fuck, she must have been so fucking worried and confused.

Not knowing what else to say, I look at her, pulling her back into a hug. "I'm so sorry, baby. I would never have missed such an important—"

"Shh. I know, pilot," she murmurs into my chest. "Don't apologize."

"What happened?"

Her smile is genuine behind still-glassy eyes. "We won. Chaz dropped the case."

Holy shit.

"What?"

She shakes her head, already knowing I'm curious. "We'll have plenty of time to talk about it later. I'm here for as long as you need me."

I stop her again, right before she gets a chance to turn the door knob. "Can you tell me why things felt off between us the past week? Was it something that happened at the party—aside from you going all Kool-Aid Man on Ally?"

Bella's shoulders slump but she recovers with a soft smile. "Later."

Why do I get the feeling I'm not going to like 'later'?

Chapter Thirty-Five

GARRETT

THE WATER SPARKLES UNDER THE MOONLIGHT LIKE diamonds are scattered over it. I stare at the dark horizon, listening to the swell of the water mix with the crackling fire in front of me and Dean strumming his guitar.

Mala, his best friend–or who the fuck knows what they are–watches his face with a look of both longing and caution.

She flew in around the same time Bella did, and while I've seen her and Dean together–from what I know, they've even been staying in the same room, but I'm not going to touch that with a ten-foot pole–I get the sense something is off between them because tension like theirs can be felt in the next town over.

Perhaps they're not as platonic as my brother would like us all to believe–though he's not fooling anyone.

The woman is not just beautiful, she'd do absolutely anything for him–sometimes to the detriment of herself. Dean must be blind, deaf, and dumb if he doesn't see what everyone else sees in Mala. But I also know the main reason why he feels his hands are tied. Do I agree with that reason? No, but hey, that's his story to figure out, not mine.

I've got mine walking over here with a beer in hand and a smile directed at me.

Bella starts to take a seat next to me in one of the Adirondack chairs Grams placed around the fire-pit in the backyard of her lake house, but I pull her by the hand so she lands messily in my lap. She yelps as some of her beer sloshes out of the bottle and lands near my foot.

She giggles as I wrap my arms around her, placing a kiss on her neck. My nose slides down the side of her neck and she shudders against my chest.

"Get a room!" Dean yells from across the fire before giving me one of his classic smirks, letting me know he's secretly happy for me.

Bella's nails scratch my neck softly, making me feel warmer than the fire ever could, while we all slide back into our thoughts.

Today was hard. Fucking brutal, to be honest.

Even after four days of coming to terms with Grams being gone, I felt that same pang inside my chest—like I was being ripped all over again—when I watched her casket being lowered into the ground.

There wasn't a dry eye at the funeral. Even Darian, who never spent as much time with her as Dean and me, got choked up when he gave me a hug afterward.

Now, Darian and Rani are on one side of me, bundled up in their blankets and sipping something hot—though it will take this breeze five minutes to cool whatever it is.

Dean speaks over the strum of his guitar, catching my eyes. "Remember how much you hated fish?"

Bella's brows lift to her hairline. "I thought you said you were a fish and grill kind of guy?"

Dean doesn't let me explain. "Oh, he is now, but you should have seen what a pussy he was back in the day."

Darian chuckles, indeed enjoying this rare occasion where he's not the butt-end of me and Dean's big brother assholery.

I give him a contemptuous look before addressing my womb-mate. "I was *five*."

"That shit went on for *three years*," Dean deadpans. "Mom and Grandpa thought you needed to see a therapist."

Oh, I see what he just did there. Whatever retort I was going to have for him dies on my tongue. Instead, I remember who took me out into the water while I held on to her for dear life. I fucking hated those slithery little fish that had no fear, coming up too close for my comfort. And yet, each time we slowly made our way in, she'd keep her voice soft and tell me she was right there. That I could hold on to her for as long as I wanted.

I take a swig from my beer. "Grams never agreed."

Dean continues strumming. "She was the ultimate believer when it came to us." He stops strumming to take a sip of his beer. "Fuck, I'm going to miss her."

"I still remember when I spent part of a summer here when I was eight or nine," Darian pipes up with a broad smile after a few minutes of us all ruminating in silence. "Every single night, your grandparents would watch WWE religiously."

I chuckle, remembering their fascination with wrestling. Most couples watched movies or TV shows. But Grams? She was obsessed with wrestling. And then she got Grandpa into it.

"No matter how many times Dean and I told her it wasn't real, that the matches were all rigged, Grams would say, 'Well, most movies and shows aren't real, either. This is no different, and it looks like a heck of a lot of fun to be tossed around like a rag doll from here to there.'"

"She was a kooky little thing." Dean laughs, but it instantly turns into a choked inhale, making everyone turn quiet again. Mala squeezes his hand, exchanging a look with him that only they can understand.

I blink to clear my tears, feeling Bella brush her lips against my temple.

We share a few more memories—of when they built this house, how we all gathered here during the summers, of Grams' love for rainbows—until Rani's loud yawn gets a giggle out of the other girls.

"Goodness, me," she says, placing a hand over her mouth. "I must be more tired than I thought."

Before she's said another word, Darian has his arm around her waist and is hauling her back into the house, giving us a wave goodnight. They have early flights in the morning, just like the rest of us, but we're all planning to at least give each other a hug goodbye then.

"I think I'm going to take a little stroll around the beach," Mala announces a few minutes later, and I notice she directs the comment more to me and Bella.

Yeah, whatever is going on between her and Dean is . . . interesting, but I've still got some questions of my own to get answered with my girl so I have plenty to keep me busy.

Five minutes after Mala disappears, Dean leans his guitar against his chair and walks in the same direction as her—*shocker!*—and Bella and I are left alone for what seems like the first time in days.

We've slept in the same room, caught up a little here and there—she told me more about the hearing—and have definitely had the comfort of each other's arms, but it's been late every night and either we're too tired or too emotionally drained to have a deeper conversation.

She lays her head on my shoulder and I curl a wisp of her hair around my finger.

"Bells?"

She hums.

"What happened last week? Something was bothering you and it fucking killed me not to know."

She grimaces. "It's not import–"

"It is to me." I tilt her chin to meet my eyes. "Tell me."

She swallows, fidgeting a little in my lap. The breeze picks up her hair, and I try not to get distracted because this woman can seriously cause heads to spin with how fucking beautiful she is. "David came up to me at the party–"

My eyes harden. "Did he try to flirt with you?" I grind out. Motherfucker has no idea who he's messing with. Chief pilot or not, I'll fuck him up if he goes after what's mine.

"No." She shakes her head before she winces. "Actually, a little, but–"

My fucking ears are ringing. "*Motherfucker*–"

Bella cups my face. "G, listen to me. That isn't the point."

"It should be. It's a *significant* point," I argue.

"He said something." She shakes her head again, looking toward the lake. "You know what, it doesn't even matter anymore. What you did in your past isn't something you can change; all I care about is your present and your future."

"Bells, look at me." I wait for her to give me her attention. "What the hell are you talking about? What did he say?"

She stabs her bottom lip with her teeth. "That you had an affair with Ally behind his back."

I wait for her to throw her head back and laugh because, if this is some sort of joke, I'd like the punchline of it soon. When she doesn't, my eyes widen in disbelief. "What? *An affair?*"

"Ally and David were married when you . . ." her frown deepens, "slept with her."

My mind whirls, trying to go back to the time I slept with Ally–more like fucked her in a tiny bathroom because she all but begged me every time we were in the same aircraft together.

I would never fucking look at a married woman, let alone help her cheat on her husband. In fact, while I'm not proud of my history of *literally* fucking around, I made it a point to look at a woman's ring finger before I ever tried to pick her up. Not that it's a guarantee that they're not married, but it's a decent indicator, and one I definitely remember Ally not sporting.

Fucking Unfortunately Ally.

My gut told me she was a whack job even after I slept with her, and again when I ran into her after four years on my trip to Vegas. But that she was cheating on her husband and involved me? *That* I never saw coming. And to top it all off, that she was married to David? I had no fucking clue!

It's my turn to cup Bella's face. God, to think she spent the entire week thinking I might have done something like that. Perhaps she even thought that if I could be a home-wrecker, then I could cheat on her, too.

Christ. I can't imagine how confused she must have been to shoulder that on her own.

"Bells, I didn't know she was married. I would never, *ever* do something like that because I actually believe in the sanctity of marriage, and I'd never want to cause anyone pain—not even a guy I have little respect for, like David. No one deserves that."

Bella clasps her hands around my wrists. "I should have told you earlier. I was just . . ." she puffs out a breath like she was holding it, "I don't know. Confused and still processing it all."

I swipe my thumbs on her cheekbones. "I get that, sweetheart. I do. But next time, process it with *me*. Give me a chance to clear up the confusion. Because you're not alone anymore; you have me and my entire goddamn heart. No burden is for you to carry on your own. You should have come to me right after you heard. We could have had this conversation *that* day and settled your mind, instead of you holding on to it for this long." I look into her eyes. "Honestly, I would have even talked to David."

Her face falls. "I'm sorry, G."

I pinch her chin, picking it back up. "Baby, I'm not trying to make you feel guilty. I'm just telling you that we're partners. *In everything.* Look at what you did for me this week."

She looks at me, perplexed.

"Despite how nerve-wracking it must have been to go to that hearing alone, despite not having received a single message from me, and despite all the things swirling around in that high-powered processor of yours." I smile, trying to get a glimpse of her dimples, which, thankfully, she flashes at me. "You rushed over here when I needed you. And I couldn't have done it without you, sweetheart. The only reason I didn't fall to my knees and cry through the hardest day of my life was because you were holding me up."

It's the truth, and she should know it.

She doesn't just give me happiness; she gives me hope and strength.

Bella latches on to me, wrapping me in a tight hug. "I love you so much, pilot. Sometimes I can't believe you're mine. Like, actually mine."

I rub her bottom lip with my thumb. "Believe it, babe. I've been yours for a long time, and I'm not going anywhere."

Her brow lifts. "You would have clarified things with David?"

As mentally and emotionally wrecked as I feel, I know this will weigh on me like a goddamn anvil until I talk to him. *Shit.* To see my ugly mug and be reminded of the man who fucked over your marriage . . .? I'm surprised he's been as civil as he has been so far.

"Yeah. I plan to as soon as we get back home."

Chapter Thirty-Six

GARRETT

"Ooh! I wanna fly that one, Uncle G!" Meera points her little finger at the model Cessna AG-wagon crop duster that has another kid hopping out of it. Like her mother, she's shortened my name, too.

She asked me yesterday how I spelled it, and when I repeated it for the third time, she grumpily declared that it was 'too long, with too many Rs and too many Ts,' and she was just going to call me Uncle G.

Well, okay then.

I help Meera into the aircraft's cockpit, leaning in to show her some of the controls, but the girl has one hell of an imagination. "Oh no! We gotta go faster, Uncle G!" She looks behind her dramatically. "The bad-guy pirates are following us! They're trying to steal our shoes!"

I refrain from telling her all the things that are wrong with that statement—including the fact that a crop duster wouldn't be the aircraft I'd use to dodge these asshole pirates. And why the fuck were they after our shoes, anyway?

Playing along, I point to the lever. "You have to increase the speed with this."

She pushes the lever, then punches a few more buttons as if she's sending out some sort of encrypted message. "Okay, phew! We got away. Thank goodness I was here to save us. We would have died if *you* were flying this plane."

Yeah, I'm just going to keep my lips zipped.

Bella and I just got back from Colorado last night, and since Meera had some sort of half-day at her preschool today, I decided to bring her to the museum while Bella was at work. Plus, I missed this know-it-all little pipsqueak.

I pull her out of the plane and we walk around, looking at a few more exhibits before waiting in line for the 3D movie. I hand Meera her glasses when my phone buzzes inside my pocket. It's a reply to the email I sent David yesterday.

Sure. Coffee sounds good, but you're buying. I'm also getting a croissant.

I roll my eyes and put the phone back in my pocket.

To say I'm surprised would be an understatement. Unless he's saying yes and what he really wants to do is break my nose, which is a fair possibility, but one I'm going to chance.

Not ten minutes into the movie and the little diva, with a family-sized tub of popcorn—which she's eaten maybe three kernels of—and a slushy, starts squirming in her seat. Okay, so maybe the historical aviation documentary isn't the most exciting for an almost four-year-old, but hey, I thought since it was 3D, she'd like it. Lesson learned.

"Uncle G!" she squeaks in her high-pitched voice, thinking she's whispering when she's really not. "Why is the man talking so funny?"

I whisper back, looking over my shoulder to see a couple of parents and their much older kids clearly trying to ignore us, "That's the narrator. Sometimes they can be a little monotonous."

She seems to like my answer, though I should have known better—the girl always has to have the last word. Unfortunately, this time, she makes sure everyone around us can hear. "When I become a pilot-narrator, I'm not going to be monogamous."

LOOKING BOTH WAYS, I run across the street to make my way to the coffee shop. I pull the door open, being hit with an aroma that really should be put into perfume bottles—espresso beans.

I spot him in the corner, studying his phone.

"David." Perhaps I could have done better than grinding out his name but between flying the past three nights and barely seeing my girl, I'm not in the mood for drawn-out pleasantries.

The only person I want to talk to today is at her company event and won't be in until later tonight. Between her not letting me have my way with her at Grams' house out of respect, and then leaving almost as soon as we got back home, I'm sporting a case of blue balls like no other. I'm already getting hard thinking about the things I have planned for her tonight.

"Garrett Meyer," David grits out with about the same enthusiasm as he gets out of his chair, putting his hands in his pockets. "You owe me a lot more than fucking coffee, but—"

"Cut the shit. I'll get you coffee on our way out. I have no plans to sit here and have a fucking book club meeting with you. I came here to tell you that I didn't . . ." I clear my throat, looking out the window next to him for a second to gather my nerves. "I didn't sleep with Ally knowing she was your wife. I had no fucking cl—"

David raises his hand, stopping me from continuing. "Save it. I already know."

My brows furrow. "Then why the fuck did you make it seem like I did in front of my wife?"

"Ally and I divorced four years ago, after I found her in our bed with the fucking pool guy." He chuckles without humor. "Yeah, talk about a fucking cliché, right? At that time, she came out and said she was sleeping with a couple of others, but she never told me who until the day before the gala." He tilts his head. "You can imagine my surprise when she mentioned your name."

I run my hand over my face. "Fuck."

He nods. "I thought, since the pool guy knew he was fucking someone's wife, then you probably did, too."

I grit my teeth. "Which is why you hit on my wife at Pete's party instead of knocking my teeth out like a real fucking man."

He shrugs. "It's been four years, and knocking you out would have only shown my cheating bitch of an ex-wife that I cared. It was only recently when she came over to suck me off that she told me you had no idea. I guess, with her going for honesty and shit, she's trying to get back more than just my dick."

I pinch the bridge of my nose. I don't even know what to do with all that unneeded information. "Well, for what it's worth, I'm sorry I even touched her. If I had known, I would have stayed away."

He rolls his shoulders back. "Apology accepted. Now, have you considered getting that wife of yours into anger management? She's hot as fuck, but damn those claws of hers. I bet they feel real nice when you're fu–"

"Finish that sentence." My molars clack in the back of my mouth and my hand itches to wrap around his throat. "I motherfucking *dare* you."

David must be smarter than he looks because he snaps his

mouth shut. Doesn't mean I don't want to punch that goddamn smirk off his face any less.

I lean closer to his ear. "Let me make it crystal clear for you. Stay the fuck away from my wife. It's the last and only time I'll be civil about it, because chief pilot or not, I'll knock you the fuck out if you so much as look at her."

David lifts his hands up. "Chill the fuck out, Captain Commando. Jesus Christ." He tilts his head toward the coffee bar on the other side of the shop. "Now, am I getting that fucking coffee or do you have more threats to shove up my ass?"

As much as I want to be out of this building and away from this dickhead, I get him his coffee. It's the least I can do for whatever he went through four years ago on my account. I can't imagine it was easy, even if he does give me douchebag vibes.

I'm just about to cross the street and get back to my car when David yells over at me, "Let me know if you want to play with the big boys, captain. Not that I care to see you any more than I have over the past few months, but I can hook you up with the right people and see if we can get you into a chief pilot position soon. And before you say you don't have the experience for it, there are ways around that. You just have to talk up your game and schmooze with the right people."

The walk sign flicks on and I start to walk across the street. "Nah, but thanks for the offer. I'm good where I'm at. Plus, I don't have the desire or the talent for sucking dick." I give him a salute. "Have a nice life, chief."

Chapter Thirty-Seven

GARRETT

It's an unusually cold day for mid-March in the Bay Area, so after grilling some salmon and vegetables on the patio, I plate and cover it before turning on the fireplace.

The cats, Brown Sugar and her mom—who I've recently started calling Terminator, because even after all this time, she still looks like she hasn't made up her mind about killing me—jump when the fire flicks on, meowing at it in unison. Their lifted fur finally seems to relax after they've thoroughly sniffed the air, waltzing away as if the fireplace has personally offended them.

I hear the lock jiggle open and see my wife enter, engulfed in her coat, scarf, and winter hat. Her dimples have my attention immediately. "Hi."

Casually, I place my hands inside my pockets, though I'm feeling anything but casual. It's been too long since I've been inside her and I'm nearly coming undone because of it. "Hi."

Her eyes stay on me when she drops her coat in the entryway before taking off her scarf and hat, then dropping them on top of it. Evidently, I'm not the only one who's hungry. "Meera's at her friend's birthday party?"

I nod. "I'll pick her up in a few hours."

Strutting over to me inside her stockings and short black skirt, Bella wraps her arms around my neck. "Thank you."

"What have I told you about thanking me?"

She chuckles. "I missed you."

I place my hands on her ass, giving her a little lift and she wraps herself around my body. I press my mouth to her ear. "Yeah? Show me how much."

She pulls my mouth to hers, tilting her head in the opposite direction to mine as she grinds her needy center over my waist. Her tongue sweeps into my mouth, searching for mine. Her arms tighten around my neck, and she moans when I caress my tongue against hers.

I set her down on the couch, kneeling in front of her before sliding my hands up her thighs and under her skirt. She writhes in anticipation and huffs out a breath when my thumb makes contact with the side of her sex. I glide my thumb along her seam, watching her pull in her bottom lip under her teeth. "You like that?"

"Yes."

"Take that sweater off for me."

She lifts her back off the couch and quickly discards her sweater, her dual-colored hair creating a staticky sound before it falls to her shoulders. I take in the sight of her round, handful-sized tits in her purple bra and my dick twitches to fucking motorboat her.

So much delicious tan skin and all for my taking.

"Pull down the cups but don't take off your bra. I want your tits bouncing when I fuck you."

"Oh, God." My wife loves my filthy words, and I'm more than happy to oblige. Her fingers hook over the seam of her bra cups before she pulls them down, giving me an eyeful of her dark pink, puckered nipples. Fuck, she's beautiful, and if I didn't have plans to fuck her for hours, I'd jizz in my pants right this second.

Keeping my thumb pressed to her warm center, I wrap my mouth around one of her nipples, plucking it with my tongue.

"Ugh!" Bella jumps under me, arching into my mouth. "Garrett."

I circle my tongue around her pebbled tip before sucking on it for good measure, building that frenzy I love seeing so much vibrating through her. Her hand tangles in my hair, and I don't have to look at her to know her eyes are shut tight.

Her skin heats under me, her breaths flowing shallowly as I continue my ministrations on the other nipple, giving it the same lap, suck, and tug.

I make my way down her belly, spending a few extra seconds lapping at her navel and making her squirm. God, I love the way she squirms under my touch.

"Please, Garrett."

Reaching for the waist of her panties and stockings, I pull them down her legs, throwing them to the side. Dragging her ass closer to the edge of the couch, I lift her knees over my shoulders. I lean down to get my first taste of her, swiping my tongue from her entrance to that already-hardening bud.

She practically thrusts her entire hip into my mouth. But I back off, kissing the sides of her thighs before growling into her heat, "You want to be fucked by my tongue and then my cock?"

"Uh-huh," she pants.

"Use your words, Bella. Tell me that's what you want."

"Y-yes."

I tweak her clit with a pinch of my fingers and she yelps, her breath hitching. "Tell me *exactly* what you want."

"For you to—" She heaves in another breath when I flick her clit with my tongue. "Oh, God," she whimpers, forgetting the rest of her sentence.

I remind her again, biting her little bud, making her drive into me again with a groan. "For you to fuck me with your tongue and your cock. Please, please fuck me, Garrett."

I smile into her wet pussy as I give her what she wants. Hell, I think I want it even more than her. Suckling her folds, I lap at her entrance with my flat tongue, making her tighten her grip on my hair. She tries to push her center into me, greedy for that orgasm almost within reach, but I'm not quite ready for her to be done yet.

Lifting up, I drag my fingers through her juices before pressing the tips of two of them inside her. She immediately clenches, locking on to them as if she'll never let them go. "So tight, so needy. You like that?"

"Yes," she pants.

I lean down again, giving open-mouthed kisses to her clit before circling it with my tongue. My fingers delve deeper, feeling her swollen walls around my pads. I pull them out a little before diving back in, curling them and making Bella growl.

"More," she hisses. "Please, more."

I work my tongue, mouth, and my fingers over her, incessantly pulling at her need until I feel her belly flex and her thighs tremble. My name leaves her lips on a wail as her sex pulses under my mouth. The flood of her juices hits my tongue and I lap at it while easing the roll of my fingers inside her.

She's a mess of heavy breaths and sweaty skin as she comes off her high, falling farther into the couch cushion. Her hands lie limply at her sides. "Oh my God. That, that–"

"Is not over," I finish for her.

Her eyes fly open and for a second, I feel like she's feeling too weak to continue and wants to take a break, but then she watches me stand. I grab a hold of my rock-hard erection through my jeans, giving myself a good tug before unbuttoning my pants and letting them fall to the floor.

I take off my Henley next, watching her eyes darken as they travel the length of me, lingering on our tattooed date on my chest to my abs, then to the guy visibly twitching to force himself out of my boxer-briefs.

Bella lifts up, reaching for my cock. She tugs the waistband of my boxers down and my dick bobs out, thick and veiny, ready to quench that hunger building inside her. "I want you in my mouth."

She rounds her hand around him, though she can't touch the tips of her fingers together, before licking the precum off my tip. Her hot tongue sends a shiver down my spine and my abs flex. She pulls the tip into her mouth, rolling her tongue around my sensitive head before pulling off with a *pop*.

She looks up at me with a mixture of desire and vulnerability, silently asking if I like what she's doing to me. The sight of my cock in her hand, so close to her bottom lip, glistening with her spit, has my mind whirling like I'm inside a cyclone. Fuck, she's almost too much.

I reach down to rub her cheek with my thumb, never taking my eyes off hers. *Yeah, I fucking like it. I love it.* "Put me back in that perfect mouth of yours and suck me off like a good girl. Don't stop until I say so."

She quickly takes me back into her mouth, her lips stretching over me again, before she starts bobbing over my dick. Her other hand strokes my base and I guide her head further down my shaft, loving the little gag that erupts from her when I hit the back of her throat.

"Fuck, yeah . . . Just like that."

I'm close, so fucking close, but I have no plans of finishing inside her mouth this time. I let her get a few more good pulls in before I haul her up on her feet. She looks dazed, but the smear of red lipstick around her mouth has me feeling savage.

"You know what you are?" I growl, pulling down her bottom lip with a rough thumb before I kiss her pouty mouth. I'm not looking for her to answer. "A witch, a sorceress, a fucking siren. It doesn't matter that I'll be up balls-deep inside you tonight, or that I'll wake you up with my tongue buried inside your sweet pussy tomorrow morning. It won't be enough. It'll never be enough. Not a single moment goes by where I don't crave you. And I'm convinced you've put a hex on me."

She smiles into our kiss, sliding her hand back down and wrapping it around my cock, still glistening from where her mouth was on it. She gives it another tug and a groan climbs up my throat. "Looks like I've been caught." Breathing away from my lips, she rolls her tongue under my earlobe before pulling it into her mouth. "I guess there's only one thing for me to do, then."

"What's that?" I rasp.

"Fuck you until you forget."

"Take off that skirt," I grind out, vibrating with my need for her.

I get on my back on the carpet in front of the crackling fire, pulling her down with me. Turning her around so she's facing away from me, I have her straddle my hips. Cupping her hips, I lift her up and she seems to follow right along with what I intend to do. *Good girl.*

Lining me up with her entrance, she looks over her shoulder, giving me the sexiest vision of her profile. And before she can say anything, I thrust up into her, filling her to the hilt in one go. We both groan as she gives in to the pressure inside her, and I give in to the feeling of her warm lips around me.

Jesus Christ, I might pass out.

She tilts forward, holding on to my thighs, taking the lead

on slamming her hips down against mine, and soon, we're moving in rhythm. I thrust up into her while she swallows me up. But when her ass goes in the air, I pull my thumb into my mouth before circling it over that forbidden hole of hers.

She tenses.

I continue to drive into her from the bottom. "Do you trust me, sweetheart?"

She hesitates for a second but then nods, her hair curtaining around her head with her bent at the waist over my thighs. "Yes."

"I promise only to make you feel good. You tell me to stop, I stop."

At her nod, I circle the puckered hole with my thumb and I wait for her body to give me an indication. She's still trying to chase her next release with my dick propelling inside her and her juices making the most delicious sounds around us.

I wait for her to climb, and right when her moaning comes to a crest, I press my thumb inside her.

Bella screams in ecstasy as her climax slams into her with the force of a hurricane, and I ram up into her, chasing my own release. I'm panting and groaning right along with her when my body goes rigid and my orgasm catapults me into another fucking planet.

A planet I have plans to visit as often as possible with my wife.

Seconds later, we're all tangled limbs around each other when a movement catches our attention. Bella and I look up to see Winky sitting on her hind legs, staring at us from across the room.

"How long do you think she's been sitting like that?" Bella asks, giving Winky an apprehensive look.

"Pretty sure the peeping Tom watched the whole show." I smirk. "I bet she really enjoyed that last part when I put my thumb inside your–"

Bella smacks my bicep before hiding her face behind her palm. "Oh, God. Shut up."

Chuckling, I pull her to me, wrapping my arms around her and kissing her forehead. My nose is inside her candy-smelling hair when I hear her stomach growl. Good thing I have dinner ready for us. "Someone worked up an appetite."

She laughs before looking back up at me. "When it comes to you, my appetite never seems to be satisfied."

I smirk, pressing my already-growing bulge against her belly. "Good, because I'd like to feed you again."

Chapter Thirty-Eight

BELLA

Four weeks later . . .

Instead of pouring only half the candy into my mouth like I usually do, I empty the entire box of my favorite lemon-flavored *Nerds* into my mouth and chew vigorously, letting the flavor seep down into my throat.

"Breathe. Just breathe." I place a hand over my belly and gulp in more air, listening to my cousin outside my bathroom.

"It's just nerves, girl," Melody says again for the third time in the past half hour. "Even though I knew I was going to marry Liam—even though I was completely in love with him—I was still nervous on my wedding day. You remember, don't you?"

I do. But this doesn't feel like nerves. This feels like food poisoning or dear God, that horrible flu I had a few months ago.

"Bells, can I get you some ginger ale? We have some set out for guests outside."

My stomach lurches again as if I'm on a shaky roller coaster, hightailing it down and feeling every freaking bump and groove.

Beads of sweat line my brows and the tip of my nose. "Yes," I grit out, like if I say another word, I might hurl.

Oh God, this is the last thing I need on such a big day. I drag in more air, trying to ease my lungs and my belly, looking at myself in the mirror of the same bathroom I was in only five weeks ago after Grams died.

Garrett wanted to honor her and have her presence close by when we took our vows again, so we decided to fly back to Colorado and have our wedding at her lake house in the presence of our close family and friends.

I run my hand down my two-piece satin white *ghagra*, which I was fortunate enough to get fitted on such short notice from an Indian clothing retailer in the city. And since Mom specifically asked that I not wear only white—since that's the color widows wear in our culture—I draped the dress with a bridal-red sash, glittering with tiny sparkles.

But even though I had my dress fitted for me just a couple of weeks ago, it feels like it's already a size too small. I undo the zipper in the back of my skirt to give myself a reprieve. How the hell am I going to make it in this for another four or five hours?

Rani did my hair and makeup, pulling my hair half up and half down and setting it with loose curls, with a few framing my face. She also did up my eye makeup, placing fake lashes over my lids and making a dramatic statement with my eyes but keeping the rest of my makeup light.

I don't look quite like myself, but I can't say I don't love it. I really do.

But what I don't love is how my outside looks and feels nothing like my insides at the moment.

"Bells." Garrett's voice outside the door has me spinning

to face it, and I realize a little too late that I shouldn't have moved so quickly when a roll of nausea goes through me again. "Open up, sweetheart. Let me see you."

"No, pilot. Go away. You're not supposed to see me until later. It's bad luck."

"Fuck bad luck. I'm pretty sure I beat all the damn odds when you agreed to marry me. And I'll do it again. Now, open up."

"Garrett, seriously, we've got it," Melody scolds my husband. "Go strut your fine ass back outside. The wedding is about to start in less than fifteen minutes. She'll be fine by then."

I hear Garrett groan like he's really not comfortable following my friend's orders, but if I know Melody, then I know she's giving him her lifted brow like he should think twice before he argues with her.

"Fine, but if you're even two minutes late coming down that aisle to me," I hear him closer to the door, knowing he's talking to me, "I'm bulldozing this door down."

"Alright, settle down, big guy. We get it. You want her tied to you for the rest of eternity. We'll bring her out soon," Melody placates.

"She's already tied to me for the rest of eternity. This is all just a formality."

With that, I hear his footsteps recede and my friends giggle. "That man is *owned*, I kid you not."

"Bells, I have ginger ale. Open up, babe," Rani insists.

I unlock my door and swing it open to reach out for the drink. I told them earlier that I just needed a few minutes alone and thankfully, they've respected giving me a bit of space—but only by a smidge with them hovering at my door.

I smile to myself as I lock the door again and pull the glass of ginger ale to my mouth. Overbearing and protective. I wouldn't have them any other way.

The first sip of the drink seems to send a soothing balm rolling down my chest, and I feel like I can breathe again. Taking another sip, I wait for the relief to consume me, but it doesn't. As soon as I take another sip, I'm rushing to the toilet in just enough time to place the glass upright on the sink and not cover my beautiful dress in vomit.

I hurl the contents of my stomach into the bowl as tears prick my eyes. Shit! This fucking sucks. My first wedding happened in the throes of a drunken stupor, and now my second will be in the throes of whatever *this* is. Maybe Garrett and I are just destined for dramatic beginnings.

"Bells! Open up, sweetie," Rani urges.

A couple of seconds pass before there's a sound like someone is MacGyvering the lock on the knob before the door swings open.

My friends gather me up in their arms, then help me wash my mouth and straighten up my hair and makeup again.

"Feeling better?" a very pregnant Melody asks with worry on her brows.

I nod, though I'm not sure how long the relief will last.

"Just take it easy with–" Melody starts to say when Rani interrupts, "Bella, you haven't missed a dose of your birth control or anything, right?"

I tense as my mind whirls. *Have I? No. I couldn't h–*

"Oh, shit." I'm sure they can see the panic in my eyes. "I did on the day after I flew out here to see Garrett when Grams died. I picked up a new prescription the day after, but yeah, I missed a dose. I didn't think–"

Melody rushes out to the adjoining room where we were all getting ready, and I follow behind her. She rummages through her bag, taking out a couple of long packets and handing them to me. "Here. I've had these in here since before I found out I was pregnant, but they should still work for you."

I look down at them. "What?" I shake my head. "I can't . . . I can't take this now! What if I'm pregnant?"

Rani holds my hands. "Then you tell him. He'll be happy, won't he?"

I huff. "I think so . . . I mean, we've talked about having more kids, but not like *right now*, you know? Oh God. What will Meera think? I haven't even asked her if she wants a sibling–"

Rani's hands tighten on me. "Babe, if I know Meera, she'll be thrilled to become a big sister, but remember, it's not up to her, either. It's a decision that you and Garrett are responsible for. And as for Garrett? Have you seen him with all the kids? He is so good with them, it's like he was born to become a father." I start to say something, but she continues, "You can take the test later if you want, but my advice is to do it now so you can put it aside for a bit and it's not on your mind while you're at the altar. You still have ten minutes before your husband comes barging in here again, breaking down doors."

I take a moment to think. What I need is several moments to think, but it doesn't seem like I have those. "Okay."

Three minutes and two wet pregnancy sticks later, the three of us are hovering over the sink, waiting for the indicators.

We look at each other at the same time when the results come through.

WITH MY HEART beating inside my throat, I link my arm with Rani's dad, my uncle. He'll be giving me away today. And as many times as I've thought about–perhaps even missed–the man who abandoned me over the years, today is the first time I truly feel his loss.

In a moment where I'm walking toward the altar and my awaiting groom–my now real husband–and the beautiful lake rippling under the sunny breeze, I wonder what it would have been like to have grown up with a father.

Without him, I grew up to be strong and independent, albeit guarded. But I also became a fighter in my own right. I grew up to believe in myself and my worth. Perhaps I would have gotten to the same place had he been in my life longer, but I can't say I'm disappointed with where I am now. Far from it.

And in the same moment that I look up and let the last bits of resentment fly into the endless sky, I let out an audible gasp.

I watch as Garrett follows my line of sight and a smile spreads over his face, rivaling the bright sky, when he sees the rainbow above.

She's here, watching. Even with the sun shining down on us, with seemingly not a drop of rain in the sky, she decided to make her presence known.

Thank you, Grams. I promise to give your grandson all the love he deserves.

I'm almost about to walk past my mom and the man she's recently started dating openly–Arthur–when I decide to stop and give her a quick kiss on the cheek. I'm happy that she's found someone to spend her time with, and I couldn't have hoped for a sweeter and gentler man than Arthur. He looks at her like she's a treasure, and it's all I can do to not get all giddy when I see them together.

And right before I get to the altar, I find my beautiful little flower girl, dressed in her most extravagant lavender dress, paired with some Dora socks and black MaryJanes.

"You look so beautiful, Mommy!" she exclaims exuberantly.

I give her a quick kiss on her forehead. "I was going to say the same thing to you. So, are you giving me your blessing to marry Uncle Garrett, then?"

She twists her mouth as if she's thinking, looking up at the man in question, who gives her a wink before flashing me her biggest grin. "I think he's perfect for you, Mommy."

I lean down to her ear. "I think so too, Meerkat."

Wrapping both my hands around the bouquet in my hand, I find the man who's been patiently waiting for me for the past four years. He helps me into the gazebo that we had converted into a makeshift altar, with beautiful flower garlands affixed to the pillars and lavender and white flower chandeliers hanging from its ceiling.

After placing a kiss on my engagement ring, he whispers with a look of concern, "You feeling better?"

I smile, taking in how incredibly gorgeous he looks in his tux, with his hair just slightly gelled back. The scruff on his jaw and the way his blue eyes mimic the lake behind us make him look inexplicably gorgeous in an almost aristocratic way. "I am now."

The exchange of our vows and 'I do's' seems to whizz by in a flash, but as soon as our officiant says, "You may now kiss the bride," I place a hand on Garrett's chest and ask the officiant if I can say a few words.

The crease between Garrett's brows, along with a few murmurs from the crowd, tells me everyone is a little surprised.

Clearing my throat after grabbing the mic from the officiant, I beg my voice not to crack as I look at my handsome and huge-hearted groom, and then up at the sky where I know Grams is still listening.

"Pilot, for years I couldn't meet your gaze. You'd look at

me and I'd look away because I couldn't explain the electricity that would course through me whenever our eyes met, and I was afraid that if I kept my eyes on you, I'd get lost in them."

I look at those beautiful eyes I'm talking about. "But if there's one thing I've learned through my time with you, it's that you'll never let me get lost. No matter how far I've been swept into the sea, you'll always, *always* find me." I take a calming breath. "And I want you to know that I'll always find you, too. I'll be by your side with every breath I take, because you own my every heartbeat, Garrett Meyer."

"I love you," Garrett croaks, but I'm not done.

I take out the little box I'd tucked into a knot in my sash while Garrett watches me curiously. Handing it to him, I continue as a tremor finds my chin, "There's another heartbeat—one neither of us has heard yet—that I'd like to tell you about . . ."

Garrett's jaw goes slack as he pulls out the rolled up note inside the empty *Nerds* box I handed him. "Holy shit." He looks at me with so much emotion and wonder, I forget the rest of my words. "You're . . . we're pregnant?"

Gasps and giggles from the audience float over to where we are, but nothing could break the connection between us as Garrett sweeps me off the floor. I yelp in his arms before bending down to kiss him, while whistles and applause burst from our family and friends. His lips hold mine for a second before his tongue gently parts them and we deepen the kiss.

He puts me down, cupping my face with glassy eyes. "Is this for real?"

I place my hands around his wrist and tell him the only truth I know. "Has there ever been anything besides real between us?"

Garrett - Eight Months Later

"G."

"Do you need more ice chips?" I pick up her half-full cup of ice chips and shake it like more ice will magically appear if I do, and then run an overwhelmed hand through my hair. "I feel like you need ice chips." I look at the nurse coming back in to check Bella's cervix for what feels like the tenth time in six hours. "I think my wife needs more ice chips. The ones in here are melting."

They're not.

But I am.

"G." Bella grits out before she does the whole pant-pant-blow breathing thing that tenses me up every time I watch it. Once she's over the contraction, her irate eyes turn on me. "Garrett! I don't need ice chips! What I need is for my husband to not lose his shit."

I rub my neck and then roll my head from side to side. "Yeah, you're right. I'm sorry. It's just . . . I thought you said this would be easier the second time around."

She holds out her hand to me and I take it. She steadies her gaze on me, sweat lining her brows and her face flushed.

"It is. Not just because this is my second time and my body sort of knows what it's doing, but because you're here."

I give her a guilty look. "Sure about that?"

"Well, not based on the past six hours but, in general, yeah."

I chuckle before leaning down and pressing my lips to hers. "I'll take that as a win."

A few minutes later, Bella's OB-GYN walks in. She's maybe five feet and possibly a hundred pounds, if that, but what she lacks in size, she more than makes up for with her huge personality.

"Alright, Momma!" She claps like she's coaching a football team, riling the guys up before they go out onto the field. "You ready for this?" She doesn't wait for Bella to respond. "I'm pretty sure you're ready for this because Nurse Gabby here says you're fully dilated and that baby is ready to come out!"

Bella's nostrils flare when she nods, and I know she's trying to make it through the discomfort. Just like she did with Meera, she refused the epidural for our baby's birth, saying that since she was pretty sure this was going to be her last delivery, she just wanted to feel it. But based on the way she's grinding her molars, I gather she might be regretting that decision. I'd probably lose my balls if I asked her though, so I keep my mouth shut.

"Oh, I see her! Hi there, little baby head!" Our doctor may just be on happy pills, but as long as she can deliver this baby, I'm not going to question it. "Now, I'm going to need you to bear down and really push for me, Bella. I bet a couple of big pushes will do it!"

Three pushes and a last scream that sounds like *Xena: The Warrior Princess's* war cry later, Bella's body slumps as the newest member of our family makes her world debut.

A silent frenzy erupts in the delivery room, where nurses

and doctors are all focused on their tasks, but my eyes are glued to the most precious little thing I've ever seen. I take that back; she's the second most precious little thing I've ever seen. With dark hair like her mom's, fair skin, and chubby little arms and legs, she's absolutely perfect.

I'm jolted out of my haze when her wail vibrates inside my chest, and Bella's outstretched arms and tears beckon the nurses to give her our baby.

"Here you go, Mom." The nurse coos at our bundled-up newborn before placing her in Bella's arms, and I watch, enraptured, as if I'm having some sort of out-of-body experience.

Bella gives her a kiss through a little sob, her exhaustion and relief evident on her face. "You're perfect, baby girl." She regards me tenderly. "Did you decide which name we're going with?"

Over the course of the past few months, we've talked about a few options, but a few weeks ago, Bella asked me to surprise her with the name. Of course, she has ultimate veto power on any name I select, but she trusted I'd pick something we would both love.

Placing a kiss on our little one's temple, I take in the curve of her perfect pout and the eyes that seem to be taking in everything in wonderment. *I get it, baby girl. I'm just as in awe of you, too.* "Rayne Ellen."

Bella's smile widens and she shifts to hand the baby to me. "Rayne Ellen Meyer. I love that we used Gram's name as her middle name. And Rayne fits her perfectly."

I place a kiss on Rayne's head, much the same way I remember doing when I came to see Meera in the hospital after she was born. "It does, but I'm going to call her Rainbow."

"Wʜᴀᴛ ᴅᴏ ʏᴏᴜ ᴛʜɪɴᴋ ᴏꜰ ʜᴇʀ?" I ask our sassy five-year-old. "She kind of looks like you, huh?"

Meera peers down at her sister in her arms. She's been holding her for the past ten minutes, and I'm getting the feeling it's not going to be easy to pry her out of her hands. "Her eyes are blue, but yeah . . . she does look like me, too. We have the same hair color."

"I bet you'll find more similarities as she grows up."

Meera bends to place her nose on Rayne's head before she whispers, "I love you, little sis."

I take a quick picture of my girls and ask if I can give Rayne back to Bella because I actually have something to ask Meera as well.

Reluctantly, Meera agrees and sits on the couch with her hands in her lap, watching me as I kneel in front of her on the floor.

I look back at Bella lying on her hospital bed with Rayne in her arms, and she gives me an assuring nod. "Meerkat, I don't know if you know this or not, but I came to see you when you were just a day old."

Meera's eyes widen. "Really?"

I tip my chin down. "I saw you, and . . . I prayed that we'd be in each other's lives forever." Taking a breath, I swallow the thickness building in my throat. "I'm glad I got what I prayed for because you're the coolest little girl I've ever met."

Meera beams at me, her smile causing her glasses to nudge up her nose.

"I hope you know how much I love you, Meerkat. I'd do anything for you. Even if you ask me to binge on episodes of *Dora* and eat cotton candy ice cream all day, I'll happily do it."

Her hazel eyes crinkle at the corners. "With crushed potato chips inside the ice cream?"

I chuckle. "There's no better way to eat it." When she

giggles, I continue, "But I was wondering if you'd do something for me?"

She leans forward slightly, concern lining her brows. "What?"

I pull out the bracelet I had made from my pocket and hold it up for her. If her eyes could widen any more, they have. I figured I'd give her a bracelet since she gave me a handmade one all those months ago. "Will you do me the honor of making me a dad twice today? I don't want to just be Rayne's daddy; I want to be yours, too. If you're okay with it, would you—"

Before I can even finish, Meera flings her arms around my neck, holding me tight before sobbing into my neck. "Yes. I want you to be my dad."

My heart expands and I gulp in a breath, holding her against me. My eyes water as I take in the happiest day of my life when I became a father two times around.

"Don't leave me and Rayne hanging over here," Bella chokes out. I turn to see her wiping her tears. "We want a hug, too."

I carry Meera in my arms, and we wrap Bella and the baby in a bigger hug, breathing in our new little family.

"What does my bracelet charm say, Mommy?" Meera lifts her wrist in Bella's direction.

Turning it so that she can read it, Bella smiles. "It says 'Daddy's girl.'"

I can see the emotion on both their faces as Meera brings her wrist back, holding it close to her chest before looking at me. "Thank you, Daddy."

I give her a kiss on her cheek. "You're welcome, Meerkat."

I won a few bets that weekend in Vegas, but the jackpot—my entire world—is right here, inside my arms.

EPILOGUE 2

Bella - 2 Years Later

You'd think being married to an airline pilot, I'd have traveled half the world already and taken long vacations to exotic places.

Nope, not quite, and not for the lack of him trying to get me away for longer than just a weekend. But with work and two busy kids, we can't ever seem to get away for more time than that.

On top of that, this past year I was especially busy helping Mom get ready for her wedding to Arthur. And even though they wanted a small and private event at the temple, my weekends leading up to it have been booked with helping her get prepared.

But as soon as she was settled in her blissful married life and I was able to take some time off work, Garrett and I dropped both our girls off at *Nani's* place and hopped on a flight to spend a much-needed week in the Maldives.

And with Garrett's airline discounts, we were able to fly business class for practically nothing. So, while I may not travel as much as I'd like, I love every moment of it because I get to do it with my best friend and the man currently smoldering at me like he's got a bad idea swirling in his head.

"Uh uh." I shake my head at him from my seat next to him. "Whatever that look is for, get it off your face."

He pulls our entangled fingers to his mouth but the gleam in his eyes is relentless, just like him. "You don't even know what it is yet."

"I don't need to. I already know I won't be able to face the other passengers on this plane if I go along with it."

His smile broadens as he unbuckles his seatbelt, shifting in his seat. "Oh, so you *do* know what it is."

"What are you doing?" I ask almost in a reprimand, shaking my head because I already know his answer.

His mouth finds my ear and there's no mistaking his words, despite the hum of the plane. "I'm going into that lavatory, and in less than two minutes, I'll either be feeding my cock to my fist or to my wife's delectable pussy. Your choice."

"G." I grab his hand, trying to hold him in place, but he slips out before I can get anything more out.

This man. He's so ridiculously pushy, I can't decide if I want to throttle him or fuck him.

But as a minute drags on with me chomping at my bottom lip and my heart trotting like a racehorse inside my chest, I know which option I'm going to end up choosing.

Trying to look as discreet as possible, I wait to make sure none of the flight attendants are near the bathroom he went inside before knocking on the door.

As if he was waiting—as if the asshole already *knew* which choice I'd make—the door opens and he practically slings me inside against him and locks the door.

I only have only a second to note how small the space is with the both of us in here when his mouth presses against my neck, sucking and kissing hard enough to leave a mark.

He slides it against my jaw and then my mouth, his hands holding my face as he ravishes my mouth with his kiss. "Do you know how seductive you are? I'm always on the precipice of losing my mind around you."

My toes curl inside my shoes, my body humming with need as his tongue dives deep into my mouth. I smile into our kiss. "Are you asking for an apology?"

His hands slide under my tunic, pulling at the waistband of my tights. "I'm asking you to fuck me."

And as soon as he has my tights and panties pulled down to my thighs, he sits down on the closed lid of the toilet. I try not to think about all the unsanitary reasons we shouldn't be doing this in here but hell, we've done it inside the gondola of a Ferris wheel, so this can't be any worse.

Garrett turns me around so I'm facing the door. "Bend for me. I need to taste you."

I bend at my waist, as much as the space will allow me, but he clearly doesn't need much because as soon as I've bent over, I feel his tongue over my soaking center. I hiss as the sensation sends a wave of electricity coursing through me, rocking over his mouth and tongue.

He pulls away all too quickly, replacing his tongue with his fingers, and slaps my ass cheek.

I hold in my yelp. "G, people are going to hear . . ."

He does it again, slapping the same cheek and then grabbing the stinging flesh with his mouth, biting it and kissing it like a man unhinged. "Let them. Maybe they'll learn a thing or two."

His fingers plunge inside me, and I can feel how wet I am just by how easily they slide in and out. "That's it, baby. Ride my fingers." He starts a rhythm with his fingers and my shoulders and neck feel heavy and weak. My knees start to wobble. "You like it, don't you? You like fucking my fingers."

"Y-yes," I hiss again, grinding my molars. "Pilot, I need . .

." I can't even think properly with my orgasm so close, but I really just want him inside. "I need more."

Not waiting for me to repeat myself, Garrett unzips his pants and pulls out his weighty erection. "Sit on me and when you do, make sure you slide right down my cock."

With his hands on my waist, I grab his thickness and angle it to my entrance before following his command and making my way down his long shaft. My sex wraps around his girth, and we both moan as I take him all the way in.

"That's it, sweetheart. Now fuck me."

Garrett puts one hand around my belly and the other on my waist, guiding me up and down his cock until we're a mess of pants and moans. I whimper when the hand on my belly slides down to my clit and he circles my nub over and over until my walls are clenching around him.

"G, oh God. I'm–" I can't even get out the words, shutting my eyes tight and letting the surge of lust consume my entire body. My orgasm rolls through me like an avalanche as I continue to rock over him. "I'm coming!"

He's only seconds behind me. A few more thrusts upwards into my body, and Garrett lets out a guttural moan with his forehead pressed on my back. "Fuck!"

We've just barely caught our breaths when there's a knock on our door. My eyes fly wide open, and I cover my mouth with my hand to hold in my yelp.

"Excuse me. Is everything alright in there?" a flight attendant asks, her mouth clearly at our door.

Garrett starts to chuckle, and I smack him with my other hand, trying to get him to shut up while my face heats like it's about to catch on fire.

"I think it's only fair that you answer her since I was in here first and you *forced* your way inside," he whispers.

My mouth falls open. "You big–"

But before I can say start calling him the list of names I

have in mind, his mouth slams against mine, making me forget it all.

The End

Your reviews matter! Please consider taking a few minutes to write a review for Ascend on Amazon and Goodreads.

ABOUT THE AUTHOR

Swati M.H. prefers to call herself a storyteller rather than an author. She lives in the Bay Area with her incredibly patient husband, two beautiful daughters, and her pitbull, Sadie Sapphire. Her days start with caffeine and sometimes end with a glass (or three) of wine.

Swati's goal as a storyteller is to distract her readers from their daily grind with stories about everyday couples finding and fighting for incredible love with the help of a little luck.

Swati loves staying in touch with her readers. Find her at www.swatimh.com or through Facebook and Instagram. Be sure to join her Sweeties reader group for daily fun.

ACKNOWLEDGMENTS

I can't remember the first marriage of convenience I ever read but I do remember the feeling I got afterward. I truly didn't want the book to end! And, that started my obsession with the trope, so much so, that if I ever come across a MoC I haven't read, I'll immediately add it to my TBR.

So, when I got the idea of Garrett and Bella having their own marriage of convenience, I was honestly beside myself. I couldn't wait to write their journey and happily ever after. They were SO much fun! Oh, and Garrett?! Oh my heart, I don't think I've ever written a swoonier hero (though, Wayland from My Beautiful Chaos might be a close second, IMO).

Thank you for reading Ascend and I hope you loved Garrett and Bella as much as I do. And whether you did or didn't, I'd love to hear what you thought about them.

As with any book I've written, it's taken a village and an army supporting me. So, without further ado, I'll start by thanking my family, especially my incredible and supportive husband. I consider myself the lucky one for having found my own HEA with him.

A huge thank you to my mom and dad for being my cheerleaders and constantly telling me how proud they are of me. A girl can do anything when her parents are right behind her every step of the way.

Thank you also to my PA, Stephanie Rash. She keeps me laughing but more than that, she keeps me organized and on track. Thank you, Steph for your continued belief in me and for supporting me through all of this.

One of my favorite parts of the writing journey is my interaction with my alpha-readers team. I cannot tell you how incredibly lucky I feel to have found them and their friendship. During the writing process, I truly live for their immediate feedback and incredible discussions through texts and voice memos and I'm looking forward to doing that again as I write Dean's book.

So, let me first start by thanking my Rachel & Rachael duo. Rachel Childers and Rachael Poxon—I cannot tell you how much fun I have when you both jump into the manuscript and start commenting on things that sometimes I don't even notice. I get giddy with your reactions and feedback. Thank you so much for always being so supportive and for keeping me energized on days that I truly need it. I appreciate you so much!

Michelle Mastandrea and Amy Crull—thank you so much for all the incredible discussions. Michelle, I was so glad to have you as part of the team this time and can't wait to continue. I absolutely loved all your highlights, insights, and even the swag ideas you gave me! Amy, thank you so much for pointing out things that I might not have even thought about —I so appreciate your thoughtfulness.

Thank you also to my beta-readers: Jerrica Martin, Melissa Schmidt, and Anita Mendeiros. I appreciate all your feedback and the fun messages we exchanged. I loved seeing your reactions to it all!

I'd like to do a special shout out to my good friend, Jenni Bara, who is not only an incredibly talented author but was also one of my beta readers. Thank you, Jenni, for helping me with so many nuances of law/litigation/custody that I didn't know before and for jumping in to read the manuscript when

I barely gave you a heads up. I truly appreciate your friendship and support.

Thank you also to my friend Yadhira G. for being my guide in through the legal aspects in this book and answering so many of my questions. I couldn't have written it with so much confidence without you.

I'd also like to thank my new pilot friend, Mr. Bradley Carey, who I'd like to award the title of "romance aviation consultant". Bradley, thank you so much for answering my million questions about "a day in the life of a pilot". They were tremendous in making me feel like I knew what I was talking about when I wrote Captain Garrett Meyer in this book :)

A huge thank you to my editor and friend, Silvia Curry. She is one of the BEST at what she does and I appreciate her so freaking much for putting up with my crazy deadlines and random questions.

Lastly but not leastly (yes, I made up that word and it's okay because Silvia doesn't edit the acknowledgments :)) I'd like to thank my author besties and the people I truly depend on to be in my corner.

Daphne Elliott—how freaking incredible, intelligent, and talented are you? I seriously am in awe and I'm so glad to call you my friend.

Brittanee Nicole—I love you to the moon. Thank you for always being such a source of sunshine and positivity. I learn so much from you.

My giggle squad (Bookies&Cookies)—Rin Sher and Monica Arya—I have literally had tears running down my face and stomach cramps from laughing because of you two. Thank you so much for the all the laughs (and forwarded videos of hot chefs) because sometimes we just need to take life a little less seriously.

Emily Silver—you are one of my OG friends and I adore

you. Thank you for always showing me the ropes. I swear you are an encyclopedia of answers!

And, my good friends SJ Tilly and Garry Michael. Not only are you both phenomenal authors but also two of the very best humans. I am constantly inspired by you and have nothing but gratitude and love for your friendship.

Thank YOU, my wonderful readers, for picking up this book and getting to this last page. I could not and would not do this without you. Thank you so so much!